COLOR, CHARM, AND STRANGENESS

A gray air of gloom and depression hung over Karpluvy Towne. Small squads of soldiers and armed citizens patrolled the streets. A worried Oskar whispered to Mamakitty, "People are staring at us. What are we doing wrong?"

"Nothing, I wager," she replied after a moment's consideration. "I think we just stand out a little bit from the typical townsfolk. They probably fear any strangers, concerned that they might be spies for the Horde."

Oskar studied their little party. Were their nonhuman origins showing? Everyone was careful to resist their innate urges. No one dropped to all fours. How could they possibly stand out? True, Mamakitty was more muscular than the average woman. And Taj blonder than the blondest north-erner. As for Cezer and Cocoa, it was difficult to tell which was the more beautiful, or who drew the more surreptitious admiring stares from the otherwise downcast crowd . . .

✳

"Amusing . . . well-written . . . anyone who enjoys an old-fashioned good vs. evil fantasy quest will want to travel on Alan Dean Foster's latest adventure." —*Midwest Book Review*

"Funny and imaginative . . . a good story that is sure to please . . . reminiscent of Gulliver's travels." —*VOYA*

ALSO BY ALAN DEAN FOSTER

The Dig

The Journeys of the Catechist series:
Carnivores of Light and Darkness
Into the Thinking Kingdoms
A Triumph of Souls

AVAILABLE FROM WARNER ASPECT

ALAN DEAN FOSTER
KINGDOMS OF LIGHT

WARNER BOOKS

An AOL Time Warner Company

WARNER BOOKS EDITION

Copyright © 2001 by Thranx, Inc.

Cover design by Don Puckey
Cover illustration by Don Maitz
Hand lettering by Carl Dellacroce

Aspect® name and logo are registered trademarks of Warner Books, Inc.

Warner Books, Inc.
1271 Avenue of the Americas
New York, NY 10020

Visit our Web site at
www.twbookmark.com.

An AOL Time Warner Company

Printed in the United States of America

Originally published in hardcover by Warner Books
First Paperback Printing: February 2002

10 9 8 7 6 5 4 3 2 1

FOR MURRAY BALL . . .
THE HOGARTH OF AOTEAROA . . .
DOG (AND CATS) INCLUDED . . .

KINGDOMS OF LIGHT

ONE

On the fertile, grassy plains of Nasid Huedril, where the fortified city of Kyll-Bar-Bennid sticks like a rough gray thumb into the broad sweep of the glassy green river Drimaud, the armies of the Gowdlands assembled to await the arrival of the Totumakk Horde. Yet for all the Horde's fierce fighting skills, for all its rumored ruthlessness and raging brutality, it was not the Horde that the defenders of the Gowdlands feared. Among their own steadily swelling number they could count numerous brave fighters and famed warriors, skilled mercenaries and professional soldiers of considerable experience and ability. These were men and women who cowered before no wielder of spear or swinger of sword. Only a name struck fear into them. A name of the Unknown, a fearful shadow given substance only by reputation.

Khaxan Mundurucu.

Reputed monster, master, and soulless slayer of men and despoiler of women, it was said. The dark arts were his province, the despair of others his pleasure. Human flesh sated his appetite and blood slaked his thirst. Where his Horde passed, the land was laid waste and the earth oozed pus. It was believed that he would not be content until all the civilized world cowered at his feet and licked the night soil from between his toes. The foulness of his countenance was alleged to send strong men into shock, his touch to cause convulsions in the most courageous of women. The gathering defenders of the Gowdlands drew encouragement from the realization that no one individual, no matter how evil and depraved, could possibly be the equal of such a reputation.

Little did they know the truth of the matter.

The promontory of Kyll-Bar-Bennid formed the gateway to the Gowdlands, with the city commanding by far the best and most accessible of the approaches to the fertile territories farther east. Twelve bridges spanned the river Drimaud, encouraging exchanges and facilitating commerce. In the months since the first rumors of the approaching Horde had changed from a whisper to a roar, trade across the great river had slowed to a crawl, and finally to barely a trickle. Now, with the advance body of the Horde so near, the swollen flood of refugees had shrunk to a few last, terrified wagonloads.

A hard man to please, the stocky, silver-haired General Goughfree was quietly gratified by the decline. The flight of civilians from the other side of the Drimaud made his work that much easier. Of the dozen thoroughfares across the river, eight were narrow or fragile enough to be held by small squadrons of determined defenders. Equipped with cannon, they could sweep any attacker, no matter how determined or accomplished, into the swift current below.

The remaining four bridges required more attention. Broad of aspect and fashioned from solid stone, they commanded the main approaches to the city and the plains that lay beyond. All four had to be held. Should even one be captured, an attacking enemy would acquire a direct route into the city. Beyond the bridges lay the town itself, circuitous of street and convoluted of thoroughfare, and beyond it the castle, whose strong high walls were well defended. Goughfree and his colleagues felt confident it could be held against any assailant. But withdrawing into the castle would mean sacrificing the city and its treasures to the ravages of the enemy. The champions of the Gowdlands had no intention of allowing the prosperous metropolis to crumble beneath the boots of the Totumakk.

As for the supposed malignant powers of this Khaxan Mundurucu, the defenders of the Gowdlands could count among their number several powerful virtuosos of the mystic arts. Having consulted with the hastily constituted council of war, Goughfree had come away convinced of the ability of these several mages and wizards to deal with this Mundurucu individual, whose arrogant reputation must perforce exceed whatever arcane abilities he might actually possess. Armies would repulse any military assault by the Totumakk, while the necromancers of the Gowdlands would repel any sorcerous affront to the city's defenses.

Thus reassured, Goughfree spent the days supervising the strengthening of the city's fortifications, concentrating on the vital bridges while not neglecting the castle or the inner wards, until he was of the opinion that, seeing the strength of Kyll-Bar-Bennid, the Totumakk might well decide it was not in their interest to hurl themselves uselessly against it.

Languorous clouds filled the sky, and the air was suffused with the dank, clinging humidity of Final Summer when scouts at last brought word of the Horde's approach. Their confirming words were not needed, since from the topmost castle heights the defenders of the city had been able to observe the expanding glow of burning fields and homes for many days now. When finally the killing teams of the Horde began to emerge from the woods on the far side of the river, the soldiers and citizens of Kyll-Bar-Bennid had their first glimpse of those who threatened their destruction.

Even on a small scale, the sight was dauntingly horrific. Bent and twisted, gap-toothed and cloven-skulled, clean-shaven or eruptive of beard, there was not a man or woman among the amassing Horde who did not reek of corruption and decay. They were a vileness upon the land—and that was only the humans among them. At least half the Horde was made up of—other things.

There were creatures with curving, slanted eyes and narrow, heronlike beaks as long as a man's arm. Black-furred bipeds reptilian of aspect boasted oval mouths fringed with long hairs that might have been borrowed from fleshy catfish, while stockier companions carried pikes and lances on shoulders hunched unnaturally forward. There were massive red-furred hulks with warty, leprous countenances and eyes devoid of lids, who gazed upon the world with unblinking ferocity. Smaller fighters in this army of the damned hopped or lurched or shambled their way into camps that sprang up around central fires, above which roasted and dripped huge chunks of meat whose origins the saner among the city's defenders made a conscious effort not to identify.

Officers in gleaming black armor moved among their diabolic troops like sharks through schools of shad. Using whips and prods, they doled out grisly imprecations and sharp blows in equal measure. None of the Horde rebelled against this harsh treatment. None dared, and there were those truly sick ones who reveled in it.

On the bridges, within the city proper and the castle on the heights above, the defenders saw, and heard, and were appalled. The hellish vision of the enemy camps was enough to induce some to desert on the spot, fleeing under cover of night, carried away by fear. Most, however, remained, their number continuously reinforced by a steady stream of resolute new arrivals. Anyone with any sense knew that here was the place to stop the invaders, before they could reach the prosperous, broad plains of the Gowdlands. Keep them on the far side of the Drimaud, and everything and everyone to the east would be safe. Let them cross, and chaos would surely triumph. To give way now was to embark upon a life of eternal, hopeless flight from an unspeakable nightmare that would never end.

All they had to do, Goughfree and his fellow officers knew, was hold the bridges. While the aspect of the Horde was certainly terrible, the invaders had so far exhibited nothing capable of instilling despair in the heart of a well-trained soldier. The enemy did not even appear to have artillery, giving a distinct advantage to the well-prepared defenders. Let them come!

On the morning of Twelfth Day, beneath a glowering sky and in defiance of a sultry, obscuring rain, that is what they did.

Goughfree had established a forward command post atop the Hidradny Tower, which defended the largest and most prominent of the bridges that spanned the Drimaud. At the midpoint of the structure, a succession of battlements had been erected, one behind the other. The same defensive bulwarks had been put in place on all of the eleven other bridges. The idea was to funnel the mass of the enemy onto one or more of the resulting narrow concourses rather than meet them on an open field. This would prevent them from bringing superior numbers to bear. Should they succeed in surmounting or battering their way through a fortification, the defenders would retreat to the next one immediately behind. In this way, the attacking enemy force would be gradually reduced at each wall, while the defenders would grow progressively stronger thanks to reinforcements waiting to be brought up from behind.

When the moment was right, Goughfree or any of the generals commanding the other bridges could draw upon well-rested reserves for a devastating counterattack to drive the attackers back across the river. The defenders would not attempt to follow, but would instead try to reduce the enemy as severely as circumstance allowed before returning to the defense of the bridges. In the event the Horde succeeded in fighting its way across the entire length of a bridge, tall entrance gates and heavily defended city walls awaited them.

It was a good plan, a sound plan, uncomplicated and easy to implement. Goughfree, Chaupunell, Zisgymond and the other senior officers had a great deal of confidence in it. With luck, it would result in the elimination of the Totumakk Horde as an effective fighting force or threat to the Gowdlands for all time.

When battle was finally joined, standing atop the Hidradny Tower and squinting through the rain, Goughfree could see that all was going as planned. Shattering the air with a frightful ululation interspersed with individual war cries, many of which did not arise from human throats, the Horde proceeded to assault all four main bridges simultaneously. If in so doing they hoped to discover a weak point, they failed miserably. Only on the Salmisti Bridge were the defenders overwhelmed by the fury of the attack and pushed back. Hastily reinforced by cavalry held in reserve for just such a purpose, the defense stiffened at the last wall before the city gate.

Taking personal charge of the counterattack, General Zisgymond of the Grand Moied of Viezshry led a charge through the gate of massed heavy cavalry drawn from four kingdoms. The impact of the armored horse and antelope on the invaders was terrible. Those who were not trampled under hoof or cut down by lance, pike, and sword either fled back across the corpse-strewn bridge or leaped into the river to escape. Those whose weighty armor did not drag them to the muddy bottom to drown were carried off downstream by the swift current of the Drimaud and away from the field of battle. It was not a defense: it was a rout. Within the city, an elated citizenry filled the air with a spontaneity of cheers.

The effect on the rest of the enemy was profound. Seeing their hitherto indomitable colleagues slaughtered or forced into the water, the columns of attackers assaulting the other three main bridges faltered in their conviction, hesitated, and were, bridge by bridge, driven back to the far shore from whence they had come. As planned, their triumphant adversaries halted there, thrusting their weapons into the air while jeering their enemy, and returning to reconstitute their defensive positions.

That evening, Chaupunell and the rest of the senior staff took the time to congratulate Goughfree and one another.

"It's not done with yet." Goughfree had been too long a soldier to sail easy upon a sea of acclaim. "They were only testing us."

"A costly test." A euphoric commander of archers was leaning against the stone fretwork, peering through the mist. The gentle rain softened the aspect of the slaughter, whose bloody aftermath still stained the rough stone of the bridges. The Salmisti and Breleshva crossings in particular benefited from the cleansing shower, restoring the sheen of their smoothly paved surfaces from bright red to flinty gray.

"We have suffered losses of our own," Chaupunell pointed out. "The wounded must be seen to, and possible weak spots shored up." He and Goughfree in concert with a pair of senior engineers set to devising revised fortifications for the endangered Salmisti Bridge.

The Horde did not wait for morning. Hoping to catch the defenders of Kyll-Bar-Bennid off guard, and before they could renew themselves with a good night's rest, the invaders launched a second attack just after midnight. Darkness allowed them to approach the defensive palisades more closely this time before they were discovered, but the surprise they achieved was only partial.

Responding with energy and determination, the defenders gave ground grudgingly on all four bridges, doing as much damage as possible before falling back where and when necessary. When the Horde threw cavalry of its own into the attack, some desperate moments ensued. Riding atop hollow-eyed hoarbeasts boasting sharp, forward-facing horns and snouts filled with serrated, snapping teeth, the Horde scattered the defenders of the previously unbreached Zhisbrechar Bridge, seriously weakening the left flank of the city's defense and threatening to breach the tower that anchored that end of the city wall. Massive as gryphons, fleet of foot as elk, the hoarbeasts were not turned by the cavalry sent to reinforce the bridge.

That was when Goughfree called forth the Shandrac Thunder. From strategically superior positions atop hills behind the city walls, the famed assembled artillery of the Twin Dominions poured fire and destruction upon the invading Horde. Explosions ripped through the rain and split the night as projectiles fell like hail on the bridge and the far shore. Terrified by the flash and sound of exploding shells, panicked hoarbeasts whirled in retreat, trampling their own reinforcements underfoot and sowing panic and confusion among all manner of befuddled attackers. When the defenders of the Zhisbrechar followed the bombardment with a furious counterattack of their own, they were met with little resistance. Debased beast and brute homunculus alike went down beneath scything sword and thrusting pike.

Once more, victory belonged to the defenders. Once again, the enemy had failed even to mount a persistent assault on a city gate. Around Goughfree, senior staff and attendant guard celebrated gleefully. Only the general himself did not participate. Though chided for his reserve, he explained that he could not bring himself to rejoice. Something worried his thoughts like a nipping eel that had clamped its jaws around his ankle and would not let go.

Where was Khaxan Mundurucu?

For the next three days, nothing more threatening than heavy rain pummeled the defenders of the Gowdlands. From a strategic standpoint, the pause made no sense. Chaupunell in particular was surprised by the hiatus—surprised and pleased, since it gave the defenders time to rest, to recover, and to repair some of the damage done to their forward defenses on the four main bridges.

Of course, Goughfree knew, the enemy was using the time to recuperate as well. The Horde had suffered terrible losses. Hundreds of bodies, some too ghastly in appearance to touch, washed up on the narrow shingle beaches at the base of the city walls and docks. The defenders, too, had suffered. But if anything, morale within and behind Kyll-Bar-Bennid was higher than ever, thanks to the unified forces of the Gowdlands having repulsed not one but two attacks of significance. And while their flow was reduced in number, reinforcements continued their steady trickle into the city.

On the morning of the fourth day after the midnight attack on the bridges, the interminable rain gave way to a light fog. Hanging over river and city, shore and plain, it imparted an eerie and unnatural peace to the panorama of devastation. Even the local waterfowl, who in the absence of battle had been slowly returning to favorite haunts beneath the bridges and along the silent shores, were strangely quiet.

The trio of forward lookouts who saw the first lumpenkin were so shocked they nearly failed to report the advance before they were cut down, torn to pieces by sinewy, muscular arms longer than their own bodies. As the towering, dull-eyed, blond-furred bipeds shambled forward, heads hanging low from long necks and the backs of massive hands scraping the ground as they walked, accompanying dramunculi swept the bridge with pyrovomitus, scorching the precisely set stones and incinerating anything flammable. Behind these striding horrors came the main body of the Totumakk Horde, even grimmer of countenance than usual, led by officers in terrifying armor who had heretofore remained in the background, giving orders without participating directly in battle.

Hastily struggling into his uniform, Goughfree knew as soon as he reached the high parapet and descried what was coming that this was to be the Final Battle. Today the Horde would hold nothing back. Today would bring the final, unconditional triumph of the peoples of the Gowdlands. It was with eager anticipation that he buttoned the collar of his weather jacket and heard the Shandrac Thunder begin to boom vigorously behind him.

Once again, explosive shells began to fall among the invaders, easy targets where they were packed together and concentrated on the eastern approaches to the four bridges. Once again, blood and bone, steel and stone, erupted in grisly fountains from the already battered but still intact stone arches and from the far shore. And then a strange thing happened.

The shells continued to fall, the Shandrac gunners plac-

ing them with unerring accuracy in the midst of the invaders. Explosions continued to split the air, and the fog
became flavored with the acrid stink of gunpowder. But
the enemy was not affected. Something was protecting
them. Gazing down in disbelief, the members of the senior
staff charged with the ultimate defense of the city and the
Gowdlands saw that the falling shells were exploding *before* they reached the ground. It was as if a transparent
shield of impenetrable glass had suddenly come into being
above each bridge, to hover above the massed columns of
advancing invaders.

"There!" shouted Colonel Borallos. The slim, dark-
haired Master of Horse was accounted the sharpest of eye
among all the general staff. Following the ramrod-straight
line of her arm, Goughfree squinted into the fog, and finally saw what she saw.

Well back in the body of each of the four attacking
columns, flanked by hairless, slate gray lumpenkin more
massive of body than their taller, blonder counterparts, and
attended by bird-things that sported quills instead of feathers and spatulate beaks lined with fine, needle-like teeth,
was a wizard. In lieu of lustrous, flowing robes, the Four
Warlocks of the Totumakk were clad in black cowls spat-
tered with crimson paint intended to simulate flowing blood.
Other than their attire, they were alike only in the evil they
served up and dispensed.

One had four arms that picked invisible somethings from
the air and flung them in the direction of the defending
troops. Another was bloated and porcine, while a third was
so squashed and profuse of jowl as to appear bodiless, as
if its legs were growing right out of the bottom of its neck.
The fourth, who was sorcerously assisting the assault on
the Salmisti Bridge, wore a high, fat red cap the same color
as its bulbous nose. Thin white wire spectacles rode that

protuberant organ, while pointed teeth protruded forward
and out from a slightly underslung lower jaw. The creature
was reading from a handful of papers, reciting in detail
those spells it had not wholly committed to memory.

In addition to sustaining the nefarious, necromantic
shields that protected the advancing hordes from the effects of the Shandrac Thunder, the four warlocks called
down burning sulfur and white-hot phosphorus on the defenders of the city. Small snapping fish fell among the
archers and crossbowmen, while biting, stinging insects be-
deviled the waiting cavalry.

As the spell-invigorated enemy threw itself against bulwark after bulwark, high on the city wall a worried
Chaupunell and Zisgymond caucused with Goughfree.

"Our soldiers are brave and determined." Along with the
rain, lines of concern streaked General Zisgymond's noble
face. "But they cannot fight incantations. Hexes do not
bleed." He gestured toward the wall, in the direction of
battle. "Already the defenders of the Salmisti and Hidradny
Bridges are being forced back to the towers. If these fall,
the enemy will enter the city. Soon thereafter, they will be
here, laying siege to the castle itself."

"Look at our people, suffering and dying beneath that
which they cannot understand." Confidence could be seen
slipping from Chaupunell's face, like a party mask whose
strap had broken. "They fight on, but their morale is de-
generating rapidly. Something must be done! Where are
our own magicians?"

"Conferencing, or so I am informed. Trying to decide
how best to counter this unexpected assault."

Chaupunell's face was set with concern as he surveyed
the field of battle. "We cannot wait for bickering oldsters
to agree upon a course of action. We must do something
now."

"Do you not think I am aware of this?" Goughfree was as troubled as any of them. "We must find a way to stop the necromancers who are leading the attack, or at the least, find a means of reducing their influence." He called to several nearby couriers, who stood waiting for orders. "Inform those commanding the defenses of the Salmisti, Breleshva, Hidradny, and Zhisbrechar Bridges that they are to hold their towers at all costs. In twenty minutes we will launch a coordinated counterattack, with cavalry, at all four points." As supreme commander of the city's defense, it was within his provenance to issue such an order. He turned to the rest of the general staff.

"I want the best archers not engaged in the immediate defense of the bridges to be formed into four squads. Each is to be escorted by heavy cavalry. When the counterattack begins, they are to be rushed forward in chariots. They must penetrate the enemy lines and kill the four warlocks, or at least cause them to retreat from the field of battle. If they can do that, I think the enemy, whose confidence has presently been restored by unnatural means, will break." He indicated the castle keep behind them. "I have the utmost respect for our own learned scholars, but we cannot wait for them to concur."

It was a sound plan, the best that could be propagated under the circumstances. Even the weather must have thought it auspicious, for when the massive counterattack began, the rain turned to a light mist that was to the benefit of the waiting archers.

The Horde was hit hard. Heavy cavalry from Blest-on-Yoor and the Kingate of Hrushpar slammed into the enemy, trampling those in front, stunning those behind, and bringing the assault on the Salmisti, Zhisbrechar, and Hidradny Bridges to a shocked halt in front of the defensive towers. Only on the bridge of Breleshva did the counterattack slow and begin to falter. Narrowest of the four main bridges that spanned the Drimaud, it offered the least room for heavy horse to maneuver.

Furthermore, the attackers there were led by the wizard of the bloated red cap. Strewing balls of orange flame in front of the counterattacking cavalry, he blinded the horses while the enemy Horde surrounded them and, one by one, brought down their armored riders. Urged forward by their bloodthirsty brethren behind, those attackers in front succeeded in pushing past and over the defenders, leaving chariot-borne archers and steel-clad cavalry bobbing behind like boats trapped in a churning back-eddy at the bend of a river.

A bleak-visaged Goughfree turned away from the unsettling scene. Though he carried the sword slung at his side primarily for reasons of ceremony, he now knew that it was soon to be employed in more prosaic pursuits.

"The tower of the Breleshva Bridge is breached, and the enemy is entering the city."

Zisgymond took a step backward. "With your permission, General, I go to take personal charge of the defenses there. There is a chance we can keep them bottled up in the Plistina District. Fighting house to house, street to street, we can prevent them from flanking and taking any of the other bridges from behind."

That was the great strategic danger, of course. Once across the river, the enemy would be able to fan out and attack the defenders of the other bridges from the rear. This posed the danger of the city's defenses collapsing completely. Of course, the castle and the plains beyond could still be defended, but glorious, beautiful Kyll-Bar-Bennid, city of elegant avenues and a thousand spires, would be lost to pillage and destruction. It was a scenario that threatened to break Goughfree's heart.

They could only pray for the success of Zisgymond's efforts. If anyone could mount a successful counterattack under such rapidly developing desperate circumstances, it was the senior officer from far Xolchis.

Zisgymond had been gone for only a few moments when a courier arrived, breathless and excited. Her expression bespoke good news, a commodity that had been sorely lacking since that morning's sodden sunrise. Whatever it was, Goughfree knew, it did not involve the struggle below. Warriors of the Horde continued to pour through the captured Breleshva tower, fanning out into the city streets behind. Already, tongues of flame and the shadows of smoke from other incipient blazes could be seen rising from homes and businesses that the Totumakk had begun to put to the torch.

Still, any good news was welcome. Absently, he acknowledged the courier's salute. "Yes, what is it?" Perhaps a prediction of worse weather to come, he hoped. A heavy downpour might help to slow the enemy's alarmingly swift advance.

The courier swallowed as she struggled to catch her breath. She was very young, Goughfree saw, and quite attractive. No time for such fond contemplations now, he reminded himself sternly.

"Noble s-sirs," she gasped as droplets of mist pearled her exhausted face, "the convocation of the Gowdland mages has deferred all action upon receiving word that Susnam Evyndd has just entered the city!"

TWO

Goughfree's eyes widened. For him, this amounted to a shout of exultation. Other members of the general staff were not so restrained. Their reactions to this news ranged from a throwing of arms joyously into the air to one colonel who fell to his knees, overcome with emotion.

The few wizards of the Gowdlands who had been recruited for the defense of the city had so far been unable to come up with a coordinated response to the attacks of the Horde. Throughout the battle, they had remained huddled within the castle keep, casting runes and seeking otherworldly inspiration. Now the news that the greatest of them all, the most celebrated and distinguished master of the necromantic arts in all the known kingdoms, was inside the city should serve to strengthen the spines of soldier and scholar alike.

It did not mean he was there to help, Goughfree cautioned himself, but it was hard to imagine why else he might have come. Surely he had not journeyed all the way to Kyll-Bar-Bennid simply to witness and observe its destruction!

"Now we have something to fight back with!" The captain of foot who spoke thrust his clenched fist forward. "Magic with which to counter magic!" He gestured contemptuously in the direction of the looming keep. "A wizard who will do battle with more than mystified mutterings. A mage of *action*."

"Great magic, too, if it is truly Susnam Evyndd." Another officer regarded the courier expectantly.

Eyes blinking as she gasped for air amid the cloaking mist, the young rider nodded vigorously as she swore. "It is truly he, noble sirs. I saw him myself, when he pulled back the curtain of his palanquin to peer out and gauge the weather."

Raundel was nodding slowly. "I have heard that his is not a countenance to be mistaken for another's." He turned to the nearest waiting couriers. "Pass the word to all defending officers that the celebrated wizard Susnam Evyndd is in the city, and will soon be involved in the fight to preserve it from the enemy." Anticipation in defense of morale was no sin, the general believed.

They were waiting, all of them except Zisgymond, when the great man finally arrived. He was dressed simply, in a manner belying his status, when he finally ascended the last step and stood among them atop the parapet. Much shorter than Goughfree had expected, the wizard strode immediately to the overlook and stood there surveying the mist-shrouded chaos of combat. Clad in shirt of plain homespun and pants of gray poplin tucked into calf-high boots of dramunculi leather, he was of ordinary build. But his face bore the scars of a lifetime of doing battle with the unknown and powerful, his eyes did not water, and his voice cleaved the dank air with the assurance of one who knows, if not All, at least a good deal more than his fellow beings were capable of comprehending. It exuded an unshakable, almost jaded self-assurance.

"When I heard what was transpiring, I got here as fast as I could." His tone indicated frustration at the delay, as if he had been personally affronted by Time itself. "I see where your problems lie. We will deal with them now."

Without hesitation or fear of the great height, he scrambled swiftly up onto the rim of the parapet. No one dared move to hold him back, or voice a warning that would clearly not be heeded. As the wizard lifted his arms, the officers of the general staff did not have to be told to step back.

Then Susnam Evyndd began to speak, addressing the unseen in a voice that boomed out over the city like a reassuring balm.

"MALORIAN NAR MACUSCO! SETHIN PAIS TAAL RA!"

The wizard's words rolled over and down the sides of the fortress and the high hill on which it stood like a peal of thunder emerging from the bowels of an arriving storm. It swept out and over clashing armies and howling warriors and echoed from the far banks of the swift-flowing Drimaud. Hearing it, soldiers of the Gowdlands looked up. Seeing a brightness beginning to coalesce on the rim of the fortress wall, piercing the omnipresent drizzle with its sharp radiance, some recognized the individual standing tall in its midst, and began to cheer. Meanwhile the masses of the attacking Horde blinked, and hesitated.

Lightning, white and pure, leaped from the billowing refulgence that had formed above the castle. In a great irregular arc, the angry bolt plunged downward to strike in the midst of the attacking Totumakk. It struck the bespectacled warlock of the bulbous red hat and, without ceremony or preamble, pierced him from front to back. A startled look transformed his supremely repulsive countenance. Slowly and without a word, sorceral or otherwise, he toppled from his seat.

Seeing this, the defenders of the Breleshva Bridge took heart and redoubled their efforts, quickly bringing a halt to the enemy advance. Once more, the well-placed shells of the Shandrac Thunder began to land unimpeded among the advancing Horde, raising havoc in their ranks and preventing reinforcements from surging across the bridge.

A second bolt of mage-bred energy demolished the porcine sorcerer, who squealed in terror as his feeble attempts to deflect the necromantic blow came to naught. Methodically working his way downstream, Susnam Evyndd next slew the third sorcerer. Each time their mystic protector was lost, the line of enemy Horde relying on him faltered. Already, the defenders of the Salmisti and Zhisbrechar Bridges were driving their attackers back across the Drimaud, recovering lost ground stone by blood-soaked stone.

Now only the four-armed warlock remained to shield the last of the enemy's attacking columns. As the wizard Evyndd was preparing to deliver himself of a fourth thunderbolt, the colonel of horse drew the attention of her fellow staff members to a spreading commotion among the Horde on the far bank. Something was emerging from the forest. It was large enough so that its general shape and size could be made out even through the light drizzle.

A giant stepped out from among the trees.

The figure was of indeterminate outline, clad from head to foot in black cloth. No gold thread adorned the massive chest, no precious gems sparkled atop the concealed skull. Though no more massive than the blond-furred lumpenkin or dark lurchers presently crowding the bridges, its oddly shifting outline inspired much comment among the onlookers. As to its identity, that did not long remain a mystery. A chant rising from the far shore began to swell in volume. Soon it was loud enough to be heard on the bridges, among the towers, and finally within the fortress of Kyll-Bar-Bennid itself.

"Mundurucu, Mundurucu, *Mundurucu* . . . !"

"So that's the legendary Khaxan Mundurucu. At last." Along with the rest of his fellow officers, General Mauf-frew was leaning against the parapet, staring across the river past the battle raging below. "He's big, but not all *that* big."

"It is not his size that should concern us." No sooner had Goughfree proffered this sensible observation than the truth of it was proved right.

Erupting from the newly arrived necromancer's right hand, a ball of orange-yellow fire soared castleward. Among shouts and involuntary screams as the members of the general staff, their aides, and waiting couriers took cover, Sus-nam Evyndd calmly turned slightly to his right and raised both hands, palms outward, the thumbs touching. No one paid much attention to the words he uttered, but they must have been powerful indeed.

A glistening, shimmering transparency materialized around him, glass and crystal come together to form a bubble of what one distant onlooker later described as clear magic. Striking this, the ravening orange fireball shattered into fiery, swiftly dissipating embers before crossing the wall.

His arm wheeling round in a great arc, the wizard flung riverward a bolt of pure sorceral force so intensely white that it verged on blue. Goughfree and the others strained to see, but it was the colonel of horse, she of the sharpest vision, who reported to them that while two dozen attending retainers had been blasted into oblivion, the black-clad figure had only been staggered by the blow, and remained standing.

It was Chaupunell who thought to look, not at the continuing pandemonium of battle or the opposing warlock, but at the valorous Evyndd. What he observed was not encouraging. The wizard was frowning, his head inclined forward, as if unable to quite believe that the tremendous blow he had just delivered had not resulted in the complete destruction of its intended target. Drawing himself up, he raised both hands high above his head, fingers pressed tightly together and pointing downward. Lightning began to crackle and take shape before his fingertips as he summoned forth a ball of energy even greater than the one he had just flung at the opposite shore. Chaupunell had to shield his eyes from it. Everyone else kept their gaze focused on the far bank of the river.

Just as the eminent Evyndd was about to deliver his blow, a cylinder of gleaming blackness shot through with internal flame struck the parapet. The result was a narrowly focused but intense explosion that knocked everyone down while rendering them momentarily blind and deaf. When Goughfree had recovered enough for his eyes to focus, he saw that a man-size chunk of wall and floor was now missing from the castle's rim. Smoke rose from the solid stone, which, unbelievably, crackled with flame in several places, the raw rock burning like kindling. Fragments of quartz within the rock had melted and run like pallid butter from the extraordinary but tightly focused heat. His throat clenched, though not from the smoke or dust.

Of the great wizard Susnam Evyndd, protector of the Gowdlands and defender of Kyll-Bar-Bennid, nothing could be seen. Then a soldier cried out, and the survivors ran to see where he was pointing. Below the wall, on the lower landing, the transparent sphere the mage had enchanted around him still sparkled in the dim light. It had preserved not only the wizard's body but those who had been standing in his vicinity. In turn, it had absorbed the full force of the strike from the far side of the river. While not strong enough to penetrate the transparent shield, that awful speeding black cylinder of unknown composition and unimaginable power had blown it and the man contained within right off the parapet on which he had been standing.

Within the sphere of protection, the wizard Susnam Evyndd had been violently buffeted about by forces no human body could be expected to withstand. As he lay unmoving on the stone paving, the pellucid bubble surrounding him made a slight popping sound—and was gone. Blood trickled from his nostrils and the corner of his mouth, staining his simple cotton clothing.

Those deliberating mages who had gathered below to defer to the greatest among them now formed a circle around the intact but motionless body. The expressions on their faces sent a cold, damp chill running down the length of Goughfree's spine. Looking up and back, one disconsolate wizard met the general's stare—and slowly began to shake his head from side to side. Goughfree's jaws tightened until his teeth began to ache. It was impossible, it was madness—Susnam Evyndd could not be dead. He couldn't be!

But he was. While the concussive power of the black cylinder had not shattered his body, its force had broken something within his skull. As the circle of melancholy mages gathered up the limp form of he who had been foremost among them and prepared to carry him safely away from the scene of battle, a distraught Goughfree realized that the defenders of Kyll-Bar-Bennid would have to make do without him.

It must be said that no one gave ground easily. The guardians of the city did not break and run. But when Khaxan Mundurucu took personal charge of the assault and started across the Hidradny Bridge, flinging fire and destruction in every direction from amorphous, black-shrouded hands, Goughfree knew in his heart of hearts that all was lost. Fears of defeat became a certainty when first the Salmisti tower, then the one on the Hidradny, fell to the invaders' relentless onslaught. To save the remainder of the army from complete destruction, and to preserve what he could of the city on the river, he and the rest of the general staff agreed to a full and complete surrender. There was nothing to be gained by trying to hold only the castle against the kind of otherworldly might they had just seen so overpoweringly demonstrated.

They met the enemy officers in the wide, central square. It was quiet, the clocks in the town towers silent, the crackle and roar of burning buildings much less than would have been the case had Goughfree and his colleagues chosen to fight to the last. Heroic bronzes of heroes and artists looked on in silence, unable to influence or comment upon the disturbing proceedings. Ranks of sullen, exhausted soldiers tried to maintain a semblance of order as they were forced to gaze across the two-inch-square individual paving stones at smirking, triumphant men, women, and spear-carrying creatures that were neither.

Standing near the center of the square, apart from the ranks, Goughfree, Chaupunell, and the others waited stoically. Their aim was to save the city and preserve as much of the Gowdlands as possible from pillage, rapine, and worse. Anxious eyes searched the lines of monsters and men for their enemy counterparts.

The forward line of the enemy suddenly parted to allow three figures to step forward. Two were men, tall of body and brutal of aspect. Goughfree was unsettled by their appearance, but did not let it show. What did he expect—court dandies fitted out in elegant silks and brocade? The third figure was much shorter, an impossible progeny of rodent and human, with a long orange-red face, a small mouth full of thin, sharp teeth, and downward-slanting, mournful eyes.

Behind them came the massive, black-clad shape of the diabolical wizard Khaxan Mundurucu. Searching in vain for a face, Goughfree and the others saw only an ambulating tower of lumpy black cloth.

"I am General Drauchec," announced the foremost of the three warriors. "Myself and generals Boroko and Feelleq-a-Qua are here to present the terms of capitulation." So saying, a mailed hand passed over a sheaf of papers that appeared to have been inscribed in blood—though the blood of what, Goughfree could not have said.

Glancing down, he began to read aloud. "This part the third," he muttered, "that concerns the turning over of stores. If we give everything we possess into your charge, what is to guarantee that my troops will have food enough to see them back to their often distant homes?"

"No guarantees, no guarantees!"

The defeated general staff of the Gowdlands looked up sharply at the source of the voice. Even the three Totumakk officers turned. None of them had spoken. The objection had come from the hulking figure that loomed behind them.

The voice, though clear and delivered with some force, had been surprisingly tinny, with an oddly reverberant echo. Almost, Goughfree thought, as if it had issued simultaneously from multiple throats.

Black cloth began to slough away from the figure. Behind Chaupunell, the colonel of horse gasped, and murmurs of confusion could be heard from other members of the staff as the true and natural aspect of Khaxan Mundurucu was at last revealed. Goughfree was no less stunned than any of them. The much-feared Khaxan Mundurucu was not a person, not an individual.

He was a *them*.

It was difficult to say which of the acrobatic goblins that together comprised the hulking form was the ugliest. One by one, they tumbled and leaped from their perches to assemble in a group on the stones of the square. Joined together by strong hands and feet, they had filled the vast black cloth in the shape of a person. Now they stood exposed for what they were: twenty-two goblinlike personages of varying size and appearance, each one of them less pleasant than the next to look upon.

A resigned, slightly fearful Drauchec confirmed what everyone could see for themselves. "May I present the Clan Mundurucu; Masters of the Mystic Arts, Commanders of the Totumakk Horde, Ravagers of the Earth and Despoilers of Kingdoms Grand and Small, Distributors of Omnipotent Unpleasantness. I, and those beneath me, serve at their pleasure." So saying, Drauchec and his two equally intimidating fellow officers proceeded to bow low in the direction of the gathering goblins, arms crossed across their chests in a gesture of utter submission.

Chaupunell leaned forward to whisper into Goughfree's ear. "Surely each of these wee creatures does not possess the power of the whole?"

"Nay," declared a dumpy figure with big ears and the frenzied face of a maniacal toadfish, "we must work together to defeat the likes of the late and unlamented Susnam Evyndd, may his pure and noble soul lie corrupted and befouled forever. It is good that our attack drew him forth to a place of openness where we could get at him. But we all also have our individual powers. See, and tremble!" Raising a hand full of fingers like unpeeled carrots, the goblin whispered a few words and gestured.

There was a poofing of air and a putrid, mephitic odor rushed up Goughfree's nostrils. Turning in horror, he saw a frantic rat with the face of one of his fellow generals scamper wildly past his feet. With a cry of delight, a goblin built like a sack of potatoes with a face banned from the land of frogs leaped into the air and landed with both broad, flabby feet on the fleeing thing that the brave Chaupunell had become. Tiny bones snapped and blood squirted out from beneath heavy, oversize boots.

Goughfree swallowed hard. Behind him, someone was throwing up. "We accept your terms," he managed to choke out, "without guarantees, relying on your mercy as victorious soldiers of noble and chivalrous mien."

"Noble? Chivalrous?" A heavily cowled something resembling a leprous monk sidled up to Goughfree and without warning or hesitation viciously kicked the general in his right knee, cracking the patella and driving the senior officer to the ground, where he lay clutching himself and writhing in pain. "We be the Khaxan Mundurucu! We take, and you give!" Thick, rubbery lips rolled into a terrifying sneer. "Give 'nobly,' if you like, but give you will!" The squat horror whirled. "Drauchec! Boroko! The city is yours. Have at it!" A great cry that was terrible to hear promptly arose from the assembled Horde.

Not everyone died that day in Kyll-Bar-Bennid, though there were many who wished they had. Some few escaped, fleeing in terror back to their farms and far cities, to spread word of what had happened, of the terrible defeat and the slaughter and destruction that had ensued. Little hope of resistance survived anywhere within the Gowdlands. The river Drimaud had been the place to stop the invaders. With most of their best soldiers and fighters now dead or in captivity, the smaller cities and communities could only try to welcome the invaders without resistance, and perhaps to buy them off. It was a feeble hope, a faint wish. Especially in light of what the Khaxan Mundurucu did while much of the city burned below them.

Ascending to the highest tower of the castle keep, the goblinish clan gamboled together while observing with pleasure and satisfaction the fiery turmoil that raged below. Most musically gifted of them all, knob-nosed Kobbod composed deviant arias on the screams that rose from the chasm of the tormented city, while his twisted sisters Kelfeth and Krerwhen put their arms across each others' hunched shoulders and gleefully cackled forth each new morbid stanza invented by their sibling.

Kobkale, generally acknowledged to be the ugliest and therefore the most admired member of the extended family, stood by the edge of the wall appraising the work of the rampaging Horde below. Kushmouth waddled over to his clanmate, his long-whiskered, flattened face alight with the pleasure to be gained from observing the final damnation of others.

"What think you, brother? A good week's work!" A leathery arm waved eastward. "All the lands of these pustulant braggarts are now ours."

"Not quite." Buried deep with Kobkale's profound repulsiveness was a mind steeped in abhorrent knowledge and sharp of thought. "Some may continue to hold out against us."

"Think you so? Genuinely?" Kushmouth frowned, an action that drew eyebrows like dead larvae halfway down over his protuberant eyes. "Don't you think the destruction of the primary city of the Gowdlands will cause all the others to bow in terror to our will?"

"Mostly, yes. But there may still be some who think it better to resist than to acknowledge our suzerainty. For them, laying waste to a town and its inhabitants will not be lesson enough." Kobkale glanced skyward. "A greater lesson may be wanting. The everlastingly stubborn must not merely be terrified: they must be reminded of that terror every day. They must be reminded of their helplessness as much as of our power." Turning from the rampart, he gathered his black-and-gray robes around him.

Depraved anticipation filled Kushmouth's grotesque face. "You have something in mind, brother!"

"Most assuredly. Gather the Clan."

They assembled atop the captured castle keep. When Kobkale put forth his proposal, there was no dissension. All present thought the notion admirable, which was to say surpassingly malign. It should ensure the subjugation of the peoples of the Gowdlands forever, and render them pleasantly malleable in the hands of the Clan and the Totumakk Horde. No chastisement more terrifying had ever been proposed by a member of the group. Kobkale was duly applauded.

This time there was no need for them to bind themselves together in the form of a giant. Instead, they gathered in a closed circle, gnarled hands clasping misshapen fingers, and focused on an imaginary point midway between them. Individually, every member of the clan could perform one kind of powerful sorcery or another. When they combined their efforts, conjoined their exertions, nothing necromantic or normal could stand before the force of their malign vision.

In accordance with Kobkale's instructions, the secret words were whispered, the special incantations invoked. In the center of the circle, unmoved and unaffected by the howls of despair still rising from the doomed city, a dark *something* began to take shape. As the chanting of the Clan Mundurucu rose in intensity and increased in volume, so did the convocating darkness. A roiling sphere of ultimate blackness congealed from the depths of places where men did not go; swelling, expanding, engorging itself on the words uttered in concert by the enclosing goblinate.

With a vast, guttural sigh, as of Death itself exhaling, the sphere suddenly spewed skyward. Reaching the clouds, it began to spread outward in all directions. Gazing at it, a delighted Kmeliog brushed back the worms that were her hair and thought of a monstrous quantity of ink spilled on a floor, only all of it turned upside down.

Where the darkness touched, the light faded, until only grayness remained. All across the Gowdlands, and beyond, natural light was blotted from existence. With the light went every suggestion, every hint of color, until all the known world found itself existing in a state of enduring grayness, permanently somber and sad. When on the following morn the sun rose, it would not shine, but instead cast only a cold ashen glow on a world cast down into an abiding melancholy.

Concluding the hex with a necromantic flourish, Kobkale and his clanmates contemplated what they had wrought, and were much pleased with their effort. None of them had ever cared much for color anyway, so its absence did not trouble them. Even the fires that leaped from building to building in the town below were devoid of brilliance, the dancing flames no longer blushing red and orange, but only an all-consuming, all-destroying gray.

"*That* demonstration of power should put an end to any thoughts of resistance," Kobkale declared firmly as the circle broke up and its component clan members proceeded to go their individual ways.

"Genuinely, genuinely!" Kesbroch clapped thick hands together in delight. Devious and irresistible were the ways of the Clan whose destiny it was to dominate the whole world.

He was not alone in his praise for their brother's counsel. Later that night, in the great hall of the castle where they had taken up residence, the other members of the Clan raised a toast of the blood of slain virgins to their noble Kobkale while they feasted on the tender meat of freshly butchered young children who had been dragged from their hiding places throughout the city.

Genuinely (as the Mundurucu were wont to say), the overarching pall of grayness that descended upon the Gowdlands sowed fear and consternation far and wide. Communities that had yet to feel the heavy foot of the Totumakk trembled and cried out as every trace and speck of color vanished from familiar surroundings. Flowers lost their tints, while paintings became as simple ink drawings set down beneath gray wash. Pinkness disappeared from the cheeks of young girls, while no longer could eager swains speak to their loved ones of eyes of dancing blue, or green, or any other hue. The world was plunged into a morbid, dreary grayness, where everyone could still see, but had lost the heart to do so.

Forced to dine on leaden grass, cattle were put off their feed and grew thin and listless, until their ribs began to show through their sides. Fungi of all manner of malformed shape and size grew large, overwhelming fields of grain, assailing orchards, and even invading the fabled, meticulously tended vegetable gardens of the kingates of Spargel and far Homim-mu. Birds ceased their singing, reduced to an occasional subdued croak, while ducks and chickens found no solace in eggs that instead of issuing forth ivory white, emerged from their cloaca ashen of aspect.

A different kind of grayness in the form of hunger began to stalk the land. Comfortably ensconced within the castle of Kyll-Bar-Bennid, the Khaxan Mundurucu received reports from Horde outriders of what their collective spell had wrought, and were mightily pleased. Town after town, city after city, submitted without a fight to their dominion, begging only that a little color be restored to them. The Mundurucu accepted these capitulations with ill grace, and maintained the full force of the malicious incantation. The despair of their newly acquired subjects was too delicious to discard. So they continued to revel in the all-pervasive grayness they had conjured forth, and to commit unspeakable atrocities within the defiled sanctity of the castle.

Kobkale had been right about more than one consequence of the Clan's conquest. Among the inhabitants of the Gowdlands were a few individuals too headstrong to realize the impotence of their position even when confronted by the sweeping power of the Mundurucu. These intractables had holed themselves up within the High Fortress of Malostranka, in the deep forest of Fasna Wyzel, and from there steadfastly refused to submit to the rule of the Totumakk. Considering it a minor matter, the Mundurucu sent a small army under the command of General Feelleq-a-Qua to subdue these obstinate ones. Finding the fortress, which was set on a sheer-sided promontory in the midst of a deep river canyon, too inaccessible to assault directly, Feelleq-a-Qua and his staff proceeded to blockade the only access, a bridge built across the tops of smaller, intervening spires, and settled down to starve out the last resistance to the Horde's rule.

The rodent-faced general was in no hurry to sacrifice any of those under his command. They had plenty of time. With the rest of the Gowdlands subdued there was no fear of being attacked from the rear, and the rich surrounding forest and countryside provided both ample provisions and good sport to the men and creatures under his command. Comfortably bivouacked, they could ravage and burn a village a week without running out of prospects for at least

a year. Undoubtedly, the garrison of the fortress would realize the futility of their position long before then, and
would request a sullen truce. Feelleq-a-Qua would gra-
ciously accept, occupy Malostranka, and then have its surviving occupants slaughtered down to the last infant.

For now, though, he was content to rest, secure in his
mastery of the immediate territory, and have his siege engineers lob occasional great stones or balls of gray fire at
the fortress. It would not do to allow its delinquent defenders time to relax, or to enjoy a peaceful night's sleep.
Idling in the chair that had been set up outside his tent beneath a canopy of gray silk, guards in attendance, he contemplated the siege as he munched contentedly on a bowl
of ladyfingers that were not made of cake.

THREE

Valkounin the Strong stood before a downcast Princess Petrine (who because of the all-pervading grayness looked more drawn than ever) and voiced what most who had assembled in the audience chamber of the castle already knew but preferred not to articulate.

"As of yesterday week, Gierash, Stenyau-by-the-Drover, the kingdoms of Roun and Rouel, Parbafan, and Grand Tecrelle have all made obeisance to the Horde." Valkounin ignored the despondent murmur that greeted his pronouncement. "We can count on no help from any of them."

"Even Grand Tecrelle!" someone muttered in disbelief. "They had the finest light cavalry in the far eastern Gowdlands."

Valkounin glanced back at the speaker. "Who can blame them for submitting? Not I. Of what use are cavalry against sorcery, lancers against incantations?" He gestured skyward, to where the formerly magnificent frescoes that adorned the high, vaulted ceiling now looked down on the assembly out of gray-gormed eyes that seemed to weep silently for their lost splendor.

"A sword cannot banish a spell. The most accurate archer

cannot transfix a hex. Without necromantic help of the first order, we are lost." Turning slowly, he scanned as many faces as he could. Some were known personally to him: others were strangers who had fled to Malostranka in search of sanctuary, or allies—or hope. The first was temporary, the second useless, and the third—the third was scarcely present.

"If only Susnam Evyndd—" a captain of fallen Partiria began. Valkounin cut him off.

"Susnam Evyndd is dead! Stunned where he stood trying to defend Kyll-Bar-Bennid. He was the greatest wizard of the Gowdlands. All students and practitioners of the arcane arts acknowledged this. Yet now he is dead, as dead as any ordinary pikeman who fought to hold back the Horde at the terminus of the Salmisti Bridge. Understanding this, the lesser wizards have fled to more congenial climes or temporalities. Still, we must find sorceral help, somewhere. . . ." His deep voice trailed away, into a silence devoid of suggestions.

Petrine was as beautiful as any princess could be expected to be, but she was also wise beyond her years. That, and her sharp tongue, had kept her unwed for far longer than was usual for marriageable royalty. Now she found herself, unintentionally and quite by accident of circumstance, in charge of the last pocket of resistance holding out against the cursed invaders in all the imposing length and breadth of the Gowdlands. It was a task she had not sought, but found herself unable to abandon. Besides, she no longer had any choice in the matter. The Khaxan Mundurucu knew who led the defense of fortress Malostranka, and everyone knew what they did to those who resisted their dominion. Better, she had long ago decided, to die fighting than squirming.

For the sake of those who had gathered together in this

last outpost of goodness and civilization, she did her best to mask her emotions. It would have been a great help, she knew, if even a very inexperienced and inconsequential wizard had been present to stand at her side and offer sage advice. But there were none. The place reserved for one trained in such arts was as vacant as the stone that waited to uplift such a brave figure. Valkounin was right about the wizards of the Gowdlands: they were fled, all of them. The demise of Susnam Evyndd had cowed them into uselessness.

"At least," she ventured, for lack for anything more positive to offer, "we are able to give the learned Evyndd a farewell befitting his courage and skill—inadequate as they may have proven to be."

"Yes, majesty." Welworthen, her personal adviser, squinted through the gray air at the gray sky visible through a gray side window. "The burial party should be soon finished with their work."

"Good," grunted Valkounin, who from the time the intention had been declared had disapproved of the dangerous and, to him, entirely unnecessary distraction. "The sooner they dispose of the remains and get back here, the better. We can use every hand that can raise a sword."

Far from the inaccessible canyon that protected the ramparts of the besieged fortress Malostranka, farther still from the ravaging host that was the Horde, deep within the ancient forest of Fasna Wyzel, a small troop of heavily armed men and women was wending its way toward a river. No homes graced its sparkling shores, no neat gardens were set carefully back from its steeply sloping banks. The depths of the Fasna Wyzel were a place of mystery, of robust rumors and ancient tales twice told. People went in, and sometimes came out, but on no account did they linger. The forest was too dark, too dense, too full of hollows and hedges where eyes peeped out at intrepid passers-by and teeth flashed when the sun fell the wrong way.

No fear of the latter now, mused an introspective Captain Slale. Green as it was once, the forest, like the rest of the world, had descended into gloomy grayness thanks to the all-encompassing Mundurucu hex. The birds that still sang in its trees, albeit fitfully and without enthusiasm, were tiny sad balls of dingy fluff. The other creatures who called the Fasna Wyzel home were little better off. Only the squirrels, charcoal to light gray of color before the application of the spell, could now revel in their natural griminess, and they chose not to do so. Since the coming of the Horde, the world was no longer a happy place, and the forest no exception.

Even the normally clear river, where the line of glum-faced soldiers turned off the main trail and headed upstream, had been reduced to a rush and gurgle of irritating drabness. No lights flashed from the small cataracts in its midst. Even the cheerful frogs had been mortified into silence by the persisting dearth of color.

In the absence of trail, Slale relied on the instructions he had received at Malostranka from the dejected minor wizard who had been one of those who had spirited the deceased Evyndd's body out of Kyll-Bar-Bennid ahead of the triumphant Horde. If these were correct, they should be very close now to their intended destination. Not that it mattered to him if they missed their goal. Nothing mattered anymore except killing as many of the enemy as possible. While serving in the defense of Kyll-Bar-Bennid, his own homeland had been overrun by the outriders of the Horde, the fine home that had been in his family for centuries had been burned to the ground, and his family, his wife and two sons . . .

He concentrated on finding a path through the trees. They grew close together here, so near the nourishing river. Moss hung from branches and sprouted like gray fur from the trunks of seasoned boles. Invigorated by the absence of normal light, monstrous mushrooms and toadstools and liverworts clambered wildly over fallen logs and old stumps. Except for the unquenchable rumble of the river, the forest was unnaturally silent, as if its inhabitants had been massively overdosed with some powerful tranquilizing agent. Slale wished for some such medicine himself. It might help him not to think so much. Thinking was dangerous, as it led inexorably to remembrance.

"There it is, sir." A weary, perspiring sergeant-of-arms rose partway in his saddle and pointed. Slale could see the house, too, peeping through the trees. He was quietly relieved. They would, it seemed, be able to do what they had come for, deliver the contents of the silver box to the domicile that lay just ahead, and return by the secret way to Malostranka. He imagined the Princess Petrine would be pleased. He hoped so. Very little pleased her these days. Even as small and insignificant a success as this would be welcomed. In that respect, he supposed, the troop's long journey was not a waste, even if he continued personally to think otherwise.

The house in the forest was surprisingly large, and of unusual design. But that was to be expected. The rear half appeared to have been hewn from the solid rock of an immense pile of boulders, while the front rose as high as three stories beneath the many-gabled thatched roof. Mullioned windows of stained glass greatly diminished by grayness gazed out across river and woods. The forest had been cleared away in front, and a small yard filled with diverse flowers would normally have greeted visitors with a carpet of color. Now their manifold petals hung low, drowned by the all-encompassing grayness.

As they approached the entrance, a dog ran out to greet them. He was of medium size, a wirehaired male who was nothing less than an energetic mass of textbook muttness. There wasn't a straight hair on his body, his tail curled back up over his rear end, and the tongue hanging out of the side of his mouth was splotched with black. Dark, lively eyes gazed inquiringly up at the tired visitors, and his whole countenance bespoke a nature that was ever sunny and alert. It raised the spirits of several of the disillusioned soldiers just to look upon this four-legged bundle of homey cheer. As the troop continued toward the house, the dog uttered a few desultory warning barks, but his heart was clearly not in it. The soldiers sensed this, and smiled. They, too, had often spent long hours on guard, with nothing to show for their efforts.

"Easy there, boy. What's the matter—you hungry?" From the heights of his saddle it was too far for Slale to reach down and pet the animal. Instead, he smiled and spoke softly, and was rewarded with toothy grin and wagging tail. The captain did not feel sorry for the abandoned dog. The life it led was doubtless better than his own.

"Dessevia," he ordered a soldier, "as soon as we're inside, see if you can find this poor friendly mongrel something to eat." It was the least they could do, he reflected, for a loyal animal whose master the visitors were bringing home in a box.

Once inside the rustic outer gate, they dismounted. Leaving half his troop to keep an eye on the horses and the forest, Slale and his remaining soldiers warily approached the house of Susnam Evyndd. The dog trotted alongside, long tongue lolling loose from the side of its mouth, spittle flecking the paving stones, eyes intent on these strange new visitors. With the silent abode looming before him, the good captain wished for the presence and advice of even a lowly wizardly apprentice, but it had been felt that none could be spared from Malostranka. The idea of entering the house of a powerful sorcerer, even a compassionate dead one, had not appealed to him from the start.

Yet there was nothing to be done but to do it, and if crossing the threshold uninvited caused him to be turned instantly into a newt, then at least he would be spared forevermore the unforgettable images of his ravaged home and defiled family that had been seared into his brain.

As his soldiers crowded tentatively close behind him he tried the front door, only slightly unnerved by the strange shapes that seemed to be swirling within the stained glass that flanked the entry. It opened at his touch, and he stepped inside. Nothing happened, except that the dog ran past him to vanish into the depths of the house. He and his troops were not blasted from the face of the earth, or transmogrified into vermin. He sighed, not entirely with relief.

"Come on," he ordered simply. "We might as well follow the dog." Clutching their weapons tightly and keeping close together, wary men and women followed in a tight knot close behind their captain.

Slale was not surprised when the animal led him straight to the kitchen. He did start slightly when he felt something rubbing up against his leg. Glancing down, he was relieved to see that it was only a very muscular black cat of average size. She had white spots on her muzzle and feet, and did not appear to be in any immediate danger of starvation.

"Must be plenty of rats and mice in a forest house like this, kitty. I expect you're better off than the dog." Reaching down, he stroked her absently, and she purred forth a grateful response. "Dessevia, Koscka; see if you can find something for these unfortunate creatures to eat." The two soldiers obediently began to poke through the multitude of cabinets, only too grateful for the duty. While the cupboards through which they were now searching might indeed contain food, they might also hold precious objects small enough for a sharp-eyed soldier to slip into a pocket.

Disappointed, they found only moldering food, utensils fashioned of base metals, and eventually, a bin marked "food for animals." The dog was almost hysterically grateful for the feed they gave it, and though they appeared well enough, the three cats who had one by one emerged from the hidden depths of the house readily joined in the feast.

The canary in the elaborate cage that hung near a far window was in more desperate need of sustenance, which the grumbling soldiers also provided. Unexpectedly, one let out a yell and nearly knocked his companion down in his sudden haste to escape the farthest corner of the kitchen, where a large wired crate sat upon a sturdy shelf among pots and bins. Instantly, weapons were drawn to deal with this new threat.

Sword in hand, the terrified soldier hovered halfway between his captain and whatever it was he had espied in the farthest reaches of the kitchen.

"What is it, Dessevia?" Slale asked tersely. Staring in the direction from which the shout had originated, he saw nothing.

"A serpent, sir! A bleeding great hideous nasty serpent!"

"It is said that wizards often keep dangerous familiars close about them," someone whispered from near the back of the invaded kitchen.

"True enough, but such sorceral servants are usually drawn from the ranks of cats and sometimes dogs, which creatures we have found here in plenty." An amateur scholar of some knowledge, Slale was proud of his book learning. "A sorcerer might keep a serpent to utilize in other ways."

Cautiously, the point of his own sword preceding him, he advanced in the direction of the cage. Oblivious to the slow approach of the uneasy soldiery, the canary had begun to sing as it cracked and swallowed the seed they had placed in its cage.

It was a snake of a type Slale recognized: impressive in appearance, it was as long as a man was tall, and of substantial girth. It lay coiled peacefully within a tightly lidded cage of glass, eyeing them out of small dark red eyes, its tongue flicking continuously in their direction.

Relieved, the captain put up his sword. "Be at ease, gentlemen and ladies. The creature is secured within its pen, and cannot get out. Furthermore, it is one of those serpents that kills by embracing its prey, and not with poison."

"You be certain of that, Captain?" The tremulous query originated with a trooper named Taree, a simple but brave swordswoman who had managed to escape the havoc that had befallen Kyll-Bar-Bennid.

"Yes. I recognize the kind." Slale stood a little straighter, his voice taking on a tone of self-importance. "I have seen such creatures depicted in a book."

The soldiers murmured softly, those who were not inherently terrified of serpents or books crowding closer for a better look. It was indeed a handsome snake, with large diamondlike patterns running down the length of its back and sides. What its natural colors might be they could only imagine: the Mundurucu hex had reduced its scaly coloration to the same sad state of washed-out gray as now dominated the rest of the world.

"I wonder if it's as hungry as these others?" the trooper commented, immediately regretting giving voice to his curiosity. His comrades were not hesitant in responding.

"Why don't you try feeding it and find out?" The suggestion from the back of the crowded kitchen sparked a minor but much needed outburst of laughter.

"Snakes of this kind need to be fed only rarely." Turning away from the cage and its inquisitive but slow-moving occupant, Slale surveyed the rest of the kitchen. "This is as good a place as any to do what we came for, I suppose. Bring forth the box."

The soldiers who had been charged with transporting the silver crate promptly wrestled it forward and set it down in front of the basin that was used for the washing and cleaning of food. Being forced to look after it all the way from Malostranka had left them with a less than sanguine opinion of its bulk, not to mention its contents.

Approaching the crate, Slale bent to unfasten the straps that secured it. Removing the lid, he gestured to his soldiers. From the midst of thick horsehair packing, they removed a smaller container. Simply fashioned of silver inlaid with an assortment of attractive but in no wise remarkable semiprecious stones, they set it gently on the sturdy wooden table that dominated the center of the room. It lay there waist-high, the silver shining dully in the muted, cursed gray light as if relieved to be free of its prison. In unblighted sunlight the carnelians and agates, amethysts and citrines that decorated its sides would have twinkled brightly. But there was no such liveliness in them now. They were as subdued as the rest of the world, reduced to lackluster lumps of rock that, like everything else, had been smothered by the Mundurucu hex.

Using his thumbs, Slale carefully pushed the two heavy latches in opposite directions and then lifted the hinged lid to reveal an inner nest of plush satin. In natural light this would have been a bright, regal red. Now it was only a wan pillowed mush. A double handful of dust reposed in a covered crystal bowl—all that remained of the venerable sorcerer Susnam Evyndd.

In accordance with wizardly tradition, the sorrowful mages who had spirited his corpse safely out of Kyll-Bar-Bennid had cremated his body upon reaching the safety of the fortress Malostranka. The remains, much reduced in volume from the original, had been preserved in the silver box. There it had been decided, by the most knowledgeable among the scholars of wizardry present, that the ashes ought properly and in the absence of any other instructions for their disposal to be returned to their owner's last known place of habitation, there to be scattered among his possessions. This also was in keeping with sorceral tradition.

Why this need be done, a number of the soldiers had grumbled on more than one occasion during the long march through the Fasna Wyzel, they could not imagine. Theirs was not to understand, however, but to do. At least they had been given the command of a rational, perceptive officer. Slale was no pompous ass, no rich noble's ambitious progeny, drunk on decorations and ribbons, but a real soldier: one the men and women under him could identify with.

"What now, Captain?" Sergeant Hyboos looked on impatiently, anxious to be away from the daunting house of magic and back to the fighting. Every hand was needed in the defense of the fortress, and they were most certainly wasting their time here. Meowing hopefully, a long-haired blond cat was rubbing up against his ankle. He ignored it until, meowing rather more forcefully, it began to dig its claws into his lower leg. He pushed it away with his other foot, ignoring it when it hissed at him softly. No one had time to comfort or caress *him*. People were suffering, and he had no time for animals.

"I'm not sure, Hyboos. The scholar Popelkas gave no

detailed instructions. 'Scatter the ashes in the house' was all I was told." Glancing at the sergeant, seeing the anxious, expectant faces of the rest of the troop, the good captain shrugged, picked up the bowl, removed the cut crystal lid, pursed his lips, and blew.

A cloud of gray ash erupted from the interior of the gleaming bowl to swirl and dissipate throughout the gray-toned kitchen. It was very fine ash, the cremators having done their task efficiently (as well they ought, having lately had all too many opportunities to practice their craft). It seemed to hang briefly in the still air of the high-ceilinged room, scattered only by the vigor of the captain's forceful exhalation. Then it began to sift down, until drifting particles of dead sorcerer could no longer be distinguished from the omnipresent accumulated dust of household inattention.

Slale waited hopefully, as did his troops, gazing anxiously at their surroundings. The lusterless sun continued to pour through the tall kitchen windows. The scruffy dog continued to crunch single-mindedly at his refilled food bowl. Cats moved silently, or claimed for their temporary territory muted patches of gray daylight. A single querulous meow ruffled the stillness. In its cage the canary chirped once from its perch and was still.

Among the silent, assembled troops, someone finally made a rude noise. The ensuing sniggers reflected only a moderate degree of discouragement. No one had really expected anything to happen.

"Let's get out of here." Frustrated and disappointed, Slale turned and directed the soldiers to pick up the valuable box and bowl. These he consigned to the care of those unlucky ones who had escorted it all the way from Malostranka. Grateful to be at last on their way, the soldiers thus charged offered no fresh objection to this duty. Who knew what might happen between house and fortress? One or two of the gemstones set in the sides of the box might inadvertently manage to work their way free of their restraining bezels.

Peaceful though it was in the dwelling's vicinity, none of the soldiers desired to linger. In more cheerful times they might have felt differently. Trapped as they were in the gloom of the hex, with the threat of final conquest by the Horde looming over all of them, they wished only to return to Malostranka to participate in the defense of the fortress. There was no time to lie by the side of the singing stream, luxuriating in its enforced drabness, on grass drained as gray and lifeless as the ashes they had just scattered inside the house.

The dog saw them off, his whiskery terrier countenance giving him the aspect of a sorrowful beggar afflicted with a mustache too big for his face. For a moment, Slale thought the animal might follow. Another time, he might have encouraged the friendly mongrel to do so. Not now. At Malostranka there was food enough only for those able to fight. A last look back, when the residence was nearly out of sight, showed that the dog had gone back inside. He hoped they had left it food enough until some friend or relative of the dead wizard thought to pay a visit to the house. Twisting in his saddle, he turned his gaze and his thoughts firmly to the path ahead. They were done with this honorable but frivolous mission, and he was anxious to be out of these endless woods and back to the fortress.

The house of Susnam Evyndd fell behind, until it was lost to sight among the trees. Despondent birds flitted between the massive boles, too dejected by their dismal surroundings to sing. Forest animals crept listlessly from den to food. In the slow eddies of the river, even the fish swam with manifest despair, barely able to muster enough enthusiasm to chase tadpoles or water bugs. A pair of dun-colored unicorns cropped absently at a purpleberry bush, their actions motivated more by instinct than actual hunger. Melancholy suffused the wood like fog and dripped from the eyes of its manifold denizens like tears.

But within the gabled house of one dead wizard, something was stirring.

It caught the attention of Oskar the dog, who had recently bid an uncomprehending farewell to the strange humans who had paid an all too fleeting visit to the humanless home. Closely resembling an ambulatory mass of dirty steel wool, the inquisitive mutt found himself sniffing curiously at a corner of the kitchen where a small pile of dust had accumulated. To his slightly addled canine mind, it smelled oh so very faintly of the intimately familiar. Atop the kitchen worktable, a slightly built calico cat caught in the process of cleaning its paws paused to watch.

The perplexed Oskar sniffed again, more deeply this time. What his doggy mind decided could not be known, but his reaction was easily deciphered. Some of the dust went up his nose, whereupon he let out an impressive and reverberant sneeze that echoed throughout the otherwise silent house.

At which point he unexpectedly found himself gazing at the world from a significantly different vantage point.

He still stood on all fours, but very different fours they were. He was more naked than even when his master had taken to shaving him in anticipation of the hottest months of the summer. Gray-tinged bare flesh met his startled gaze. Sitting back, he found his head and upper body rising of their own accord, until he was standing, yes *standing,* on his two hind legs. His eyes looked down at the world from a height considerably greater than before. Stunned quite beyond anything in his open, good-natured experience, he let out a howl of surprise.

"By the mother of all litters that ever peed in their sleeping box, I never—!"

He broke off the howl halfway, eyes wide, one paw snapping back to cover his shocked mouth. Except it wasn't a paw. It was a hand. A hand not unlike that of his master Evyndd, only younger and smoother of skin. And his muzzle, the very same muzzle he used to locate deliciously dead animals and putrefying old bones—his muzzle had been squashed flat. It, too, was naked like most of the rest of him, except for the thick, drooping mustache that grew beneath his nose. His nose . . .

His nose was warm and dry when it ought to be cold and wet. Even so, he did not feel sick.

Slowly, fearful of falling over, he turned to examine his surroundings. They, at least, had not changed. There were the familiar cleaning basins and the spigot from which cool, fresh water flowed at the touch of a lever. There the shelves, with their dishes and utensils. There the main food preparation table, atop which the cat Cocoa liked to sprawl and clean herself. She was sitting there as he stared now, licking herself between the toes of her right forepaw, her tongue carefully moving up and down in brisk, efficient cleaning movements. She glanced up at him out of bright, alert eyes that were forest green when everything wasn't gray.

"Meowrrr—are you ugly! You look—"

Breaking off abruptly at the sound of her own voice, she looked down at herself. In place of the mottled, multicolored cat, a very beautiful and wholly human young woman sat cross-legged atop the worktable. Like Oskar, she was mostly hairless and entirely naked.

"I look what?" Adopting a slightly twisted grin, he put his forepaws (no; his hands, he corrected himself) on his hips and regarded his formerly feline companion expectantly. His joints bent in all the wrong directions.

Stunned, she slid awkwardly off the worktable to land perfectly on all fours. Hesitantly she stood up, imitating his posture, and slowly began to examine herself. She was manifestly not pleased with her initial discoveries.

"Where," she declared in outraged bewilderment, *"is my fur?"*

"Gone the way of much that is cat," declared a strong, somber, and surprisingly deep voice.

"Does this mean that from now on we exchange kisses instead of hisses?" added a second.

As one, Oskar and Cocoa looked in the direction of the doorway that led to the inner rooms of the house. Two more humans were standing there, also naked. Oskar sniffed. His nostrils seemed not to be working quite right, as if a cloth had been laid over his face. But he could still recognize a familiar body odor when he encountered one, even from across the room. Though entirely human, he knew both of those who had spoken.

The strong, deep voice belonged to Mamakitty. Though senior among the wizard's cats, she was deceptively sleek of flank. From frequent friendly tussles, Oskar knew she was fashioned of the cat equivalent of corded steel. Standing there in the doorway, black as always and with the same white patches ornamenting her muzzle, feet, and hands, her nude form reflected both her maturity and her remarkable physical condition.

Next to her, experimenting with his human arms and hands by taking great silly swings at the empty air, was Cezer. His hair was as proportionately long and blond as it had been when he had walked on four paws, though now it was by and large restricted to the top of his head. Delighting in the utterly unexpected transformation, he began leaping about, letting out occasional shouts of delight as he reveled in his bipedal vantage point and prehensile fingers.

"Look!" he shouted gleefully as he picked up first a soup ladle, then a mixing bowl, "I can hold things! No more just pushing them around—I can pick them up! And throw them!" Demonstrating, he heaved the ladle in Oskar's direction. The dog-man ducked, leaving the ladle to bang noisily off the back wall of the kitchen.

"That's not all I can grab." Taking a step toward the worktable, Cezer raised both human hands.

A familiar warning hiss emerged from the throat of the transformed Cocoa. "Keep away from me, you lecherous freak! I'm in no mood to play."

"This isn't about play." Striding with her usual innate majesty into the kitchen, Mamakitty cuffed the ebullient Cezer sharply on the side of his head. Though he was bigger than she, and stronger despite her size and condition, he did not hit back. He had too much respect for her. They all did, Oskar included.

When a very different kind of hiss sounded from the far corner of the kitchen, they realized with uneasy certainty that whatever unknown incantation had transfigured them had not yet finished with its transforming work.

The naked man who rose slowly and unsteadily but with increasing assurance from a low crouch was massively built, and far taller than anyone else in the room. His face was as chiseled as the rest of his body, and unlike the rest of them, he was absolutely hairless, even to the eyebrows. The newly rendered humans did not identify him immediately. This was not surprising, since in their previous embodiments they had had very little contact with him even though he had lived always in their midst.

Realization struck Oskar first. After all, only one denizen

of the wizard Evyndd's menagerie had been both hairless
and fashioned of solid muscle.

"Great offal—it's Samm!"

"I never would have guessed." The beguiling Cocoa was
eyeing the naked mass of muscle admiringly, much to the
well-formed but far smaller Cezer's evident irritation.

Not knowing what else to do, and wishing from the very
beginning to preserve harmony in their altered states among
all, Oskar approached the man-serpent. Imitating a gesture
he had observed the Master exchanging with his guests, he
tentatively extended an open hand.

"Samm the snake. How strange that after all these years
we should only now truly be able to communicate."

Bending low to avoid banging his bald head on the ceiling, the giant's expression reflected serious confusion.
Oskar immediately found himself sympathizing.

"It's all right. I think all of us who have been transformed by the Master's magic are capable of speech. Try
it."

"Wasn't worried about speaking," the giant grumbled.
"Just not sure yet how to use these." He held out both huge
hands, gazing at them as if he had suddenly sprouted cac-
tus spines instead of fingers. Which he might as well have,
Oskar reflected. To a formerly limbless creature arms and
legs, hands and feet, would be more of a novelty than even
human speech.

Reaching out, he took one of Samm's hands in his own
and squeezed gently. Emulating the gesture, the giant
squeezed gently back, his grip completely enveloping
Oskar's. The dog-man winced at the pressure but held on
long enough to shake the other's hand. He was relieved to
have his own back in one piece.

"What has happened to us? What is this?" Like the serpent he had been, Samm was a creature of few words.

"The work of the Master. It has to be." Mamakitty strode farther into the room, scanning shelves and starting to poke into cabinets. "There must be reason behind all of this, or it would not have happened."

"Where is the old tomcat, anyway?" Leaning back against the worktable, Cezer struggled to scratch under his chin with his rear leg. While he could manage the feat, he found it much easier to use one of his new hands. "If he's making magic, he should be here."

"He is here." Oskar eyed the younger man somberly. "I know—I smelled him. Inhaled some of him, actually."

Cezer frowned and stood away from the table. "What are you talking about? That dust—?" Oskar nodded slowly. "But that would mean—?"

"The Master is dead." Clawing open a bottom drawer, Mamakitty found it contained only onions. "He would not have caused this to happen to us without a reason. Somewhere in the house there must be an explanation for what has happened to us. When we find it, we will know what to do next."

Placing a firm hand on the back of Cocoa's neck, Cezer smiled invitingly. "I know what I'd like to do next. This shape offers all sorts of interesting new possibilities."

Whirling, she slapped his hand away. "For once in your lives be serious, Cezer! This thing that has happened is a bigger thing than any of us!" Under her breath she added, "Master Evyndd should have had you fixed last year, when he was thinking about it."

"I heard that!" Cezer replied accusingly.

"Both of you!" Mamakitty growled commandingly, "stop fighting and start looking."

"Looking for what?" Spreading his hands in an unconsciously perfect human gesture, Cezer eyed her questioningly. "Even if we found something, how would we know what we were looking at? Cats can't read."

"I have this inescapable feeling that we can now, just as we can speak." The older woman tossed a sealed jar in his direction.

Catching it effortlessly in one hand, Cezer glanced at the handwritten label. "Sweet pickles. I hate pickles." His eyes widened as he realized what he had just done. "*Fssst,* you're right! We *can* read!" He examined the warm, familiar kitchen anew. To the usual sights and smells, little had been removed while' much had been added. "I wonder what else we can do?"

"Besides babble inanely?" Cocoa was helping Mamakitty with her search. "Why don't you help us and find out? There must be something the Master left behind that will tell us what to do next." In a cheerful daze, the long-haired young man proceeded to join in the search for they knew not what.

Leaving Samm to cope by himself for the moment with the complicated and somewhat daunting business of learning how to use hands and feet, Oskar started to join the others, only to be stopped by a plaintive voice from overhead.

"Hey—what about me?"

Despite the human words, there was no mistaking the golden, mellifluous tone. Glancing up, Oskar saw a very slim, very pale blond young man clinging rather desperately to the highest rafters of the kitchen.

"Hello, Taj, and welcome to the world of human form. Come down and be with the rest of us."

"Come down—how?" Extending a slender arm, the former songbird fluttered fingers with extreme rapidity and to absolutely no effect. "My wings are gone! In their place I have these—these finger things. Good for picking up seed but useless, I fear, for flying."

"It's only a short drop. Just let go and land on your feet."

"Easy for a dog to say," the former canary grumbled. "If I come down, you promise to keep the cats from attacking me?"

Oskar shook his head resignedly. That gesture, at least, felt wholly familiar. "As you can see, everything's different now, Taj. You're as big as any of the cats-that-were." This human speech, he reflected, was much more efficient for purposes of communication than barking. The only response barking at Taj, for example, had ever provoked was a squirt of something from the high-hanging cage that was not especially eloquent.

"Yes, but not as strong, I fear."

"Well, you can't stay up there." Mindful of Mamakitty's directions, the dog-man bent and began rummaging through the lower kitchen cabinets.

Taj waited another couple of minutes before hanging momentarily from his hands and then dropping to the floor. He landed without difficulty on his bare feet. "Say, that wasn't so bad."

"I didn't think it would be. Master Evyndd caused us to be changed, not helpless." Oskar looked back from where he was searching. "Now, help the rest of us look."

"What are we looking for?" Taj ambled close to peer over the other man's broad shoulder.

"Something to tell us what we're supposed to do next."

"What makes you think we're supposed to do anything next?"

"Because . . ." Oskar hesitated. It was not an unreasonable question, and it took him a moment to come up with an answer. "Because Master Evyndd wouldn't have caused this to happen to us without there being an important reason behind it. I don't recall him ever doing anything without a reason."

"Then maybe we're looking in the wrong place." For a mere bird, Oskar felt, Taj had often demonstrated exceptional intelligence. "Shouldn't we be searching the study?"

The study. Oskar tried to twitch his tail at the thought of it. The absence of a tail was disconcerting. Still, he mused, there were other appendages he would have missed more. Be grateful for what you have, he told himself. While Evyndd's pets had been allowed in that sanctum sanctorum, it was only when the Master was present. Woe unto any animal who was caught there without permission! Mamakitty relieved him of the need to contrive a response.

"Taj is right. The study is where Master Evyndd kept all of his most important things. We should look there." Turning, she gestured with a hand as fluidly as if she had been doing so all her life. "Everyone follow me."

Oskar was more than willing to let the senior cat go first. As they stood confronting the open portal, ingrained training warning them to stay back, he observed that Cezer was standing very close to the equally tall but much less muscular Taj.

The former songster finally noticed the other man's intense, unwavering stare. "Is there something on your mind, cat-man?"

"*Yesst*. I have this overpowering urge to rip your throat out and gnaw on your brains."

"Repress it." Oskar felt no compunction at intervening. "If we're going to survive what's happened to us, we're going to have to rely on each other's help."

"Besides," declared Taj boldly, "I'm big enough now to fight back."

Eyeing the other male, Cezer let out a disdainful snort. "Maybe."

A heavy hand fell on his shoulder. Looking up and back, Cezer's eyes widened to take in all of Samm, who had come up quietly behind him. Even in his new, massive man-form, the former snake moved with uncanny silence.

"Leave him alone," the giant hissed threateningly. "Remember—if given a chance, I would also kill and eat cats."

"All right, take it easy, musclehead!" Shrugging off the oversize hand, the irritated Cezer stepped aside.

"Quiet, all of you!" Cocoa's attention was focused on the interior of the sacrosanct chamber. Crowding close together in the doorway, they stared in silence as Mamakitty tentatively but with increasing assurance moved into the study.

The manifold shelves that lined the chamber were crammed to overflowing with books and beakers, fragments of unknown creatures dried and jars of organic matter preserved. In the center stood a table of polished dark walnut. Boxes of strange powders jostled for space with bound bundles of desiccated plants and twigs. High overhead, a single stained-glass dome of singular design allowed wan sunlight to penetrate. It was as gray as everywhere else, and the magnificent stained-glass segments were likewise utterly devoid of color.

Finally, Mamakitty rested both hands on the back of the high, thickly upholstered chair. "I think it's safe. It looks safe. It smells safe. Everyone, come and help search."

They filed into the room, still uneasy at the thought of rummaging through the Master's belongings. Only Taj seemed at ease. But then, Oskar remembered, the Master had often taken the canary into his study to entertain him with song. For that reason, Taj was probably more familiar with the study and its contents than any of them. As they hunted and the floor did not fall away beneath them, their confidence grew. But loose papers yielded no immediately useful information, and none of the hundreds of books and scrolls glowed with revelation.

"There has to be *something*." Mamakitty wiped a forearm across her face. The advent of perspiration was another new, and unpleasant, consequence of their recent transformation. Wherever her much less flexible neck would permit it, she licked the salty droplets from her bare skin.

"If I have to look through one more moldy old book, I think I'll throw up." Cocoa took a deep breath. "This room stinks of age. Besides, all this work is making me hungry. The bookshelves are full of wonderful mouse smells."

"I'm hungry, too." Oskar brightened. "Wait a minute. If I remember right . . ." Walking back to the Master's desk, he started pawing at the drawers on the right side before he remembered to use his fingers.

"I've gone through those already." Mamakitty made the comment idly. "There's nothing in there."

"No? What about this?" Triumphantly, he held up the opaque glass jar of tasty snacks from which their smiling master had so often dispensed special treats. Grinning, he started to bite the top. Remembering how the Master had done it, he carefully unscrewed the lid. "Couldn't do this with just paws." Reaching inside, he grabbed a couple of favorite pieces and popped them in his mouth. As he chewed, his expression faltered.

"They don't taste the same, somehow."

"Dogs! Can't think beyond food. Don't hog everything for yourself." Stepping forward, Cezer staked a claim on the jar. As he reached for it, Oskar tried to pull away. Caught between their efforts to establish possession, the jar was pulled loose. Falling to the floor, it bounced once and began rolling across the carpet, spilling treats as it tumbled.

"Now look what you've done!" Oskar barked.

Suddenly, Mamakitty was striding forward, but not to recover edibles. Bending, she reached into the jar and pulled out a half-revealed piece of paper. It was neither large nor lengthy, but it was enough. It was what they had been looking for.

"What better place to leave instructions for one's animals than in their treat jar?" Carefully she unfolded the single sheet, using both fingers and tongue. "What more likely place for spying intruders to ignore?" In the silence that ensued, she read hungrily, her green eyes focusing on the paper's contents as intently as if they were rat tracks.

Unable to stand the ensuing silence for more than a minute, Cocoa moved to stand alongside the older woman and read with her.

"What does it say?" Taj asked finally. "I remember seeing that paper, but never thought to look at it." He sniffed. "There are no canary treats in that old jar."

Mamakitty looked up, her expression solemn and serious as always. "Many things, minstrel. It says many things. But you won't believe what it expects us to *do*."

FOUR

They crowded around Mamakitty and the revelatory note. Rather than try to read it himself, Oskar waited for her to explain. Strange, he mused, how perfectly her human speaking voice mimicked the serious tone of her erstwhile meows.

"'If you are reading this,' it says, 'then it means that I am dead, and will not be coming back to you, my closest and dearest companions.'" Mamakitty paused, but no one could think of anything to say—though Oskar thought a small chirp might have escaped Taj's lips, and Cocoa was visibly choked. To cover the naked emotion, she licked the back of her right hand and began wiping at her eyes with it.

"'I have always felt there was more truth, honesty, love, and common sense in what are commonly misidentified as the lower orders of animal than in a highly conflicted and combative humanity. That is why I never married, but instead surrounded myself with your kind. But now that I am gone, I regrettably must ask you to don human shape for a while, until you have hopefully accomplished that which I could not.

"'The Gowdlands that are home to us all have been invaded by a most dreadful menagerie of creatures human and otherwise known collectively as the Totumakk Horde. They are led, I ascertain, by a necromancer I do not know and whose identity I cannot perceive. Such cloaking power signifies a sorcerer of uncommon strength and ability. I believe that when the ultimate moment of confrontation comes (as it must) that I will be able to defeat him. If you are reading this letter, then it means that I was wrong in the most profound manner imaginable. Though I am loath to transform you into that for which I have sympathy but little love, I have no choice. In your original and natural form there is no way you can successfully do that which I must now ask of you.'"

"And what might that be?" wondered Taj, who despite his slender build seemed more at ease in the room than any of his companions.

Mamakitty glanced over at him, then read on. "'Should I fail, it will mean that this Khaxan Mundurucu and the Horde that he leads will perforce have overrun the Gowdlands and taken from it all color, for such was the terrible consequence the runes predicted would come to pass in the event of my possible defeat. The tint of Truth, the brilliance of Righteousness, the panoply of the spectrum itself: all will be stolen away. To throw back the Horde into the dark depths from which they have come, color must first be restored to the civilized lands. Somehow, you must find the pure light of true coloration, wherever it survives, and bring it back.'"

Gray-green eyes flashing, expression solemn, Mamakitty carefully folded the letter. She started to put it into her mouth for safekeeping, then realized that her new fingers would do just as well. "That's it, then. That's our obligation."

"Old dead Master doesn't want much, does he?" Oskar

snapped at hovering dust motes, scattering them in the light from above. "Bring back some color, is all. As if we could catch such a thing with our bare hands and stick it in a bottle, like milk. Now, if it was a bone—"

"Regardless," the dusky woman growled, "it is our departed master's last wish. We have an obligation."

"*Obligation?* That's a human word." Sniffing pointedly, Cezer spun around to take a playful slap at Taj, who ducked instinctively and slapped back. "What 'obligation' do we have to humans? None! Don't get me wrong—Evyndd was a good master, as masters go. But remember some of the other humans who came to visit! They would push us away from them, and when the Master wasn't looking, sometimes they kicked and cursed. We all know that there are other humans who do even worse than that to our kind." Spreading his hands wide, he executed a perfect experimental back flip for the sheer joy of trying it on only two feet.

"Let this Horde keep its grayness! I myself can still see and enjoy all that I need to. So can you," he told Cocoa and Mamakitty, "and you," he added with a nod upward in the direction of silently watching Samm. "And you well enough," he told Oskar. "Believe me, all this business about 'color' is overrated. We can see enough of it to get along. Obligation to help humans? I don't think so!" He threw the powerfully built older woman who had read the letter a challenging glance—while keeping prudently out of reach. Though somewhat reduced, she still had claws. "What about it, Mamakitty? How many of our remaining lives do we owe a dead master?"

"We owe him the fact that there will no longer be a master over us." All eyes turned to Oskar. Cezer frowned and wrinkled his nose.

"But you were just saying—"

The other man cut him off. "I was decrying the difficulty of the task Master Evyndd has set before us—not saying we shouldn't do it. Look at us." He gestured meaningfully.

"I'd rather not, if you don't mind." Taj gave a slight shiver. "I miss my feathers."

"We all need human clothing," Mamakitty observed. "Not only for warmth and protection, but simply so we can move about in the world of humans without drawing attention to ourselves. You've all seen how they 'dress.'"

"Clothes!" Cezer shuddered, and not from the cold that afflicted Taj. "Human things."

"Like it or not, we are human now. Maybe we'll be human forever," Oskar pointed out. "It all depends on the Master's spell, about which we still know very little. The sooner we get used to the idea, the easier it will be for us. Think of it. No masters anymore."

"Except for this Khaxan Mundurucu," Mamakitty reminded them.

Oskar nodded, his thick gray mustache bobbing. "Think of all the bad masters who visited here. Now imagine them multiplied a thousandfold and set over not only animals such as ourselves, but over all humans as well."

"Masters above masters?" Cezer muttered. "I admit that's not a very appealing notion."

Oskar nodded somberly. "If we do what Master Evyndd wishes, maybe we can prevent that from happening. All we have to do is bring color back to the Gowdlands." He eyed each of them in turn. "Myself, I wouldn't think we could do such a thing—except for the fact that Master Evyndd apparently believes that we can. We must at least try." He looked to Taj. "You see color better than any of us, so you know best what is missing and needs to be recovered."

The songster nodded slowly. "I wish I could make you all understand what the full range of color is like. Then you'd know why it's so important that it be restored to the world."

Hopping up on a table, Cezer performed a swift pirouette, rendering himself delightfully dizzy in the process. "If you say so. Never having taken anything too seriously, I guess I can't do so even with my own objections. But I warn you now: at the first sign of serious trouble, I'm taking my leave. For all I care, the Gowdlands can stay forever dark and gray. I can see just fine."

"Seeing without color is seeing without joy. I wish I could explain it to you," Taj responded. "There's no joy without color to dance with. Remember the day that orchestra of humans came to play for the Master on his birthday? Each instrument makes a sound like a different color."

"I would so like to dance to all the colors and not just the ones that we can see," Cocoa murmured dreamily.

"I can always dance in your eyes, my little mouse." Cezer's twinkled.

"It's settled, then." Oskar scanned the study. "We need to prepare. First, as Mamakitty has pointed out, we need human clothes to hide our furlessness."

A rumbling hiss of uncertainty commanded his attention. "What about me?" wondered Samm.

"We'll put something together for you." Mamakitty contemplated the problem of the man-snake's size with her usual confidence. "All of us are going to have to learn how to adapt." Her tone turned disapproving. "For one thing, we will have to learn how to avoid distractions. Cocoa, stop wasting time at that mousehole."

Looking abashed, the exquisite young woman rose from where she had been crouching beside a dark spot in the baseboard. "Sorry." She waved a hand. "I just thought that with this longer reach I might finally get my claws on the tricky little blood pouch."

"Weapons." Oskar's heavy eyebrows furrowed. "We'll need weapons as well as clothes. I've watched humans play-fight. They don't bite each other. At least, the adults don't. I wonder if that means that younger human children are more like cats and dogs."

Cezer was trying, with little success, to lick the end of his nose. "I'm not flattered. Human infants pee wherever they feel like it. No discipline."

Ignoring the other man's comment, Oskar indicated a second door set in the rear wall of the study, behind the Master's desk. "Let's have a look in the storeroom. I always liked to lie in there, especially on hot days. Now it seems I'll have to dig through it to find what we need."

"I'll lend you a paw, Oskar." In a single effortless bound few humans could have equaled, Cezer was off the table and standing alongside his old roughhousing playmate. No one in the room thought the prodigious leap anything remarkable. "Maybe while we're searching for 'clothes' we can find a container that will hold color."

"I'll settle for one that will hold water." Muttering thoughtfully to himself as he followed in the wake of his companions, a dejected Taj resumed his examination of his new hands. "No feathers, no wings—no flying. Maybe the Master's magic has empowered the rest of you for the better, but I feel downright clipped."

A mass of muscle nudged him from behind. "And I feel—liberated," Samm told him. "Don't complain until you've lived all your life as a virtual quadriplegic, and then somebody suddenly gifts you with useful hands and feet. For me, just walking and being able to pick things up with something besides my mouth is a miracle that never ends." He gazed down at the songster. "Perspective is better from up here, too."

"Don't be so sure humanness is such a great present,"

the songster snapped. "We've only possessed it for a few minutes." He swatted at the pinkish appendage the giant flicked in his direction. "And keep that tongue away from me! Yuck!"

"Sorry." Samm was apologetic. "Old habits, you know." He looked thoughtful. "Just as I've always thought, though. You *do* taste good."

Not that he felt there was *really* anything to worry about, but a wary Taj nonetheless edged a little farther away from his towering companion, putting Mamakitty between himself and the giant.

The storeroom of Susnam Evyndd was no afterthought; no cramped closet space filled up with old books, forgotten furniture, and discarded memories. The spacious, windowless chamber was lined with deep shelves and tall cabinets stuffed with incomprehensible arcana. Cocoa shuddered as she passed uncomfortably close to something gray-green and ichorous floating within a translucent, badly scuffed glass globe. The marks, she noted uneasily, were on the inside of the glass. Even the intrepid Cezer shied away from a tapering cone of dark wood from whose interior faint, insistent scratching sounds could be heard.

Scattered among the intimidating were more familiar and less frightening shapes and objects. Having spent more time in the cool depths of the storeroom than any of them, Oskar led the way. Radically altered his appearance might be, but he retained his memories intact. Sure enough, in the very back they found racks of clothing: the majority intended to be worn by the wizard, but also some items that had been maintained for guests, or left behind by previous visitors. The women's attire would require some minor modifications, but Cocoa and Mamakitty would be well garbed. As for the rest of them, while Taj found himself lamenting the absence of style, there was enough that would be suitable.

The notion of donning artificial skin caused them more grief than the finding of it. As she slipped into traveling pants and jerkin, Mamakitty writhed as if being subjected to a soapy bath.

"This is too tight."

"It's all too tight." Oskar was having trouble with the belt he had chosen until he thought to think of it as a leash on his pants instead of his collar. That narrow band of leather still encircled his neck. The idea of removing it was still somehow—obscene. "If it was loose enough to be comfortable, it would all fall off." Gingerly, he placed a loose velvet cap on his head, forgetting that there was no longer any need to be concerned about objects pressing down on his ears now that they protruded from the side of his head instead of the top. He found they no longer rotated very well, either.

"I don't see what you're all so aggravated about." Hunkering ponderously down before a tall antique mirror, Samm admired the cloak and hood he had cleverly improvised from a huge blanket. "I am enjoying this."

"Why should it aggravate you?" Mamakitty wrestled awkward new body parts into constricting silk. "You're used to shedding old skins in favor of new. We're not."

"You will find that the habit grows on you. Personally, I feel quite refreshed." Pulling the makeshift hood over his head, the giant resembled a marble sculpture that had somehow broken free from a castle portico.

"Weapons?" Making a face, Cezer gave one last desultory tug on the bottom of his shirt. Oskar thought the cat-man looked quite fine. He, on the other hand, felt as disheveled as he had in his wiry gray fur. That was just the way things were, he sighed. Some creatures were destined to look sleek and handsome no matter their circumstances. Then there were those like himself to whom the term *well-groomed* would never apply.

He put the thought aside. They were not going to a fancy dress ball. "Over this way," he told them.

An offshoot of the storeroom, the wizard's armory was small, befitting Evyndd's reliance on abilities that did not require the application of muscle. But there was enough gear to outfit them all, albeit not always to their individual tastes. Cezer immediately laid claim to a bejeweled, high-pommeled sword that had been a gift to the sorcerer from a grateful client. Cocoa settled for a similarly well-decorated rapier and matching stiletto, while Mamakitty was content with a far less flashy sword. Satisfied with the leavings, Oskar struggled to buckle on the remaining blade. He was still having trouble learning how to use fingers.

They had to cajole Taj to carry any weapon at all. "I'm a singer and a thinker, not a fighter," he kept protesting. In vain, it turned out, as Oskar and Mamakitty outfitted him with a brace of small throwing knives. As for Samm, spears and swords looked like toothpicks in his massive hands, and might have proven as effective.

"These are too small." He laid them aside. "I will improvise something suitable for my size and appropriate to my nature." But with the tiny armory all but gleaned, there was little left to choose from. "I have an idea," he announced cryptically. Exiting the storeroom, he left them to proceed with the next step in their search.

Though they examined every corner, even searching behind the tall wooden vessel from which emanated threatening scratching sounds, they found nothing that looked like a suitable vessel for the capturing and holding of color.

"Would we even know one if we saw it?" A weary Cocoa wiped sweat from her forehead and proceeded to lick the moisture from the back of her hand, lamenting the much reduced reach of her new tongue. "We're nothing but a wizard's pets, and have little of his knowledge."

"I should have paid more attention to the things he was doing and slept less." Mouth set, Mamakitty rested hands on hips and surveyed the chamber. "We'll just have to find something appropriate to store this color in after we've collected it."

"Then that's how we'll deal with it. The next thing we have to do is choose a leader." Pausing in the doorway that led back to the rest of the house, Cezer struck an aristocratic pose, head up, one hand on the pommel of his magnificent jeweled sword, ears pointed as far forward as he could force them. "I hereby nominate myself. Who votes for me?" When not one hand or voice was raised in support, his expression changed to an irritated pout. For a moment, he thought about spraying the lot of them, but somehow that no longer seemed an appropriate response. "All right, then—if not me, who? Who is better qualified as a fighter?"

"Better in this instance to ask who is better qualified as a thinker?" Turning, Mamakitty indicated the scruffy individual standing by her side. "I propose that we confer the distinction on Oskar."

"Him? The living doorstop? The dust mop that eats?" Cezer almost broke out laughing. "You can't be serious! Who ever heard of a leader of a desperate adventure named 'Oskar'?"

"Why not you, Mamakitty?" proffered Cocoa shyly.

"Because I can be too impatient," the older woman replied. "I suspect there will be times ahead of us when calm and reflection are more important than sheer brain power. Oskar is by far the most even-tempered of us all. The most mellow, if you will."

"Also the ugliest," Cezer put in, "though I don't see that as a qualification."

Glaring at the younger male, Mamakitty concluded, "I cast my vote for Oskar."

"If you think he's the right one—" Cocoa shrugged. "Very well. I'll vote for him as well."

"Thank you—I think." Running fingers through his thick, undisciplined patch of remaining fur, Oskar came to a decision and tossed the cap aside. Though light enough, even the slight weight on his head irritated him. So his scalp would get wet—he had never minded it before. "If this is what you all want"—Cezer held his tongue—"then I will do the best I am able. What say you in this matter, Taj?"

"I don't care." The singer was not happy. "We're probably all going to die anyway, so what difference does it make who leads us?"

"Thanks for that vote of confidence." Gazing past the slim-bodied cynic, Oskar squinted. "Where's Samm? His opinion counts in this as much as anyone's."

"He said he was going to try and find something to arm himself with," Cocoa reminded them. "I wonder if he's had any luck?"

Still miffed by his rejection, Cezer snorted derisively. "Probably trying to figure out how to make a dirk out of a fork. His kind aren't too bright, you know."

They located the giant behind the house, by the guest stables. Cowl pushed back to expose his bald head, he proudly displayed his handiwork. The impressive appliance he had fashioned for himself consisted of a single massive granite wedge wrenched from the foundation of the stable. A hole ran through the center of the wedge-shaped stone. Using the tough leather straps of old unicorn tack, the man-mountain had fastened the block securely to a thick pole chosen from a pile of cut logs stored by the side of the stable. Water dripped from the imposing apparatus. Several such soakings, Mamakitty knew, would cause the leather straps to tighten even more securely around the rock.

"That's quite an axe," she told the giant admiringly. "It suits you."

Cezer could still not quite bring himself to compliment his newly limbed companion. "Simple is as simple does," he sniffed. "There's no elegance in it."

Samm hefted the immense adze in both hands. "I did not fashion it for beauty, meower of meticulous complaints."

Mamakitty stepped in before Cezer could respond. "That's enough, you two. We're likely to have to fight some of this Horde, and maybe an evil necromancer or two. Save your belligerence for that." She turned to Oskar. "Time to go."

"Go?" A baffled Oskar scratched absently at his hip. "Go where?"

"Yes, where!" Cezer snickered gleefully. "Lead on, O stalwart and intrepid leader! I hereby knight thee Oskar the Oaf. Lead us—if you can even pick a direction!" Leaning forward, he lowered his voice to an acerbic whisper. "Why not use your great oversize nose, and simply smell us a path? You always were good at ferreting out the most remarkable stinks."

"Though rude as always, Cezer has a point." Looking ravishing (to another human, at least) in her riding pants, boots, and long-sleeved tunic, Cocoa eyed Mamakitty questioningly as they returned to the house. "Do we even have an idea where to go to find this color we're supposed to bring back?"

"Yes, and once we've found it—" Samm began.

"If we can find it," Taj interjected.

"—how do we 'catch' it, what do we put it in, and how do we bring it back?" the giant finished concernedly.

Everyone's attention swung to Mamakitty. She considered silently, then shrugged her broad shoulders. "Hey-ho, *pssst*—we'll catch each fish when it swims past. Cocoa's right. First we have to figure out where to find this batch of color. After that, everything will follow naturally."

"Unnaturally, you mean."

"Don't be so pessimistic, Taj," Oskar chided his friend. He had always enjoyed Taj's singing, but now was not the time for coddling. "If Master Evyndd believed we could do this thing, then do it we will."

"Boldly spoken!" Drawing his sword in a single supple motion, Cezer thrust it skyward. "Onward, masters of an empty house! Onward to—" He gazed pointedly at Oskar. "Excuse me, dear Leader, but you still haven't said where we're going?"

His brows drawing together, the other man pushed out his lower lip defiantly as he engaged in a momentary orgy of contemplation—after which he turned helplessly to Mamakitty. "We have to have a destination. What kind of color might be immune to this world-spanning incantation of the invaders?"

"How should I know, dog?" Troubled, she walked over to the kitchen window and gazed out at the creek. The rippling water was gray, the trees thrusting up from its banks gray-green, the grass dim and dingy, the wildflowers different shades of dusky gray. Nowhere was there a hint, a suggestion, of the color that had been stolen from the world. Natural light would bring back that color, she knew. To have color you had to have the right light. But in the absence of color there was—

She let out an abrupt, unexpected yowl so loud that it stiffened the hairs on Oskar's neck, caused Cezer to drop to a fighting stance on all fours, and made Cocoa leap instinctively onto the table. Samm did not stir, but Taj took immediate refuge behind the giant's bulk.

"I *know!*" Mamakitty's gray-green eyes flashed, and her face was flushed with eureka. "There is a place where there is always color. Always! So if the color is still there, then the light that contains it will be also, and we can try to capture it."

Sheathing his sword, a still dour Cezer could not restrain his curiosity—a characteristic retained from his previous state. "There is no such place. Certainly not around here, and where else have we ever been?"

"Speak to your own experience, youngling." Mamakitty was reaching now into the depths of a maturity he did not possess. "I have often gone with the Master, to keep him company on his travels."

"As have I," observed Oskar.

She turned to him. "Then you might remember this place as well." As everyone crowded around, Samm having to bend low to avoid the ceiling, she explained. "I remember it clearly. It was sometime last year, when Master Evyndd went to visit the minor wizard Matthias Seifert in the town of Zelevin."

"Yes, I remember that trip," Oskar commented thoughtfully. "I rode on top of the coach. The footman was very nice." He rubbed the back of his head in remembrance.

Mamakitty nodded and continued. "It took more than a week even by fast coach just to get to Zelevin. But that town is of no importance in this. What matters is the place where the river Shalouan spills into the beginnings of the Eusebian Gorge. Do you remember that place, Oskar?"

"Of course. The road became very steep there, where it winds its way down the canyon. The river was loud, and there were many new fresh smells."

"Where the river plunges into the abyss there is a great waterfall, and always in attendance to the waterfall, or so the Master said when he was admiring it as we passed, there is—"

"*A rainbow!*" Oskar barked eagerly. "A grand, gorge-spanning, gorgeous, permanent rainbow! Colors, such bright colors, I remember, and"—he met her gaze enthusiastically—"the light that contained the colors. Or at least, those few that I could see."

"Is that all?" Cezer sniffed and wiped his face with the back of his left hand. "There can be no rainbows in light of this hex, and if by chance there is one at that place, it's gone all gray by now, like everything else."

Mamakitty refused to be dissuaded. "I recall the Master murmuring to himself that so long as the river leaped into the canyon, there would always be a wonderful rainbow in that place."

The other cat was not persuaded. "This is the same Master Evyndd, mind, who also wrote that he expected to defeat the Horde and Khaxan Mundurucu."

"Not even wizards are perfect," Oskar reminded him. "You have a better notion?"

"What—who, me?" Mock-startled, the younger man put a hand to his chest. "Who am I—the leader of this misbegotten outing? No, I haven't a better idea. Because there *are* no better ideas." He looked to Mamakitty, unable to keep the respectful tone entirely from his voice. "So we might as well pursue yours."

She nodded. "I'm glad you feel that way. Let's find some sacks in which to carry provisions, take what we can carry, and be off. The sooner we return with this light of color, the better the world will be for it."

"We should look for one other thing to take with us that

we may need in the world of humans." Tongue hanging out, Oskar looked thoughtful.

"Like what?" Cocoa wondered aloud.

"The Master did not speak of it often, but his visitors did. It is called money."

"Yes, we'll certainly need some of that!" The top of his head now being too high for her to reach, Mamakitty settled for patting him on the back. "Good that you remembered it, Oskar."

"We have to have money," he remarked diffidently. "Apparently all humans have some. I wonder how it's used?"

"In trade, and I'm sure we can manage to work out the details." Bending, Taj began searching the drawers of the wizard's desk. "I know what it looks like, and I think I remember where the Master Evyndd kept some. The rest of you, get the food and water together."

Though they thought themselves prepared, it was still something of a shock when, as well equipped as they could manage, they stopped beyond the main gate to look back at the only home any of them had ever known. Now utterly empty of life, in the diffuse gray light the many-gabled house wore an unmistakable air of loneliness.

"This feels so strange." Cocoa uneasily eyed the narrow forest path that stretched out in front of them. "I keep waiting for someone to tell me what to do next."

"Like get back to the house?" Wearing cockiness like an embroidered cap, Cezer started resolutely forward. "We don't have to worry about that anymore. We can go where we please and do as we want. From now on, that's exactly what I'm going to do!"

"So long as you do it on the road to the Shalouan Falls," Mamakitty reminded him. She took an admonishing swing at his head, which, as he had so often done in the past, he nimbly avoided.

FIVE

Deep within the forest they kept close together—not so much for protection as for mutual reassurance. All except Cezer, that is, who in spite of an anxious Mamakitty's repeated warnings scampered and darted off on unpredictable tangents of his own, eager to explore every hollow tree, every rocky crevice, every new sight and sound and smell. Birds drab of color and glum of song tracked their progress, mildly intrigued by a party of travelers who looked human but acted and smelled very much otherwise. When certain members of the party cast unusually intent glances upward into the trees, something deeply felt told the birds to keep their distance.

"I'm hungry," rumbled Samm. "I haven't eaten in weeks."

"What are we supposed to do about it? Give you all our provisions on the first day?" Leaping effortlessly over a fallen log, Cezer did not bother to look in the giant's direction. "Besides, wouldn't you rather have live food? Go eat a bear or something. If you do, save me the liver."

"We can't eat like that anymore." Mamakitty's expression reflected inner turmoil. "For one thing, it somehow doesn't sound so good to me now. For another, if we're going to capture this color and bring it safely back, we may very well have to interact with other humans. That means learning and miming their ways."

"You learn and mime their ways. Doesn't interest me. I still feel fully feline. *Hah!*" Thrusting his face toward a crevice in a huge tree, the mischievous youth nearly gave the golden squirrel dozing within a small heart attack.

"Mamakitty's right." Though not so agile as his naturally acrobatic companions, Oskar trotted easily through the woods, enjoying its sights and smells from an entirely new perspective. His ability to remain upright at all times without falling over was a source of continuous amazement to him. Still, he had to fight the urge to drop to all fours and break into a run. "The last thing we want to do is attract attention to ourselves. Word might get back to this Mundurucu creature."

"Let it come!" Leaping high into the air, a grinning Cezer promptly whacked his head against a low-hanging branch and tumbled unceremoniously to the forest floor.

"You see, piss-for-brains?" Cocoa was chuckling softly at him, the sound rising from within her half laugh and half meow. "We have yet to master our new selves."

Rising, Cezer felt gingerly of the top of his head, relieved for the moment that his ears were now located on its sides. "I'll master yours, if you'll let me."

One lissome hand caressed the pommel of her sword. "I don't think so, Cezer-man. I may only have one claw left to me, but it's a mighty big one."

"Speaking of mighty big ones—" he began.

Ignoring him, she looked over at Mamakitty, striding powerfully along beside her as though she had always walked on two legs. "His snideness makes me wonder, though. When am I likely to come into heat?"

"I don't think humans come 'into' heat," the older woman replied after a moment's careful consideration. "I think they're sort of ready all the time. It's a different state of being."

Cezer grinned enthusiastically. "Sounds like a state I could reside in."

"How does instant evisceration sound to you?" Cocoa glared at him meaningfully.

He skipped easily out of her reach, wagging a finger in her direction. "Decidedly unromantic. Your feelings will change, you'll see. They do every month." Turning away from her, he found himself attracted to a bush that rustled with unseen small inhabitants.

Oskar observed the byplay in silence. Although they were now technically of the same kind, the thought of congress with Cocoa did not appeal to him, despite her obvious human charms. Having known her only recently as feline, the thought of—he forced himself to focus on the route ahead. Though the forest was amiable and the weather benign, it was still a long walk to the Eusebian Gorge.

By the end of the sixth day it was apparent they had made the first major miscalculation of their quest. Mamakitty had been correct in her remembrance: it did indeed require a week of travel to reach the city of Zelevin—by fast coach. When it occurred to her that they were progressing far more slowly, she was forced to revise her estimate of the time that would be required to reach the Falls.

"At least another week, maybe two," she ventured in response to a tired Taj's query.

"My feet hurt," the songster complained. "This walking is *not* for the birds." He gazed longingly skyward. "If I still had my wings—"

"You'd be shot down by some curious hunter and like

as not popped as a sweetmeat into a roasting pie," Oskar reproached him. "Be content with what you are—alive." He looked at Mamakitty. "Our supplies will not last another week."

"I know." She heaved a matronly sigh. "There's no avoiding it: we're going to have to go into Karpluvy to re-provision." In response to several curious stares she added, "It is a town that lies between here and the Gorge. I remember stopping there for the night with Master Evyndd."

Oskar nodded. "I remember it, too. It will be interesting to visit it as a human."

"We have human money." She jingled the purse that was slung at her belt. It was heavy with coins taken from the Master's study. "We can buy food, and for a change will be able to sleep under cover instead of out in the woods. But we must be careful. Like the Master when he would travel incognito, we must practice Takiyyah, the art of concealing the truth about ourselves. No one must learn who we are, what we were, or where we are going."

Cezer drew himself up indignantly. "Hey—why are you all looking at me?"

They camped that night on the edge of the forest. In the distance, the lights of Karpluvy twinkled like stars that had fallen to earth. Oskar surveyed the scene with a mixture of excitement and apprehension. Would they be able to pull this off? Each of them was clad in human costume that ran much deeper than the clothing he or she wore. He could not speak for the others, but he still felt like a dog, saw the world through the mind if not the eyes of a dog, dreamed dog dreams.

He did not want to wander the world of humans on two legs. What he wanted more than anything else was to be lying in front of a crackling fire in the house, with the Master sitting in his big easy chair nearby, reading from one of the innumerable weighty tomes taken from his study. If an occasional crumb of bread or pat on the head came his way, he would be content.

Instead, he found himself burdened with complex thoughts, colliding ideas, new notions, and this damnable Obligation. Watching Cezer gambol among the trees, terrifying small creatures with inherent sadistic delight but without malice, he almost wished he was a cat. Confidence was part of a cat's natural makeup, he knew. Cats acted as if they owned the world, and everything within it existed on their sufferance. Cezer would confirm that opinion, he knew. In contrast, dogs lived with uncertainty, with questions. A sudden thought made him feel a little better.

That meant, based on everything he knew, that dogs were more like people than cats. It was a reassuring realization.

"How are you doing, Taj?" he inquired of the smallest member of the group.

The songster stopped humming and bent momentarily to peck at an itch on his upper right arm before replying. "It's difficult, Oskar." He gestured overhead. "I feel I should be sleeping up in a tree instead of down here on the ground. Everything in my being tells me I'm in terrible danger down here." He nodded at the other side of the campfire, where Mamakitty and Cocoa sat conversing. "Bad enough I have to try and go to sleep surrounded by three cats."

Oskar considered the tree above them. "Why not try sleeping on a branch, if it'll make you feel better?"

"And if I roll in my sleep and fall out?" Taj was downcast. "I'll hit the ground. Actually hit the ground! That's never happened to me, Oskar. You don't know what it's like, this fear of falling. Cats may land easily on four feet, but birds land as lightly and easily as—well, as a feather.

The thought of not being able to slow a descent, or stop a fall . . ." His eyes were tortured.

"At least you're used to standing on two feet," Oskar encouraged him. "So you can't fly. I understand that. But if you've never fallen off a perch in your sleep before, what makes you think you'll do so now? Why not give it a try, on a low branch. If it works, you can sleep in a higher place tomorrow."

Taj considered, then nodded slowly. "You take a long time to get to a point, Oskar, but when you do, it's usually worth the journey. Thanks, I will." So saying, he got to his feet and shinnied up the trunk behind them. Choosing a large, low-hanging branch, he promptly dropped his chin onto his chest, let his arms hang at his sides, and closed his eyes. He rocked slightly but didn't tumble. Soon he was fast asleep, a small smile fixed on his face. Oskar was much pleased.

He had begun to pace off tighter and tighter circles preparatory to retiring himself when a shape materialized at his side. It was Cocoa. He hadn't heard her approach, which was hardly surprising. Cats didn't walk up to you. They simply appeared. Even in the absence of natural light, her eyes were luminous. He blinked repeatedly: she did not.

"Oskar, I have to ask you: do you find this form attractive?"

He hesitated. He didn't want to be scratched, even by nails greatly reduced in efficiency. "Cezer does," he replied quickly.

Her expression was one of distaste. "Cezer thinks everything with a tail is attractive. I'm asking you. You know how important looks have always been to me. You've seen how much time I spend grooming and cleaning myself."

Her expression twisted delightfully. "I can't even clean everyplace in this body."

Ignoring the implications of that observation, he plunged ahead as best he was able. "I've always thought you, um, pretty, Cocoa. Just not my type, that's all. I mean, you're feline."

"Not anymore, I'm not. I'm human—and so are you." Curiosity flickered behind her eyes as she moved closer to him, very close indeed. Panic rising within him, he looked past the fire, but Mamakitty was already asleep, curled up with her back to the flames. The curves and lines of her back were highlighted by the blaze, a fact which he suddenly realized was . . .

This sweating business, he reflected anxiously as beads of perspiration broke out on his brow, was decidedly irritating. On the other hand, he realized, he would not have presented a more confident picture with his tongue hanging out and drool dribbling from his jaws. He noticed that he was, however, panting noticeably.

"All right, yes—I do find you attractive in this form. But it just doesn't seem right somehow. I mean, I feel I should be chasing you, not—"

"Not what?" The smell of her was powerful, a confusing, conflicting blend of human and cat. "Biting me? You can bite me if you want, Oskar. I never realized how big you were before this. I was always trying to ignore you, or get away from you." Her lips, devoid of fur, were very close to his as she stretched upward on tiptoes to bring them nearer to his own. "Come on, Oskar. Why don't you take a little nip? Just—don't—bark at me."

Laughter suddenly split the night air. They pushed apart to see Cezer, pointing and chortling. "Now *there's* a sight to tickle a cat's funny bone better than catnip! I always thought you had better taste, Cocoa. That close to the floor mop that walks, I thought your fur would be up."

Stepping back, she brushed at her blouse and with great dignity, turned to walk away, moving to rejoin Mamakitty on the other side of the campfire. "For your information," she replied acidly, "my fur *is* up."

The laughter died in Cezer's throat. "Hey, I didn't mean ... what I was trying to say was ..." Growling, he advanced to confront Oskar. The older man did not move. "Listen here, bone-farts: you're a dog, I'm a cat. Cocoa's a cat. Is that too complicated for you to understand?"

Reaching out, Oskar quietly gripped the front of the younger man's shirt in his clenched fist. Fingers were a poor substitute for teeth, but they would have to do. "Not anymore, hysteria-for-brains. She's human, as are you and I. If she wants to explore communication in this form, I'm not going to tell her she can't. And neither are you."

Cezer's right hand dropped to the pommel of his sword, then drifted away. Pulling free of Oskar's grasp, he straightened his shirtfront. "I don't like you, dog-man. I never did."

"The feeling's mutual. But for the sake of this journey, we had better learn to turn our anger outward, away from the group."

Cezer nodded slowly. "Fine. Just keep away from Cocoa."

The older man casually crossed his arms over his chest. "I'll keep away from Cocoa the cat. If Cocoa the woman wants to talk to me, I'll make myself available."

"Master should've had you fixed." Muttering to himself, Cezer moved away. Oskar watched the younger man until he had lain down and closed his eyes. You couldn't trust a conscious cat.

With a sigh, he decided he had better find a place to sleep himself. Samm looked content, curled into as tight a

ball as he could manage, his head resting on one massive
arm. Tomorrow they would enter a human town. They
would have to pass themselves off as humans without a
master to tell them what to do, how to act, or how to behave. If they failed, and drew unwanted attention to themselves, their journey might find itself compromised before
it had even begun. Finding a soft pile of leaves, he paced
a few circles, settled down, and dropped into a deep but
far from dreamless sleep. Occasionally he would whimper
softly, and kick out with his right leg. Only when he rolled
onto his back and thrust hands and feet into the air did the
unsettling dreams finally cease.

With its narrow streets, innumerable decorated shopfronts,
shuttered pubs, and a general level of activity that bordered
on the somnolent, Karpluvy Towne was not the noisy, ex-
citing contrast to the deep silences of the Fasna Wyzel that
they had expected. The same gray air of gloom and depression hung over the township that gripped the rest of
the Gowdlands in its melancholy embrace. Small squads
of soldiers and armed citizens patrolled the streets, windows remained closed and shuttered, and people spoke in
whispers of the coming of the Totumakk Horde. Their greatest hope appeared to be that the terrible Horde would overlook so small and isolated a community as theirs, and pass
to the north and south of it.

As they entered upon the cobblestone streets, a worried
Oskar leaned over to whisper to Mamakitty. "People are
staring at us. What are we doing wrong?"

"Nothing, I wager," she replied after a moment's consideration. "I think we just stand out a little bit from the
typical townsfolk. They probably fear any strangers, concerned that they might be spies for the Horde." She studied their surroundings thoughtfully. "I remember Karpluvy

as being full of life, and light, and happiness. See what the loss of color does to human beings?"

Oskar studied their little party. Were their nonhuman origins showing? Everyone was careful to resist their innate urges. Cezer had put a leash on his feline exuberance, and no one dropped to all fours. Samm had a tendency to slide down the street until Taj reminded the giant to pick up his feet. Surely they had managed to blend in. How could they possibly stand out? True, Mamakitty was more muscular than the average woman. And Taj blonder than the blondest northerner, even in the dim gray light. As for Cezer and Cocoa, though it pained him to admit it, it was difficult to tell which was the more beautiful, or who drew the more surreptitious admiring stares from the otherwise downcast crowd—from both men and women.

Come to think of it, of them all, he was the only one who looked remotely average. This realization made him feel neither slighted nor overlooked. He had always been commonly, even exceptionally, ordinary.

So it was fitting that when they finally settled on a slightly less than funereal taverna in which to dine and re-stock their nearly barren store of victuals, it was he who entered first, made hesitant but easygoing contact with the proprietor, and secured them a table near the back. His mastery of language might be lacking, but his inherent friendliness overcame the owner's initial uncertainty. Maybe he was not as handsome as Cezer, but the personality people had instinctively liked when he was a dog had carried over to his human shape. It was a puzzled proprietor who wondered at his sudden urge to reach across the counter and pat this scruffy, smiling customer on the head.

While Mamakitty discussed the purchase of jerked meats, assorted fruits, dried fish, salt and other spices, and assorted individual items from the slightly bemused owner, the rest of them retired to a table and ordered food from a jaded serving wench no less depressed than her fellow townsfolk. Try as she might as she recorded their order, she could not keep her eyes off the rakish profile and lean muscularity that was Cezer.

As for their larger purchases, if the shopkeeper found any of them curious, especially the large bag of fish heads that the dark woman ordered up, he kept his opinions to himself. Not only did he find the handsome broad-shouldered customer herself intimidating, but the man-mountain hovering wordlessly behind her ensured that he held his peace. As the merchant filled and packaged the order, he tried not to glance in the direction of the curious colossus. The man-mountain's unconsciously intense stare was more than a little unnerving; it bordered on the hypnotic. Didn't the giant *ever* blink? And why did he seem unable to keep his tongue inside his head?

Mamakitty and Samm were still busy accumulating supplies for the journey ahead when food finally arrived at the rear table of the extensive establishment. In her absence it fell to Cocoa to hiss a warning at her two male companions.

"Stop that!"

Pudding in hand, Oskar frowned at her. "Stop what?"

"Eating like that. With your fingers." She cut her eyes sideways, indicating nearby tables full of muttering, suspicious townsfolk. "Among humans, certain foods can be eaten by hand, but others demand the use of utensils. Didn't you two ever watch the Master and his visitors eat?"

The two men exchanged a glance. "Not really," Oskar confessed. "I was more interested in following the path of overlooked table scraps."

"What does it matter?" Grinning defiantly, Cezer deliberately shoved his hand into the middle of the large hot pie that presently occupied the center of the table and extracted a heaping fistful of steaming vegetables and bits of meat. This he conveyed with careful deliberation to his waiting mouth, thick gravy oozing out between his fingers.

Struggling with unfamiliar knife and fork while wishing she could simply bend over and shove her face into her plate, Cocoa lowered her eyes. "You disgust me!"

"She ain't the only one."

The amused voice came from nearby. It was difficult to say who were the roughest-looking individuals occupying the table across from the travelers': the heavily bearded men, the women with their manifold painful piercings, or the pair of horned mogs freely sharing their food and drink. Oskar opted for the women.

Fumbling a piece of chicken into her mouth, Cocoa kept her gaze lowered and her voice down. "Just ignore them."

"You ignore them." Grease and gravy threatening to stain his elegant tunic but never quite adhering, Cezer rose from his chair, shaking off Oskar's cautioning hand. "Excuse me, offspring of an indeterminate parentage: did you say that I disgust you?"

It grew very quiet very quickly at the neighboring table. Still tugging at his companion's shirt, Oskar growled his own warning. "By the Whiskers of the Great Mother, sit down!"

Cezer spoke without looking at his companion. "Not until this boorish lout apologizes. To Cocoa if not to me."

Smiling wanly at the grim-faced group seated across from them, Cocoa declared reassuringly, "That's all right. No apology necessary."

One of the mogs was starting to rise. Jingling more chain than a clutch of convicted pickpockets, so did the blue-painted woman next to him.

"Drinks are on the house!" Oskar suddenly shouted as he pushed his chair back and straightened.

Toothy mog, blue woman, and puzzled companions stared at him. "You can't say that," rumbled one of the men. "Abnyk is the owner of the White Ass. Not you."

Grabbing Cezer around the neck, Oskar nodded in the speaker's direction. "I know, but I needed the moment."

"Let go of me, you fatuous cur!" Whirling around, an enraged Cezer swung one fist in a sweeping arc that caught the startled and still seated Taj on the side of his head. Reeling but not releasing his grip, the older man stumbled backward, still holding tightly to his outraged companion.

"By Master Evyndd's beard, that's enough!" Putting utensils and further thought of food aside, Cocoa leaped across the table to join in the fray. Her weight was enough to send all three of them crashing to the floor in a noisy upwelling of dishes, goblets, drink, and condiments. Caught in the middle and struggling to escape the fray, Taj succeeded only in being drawn in deeper.

Confronted by this display and uncertain now exactly how to proceed, the ominous throng at the other table hesitated. By the time one of the men started to draw the knobkerrie slung at his belt, Mamakitty had arrived. More importantly, so had Samm. The giant put a hand on the would-be combatant's shoulder.

"Let's everyone just keep calm, shall we?"

"Snolwraith! I'll not have anyone telling me to—" At this point the eager bruiser noted that the hand on his shoulder was quite large enough to envelop his entire head and squeeze it like a pimple. His voice and testosterone level plunged in concert. "On the other hand, maybe I will."

The nominal leader of the seated rogues shrugged. "No need for us to thrash them, Gelgirth. They're doing a good enough job of it themselves." Watching the brawl, a couple of the women had begun to giggle. Vestigial wings smacking appreciatively against one another, the mog seated between them began to shout encouragement and suggestions to the combatants.

Observing the chaos, Mamakitty uttered a sigh of dismay. "What the canary is doing in there, I can't imagine. Samm, clean it up."

"Yes'm." Lurching forward, the giant deftly but firmly began to disengage the cursing, spitting, disheveled belligerents.

"Outside." To the now grinning spectators she added, "Sorry for the disturbance."

"Not disturbance." With a sharp claw, the other mog picked something revolting out of his front fangs. "Enjoyed the show, I did."

"Rightly so." A human comrade slapped the mog on the back, between its folded wings. "Fought like cats and dogs, they did!"

Once they were outside, while Samm strove to balance an enormous canvas sack of newly acquired supplies on his expansive back, Mamakitty proceeded to upbraid her abashed companions.

"What were you thinking, fighting in there like that?" There was no response from the now contrite combatants. "The one thing we don't want to do is draw attention to ourselves, and you four promptly start a fight!" She glared furiously at the leanest member of the indicted quartet. "And even you, Taj—I'm surprised at you."

"I wasn't—" The singer was not given a chance to explain.

"We were insulted." His honor but not his tunic stained, Cezer methodically flicked chopped carrots from his collar. "I was merely attempting to redress the situation."

"You would've been redressed, all right," Oskar growled at him. "In blood. I had to stop you."

Taking another tack, Taj blurted, "It was Cocoa who saved us. By jumping in and keeping us fighting among ourselves, she gave those at the other table no reason to participate." He eyed the young woman admiringly, his thoughts oddly unbirdlike. "That was very clever of you, to fake a real fight to create a diversion."

She frowned in confusion. "What 'fake'?"

"Oh, come on, all of you! I want to be well out of this misery-drenched town by nightfall. Before any of you can cause any more trouble." Pivoting smartly, Mamakitty started down the main street, resuming the march south-eastward. The others followed.

"Should've kicked your butt," Oskar muttered.

Cezer hissed at him. "You and what pack of offal-rolling mongrels?"

"Shut up, the both of you!" Lengthening her stride, Cocoa caught up to Mamakitty and engaged her in con-versation, ignoring the two men. Oskar went silent to oblige her, while Cezer did the same so he could concentrate on watching her walk.

Behind them, in the White Ass Tavern, mogs and men had already forgotten all about the contretemps that had taken place at the table beside them. Those of the other patrons who had observed the fracas had returned to their respective drinking and conversations. Once more, the gray and depressing atmosphere was broken only by occasional whispers.

Only one patron left his seat. Easing away from the ragged counter, he was already composing the message he would send via aireq bird to distant Kyll-Bar-Bennid. It had been known for some time that the generals of the Horde and the necromancer Khaxan Mundurucu would pay well for any information that would help them to ferret out the remaining small pockets of resistance to their otherwise all-dominant rule. Surely any armed, purposeful, combative travelers who as they were fighting among themselves swore by the name of the dead wizard Susnam Evyndd were worthy of the Horde's attention?

In addition to being keen of eye and ear, the quisling was also sensitive of nose. When seated, the belligerents had smelled as human as anyone else. But when they had been battling with one another, a powerful odor of cat and dog and something fowl had suffused that portion of the taverna. Whether that information would be of any use to the Horde he did not know, but wishing to be as thorough as possible in hopes of receiving an appropriate reward, he had included it in his missive as well.

Like the rest of its arboreal brethren, the aireq bird was in a less than cheerful mood when the eager eyewitness attached message and directions to its leg. It sat on its perch, face nearly as long as its wings, and waited apathetically for instructions.

"Go now," the former resident of the taverna commanded. "Fly swift to the fortress of Kyll-Bar-Bennid, deliver this message, and hurry back with our reward. Your share will feed you well."

The aireq sighed and fluttered its sleek blue-black wings in the subdued gray light. "Might as well. I could use the exercise." Whereupon it lifted from its perch by means of the two smaller wings attached to the sides of its skull, rose into the air, and flew straightaway out the open window.

It was the opinion of the soldiers guarding the castle among whom the aireq landed that they should skin the unexpected arrival for its fine feathers, which could be sold in what remained of the city market, and then add the plucked body to the communal stewpot. Fortunately for them (not to mention the understandably agitated aireq) an officer of the Horde with some knowledge of such things and a good deal more insight into matters of advanced communication interrupted the incipient plucking and rescued the bird. Upon hearing its tale, the officer promptly conveyed it to the fortress keep where the general staff of the Totumakk and the horrid Khaxan had established their headquarters.

Kelkefth relieved the aireq of its communiqué, considered eating it herself (raw), and was stopped by her sister Knublib. "What kind of information would we glean if word were to spread that we devour the messengers?"

"Pagh!" Wiping green snot from the end of her exceedingly bulbous, tumorous nose, the other Mundurucu spat at her sister. "It be only a bird."

"Messenger still." Seeking to settle the argument, Knublib added, "Let Kobkale decide."

When presented with the message and its attendant controversy, that distinctively overbearing but perceptive goblin quickly validated Knublib's perspicacity. Left unconsumed, the greatly relieved aireq was sent on its way in possession of a suitable pouch of gold coin to reward its tattler of a master. In its absence Kobkale, Kieraklav, and the Hairy Kwodd debated the significance of the missive that had been delivered to them.

"So fighting travelers who spoke of that miserable dead amateur, Susnam Evyndd, stank of cat and dog." Kieraklav's nose itched, and she rubbed her flat face with a palm big enough to easily cover the entire grotesque countenance. "So what?"

"Not just of Evyndd." Hairy Kwodd always sounded as if he was speaking from the bottom of a well because he was entirely covered from pointed head to protuberant toe with a cascade of dirty white hair. No one, not even his fellow Mundurucu, knew what he really looked like. This caused no problems because no one was sure they really wanted to know. "According to the message, these strangers referred to him as 'Master' Evyndd. That suggests a connection that is deep and personal rather than casual."

"I agree." Kobkale was sucking the marrow out of a human bone of indeterminate age. "Not that any such as are described in the report appear to present much of a danger."

Kieraklav shrugged blunt shoulders, and unpleasant things shifted beneath her leathery blouse. "Tell Drauchec. Have him send a detachment to find these apostates and remove their faces."

"Rush to judgment, be it now?" Kobkale struck her a capricious blow that sent her spinning. Landing on her feet, she straightened her jumbled attire and voiced no umbrage at the reprimand. Among the Mundurucu, kicks and punches were often used in place of more formal grammar to punctuate argument. "I think not," Kobkale went on. "There may be more here than meets the eye."

"What say you, brother?" gurgled Hairy Kwodd.

Kobkale gnawed on a fingernail that was blunt, sharp, and filthy. It required daily refilthening to keep it that way. "I say that while Susnam Evyndd might have been an amateur, he was a talented one. The Mundurucu differ from other goblinish necromantics because we have acquired wisdom as well as talent. There may be nothing to this tale— or there may be something to learn. Learn first, kill later, says I."

Kieraklav grudgingly grunted assent. "I prefer to kill right away, but it is not worth arguing about."

"Whether it is worth anything remains to be seen. That

is my point." Kobkale squinted at a high, narrow window. Outside the castle keep, all was gray, dank, and wretched. Just as things ought to be, he reflected contentedly. Only an occasional scream wafted weakly up from the occupied city below. Not even the stubborn resistance of the company of humans holding out in the distant fortress called Malostranka could spoil his humor.

"I would not put a postmortem transforming spell beyond the capabilities of the extirpated amateur Evyndd. Is it known if he kept any familiars?"

Kieraklav exchanged a glance with Hairy Kwodd—or feigned one, since his eyes were hidden behind his hellacious hirsuteness. "If he did, he brought none of them with him to the battle."

"The travelers described in the traitor's missive could not be very effectual familiars." Hairy Kwodd shuffled barely visible oversize feet. "They have done nothing to avenge the dead amateur."

"And yet." Kobkale had not achieved the standing he held among the Clan by rushing to judgment, or by taking opponents—any opponent—for granted. "It is true this may amount to nothing. The informer may have heard wrong, or smelled wrong. But it is better to ensure that there be no threat to us in this."

"Should I tell Drauchec?" Kieraklav quite fancied the Horde general, his expression of revulsion when she touched him notwithstanding.

"No." Kobkale's deviant mind was hard at work. "If there are animals involved, they may well be able to avoid or to fool the simple minions of the Horde. Our bloodthirsty brethren are most righteous killers, but they are not particularly perceptive. Kind to kind, like to like. Set similar to catch same, says I."

Kieraklav frowned, which made her appearance even

more distasteful to look upon than usual. "You wish me to find among the Horde cats and dogs suitable for transmuting?"

"No, not cats and dogs. Besides, I have seen cats and dogs among our retinue within the Horde, and they are kept for food, not as pets. Search among them for attendant animals, yes, but not cats and dogs. I will describe to you the type that I would like to have for this spell."

So Kieraklav and several other of the Mundurucu went among the fighters of the Totumakk, careful in their questioning not to interrupt the looting and torturing and rapine. This was not difficult, since by now there was very little left to loot, and few left to rape. The Horde was compelled to resort to casual torture for amusement, an undertaking at which they were adept if not imaginative. They were always grateful to receive suggestions and pointers for improving their skills from the far more inventive Mundurucu.

When at last Kieraklav and Hairy Kwodd reported back to Kobkale, it was with suitable subjects in tow.

"We could only find three who fit anything of your description," she complained.

Kobkale promptly smacked her halfway across the room. Picking herself up immediately, she dusted off the new, fungus-infected dress she was wearing and rejoined him. Kobkale did not deal Hairy Kwodd a similar blow because no one had ever seen that shaggy individual knocked off his feet. Also, Kobkale sensed instinctively that it would not be a good idea. Like the rest of his brethren, he did not want to see what really lay beneath that enigmatic, tangled, ambulatory thicket.

Instead, he proceeded to examine the confused but combative trio of creatures his kinfolk had procured. "They'll do," he announced finally. Lifting both arms, which in the case of even stout goblins is not very high, he raised his voice. That was not very high either, but his words still resounded off the walls of the keep. Below, shackled humans heard, and shuddered at the import of the fresh evil they could feel sifting through the fortress.

Lowering his hands at last, Kobkale joined fingers with Kieraklav and took hold of a fistful of Hairy Kwodd's cascading whiskers. Both of them joined him in the concluding chant. Stuttering green-gray light suffused the room and focused on the three restrained creatures in their midst. There was a sound as of paper ripping, a distant, forlorn yowl, and then silence.

Where the three confiscated pets had clustered defiantly together there now stood three naked human figures. The taller male and one female were slim, muscular, and possessed of devastating smiles that reflected not an inner good nature but preternaturally long canines, a legacy from their former state as vampiric night fliers.

Standing between and slightly in front of them was a stocky, long-jawed man with red-brown hair spotted with white. His eyes were large, luminous, and penetrating. He, too, was smiling, showing teeth that were sharper than they should have been. Every move he made, every motion of his body, oozed barely restrained power and strength. Standing before the three Mundurucu, he was a coiled spring of ferocious, inimical energy. Not surprising, Kobkale knew, since he had been transformed from one of the nastiest, most foul-tempered creatures in nature.

"These two have names." Kieraklav proceeded to identify the closely related male and female. "The one with the balls is Ruut, and his companion is called Ratha." With a gnarled finger she indicated the third member of the quietly defiant trio. "That one doesn't have a name."

"Then we will call it by what it is." Kobkale approached. "Tell me, Quoll, how do you like your new circumstances?"

"I like them fine," the quoll replied, whereupon it exhibited blinding speed in leaping straight at Kobkale, both hands outstretched as they reached for the Mundurucu's exposed throat.

Something thin, scabrous, and unholy whipped out from within Hairy Kwodd's mantle of kink to wrap several times around the quoll's wrists. Snarling, the new-made man found himself yanked around. Eyes ablaze, he prepared to strike at his captor even with his arms bound and helpless. Something in the aspect of Hairy Kwodd told him that would be a bad idea. So he stood still and held his peace, simmering and boiling like a pot kept too long on an overheated stove.

"Temper, temper." Though a little rattled by the suddenness of the attack, Kobkale knew it boded well for the trio's mission. "Why did you jump at me like that? Are you so displeased with your metamorphosis?"

"Not at all," Quoll replied, his arms still secured. When Hairy Kwodd released him, he stood naked where he was, rubbing his wrists lightly. "I just wanted to kill something, and you were the first liveness I settled on."

"You will have your opportunities to kill, I promise you. That and more, if you and your new friends conclude one simple task to the Mundurucu's satisfaction. You may even keep your human bodies, which are more conducive to murder than your former animalistic forms."

Behind Quoll, Ratha grinned contentedly. "Very sweet that would be." She licked lovely, but very dark, lips. "Speaking of sweet, my throat is quite dry."

"Transmogrification is a thirsty business." Kobkale nodded at Kieraklav, who was eyeing the naked Ruut ardently. "Find blood for these two, and flesh for the other. Then suitable attire." He pursed thick lips, causing the upper one to submerge half his nose. "Come to think of it, take them on a stroll through town, and you may find everything you need in any one suitably populated house." Approaching Quoll, he looked up at the new man, whose countenance seemed fixed in a perpetual glare.

"I know you would like to rip out my throat and wallow in my guts, but you're going to have to be able to restrain yourself, or you'll never succeed in carrying out the relatively simple task I have in mind for you."

"Don't worry about me. I can control my urges when I have to." Even in the repressed gray light of the chamber, the goblin could see that the man's eyes were as much blood red as they were blue. "When I have to."

Kobkale was pleased. He was confident that when they sent this trio on its way, he and the rest of the Mundurucu could forget about this business of cat- and dog-smelling humans who venerated a dead enemy.

In fact, he would have pitied them—had he or any of the Mundurucu been capable of expressing so alien an emotion.

SIX

As was usual with examples of active hydrology, they heard the falls before they saw them. All morning, the road to Zelevin had been narrowing. Formerly negotiable slopes on their right grew more and more perpendicular, until they were striding along with a sheer wall of black basalt on their right hand and steep drop-offs immediately to their left. Moisture-loving trees and bushes, ferns, and mosses clung to the mountainside and overflowed the gorge below. Water dripped in sparkling streams from leaves with pointed tips, as if the ferns were fountains whose spigots had been left ever so slightly open. Dominating everything else was the sheer-sided plug of weathered volcanic rock known as Temmerefe's Sky-Reef, usually emerald-crowned, now reduced to a gloomy gray mass no different from the less spectacular peaks that surrounded it.

Normally, hummingbirds and sunbirds gathered in profusion to feed on the flowers that clung to the sides of the Eusebian Gorge, their shimmering metallic throat feathers glistening like enameled porcelain, while translucent flequins soared high on the rising currents of moist air and cried for carrion. Now only a few desultory cheeps and squeaks reached the travelers, so benumbed were the arboreal denizens of the gorge by the absence of color. Espying one lonely sunbird flitting moodily from vovix blossom to perapa flower, Oskar wondered how in the absence of gender-specific tints males and females could tell one another apart. Cezer wondered if the lack of color would change the taste of the high-soaring fliers' flesh. Taj gazed longingly at his distant relations, while Samm wondered . . .

Did Samm wonder, Oskar mused? And if so, what did the giant wonder about? He made an effort to imagine snake thoughts, failed, and returned his attention to the ground. Traveling on only half the usual number of legs, it would be easy to slip on the damp, sometimes muddy road. It was getting easier, but was a long way from being second nature. This upright human posture still found him unsteady. The urge to drop to all fours when traversing the most difficult spots had not left him. The cat folk were not troubled by the steep slope or precipitous drop. Whether on two legs or four, they remained completely at ease in high places.

"I don't see any rainbow." For the past hour, Taj had been whistling (and whistling wonderfully) to keep their spirits up.

"It's here. We're not at the falls yet." Mamakitty strode along smoothly, seemingly untroubled by her newly enjoined verticality. But then, Oskar reflected without jealousy, she and Cezer and Cocoa had cat senses. He was only a dog, with all the fears and worries dogs were heir to.

The travelers did not hear the roaring until they turned a sharp corner on the mountainside, and did not see the falls for another two hours, during which time the road angled sharply downward as it descended into the gray-green depths of the canyon. Then the tall trees that sprouted from the edge of the gorge gave way to smaller bushes and thickets of color-drained flowers, and the clamor that had been growing in their ears all morning suddenly doubled in intensity.

"Oh—how beautiful!" Cocoa stopped by the side of the road, which was now barely wide enough to allow a coach to pass, to admire the thundering cataract.

"Magnificent." Taj shook droplets of water from his hair. He would have lifted his arms to embrace the spray, but clad as he was in clothing instead of feathers, the gesture seemed certain to give rise to more difficulty than pleasure. "As is your rainbow, Mamakitty."

"If I didn't see it, I wouldn't believe it." Oskar gazed in fascination at the band of multihued brilliance that stretched from one side of the gorge to the other, fronting the white-foamed waterfall like a belt across the belly of a pallid stranger. It was like nothing he had ever seen before. Viewing it in passing on his previous visit in the company of Master Evyndd, he had been able to see it only through the color-limited eyes of a dog. Even so, his astonishment at the multihued revelation was as nothing compared to Samm's.

The giant threw back his broad chest and inhaled deeply, his tongue flicking out from between his parted lips. "So *that* is what real color looks like! Never in my wildest dreams could I have imagined such a thing. It tastes—hot."

Cezer frowned. "What does?"

The giant looked down at him and smiled. "Color."

Oskar continued to stare quietly. "This rainbow may be the last remaining object of real color left in the Gowdlands."

"But why should it be so?" Samm was clearly, and

unashamedly, puzzled. "Why should color here alone remain, in this form?"

Though she was no scholar, Mamakitty did her best to offer an explanation. "I can't really say, except that rainbows aren't like painted walls or dyed clothing or even spotted fur. According to the Master, they exist from moment to moment. Maybe the ability to constantly renew itself through the varying action of the falls allows it to elude the effect of the Mundurucu hex."

"I suppose that makes sense, of a sort." Turning from the rollicking, booming torrent to face her, Cezer smiled expectantly. "So—how do we capture some of it and carry it back with us to the forest? Or anywhere else, for that matter?"

Oskar taunted his companion. "You once told me that, given a clear shot at it, you could catch anything in your paws."

The younger man held up his human hands. "In my *claws*, long-face." He indicated his blunt human nails. "With these I would be lucky to catch spaghetti."

Mamakitty had been giving the matter some thought. "Ever since we left the Fasna Wyzel we have been within a day's walk of pond, or stream, or town. So we don't really need these heavy water bags. We can empty them out and use them to catch and carry rainbow."

"I'm all for that." Samm grunted approvingly. Which was not surprising, since he was carrying nearly all the water and the bulk of their supplies by himself. The weight would have been better distributed if he had been able to crawl. Traveling upright had disadvantages as well, he mused.

"Why, what a fine idea!" Cezer gestured expansively into the gorge. "We'll just stroll over to that vaporous band of blurry light, pluck colors from it the way Master

Evyndd's visiting help used to pick grapes from his vines, and stuff them in our water bags." His voice dropped to a huskily sardonic, but nonetheless still attractive, murmur. "There's nothing to it. All we need to do is figure out how to catch light with our bare hands."

"If anyone can do that, a cat can." Pushing past him, a determined Cocoa followed Mamakitty down into the bushes that lined the canyon. Lilting fragrances from the flowers they disturbed rose up toward the road. Color might have vanished from the world, but there was still sweet fragrance aplenty.

Oskar clapped Cezer on the back. "Come on, fuzzball. Let's see if you can keep your dainty costume spotless while slogging and sliding down through soggy vegetation and muddy hillsides."

Tugging at first one lace-trimmed sleeve and then the other, the younger man sniffed haughtily. "With the greatest of ease, my rough-hewn friend. Watch, and marvel at natural grace at work."

Samm and Taj followed behind them. "Those two have always argued, no matter what kind of body they happened to be occupying. Up in my cage, I was able to see and hear everything."

"Lucky you, living in a penthouse." Unable to fit between two trees, Samm simply shoved one aside. Upturned roots bled mud and worms as it crashed to the ground. "As for myself, I find I quite like this new perspective."

"We're all going to have get used to these new forms if we're going to fulfill Master Evyndd's last wish." Taj hopped nimbly over a small stream. "And stop staring at me like that! You're making the back of my neck burn."

"Sorry." The giant contritely shifted his gaze.

It was not an easy descent, but by relying on their natural instincts they crossed obstacles and surmounted barriers that would have given even very agile humans pause. By nightfall they had reached the base of the cataract. While the perpetual mist that rose from the water-worn rocks at the bottom of the falls did not bother Samm—much less Taj and Oskar, who reveled in it—the other members of their party were adamant about finding a drier place to spend the night. A small rocky overhang surrounded by dense vegetation provided the shelter they were looking for. Close at hand, falling water plunged earthward behind the diffuse arc of muted color that was the rainbow they had come to find.

Somewhat to everyone's surprise but to Cocoa's especial delight, Oskar proceeded to make a fire. Their amazement surprised him. "If you'd watched as many of these being built as I have, you'd understand." While he tended to the comforting blaze, the rest of them set about gathering the driest plant matter they could find with which to fashion temporary bedding.

"In the morning," Mamakitty announced, "we'll start working on how we're going to capture some of that colored light to bring back home with us. If empty water bags won't serve, we'll think of something else. Once we've gathered our fill of color, we can seek out other masters like our Evyndd. They will know best how to spread it through the Gowdlands and beat back this hex of the invaders."

"I don't think the water bags will work. I still think we need a special kind of container. Something that will hold anything." For once, Cezer was not being sarcastic.

"I wonder if we could make something?" Taj mused.

"Too bad we're not bringing back sound." Cezer's serious mien had not lasted long. "Then we could just grab it and shove it down your throat. You being the master of song, and all."

Having come so far, and participated in at least one fight (even if it was among friends), Taj was no longer so easily intimidated. "I'm composing a special song just for you, tyrant of baby mice."

As Cezer's expression tightened, Oskar stepped in front of him. "Since you're so full of suggestions and energy, why don't you help me gather some more fuel for the fire?" He indicated the cheerful but modest blaze. "That is, unless you fancy waking up cold sometime before dawn."

"No, that doesn't appeal to me." Joining his companion, Cezer added, "The Master knew what he was doing. Ordinary humans would have difficulty spending the night in a place like this, but not us. We're all used to sleeping on the ground."

"Speak for yourself." As the other men disappeared into the bushes, Taj started looking for a comfortable tree in which to make his bed.

The relentless rumble of the falls served to hasten everyone's sleep. Not that help was needed. The difficult descent down the mountainside to the river below had exhausted everyone. A short evening meal was followed by rapid dispersion to individual beds.

Oskar was the last to allow himself to relax. By the time he had finished thinking, and planning, everyone else was already asleep around the fire. Samm had gone off by himself, to find a separate clearing where he would have enough room to make himself comfortable—and also so that he would not roll over in the middle of the night and crush one of his more fragile companions.

With a sigh, Oskar rose and walked over to the berth he had fashioned for himself out of leaves, smashed twigs, and other forest floor detritus. It was not his soft, padded bed back home in the Master's house, but it was better than the bare, rocky ground. Nearby and not far below the

site of their campsite, the river Shalouan foamed its way
eastward, toward Zelevin and Sibrastkou and the other
mountain communities that had so far largely escaped the
most devastating effects of the Totumakk invasion. Eventually, he knew, the Horde would extend its hand here as
well, to these peaceful hillside towns and river communities, to pillage and despoil. Before that happened he hoped
he and his companions could furnish the means for fore-
stalling any further abominations.

Stepping into the center of his bed, he paced his ever-
tightening circles before finally sitting down and curling
into a sleeping position, his head resting on his hands, legs
stretched out away from him. The resounding music of the
cataract overwhelmed all but an occasional *crack* of burning wood from the fire, and lulled him into a deep and unforced sleep.

When he awoke, it was still dark out. Not the dark induced by the Mundurucu hex, but true middle-of-the-night
dark. A sound had disturbed him. As he rolled over onto
all fours preparatory to rising, he saw Mamakitty standing
protectively alongside Cocoa, with Taj and Cezer hovering
nearby.

Confronting them were a pair of tall, slender shapes clad
in black capes and matching caps. Each held a crossbow
trained on his friends. Reaching down and behind him,
Oskar silently felt for his sword, which he had removed
for sleeping. It was not where he had laid it, nor was his
dagger in its sheath on his belt. Both, he quickly saw, lay
in the heap of confiscated weapons piled beside the two
caped figures.

In front of them, twirling a small but nasty-looking mace
like a conductor warming up with his baton before a concert, stood a slightly shorter but far more muscular individual. His long jaw and nose combined to create an

extraordinary silhouette. But it was his eyes that drew Oskar. Even in the reduced light at the bottom of the gorge, they burned with a maniacal fury.

As he rose, that gaze turned to confront him. "Ah, the last drowsy wayfarer awakes. Please to come forward and join your friends, Mister—?"

"Oskar." Walking slowly over to stand next to his companions, he considered making a jump for his sword.

His unspoken intention amused the leader of their captors. "Please to try it." The mace ceased rotating. "I can crack your skull three times before you reach your weapons. I would very much enjoy doing so, to hear your bones break and see your blood gush. But I am constrained by those whom I serve."

"No need to ask whom that might be," a disconsolate Cezer muttered.

"How did you find us?" an angry Mamakitty wanted to know.

It was Ruut who replied, the cocked crossbow held easily in his exceptionally long, limber fingers. "Did you really think anything of note could escape the attention of the Khaxan Mundurucu? They are alert to even so insignificant a threat that such as you might pose. Quoll speaks the truth when he says he would like to break your bones. But we are commanded to bring you back with us to Kyll-Bar-Bennid. The Mundurucu wish to know what you intended to do, you who mouth the names of a dead wizard."

"We're not doing anything." Taj took a step forward. "When we heard that our master had died, we felt free to leave his house. We travel together to seek gainful employment in Zelevin."

"Really?" Ratha's lips hooked upward in a humorless smile. "That's all?"

"That is all." Taj nodded and smiled back.

The crossbow bolt grazed his left side, slicing through the flesh and bringing forth a swift flow of blood. Clutching at his ribs, Taj looked down uncomprehendingly. Warm redness oozed out between his fingers.

"You—you shot me," he mumbled in stunned disbelief.

"No." Ratha was already reloading her weapon. "I *almost* shot you. That was just a tickle, to show you how we treat those who think us stupid. If I'd really shot you, you'd be lying on the ground now, with a metal shaft sticking out of your guts, squealing like a pig on the killing hook."

"Why?" Mamakitty trembled with anger.

"We want to move quickly. That means we don't have time to waste on foolish lies. Personally, I don't care what your real intentions were." Sharp teeth flashed briefly in Quoll's mouth. "It is not our business to find out. Only to bring you back." Red-gray eyes burned. "So long as one or two of you survives to answer the Mundurucu's questions, they will be content. I don't care which two." He jiggled the heavy, spiked end of the mace, bouncing it up and down against his open palm. "Come to think of it, five is an unwieldy number. It cries out to be reduced." He spoke without looking back at his companions. "Please to tell me what you think?"

"I think six is even more unwieldy," hissed an unexpectedly sonorous voice.

Samm did not burst from the woods so much as throw himself into the clearing. One massive foot landed in the fire, sending a whirlwind of orange-red sparks flying. The iron-tipped bolt that caught him in the right shoulder, he ignored. Swiping downward, he snatched the other crossbow away from Ruut. Fingers contracted tightly, and the sound of snapping wood and tortured metal rose above the roar of the falls.

Oskar made a dive for his sword. As he did so, Quoll darted with astonishing speed to intercept him, the lethal business end of the mace rising high above his head. He let out a stiff, startled squeal when Cezer slammed into him from the side. Its trajectory altered, the mace struck only bare ground. Snatching up his blade, Oskar rolled quickly onto his feet, ready to thrust and hack with abandon.

But the fight was already over. Capes flashing briefly in the glow from the fire, their extraordinary assailants had vanished into the undergrowth. Contorting his body with incredible abandon, their leader freed himself from Cezer's grasp and rushed after his companions, moving through the dense brush faster than even a rearmed Mamakitty and Cocoa could follow.

By the time the two women returned, Oskar and Cezer had already extracted the crossbow bolt from Samm's shoulder and were applying a makeshift patch to Taj's side.

"That was brave of you, to try and dissuade them with a lie." Cezer tugged the bandage tighter around Taj's injured flank. For once, the cat-man spoke without sarcasm.

The smaller man shrugged, then winced. "I wish I had spent less time singing and more listening to Master Evyndd. Who knows? Perhaps I might have picked up a useful spell or two."

"Foul creatures." Mamakitty put her sword aside and wiped sweat from her forehead. "So the Mundurucu are aware of us. That's not a good thing."

"But they don't know our intentions." Finishing up the bandage, Cezer gave it a little pull to make sure it would hold. Taj winced at the contact, but did not cry out.

"Small comfort." Oskar found himself gazing intently into the dark woods. "They know enough to want to stop us." He glanced back at the largest of his comrades. "Your arrival was timely, Samm. You probably saved us all."

The giant tried to shrug, but his bandaged shoulder would not permit it. "Not timely enough." A cumbersome finger pointed. "Taj was almost killed."

"But he wasn't," Cezer announced brightly. "Just got a scratch."

"Scratch *you,*" the songster muttered in pain.

"We can't stay here." In the darkness, Mamakitty had begun gathering up her few belongings. "We have to go."

"What—now?" Cezer eyed her uncertainly. "In the middle of the night? You really think they'll be back, and so soon?"

She met his gaze. "If you had been given a task by this Mundurucu, would you return and confess to failure? I don't want to be shot at in my sleep, or surprised by whatever other skills these empowered predators may possess. Or did you think they were regular people?"

"No," Cezer admitted. "They are transformed, like us. The smells of the caped ones I recognized. The other—his scent is new to me. As new as it is unpleasant."

Mamakitty nodded knowingly. "I sniffed the same. We move now."

While Cocoa and Oskar kept watch, they hastily loaded up their supplies—with Samm, as usual, hefting the bulk of them. When all was in readiness, Mamakitty led the way through the moonlight while Oskar and Samm guarded the party's rear. Several times Oskar thought he sensed movement in the sodden brush, but when he looked in the appropriate direction, he saw nothing. Nor did Samm, whose eyesight was sharper still. Unfortunately, the giant could not also make use of his exceptional sense of smell, or his unique ability to sense the heat given off by living things. At the bottom of the gorge, individual odors and temperatures were masked by the omnipresent mist generated by the falls.

The air grew steadily damper as they forced their way through the thick vegetation and approached the base of the cataract. Trees and bushes gave way to expanses of bare, slick rock, and the revealed moon brightened their surroundings. Cocoa hissed with delight when their objective finally came into view from behind a quartet of blooming mistberry trees.

"You were right, Mamakitty! It *is* permanent! I never would have thought you could see a rainbow at night."

The older woman surveyed the band of color, subdued but unmistakable, that arched across the roaring river. With her humanized eyes, she could for the first time see *all* of it. In so doing, she could at last understand why humans always stopped to marvel at the sight.

"At night it would more properly be called a moonbow, I should think, but they are one and the same thing. Don't credit me with overmuch knowledge. If you had spent more time in the company of Master Evyndd, you would know as much as I do."

"He was always pushing me off his lap," Cocoa replied regretfully. Using caution, she approached the edge of the ledge onto which they had emerged.

"Same with me." Cezer was equally entranced by the nocturnal spectacle, though he tried hard not to show it. "I was always too busy with more important matters. Chasing dust motes or hunting vermin, for example." He leered good-naturedly at the fine young woman beside him. "Bet he wouldn't push you off his lap now."

"Cezer, you are incorrigible!" She edged sideways, beyond his reach.

"Actually, I'm a tabby, but what's a whisker or two between friends?"

"What do we do now?" Oskar found that he could approach the rainbow quite closely. It seemed to him that this was an unusual quality for a rainbow, which he had thought tended to retreat whenever a person drew near. This one, though, remained fixed in place as if cemented to the rocks, the muted colors growing brighter and more intense the closer he came.

Unslinging her collapsed water bag, Mamakitty advanced to join him. "This is empty. Let's try making use of it and see what happens." Holding open the spout, she encouraged him with a nod.

Nothing to lose, he thought as he reached out with both hands. Holding them tightly together in the manner of someone preparing to scoop water from a stream, he pushed them forward into the moonbow. Something might have tickled his fingers, but he couldn't be sure. As he drew back his cupped hands, the movement seemed to stretch the edge of the glowing arch ever so slightly, as if the diffuse, colored light possessed some slight viscosity of its own.

His curving palms, however, were empty of light or color, and contained nothing to place in the waiting water bag.

"Well, that didn't work," he murmured. "I thought I could feel something when my hands were inside, though."

"Feel what?" Though still dubious of the enterprise, Cezer was intrigued.

Oskar considered. "Hard to say. A kind of stickiness. It was barely perceptible. I don't think an ordinary human would have noticed it. We dogs have a more sensitive touch."

"Now there's a contradiction," Cezer sniffed. "A sensitive dog."

"There's something there." Mamakitty studied the nearby

band of coloration. "We just have to figure out how to draw out some of it."

"Here, let me try." Hands extended, Cocoa pushed past both of them.

"No more time for experimenting, I'm afraid." At Samm's unexpected warning, everyone turned to follow his gaze.

Something was dropping out of the moonlit sky. A pair of massive winged shapes had wheeled around above the northern horizon and were now diving straight toward them. Identifying the specters from a picture he had seen in one of the Master's open books, Taj went cold in his belly.

Morggunts. With riders. Riders he recognized.

The two caped assassins sat just behind the long necks of the morggunts, feet pointed forward, bodies arched over the heads of their mounts. Long silvery teeth protruded above and below the lip line from narrow, crooked jaws. Membranous wings caught the rising air of the gorge, imparting profound maneuverability to the nocturnal fliers. Tripartite black tails whipped the clouds, and nostrils flared. Like all morggunts, they had no eyes.

Clinging more tightly to the third monster was the quoll. No flier he, the airborne assault was less to his liking than that of his companions. Nevertheless, he clung gamely to his terrible steed, relying on its teeth and claws to do all necessary work.

The morggunts were big enough to pose a real threat even to Samm, Oskar reflected as he fought to unsheathe his sword. Assuming a defensive pose, he found himself lamenting the absence of an archer among them. Not that arrows or bolts would have done much more than irritate a diving morggunt. What they really needed was a cannon.

In lieu of artillery, Taj shouted at them from behind. "Here, this way! I think I've found something!"

Ordinarily, Cezer would never have been so quick to follow the songster's lead. But with only seconds to go before the morggunts and their riders were in among them, Taj's disdainful companion was the first to follow his suggestion. Mamakitty and Cocoa followed close behind. Samm unleashed one swing of his colossal axe, forcing the morggunt carrying Quoll to back air. The eyeless demon struck with its snakelike neck, and teeth ripped the giant's cloak. A sound testimonial, the frantic Oskar reflected, for wearing loose-fitting attire in time of battle.

Demonstrating remarkable agility for one so large, Samm stumbled backward along the route taken by his companions, covering their flight. Oskar remembered swinging his sword two or three times. The wild blows did not make contact, but they kept Quoll's own rapier at bay. By the time the three morggunts had landed and were massing fang and claw for an overwhelming attack, their quarry had vanished.

Vanished? Vanished where? Oskar found himself wondering. That they *had* vanished could not be denied. Or maybe it was the world around them that had vanished. One minute he was swinging his sword wildly when his guts told him to leap and bite—and the next, he was drowning in color. Seeing color, breathing color, hearing and smelling color. Samm was right about the latter—it *was* hot.

The moonbow, he realized. They had not stumbled through the moonbow, but *into* it. As if trapped in a powerful stream, he felt himself caught up and swept toward the top of the arc. Color roared blue in his ears and burned yellow against his eyes. Then he was falling, falling, down through hue after warm dampish hue. Purple cushioned his plunge. Tiny moonbows sparkled in his eyes as he steeled himself to make contact with the rocks on the far side of the river.

When he finally did hit, the shock blew the little moonbows away from the inside of his eyes. The roaring blue left his ears. The ground beneath him was hard, but it did not feel like water-slicked rock. For one thing, it was sandy. For another, it was dry. But that was impossible. Here at the bottom of the gorge, at the base of the falls, everything existed in a state of perpetual clamminess.

As the last of the miniature moonbows faded from sight, he saw that not only was it no longer damp—it was no longer night. In front of him, in broad daylight, his friends were spreading out, forming a small circle as they marveled at their wholly unexpected if timely transposition.

Broad daylight. *Normal* daylight. For a wild moment, Oskar thought that color and natural light had returned to the world. Looking around, he realized that more than the light had changed. The world had changed. There was no sign of the moonbow, or the waterfall that sustained it, or even the Eusebian Gorge.

They had gone through the moonbow and come out on the other side. The only problem was, the other side was not just the other side. It was another side entirely.

Another world. Or at the very least, another place.

Collecting himself to examine his new surroundings, Oskar exulted silently in the realization that if he was confused, their pursuers must be even more so. Because wherever they were now, there was absolutely no sign of morggunts, black-clad riders, or the red-eyed, maniacal Quoll.

That individual was presently feeling even more surly than usual. Dismounting from his morggunt, he strode quickly to the base of the moonbow. Around him, the river Shalouan crashed and bounced over the jumble of boulders that formed the base of the falls. Behind, he could hear his bemused comrades puzzling over the abrupt disappearance of their seemingly cornered prey.

"Where did they go?" Ratha slid lithely from the neck of her mount. "I saw no flash of necromancer's light, heard no outbreak of sorcery."

"There wasn't any." Black cape billowing in the damp wind from the falls, Ruut moved forward to stand alongside the stockier Quoll. "They all stumbled backward, and went away."

Murderous red eyes glared up at him, and the shorter man's nose twitched. A quoll's nose was always twitching, always searching, but in this instance it smelled nothing but water. Even their quarry's odor had vanished with them.

"Is that what you want to tell the Mundurucu?"

What little color there was drained from Ruut's pale countenance. "No, but what else can we do?" Long, spiderlike fingers gestured fruitlessly. "They have gone."

"Then we must follow. Somehow." A deliberate hand held out before him, Quoll slowly advanced on the moonbow. His fingers made contact, sensed a slight tackiness, and continued to penetrate. Taking one step at a time, Quoll walked completely through the moonbow's edge. Pivoting, he repeated the exercise, until he was once more standing alongside his two gaunt comrades.

"They have gone through the rainbow. For them, it was a door. For us, it is nothing more than light reflecting from droplets of water. Something turned it, for them, from a phenomenon of the natural world into a means of escape." Bushy eyebrows shadowed those icy, penetrating eyes. "Or someone."

"Someone?" Ruut exchanged a glance with his equally mystified mate. "But the wizard Evyndd is dead, slain by the glorious Mundurucu at the battle for Kyll-Bar-Bennid."

He indicated the place of disappearance. "You saw how they fled from us."

"I also smelled their fear, which was strong enough to rise above this accursed dampness. There is no sorcerer among them. The wizard Evyndd has not risen from the dead to save them." Sitting down on a rock and tucking his legs beneath him, a thoughtful Quoll sat as still as he was able and contemplated the enigmatic moonbow. "They truly smell of cat and dog, as the informant insisted. Apropos of that, sorcerers and witches of different stripe often have certain elements in common. Familiars, for example. Working with a necromancer, alongside one, such creatures are known to sometimes pick up shards and fragments of their master's skills."

Ratha nodded slowly. She would have been truly beautiful had she not worn unsheathed savagery like eye shadow. "So you think the wizard Evyndd's familiar may be among those we pursue, and that it has worked some strange alchemy to preserve them?"

"Do you think they crossed a bridge over this river where none exists? Did they transform themselves into puffs of cloud and drift away downstream?" Quoll's lips parted, exposing teeth shaped and pointed like white needles. "Please to realize that there is impressive thaumaturgy at work here." Rising, he headed deliberately toward his quietly salivating, waiting mount.

"I will take it upon myself to return to Kyll-Bar-Bennid. When it flies level with the ground, the morggunt flies slowly, but it will still be far faster than walking. I will describe to the Mundurucu the events we just witnessed."

The terrible-visaged Ruut was impressed. "Are you not afraid?"

Pausing with one leg half-raised as he prepared to mount, Quoll glared back at him. "My kind are afraid of nothing—not even the Mundurucu. We live to kill, and so deal daily with death. I know the Mundurucu can do worse, but the keen ones among them think before they slay. They want dead those whom we hunt; not me and thee. I think I will return with most of my limbs intact, together with the means for following our bumbling but opportune pilgrims. When we identify the one who is the familiar that travels among them, we will deal with it first. Once that individual has been slain, the others will quickly submit or perish."

Swinging his leg over the narrow neck of the morggunt, he whispered into its upthrust, spike-fringed ear a word that must go unmentioned. Snapping at the dank air of the canyon, the demon of the night sky lifted its head and spread its wings.

"Until I return, you must keep watch. Perhaps there is no air where they went, or food, and they will be forced to come back out the way they went in. In that event, you must be ready for them."

Ratha nodded, one hand falling to caress the red metal of her sword. She stood close to Ruut as the morggunt rose into the air. Circling to gain altitude, it was visible for several minutes before, at its rider's urging, it straightened out and disappeared over the rim of the gorge, heading northwest.

Turning, Ruut considered the moonbow. Falling water was clearly visible through the wide bands of diffuse color. Reaching out, he waved one waxen hand through the edge. It came away damp, without penetrating to unimaginable realms beyond.

Disgusted, he looked away. "We can make a camp in the shelter of the trees, and there is plenty here for the morggunts to eat." He tapped the crossbow now slung against his back. "If they show themselves here again, we will take out their legs."

Ratha nodded agreement. "The giant first, since we don't know which one is the familiar. Aim for his ankles. The others we will take in turn."

"And if they don't come back out, we will go in after them." Ruut was feeling more and more confident. "From the Mundurucu, Quoll will acquire for us the means of following." Striking out suddenly with one hand, he snatched a salamander from its resting place among the rocks, popped it into his mouth, and chewed noisily, spitting out small bones one after another.

His kin and companion watched enviously. "That reminds me: I'm hungry, too."

"A tidbit." Plucking the small, now bloodless skull from between his lips, Ruut cast it absently aside as he glanced back over his shoulder. "As Quoll said, the Mundurucu will want only one or two to question before they dispose of them. The rest will be ours, to drink at our leisure."

Contemplating the vision, Ratha felt better. As viewed through her red-stained thoughts, the anticipation was delicious.

◊ SEVEN

There was much to see in the place where their swift journey through the moonbow had deposited them, and much to think about, but what struck Oskar immediately after the light and color was the heat. Compared to the damp coolness at the base of the Shalouan Falls, the air was as brutally hot as it was dry. Around them in all directions stretched a gravel plain dotted with plants the likes of which he had never seen before. Some were twisted together like entwined ropes, while others grew straight up toward the sky, with thorny branches that grew out at right angles to the trunk. A third group of large growths resembled the cracks that formed on the surfaces of thinly frozen ponds, while the flowers that bloomed on them in spite of the temperature sprouted their own shade leaves.

Not only was it hot, he realized, but in this place at least, natural color had returned to all their surroundings. Gradually he became convinced that they were no longer in *the* world, heretofore the only one he and his companions had ever known, but in another. As the initial shock of their unexpected transposition began to wear off, he remembered their murderous pursuers. Whirling about, he sought the pale, malign faces of the black-caped morggunt riders and the pinched, feral smirk of Quoll. Neither was present to leer back at him. There were only his friends and traveling companions, standing dumbstruck as himself beneath a scorching scarlet sky.

Color. Wherever they were, whatever the name of this fiery place, it had color. Colors such as he had never been able to see out of dog eyes. So this was what humans meant when they spoke of the color of something. To one who had lived knowing only the limited hues available to his canine kind and then the grayness of the world as cursed by the Mundurucu, it was more than a revelation. It was a whole new kind of being, like tasting a dozen novel food flavors all at once. The hex of the Mundurucu had not reached here, or had never taken hold. Glorious it was to experience a world saturated with bright hues, so profound as to be almost blinding. Wonderful also it was to realize that, however great their power, the Mundurucu were not omnipotent. There was only one thing wrong.

Magnificent as the coloration was, it was all variations of the *same* color.

Everything—sky, ground, plants, the line of flat-backed beetles clustering around fallen fruit, the distant hills, the clouds scudding turgidly overhead—was suffused with redness. The beetles were pink and cerise; the rotting melon-size fruit into which they were burrowing, brightskinned as fresh cherries; the distant hills, frozen in permanent sunset even though the sun was still high overhead and it was far from eventide. Carmine blossoms sprouted from maroon tree limbs, while through the sky a gaggle of shocking pink grouse groused a raucous route toward the eastern horizon. Even his friends had acquired a distinctive roseate cast.

"You look like you've been in an accident," he told Mamakitty. Naturally darker of color than any of them, her skin appeared as if viewed through blood-stained glasses.

"You should see yourself," she shot back testily. "All red and pink streaks. And pull in your tongue. I know it's hot, but remember that we don't have to pant anymore. We get to sweat instead."

"I prefer panting—it is a far more elegant way of dealing with elevated body temperature." Cezer was sipping from his water bag. In the absence of commonplace mountain and forest streams, the water they carried with them had suddenly assumed real importance.

Of them all, Samm, with his mottled, patterned skin, had taken on the most interesting appearance. "You look like you were designed instead of born," Taj commented. The songster was fortunate in having a relatively uniform skin tone. In this place it was no more striking than a pale reddish tan.

"Where are we?" Kneeling, the tip of her scabbard scraping the hard ground, Cocoa fought down the urge to go and chase the beetles. Instead, she picked up a handful of red-tinged pebbles. They filled the delicate bowl of her palm with more than gentle warmth, and she quickly cast them aside. "Not anywhere near the Eusebian Gorge, I'll wager."

"Nor anywhere known." Mamakitty studied their surroundings, searching for signs of life. "I believe we have gone into the rainbow."

"It being formed of moisture, I would've thought the inside of a rainbow would be cooler than this." Reaching up to caress his forehead, Samm marveled silently at the unfamiliar perspiration that beaded his skin.

"We're inside color, not moisture." Oskar squinted at the sky, his bushy eyebrows affording him some protection from the unrelenting glare. "We fell into the near end, which is red, and were carried by a current of red all the way up and over and down the other side—where I am guessing we fell out. Which I suppose explains the restricted variation in the coloration of our surroundings."

"Is this enough to take back with us, do you think?" Cocoa tried to grasp a handful of red air, with no success.

Mamakitty shook her head. "Even if we knew how to confine some of it, I don't see how it could be sufficient. The Mundurucu hex stole all color from our world, so we must somehow get all of it back. How we are to do that I still haven't figured out."

Silence greeted her observation until Oskar avowed, "I once saw Master Evyndd break up ordinary light into rainbows with a special piece of glass he called a *prism*. If ordinary white light contains all colors, then that is what we must bring back to our world."

To his dismay, Cezer found himself agreeing with the other man. "You make good sense, snot-nose." He gestured with one hand. "Trouble is, we are entirely in the red here. I see no ordinary, or white, light in this place."

"Then we must search until we find it," Mamakitty declared firmly. "And along the way, we must look for a means to capture and carry some of it back with us after we have found it, in the event our water bags do not serve." She kicked at the hardscrabble ground with one foot. An awkward place for a cat to go to the bathroom—but not, she reminded herself, a human. "It is fortunate only I emptied my bag, or else we should be in truly desperate circumstances."

"Maybe," Cocoa wondered hesitantly, "we should leave this place and look farther afield in our own world. Maybe we should try harder to acquire color from the whole rainbow that spans the gorge."

"A fine notion." Eager to return home, Cezer was in ready agreement. "Taj, you're the one who led the way in here. Now you can show us the way back."

The songster lowered his eyes. "I'm afraid I can't do that. I thought I saw a path leading behind the falls. I ran for it, and instead found myself caught up in the rainbow and dumped here. I certainly don't know how to get back."

Cocoa looked over at Samm. "You always said that color smelled hot. It certainly fits this place!"

In the stricken silence that ensued, Oskar was moved to point out that there was no sign of their malevolent pursuers, either.

"If Taj doesn't know the way back," Cocoa observed with inexorable logic, "then even if we can find and collect some white light, how are we going to return it, and ourselves, to our home?"

Mamakitty was ready for that one. "First things first, my dear. One impossible task at a time." Bending forward to shake sweat from her face, she straightened and scanned the horizon. "First we must find a way out of this dreadful heat. I like lying in the sun as much as the next cat, but not the whole day long."

"I don't know what you're all so·worried about." Eyebrowless Samm inhaled deeply. "I think it's quite pleasant here."

Oskar found himself envying the giant his natural tolerance for heat. "I wonder if anything lives here besides misshapen plants and flat-backed bugs? If we could find someone to talk to, we could ask them about the presence of white light. If not here, in this land of everything red, then perhaps somewhere else."

"Not a problem." Cocoa was pointing with a slim, girlish hand. "We'll just ask them."

The cart that was coming toward them was drawn by a pair of short-legged, warty, carmine-colored creatures that looked like frogs who had been stepped on. Repeatedly. Instead of straps and buckles, they were harnessed in red-black nets that restricted their movements even more than normal tack would have done. Bulbous eyes bulged so far from the sides of their skulls that they were equally capable of looking backward as well as forward.

The wagon they were pulling rattled along on eight wheels whose individual diameter was no greater than the length of Cocoa's arm. The bed was piled high with neat bundles of firewood and a couple of barrels that, even at a distance, reeked powerfully of distilled spirits. As for the pair of drovers, they were no taller than Taj but far more stoutly built. Their wide, flattened faces looked pushed in, their teeth were broken snags, and their eyes small and beady. One wore pants, shirt, and a wide-brimmed, floppy hat of some material resembling felt. The other was clad in shorts, suspenders, and a long-sleeved shirt that defied both the heat and common sense. His bonnet boasted fore and aft rims that shielded him somewhat from the merciless sun.

Espying the cluster of travelers, their expressions reflected mutual surprise. Repressing a sudden embarrassing urge to chase the wagon and bark at its wheels, Oskar approached the slowing vehicle, his right hand upraised.

"Uh, hello there." Flashing a wide smile at the pair of homely countenances perched on the bench seat, he extended his open palm to the driver in the manner of human greeting, even though the creature was manifestly not human. "We're strangers in this country, just recently arrived, and we could use some help and some directions."

The gross drovers exchanged a glance. Then the driver looked down and smiled. It did not much improve his appearance. "Of course we'll help as much as we can, visitor. The Warrow Plains ain't no place to be wandering about. Better you come follow us." Raising a short-handled club, he gestured over the heads of the stoical team. "You're lucky. Pyackill is just through those there hills. You'll find staying places there, and food, and water."

Cezer had moved up to stand alongside Oskar. "Listen, my good ma— well, whatever you are. What sort of reception are we likely to find in this Pyackill? Us being strangers, and all."

The drover's smile widened. Mildly curious, Oskar tried to count the number of teeth in the impossibly wide maw, giving up when he reached forty-two.

"Why, surely it's strangers you are! Pyackill's one of the friendliest towns in the Red Kingdom. You'll be greeted regular by folks in the street, and people you've never met will reach out to help you." Whereupon he brought the club down hard on Cezer's unprotected and unsuspecting head.

Caught completely off guard, the cat-quick swordsman went down in a heap. Oskar lunged reflexively at the drover, only to feel the fist of the other musterer intercept his face with surprising force. Cocoa was at his side in an instant, as was Mamakitty.

The rowdy brawl quickly spilled out onto the rusted earth as drovers and travelers, bound up together in a ball of flailing arms and kicking legs, tumbled off the wagon's seat. Samm was able to separate them before more than a few drops of blood had been spilled. Clothes had been dirtied, flesh scratched, feelings bruised, and in the course of the fight an embarrassed Cezer had hacked up what turned out to be a couple of old hairballs.

Brushing rust-colored dust from his pants, Oskar glared at the local who had punched him. Before he could speak, the squat drover advanced on him anew. Oskar flinched warily, prepared now to defend himself, but the creature only reached up to clap him on the shoulder.

"Welcome, friend. I'm Baldrup." A thumb jerked in his companion's direction. It resembled a week-old sausage that had been seriously dog-worried. Though it reminded Oskar he was hungry, he resisted the urge to chomp down on it. "That's my brother-in-law Snicklie. Nice to meet you."

"Nice to—?" Struggling to comb dry twigs out of his long blond hair, a fuming Cezer had to be restrained from drawing his sword. "Is this how you greet all your 'friends'?"

Snicklie chuckled, an unexpectedly childish gurgle. "Of course not." He indicated Samm, standing silent and alert behind him. "But your great lumbering colleague here interrupted us before we could finish."

Frowning, Mamakitty delicately fluffed her own black curls, regretting that her fingers were not as adept at the task as her tongue would have been. "Are you trying to tell us that this is your way of showing friendship?"

Baldrup gazed longingly at the club Samm had gently but firmly removed from the drover's grasp. "How else does one greet good friends?"

"And this is how everyone here acknowledges guests? Including those 'friendly' folk you spoke of who inhabit the town we're about to enter?" When both blithely smiling drovers nodded in unison, Mamakitty hastily called for her companions to gather around her. "Would you excuse us for a moment?"

Still straightening their rumpled clothing, the disconcerted travelers stepped off to one side to caucus quietly.

"This doesn't make any sense." Taj was both worried and bemused.

"Sure it does," argued Cezer. "They're crazy. This is a crazy place, so what more normal than for it to be inhabited by crazy people?" His whiskers would have been twitching nervously had he possessed any.

"They're not crazy." Cocoa spoke softly but with the feeling that she was right. "They just have different customs."

"*Different* is too fine a word for it," commented Oskar. "We're going to have to be very careful here. The more someone 'likes' you, the harder the hit they may expect you to absorb." He glanced back at the two drovers, who stood waiting patiently for their new acquaintances to finish conferencing. "I mean, a friendly nip is one thing, but that wasn't exactly a pat on the head."

"He's right," agreed Mamakitty. "And we may very well be expected to hit back, lest we be accused of being standoffish. Or worse, deliberately unfriendly."

Rubbing his elbow where he had landed when everyone had tumbled off the wagon, Cezer wore a grim expression. "That I can do. In fact," he added warningly, "if we run into any more of this local 'friendliness,' they may find me the most polite individual ever to visit this town."

Oskar whacked him on the shoulder, and the other man whirled sharply to confront him. "Just being friendly, old friend. If we're going to get through this and find the white light we need to take back with us, we're going to have to learn how to adapt to local customs."

"How about I adapt your nose?" Cezer growled.

Mamakitty took a firm grip on his arm. "Not now. Let's thank these two for their offer of assistance, tell them we'll be delighted to follow them into the city, and see if they can supply information as well as guidance. And remember: be courteous."

"With pleasure." Allowing her to hold on to his arm, Cezer ground one fist into the open palm of his other hand. "Just tell me when you want me to be friendly, and to whom."

"I will," she assured him, "and you need to trim your claws—um, nails."

Oskar accompanied Cocoa on the walk back to the wagon. "It makes sense, I suppose. In a red country, what more natural than that everyone should be red-tempered?"

"I fear there will be many times before this search is over when we're going to have to suppress our natural instincts and think and act the reverse of what is normal." Her musk was subtle and distinctive in his nostrils. With a start, he realized that the drovers and their dray animals had hardly any body odor at all.

"Easy to say," Oskar commented. "But which 'natural instincts' do we repress? Mine are canine, yours are feline, and Taj and Samm's instincts are completely different from either. Do we repress those instincts, or those of humans, or both?"

It not being any easy question, she had no ready reply for him. "Well, for a start, try to remember not to pee on anybody's leg."

He responded with a sour smile. "Thanks, Cocoa. I think I could have figured that one out for myself." Silently, he started looking for a bush to complete the business that had begun to preoccupy another part of his thoughts.

"It's very nice to meet you, and we'll be glad to follow you into this Pyackill, and to listen to any other advice you have to impart." Mamakitty nodded at Samm. "Give him back his cudgel."

Baldrup accepted the club with a thankful nod, hefted it briefly, and considered its proximity to Mamakitty's head.

"Don't do it," she warned him as she took a step back. "I'll scratch your eyes out."

The drover looked hurt. "Oh, well. If you want to be formal about things." Picking up the knotted ends of the netlike reins, he pursed rubbery lips and blew a sharp whistle. The low-slung, lumbering dray animals lurched forward, and the wagon began to move again. Not wishing to become too painfully chummy with their newfound friends, the travelers were careful to keep close to the vehicle but well beyond arm's length.

Pyackill was more city than town. It reminded Mamakitty and Oskar of the visit they had once made to Zelevin in the company of Master Evyndd. There were more people and activity in one place than either of them had ever seen before. Suffused in the local tones of red, it projected an air of normalcy they had not experienced since the Mundurucu had banished color from the Gowdlands. As for the other travelers, from Cocoa to Samm they were overwhelmed by the profusion of unfamiliar sights and sounds and smells.

"And I used to think that the world was a big place when Master Evyndd let us roam the forest beyond the yard fence." As Cocoa marveled at the multistoried buildings of red brick, the peaked slate roofs, and the hard squarish stones that paved the streets, she had to fight down the urge to go climbing.

"Think how Samm and I must feel." Taj indicated the

bustling two-way traffic flow of massed humans and animals and beings he did not recognize. "At least all of you were allowed out of the house. We were but rarely let out of our cages, and that always inside."

"There is so much more to see." The giant trod behind the wagon, careful where he put his feet lest he step on some unwary citizen. He was still getting used to legs as a means of locomotion.

"Especially from your vantage point, so unlike that of the worm's-eye view you had before," Cezer indelicately pointed out.

Samm was not offended. "No, that is not so very different. If you will remember, when Master Evyndd used to let me out of my cage, I was fond of ascending to the very top shelves of the kitchen and resting there."

"I can attest to that." Taj gave his new companion a tentative jab in the ribs that the giant hardly felt. "It wasn't very comforting to have you staring at me eye to eye from across the room."

Samm gazed down at the much smaller songster. "I could never reach your cage. The gap was always too great. Master Evyndd knew that." He smiled reassuringly. The expression came naturally to him, since snakes are very good at smiling. "Anyway, you never really tempted me. You weren't enough of a meal to be worth the effort." From behind, he gave Cezer a nudge that sent the other man stumbling. "In *your* original state, however, you would have made a filling repast. I often imagined all that fur sliding down my throat."

"Very enlightening. And quit staring at me."

"Sorry." The giant averted his gaze. "I wasn't aware that I was."

"Though I have little personal experience of such things, this seems to be a prosperous community." Ignoring her companions' irrelevant verbal byplay, Mamakitty was studying their surroundings, absorbing the look and feel and smell of everything they passed. For their part, they drew a few stares of their own, mostly due to Samm's unignorable presence among them.

"Oh yes." Baldrup smiled down at her. "Pyackill is the most important trading center in this part of the kingdom. Everyone who is anyone comes to Pyackill." Reaching over, he smacked her on the back of her neck. Thick black curls cushioned the impact somewhat. Rubbing the place where the drover had made contact, she did not hesitate to punch him in the leg. He was plainly delighted by the blow.

"And beyond Pyackill," Oskar inquired curiously. "What lies beyond here?"

"You really are strangers, aren't you?" Snicklie rubbed his squashed nose with the flat of one hand, making squeaking noises. "The kingdom stretches as far as one can imagine to north and south. To the west," he pointed, "it goes for only a short distance before fading into the Sere Desert, where it is too hot for anything to survive."

"Hotter than this?" Taj had just finished taking a sip from his water bag. In general, he dipped less frequently into his supplies than did his companions. This was only to be expected, since he drank like a bird.

"Hotter than you can imagine. Too hot even to breathe. Nothing lives there." Leaning over the side of the wagon, Snicklie spat something pinkish into the street, just missing an outraged pedestrian. "To the east is the Kingdom of Orange."

Oskar nodded thoughtfully. "That would make sense. And beyond that I presume there are other kingdoms both distinctive of and defined by color?"

Snicklie made a face within a face. "I wouldn't know

about that. My brother-in-law and I are simple farmers, not world travelers."

"What seek you here?" In spite of the seeming handicap imposed by his stunted arms, Baldrup was doing a skilled job of directing the wagon through increasingly boisterous traffic.

"White light. A baneful hex has banished all the color from our kingdom. We have been charged by our former master with returning it. To do that we have determined that we need to bring back to our kingdom as much white light as we can carry, since white light contains all the colors that are now absent."

The two homunculi exchanged a doubtful glance. "I don't see how such a thing is possible." Snicklie was leaning over, but despite his feelings of sympathy, he did not strike out at Oskar. "Even if it is, you won't find what you're looking for here. There is no color in the Kingdom of Red but red."

"That is the way of things, and how they should be." Baldrup hesitated but briefly before continuing. "Though on business I myself once crossed the border to visit the Kingdom of Orange."

"What was it like?" Cocoa asked him.

"Personally, I found it chilly, and the folk there not very friendly. There is little commerce between our two kingdoms, though we get on well enough with one another. They keep to themselves, and we to ours, which suits us both." He was nodding absently to himself. "Colors should not mix."

"Oh, I don't know about that." Cocoa looked thoughtful. "If you mix red with—"

Mamakitty cut her off with a warning look. "Now Cocoa, we're here as visitors, as guests. We don't want to offend anybody's beliefs."

Cocoa was not so easily silenced. "Color isn't a belief. Color is—just color. Mixing them doesn't hurt—"

"What lies beyond the Kingdom of Orange?" Oskar asked hastily.

"I don't know." Baldrup shrugged broad shoulders. "There are rumors, and I hear stories. Some are hard to credit." His smile returned as he chucked the shards of net rein gripped in his left hand. "Red I have always been, red I will always be, and red-on-red is good enough for me."

"Greetings, visitors! Buy my fresh produce?" An old crone with a remarkably attenuated face held out a small, triangular fruit from the oversize sack balanced on her bent back. Or maybe she was an old crow. Attempting to estimate the length of her astonishing beak, Oskar couldn't be sure.

"I'm not hungry," replied Cezer, keeping aloof.

"Well, you look like a nice biped. Have a taste on me." She passed him the fruit with one withered hand and struck him square in the snout with the other.

"Why, you vicious old bitch!" Startled and hurt, Cezer raised his fist to strike back. Oskar noted the elderly peddler's expectant smile.

"Go on, Cezer—hit her. One good turn deserves another." He was smiling hugely at his companion's discomfort.

"*Psst*, that's right—I forgot." The other man promptly lowered his raised arm. "Madam, despite the provocation, I am a gentleman, and I am not going to hit you."

The crone (or crow) spat at his feet and her expression twisted. "Ill-mannered and disrespectful to your elders, is it?" Reaching out, she snatched back the fruit she had given him. "Buy from another, then. You won't find fresher produce."

"Got any seed?" Taj inquired. The long-snouted head shook regretfully.

Bewildered and troubled, Cezer edged closer to the wagon, head bowed, back hunched, hands clasped behind his back. "I do not like this place: no, I do not."

"Don't be downcast. Pyackill's as friendly a community as is to be found in the south of the kingdom. You'll soon settle in." With this assurance, a cheerful Snicklie extended a friendly hand of his own. The stick it held caught the brooding Cezer on the side of his head, sending him stumbling forward. Oskar had to take hold of the other man to keep him from drawing his sword.

With an effort, Cezer let the several inches of steel he had exposed slide slowly back into their scabbard. "I don't know how much longer I can take this, Oskar. Everything here is backward." He rubbed his nose. "And for us, that makes things doubly backward."

"Which should make them forward again," Oskar responded unhelpfully. "To us the local ways seem strange, but they are otherwise to the people who live here. Whose help," he reminded his friend, "we need. Just remember that they see everything through red-colored glasses." Convinced that Cezer had regained control over his emotions, Oskar let him go. "Maybe to get along here successfully we just need to be a little less human and a little more like our natural selves."

"Okay." Wetting one palm, Cezer used it to straighten his hair where the stick had mussed the blond locks. "But no matter how 'friendly' we have to become, I'm not biting anything like these two on the back of their neck."

"I'll handle the formal greetings for you," Oskar assured him. "I used to quite like pawing new acquaintances."

"We have to find not only a respectable quantity of

white light," Mamakitty was telling Baldrup, "but white light we can carry back with us."

"Light you can carry." The drover looked dubious. "A difficult task, surely. But now that I have had time to ponder on it, perhaps not as impossible as first I thought."

"You know where we can find such things?" Cocoa eyed him eagerly, at the same time taking care to keep out of club range.

"No." At her crestfallen expression the drover added, "But I can tell you the best place to look." He nodded forward, over the low-slung heads of his team. "In the central marketplace, where we are only now arriving. If it's not for sale there, it's not to be found anywhere in the Kingdom of Red."

If the travelers thought the city was lively, the marketplace overwhelmed them. Stalls, shops, carts, individual traders, all hawked red-tinged goods and unfamiliar services in the vast paved square that surrounded the single lengthy two-story structure that was the original market. There was so much to see that it was impossible to take it all in. They saw no one selling light, white or otherwise, but Baldrup advised them such eclectic specialties might best be searched for within the main market building itself.

To show their thanks, the travelers helped Baldrup and Snicklie to unload their wagon and set up their stall. Formal farewells and thanks they left to Samm, who could best absorb the neighborly blows the two escorts proceeded to rain upon his legs and belly. Surrounded by traders and peddlers who walked, lurched, humped, waddled, hopped, and slithered about the square, the visitors from Fasna Wyzel made their way toward the crowded market building.

Within those high, narrow walls, the noise level of

chatting, complaining, and trading was magnified to such a degree it had Oskar marveling that any business could be conducted at all. It was impossible to know where to begin.

"Let's try that booth over there." Mamakitty pointed. "At the moment it doesn't appear to be too crowded, so the proprietress may be willing to talk."

"Talk is fine," murmured Taj. "But I'm standing back. In case she decides she wants to get friendly."

Aside from being as naturally red-faced as her fellow merchants (face rouge would not be a big seller in this kingdom, Cocoa reflected), the proprietress in question differed from anyone they had yet encountered. She had the broad, flat face of their benefactors Baldrup and Snicklie, but there any similarity ended. Unlike them, her countenance was not in the least humanoid. Spinelike whiskers protruded at least a foot from the sides of her huge, dark mouth. This somewhat intimidating maw was lined with slender, needle-like teeth that made those of the quoll look blunt. Her eyes were wide and wild, with enormous dark pupils. In contrast, the dress and apron she wore were pure homespun.

"Ses sirs, ses sirs, what will it be for thee today?" Her voice was a mewling cackle, soft yet sinister. Except for the friendly blow she aimed at Cocoa, her demeanor was pleasant enough. It was the only thing engaging about her. The opaque jars stacked on the rickety shelves behind her did not invite closer inspection. "Sou be hungry, I see. Biski, she can tell a hungry traveler when she see one!"

"We really just need some information," Oskar began, only to have Cezer elbow him aside.

"Speak for yourself! Me, I'm starving!"

"A sample for the gentleman?" Holding out a spine-tipped hand, the creature passed something unseen to the eager cat-man. Hardly sparing it a glance, he gave a shrug, and downed the free offering in one swallow. His companions watched and waited expectantly.

"What are you all looking at?" The young man smiled contentedly. "Tastes like chicken, with a hint of pepper and sage." His smile fluttered somewhat. "Quite a lot of pepper, actually. No, it's not pepper." Now thoroughly absorbed by what he had swallowed, his expression changed to one of intense introspection, then uncertainty, and finally amusement as he burst out laughing.

"What's so funny?" Samm wanted to know. Despite what his friends thought, the giant did have a sense of humor. It was not his fault that his former throat did not allow for laughing.

"Don't—know." Cezer was chortling so hard he found it difficult to talk. "Something—inside—tickling!"

"Of course." Tugging a protective cloth aside, the merchant Biski exposed her samples to the sun—and to full view of her potential customers. "Tastiest eat-treats in all of Pyackill. And the most active, ses!"

Oskar leaned forward and stared. The countertop she had exposed was full of food—and full of motion. That in itself was not so very unusual. What was unsettling was that they were one and the same. All of the food was perambulating; in different ways, by different means.

There were plump round red globes with taut skins that resembled cherry tomatoes—except that each floundered on dozens of highly active, tiny feet. Baskets of berries were covered with fine cilia that kept them in constant motion. Corpulent vegetables skittered back and forth and bumped into one another on appendages that resembled stiffened fish fins. Some of the minuscule limbs were of familiar design; others were entirely new to the travelers.

"Your food—walks around," Mamakitty observed

aloud. The urge to swat at the ambulatory foodstuffs was almost overpowering. A human would not do such a thing, she reminded herself.

"Welp, of course it walks! Or crawls, or slithers, or otherwise moseys about." Huge dark pupils narrowed slightly. "Mean to tell Biski that sou don't like food that moves after you've eaten it?" Cocoa was leaning fretfully over Cezer, who by now was lying on the ground writhing in pain from laughing so hard.

"It isn't that," Mamakitty explained delicately. "We're new to the area, you see, so we're new to the food as well. Your offerings in particular are certainly—exceptional."

Oskar's concern as he indicated the prone, thrashing Cezer was more immediate. "Exotic new foods can be hard to digest. Our friend seems to be having some trouble."

Biski leaned over the counter full of meandering foodstuffs. "Too rich for him, is it? Maybe I shouldn't have offered him a nokus on an empty stomach." She indicated a dish full of lustrous fruits that resembled olives on wheels. They kept racing around the dish and banging into one another. "He'll be all right in a few minutes, once the nokus rollers have started to dissolve in his belly. Though I must say I disagree with your opinion. Your friend isn't exactly suffering."

Gazing up out of frantic eyes, Cezer continued to cackle hysterically. Oskar smiled back, ignoring the other man's look of murderous rage, and reached out to catch the curious vendor with a solid right hook across her long face. From where she was kneeling beside Cezer, Cocoa looked startled, and even Mamakitty was taken aback.

Not Biski, though. Staggered by the blow, her huge mouth made gulping motions, like a fish out of water fighting for oxygen. "Now that's more like it, stranger-man! For a while there I thought sou were going to play the patrician with me, like the richy folk who always have their sniffers stuck high in the air when they deign to visit the marketplace." She rubbed spine-tipped fingers together. "What can I sell sou?"

"As we said," Oskar repeated. "Some information."

"What we need to buy, sou— you don't sell," added Cocoa.

"Mnmph, is that so? Try me. What be your pleasure, then?"

Oskar wondered if those enormous pupils let her work her booth as effortlessly at night as in the daytime. "We come from a land of many colors."

"Many colors!" The elderly crone wiped dirty spines against her apron. "Who ever heard of such a thing! But it is true that I am not well traveled, and what do I know of the greater world? Many colors, say sou? Even in such a place, though, red is still best, ses?"

"Yes, of course," agreed Mamakitty diplomatically. "But a hex has been placed on our kingdom that has wiped out nearly all color. To restore what has been lost, we need to return with a quantity of white light, which contains within it all colors."

Once more the gaping beak gulped air. "Many colors, white light—what strange places exist beyond Pyackill!" As she stood behind her counter of animated food contemplating their request, the rubbing of her wide chin by one spiny hand produced a sound like a fly trying to force its way through a metal grate. "Light is not my specialty." Raising her other hand, she pointed to a stall at the very end of the long building.

"See that red flag hanging there?—well, they all be red, I suppose—try Phuswick's booth. He gets around a good deal, he does. Has superior taste in victuals and always buys the best from me. If anyone in Pyackill can sell sou white light, Phuswick it be."

"Thank you." To add emphasis to his gratitude, Oskar tried to kick her under the counter, but it was too wide and his foot would not reach her spindly, spiny legs. Noting the gesture, she gargled merrily at him, a twinkle in one enormous eye. Reaching up with a finger, she removed the irritation and flicked it aside.

"That's all right, stranger-man. It be the thought that counts."

EIGHT

With a name like Phuswick, Oskar expected the occupant of the booth to be fully human, perhaps plump of
form and amiable of aspect. He was neither. A Very Large
Bug presided over the contents of a gigantic antique shop
whose inventory had been squashed and smashed and
squeezed down to fit into one of the fifty or so booths that
lined both sides of the market building's busy interior. The
variety of goods on display in the stall was breathtaking,
as was the efflux that emanated from their owner.

Delighting in the opportunity to visit the interior of a
covered structure with a ceiling high enough to allow him
to stand without bending, Samm stood in the middle of the
mob, customers and tourists and merchants swirling around
him like penguins cavorting madly about an iceberg. Taj
remained at his friend's side, while Cezer and Cocoa were
happy to stay in the background. That left it, as usual, to
Oskar and Mamakitty to endure the majestic stink as they
queried the proprietor.

"You're Phuswick?" Oskar half hoped the bug would
reply in the negative.

"I am," hummed the recipient of the inquiry. His voice

was smooth as maple butter, a startling contrast to his fetor and appearance. Big red-black compound eyes regarded the new customers. Between them, a mucousy proboscis probed a plate of chopped bits of something whose identity Oskar preferred not to know. It was no revelation that this trader would be a good customer of Biski's hyperactive cuisine.

"What can I interest you fine people in today? Perhaps a—" Leaning back in his hard wooden chair, the vendor reached for a quivering object that was languishing on a middle shelf.

"No, don't touch that!" Though far from squeamish, even Mamakitty had limits to her fortitude. "Please don't touch that." Eyeing the proprietor, she felt a surge of guilt at all the bugs she had toyed with and crunched in the not so distant past.

"Well, all right." Straightening in his chair thrust his body odor even more forcefully in the direction of his customers. "What, then? Or have you come to try and sell me something?" A clawed foreleg indicated the overflowing stock. "I am in need of nothing today. As you can see, my inventory is quite high at the moment."

Maybe if you used some perfume, or scented lotion, you'd have more customers, Oskar thought. Actually, once you got used to it, the smell wasn't so very much stronger than wet dog. Aloud, he inquired straightforwardly, "Biski sent us. She said that if anyone in Pyackill had what we needed, you would be the one to see."

"Ah, Biski!" the vendor buzzed. "Lovely Biski. Almost arthropoid, I like to think of her. Breeder of the best stubbleblips in the kingdom, too." Focusing on Oskar, much to the latter's olfactory discomfort, the merchant hummed, "What is it you need?"

"White light," declared Mamakitty flatly, sacrificing her momentary anonymity to spare Oskar the full brunt of the vendor's stench. "We need to acquire a large quantity of white light."

"And something to carry it in," added Cocoa from behind.

Having nothing to frown with, Phuswick had to settle for emitting a series of uncertain buzzes, as if he were aloft and abruptly losing wing power. "White light? You want to buy white light?"

"You don't know what it is." Cezer sighed in disappointment.

Looking past Oskar, the vendor replied sharply. "Of course I know what it is! Do you think me ignorant, one-lens? White light," he muttered, "is the light of all lights."

"Yes, that's it!" Pushing forward, an excited Cocoa tried to descry which of the dozens, of the hundreds of jars and alembics, pots and bottles, might contain the vital ephemera they had come to find. "Where is it?"

"Not here," the vendor snapped. "I'm a shopkeeper; not a theurgist. You won't find something as evanescent as white light for sale in a stolid, workaday place like Pyackill. If you really mean to have it, the acquiring will require more from you than money. It demands courage and skill, boldness and stealth."

"Then you know someone who does have it for sale?" asked Mamakitty as she slapped away the filching fingers of a would-be pickpocket. The tousle-haired boinkle grinned up at her as he hopped beyond her reach.

"Nice to meet you, too, stinky lady!" He smirked.

"I know of someone who *might* be able to tell you where to find it." The fetid vendor rubbed his rear wings together.

"Then all we have to do is ask?" inquired Oskar eagerly.

"In a manner of speaking. You need to talk to those who

guard our border with lands of other light. You need to talk to the Red Dragoons."

Oskar nodded to indicate his understanding. "Doesn't sound too difficult. Where do we find these red dragons?"

"Not dragons—dragoons. On the border with the Kingdom of Orange, due east from here," Phuswick explained. "Be on your best behavior. You know how soldiers can be."

"'All we have to do is ask.'" Cezer made a disgusted noise. "The Master once had a group of soldiers stay several days with him, discussing how knowledge sorceral related to matters military. I didn't like them. They wouldn't let me sleep in their laps, or scratch on their boots."

"This lot probably won't either," Oskar pointed out dryly. "Better get used to the idea now."

Cezer nodded tersely. "Don't worry. This shape doesn't seem suited to such pleasurable activities." He grinned at Cocoa. "Bet they'd let *you* sleep in their laps, silky-skin."

She made a face. "I'd rather scratch boots."

"We'll do it." Mamakitty's tone was firm if not entirely assured. "We'll question these soldiers, find the white light, and take it back with us."

"But not today, for I'll wager this outpost doesn't lie close to the city limits."

"Hardly," murmured Phuswick. Rising from his chair, he lurched forward until he was standing fragrantly close to Oskar and Mamakitty. "I'll draw you a map, as best I can recall from what I know. Beyond that, you're on your own. I can give you no further help. I don't do much buzzing around soldiers." Reaching out, he gave Oskar's nose a severe twist. "But I'm only doing this because I like you," he finished as Mamakitty, palm cupped protectively over her face, ducked back out of his reach.

* * *

The narrow road through the Glavieb Hills was surfaced with reddish clay. For several days subsequent to leaving Pyackill, traffic grew progressively thinner, until a last trio of farmers parted ways with the travelers not far back up the road.

"This must be harsh country in which to raise crops." Taj was striding along easily, one hand shading his eyes from the sizzling red sun as he studied the rugged hills through which they had been climbing for the better part of the day.

"Depends on local conditions, I suppose." Nudging a rock aside with one booted foot, Cocoa exposed the carmine-colored cockroach that had been hiding beneath. It scurried off in search of a more secure place of concealment. No ordinary human would have heard the skritching of its tiny feet, but like her companions, Cocoa was neither ordinary nor entirely human. She fought off the urge to chase down the cockroach, trap it under one hand, and eat it.

Something came screaming down the slope toward them. Mamakitty ducked, while Oskar and Cezer reacted by drawing their swords. The bird was red-blue, with enormous splayed wings and a single eye set in the middle of its skull. There were tiny teeth in its beak, and as it rocketed past the travelers it snapped at Mamakitty's curls. Then it was gone, an ominous presence soaring out of sight below boulders and ridges they had just traversed.

Straightening, Mamakitty felt gingerly of her coiffure. It was intact, as was her scalp. "Never saw anything like that before."

"Maybe it was just trying to be 'friendly,' in the local manner," Cezer suggested dryly. "Maybe it wasn't even a bird."

"Oh, it was a bird, all right." Taj spoke with some authority on the matter. "Not a seed-eater, either."

Though the unexpected and brief assault had harmed no one, they remained on high alert as they continued to ascend, scrambling over boulders and rocks with effortless agility. Only Taj, unaccustomed to climbing, had any trouble with the ascent, and he was helped over the rough spots by his companions.

It took several days of steady tramping to reach the border country, during which time the harshness of much of the terrain slowly gave way to increasingly lush vegetation. Rivulets became streams, streams became rivers, as the entire character of the landscape through which they were marching lost its rough edge.

It also lost some of its all-pervasive color. The hardy red tint that had stained everyone and everything they had encountered since Taj had first stumbled into the rainbow at the base of the Shalouan Falls grew muted. They were entering a region where two colors of the rainbow melded, as one kingdom gave way to another.

Oskar was especially pleased by the transformation. Not that he particularly disliked the color red, but in addition to the heat it seemed to amplify, its multiple variations had a way of sanctifying the kind of mannered hostility they hoped to leave behind.

Certainly the coloration of the atmosphere, as well as the countryside, was becoming noticeably softened. In the distance, rolling hills covered with thick vegetation took on a distinctive orange hue. Perhaps, he hoped, they were about to enter a land where courtesy was not founded on the prickliness of physical contact. But first they had to make certain they were traveling in the right direction.

There was no need to spend time searching for the Red Dragoons. As soon as they reached the main river, they found themselves confronted by a pair of those splendidly uniformed border guards.

"Travel documents, please." Cerise light glinted from the brightly polished helmet of the young man who bent low in the saddle of his kudu to query Oskar.

"I'm afraid we don't have any documents. We're strangers here, having come from," he thought rapidly before concluding, "far to the west. From the other side of the Kingdom of Red."

The dragoon's companion laughed softly at this, but the one asking the questions did not smile. "Oh, come now, traveler. What do you take me for? There are no kingdoms to the west of Red. Beyond that farthest border the climate grows too hot for intelligent life. Nothing can survive there."

"Nevertheless," put in Mamakitty, sensing that Oskar needed support, "that is where we come from. But our country is not so very hot. Not even as hot as this. We traveled hence by means you would not understand."

"Ah!" The dragoon sat up straight in his saddle. "Then you are magicians!"

"We certainly owe our presence here to magic," Oskar admitted truthfully.

"They don't look like magicians." The other rider spoke for the first time. Oskar noted that he had four horns protruding from his head, a third eye in the center of his forehead, and only three long fingers on each hand. "And they smell funny. Especially that one." He indicated Oskar, who looked hurt.

"It's not for us to decide." The soldier who had carried the conversation backed his steed a couple of paces. "You must come with us to the post. Captain Covalt will decide what is to be done with you."

"That's fine with us," Oskar replied amiably. "We have a question or two for him as well."

The dragoons' base consisted of a cluster of tents and small wooden buildings surrounded by a stockade of flexible red trunks and branches that had been interwoven together horizontally as well as vertically to form a strong, impenetrable barricade. It was the first wall Oskar had ever seen that looked as if it had been braided rather than built. From its location atop a sloping but dominant hill, the post commanded a fine view over the surrounding countryside, including the wide, slow-flowing river that ran from north to south on its western flank. As well as sky and clouds, the flora on the far side of the river had a distinctly orange cast.

Dragoons busy with washing, or maneuvers, or drilling paused in their tasks to observe the escorted newcomers' arrival. Particular attention was paid to Samm, since it is natural for soldiers everywhere to instinctively size up the most formidable of any potential opponent. The giant's imposing stone axe garnered murmurs of admiration.

The travelers were not troubled when the stockade gate was shut behind them. Having committed no offense, they had nothing to fear. They were here to answer questions, and to ask one or two of their own.

Their escorts disappeared into a single-story stone structure. Water was provided to the waiting guests. Within moments a trio of officers emerged, resplendent with polish, paint, and attitude. Only one was human. A second had the wide, flat face so typical of the city dwellers the travelers had encountered in Pyackill. He also boasted a long, naked, ratlike tail that emerged from the seat of his trousers, and two finger-thick whiplike antennae that protruded from his forehead. His companion was barely three feet tall, with a face like a carp and an inability to stand still.

As for the post commandant, Captain Covalt, he was of moderate height and dark of skin, with a bald head and two furry ears that thrust upward from either side of his skull. His jaw line flaunted an unfortunate natural downward curve that afflicted him with a permanent frown, and he had no visible nose. A wide mouth overfilled with small whitish teeth completed the countenance, which despite its somewhat forbidding features was not overtly malicious.

"So, you claim to come from west of the kingdom, and by means sorceral?" Though he spoke to Oskar, his gaze was fastened on Cocoa.

"We entered into this realm from a land where no one color is dominant," Oskar replied. "I know that may be difficult for you to accept, but—"

"It is not difficult to accept: it is impossible to accept. *All* kingdoms are cloaked in a preclusive dominant color. That is the way the world was made. As well as being a soldier, I am also something of a scholar of such arcana. Call it a hobby, with which I try to while away the long lonely hours in isolated outposts such as this." Approaching Cocoa, he smiled a dentist's dream, took her hand, and kissed it. Given the width of his jaws, he could just as easily have swallowed it. "And what might your name be, my dear?"

"Cocoa." She tried not to show the revulsion she was feeling. This was not due so much to his hybrid appearance, so different from anything they had yet encountered, as to his smelling strongly of onions despite the fact that there was nothing in the least tuberous in his mien.

"A lovely name for a lovely lady. I request the honor of sitting next to you at dinner tonight." He struggled to smile, wrestling with the natural arc of his lips. "You will be our guests, of course."

"That's very kind of you," she replied courteously, "but we're in something of a hurry."

"Such a pity." She finally managed to free her hand. His touch was greasy. "Tell me: what compels you to flee the dragoons' hospitality so precipitously?"

"White light." Without openly jostling the captain, Oskar did his best to worm his way between him and the patently uncomfortable Cocoa. "We have to find some, and take it back with us to our country."

"White light? As an educated person I know of the existence of many colors, but not white." Turning, the captain gestured in the direction of the river. "Certainly there is none such to be had in the Kingdom of Red, but I have heard tales—old people's fancies, travelers' stories—of the many wonders that lie far to the east. The Kingdom of Purple especially is rumored to contain many marvels. I was once told, by a venerable and experienced traveler, of a temple there that contains within its walls examples of everything that is, or ever was, or that can be imagined. If your white light is to be found anywhere within the kingdoms, I would think that would be the place. You will assuredly not find it in the Kingdom of Orange that lies just across the river, which we know well."

"We'll cross whatever lands we must," Mamakitty informed him. "We can't go home without it."

Furry ears twitched as the captain bobbed his head. "I'm sure your quest is a noble one, though for the life of me I can't imagine why anyone would need to acquire such a mysterious intangibility." Reaching out, he took Cocoa's hand before she could avoid his grasp. "You have no travel documents. A fact I am willing to overlook."

"That's real neighborly of you." Oskar noticed that a number of the dragoons in their immediate vicinity had stopped laboring at their daily tasks and were slowly picking up their weapons. A new scent was in the air, and it was not onions. "We'll be going now."

"By all means," agreed the captain. "Take your leave. However, in the absence of documents I am afraid the kingdom demands security of another kind. One of you must remain behind to guarantee the good conduct of the others." His grip on Cocoa's wrist tightening, he nodded at her and grinned alarmingly. "This one. She will not be harmed, and will be treated as an honored guest until you return."

"We can't do that." Mamakitty stepped forward. "You see, we're kind of used to each other's company. Also, we believe that it's important to the success of our quest that we stay together. We pose no threat to the Kingdom of Red, or any other kingdom."

There was no mistaking the intent of the circle of dragoons, who, though incompletely attired and out of formation, were now closing an armed circle around the travelers. As unobtrusively as possible, Oskar let his right hand fall toward his sword. Samm made a show of unlimbering his great axe, while Taj gripped one of the rather insignificant-looking knives with which he had been outfitted.

Disdaining any further diplomacy, Cezer pushed his way forward, sword already drawn, eyes ablaze, teeth bared. "Take your hands off her, sir! It is no gentleman who designs to hold a lady against her will."

"Well and stupidly spoken." Releasing Cocoa's wrist, Captain Covalt slowly drew his own blade. "Obviously, you are unaware of my reputation as a swordsman."

"And you are unaware of mine!" Relaxing into a fighting stance, Cezer prepared to defend Cocoa's honor, ignoring the fact that she had drawn her own sword.

"You have no reputation," Mamakitty hissed at him.

"I will in a few moments—I hope," the would-be cavalier responded tightly.

Slowly shaking his head, Captain Covalt removed his splendidly embroidered jacket and handed it to one of his attachés. He was solidly built; his would not be an easy defense to penetrate. Oskar tried to conceal his concern. Though enthusiastic and energetic enough, Cezer had no formal training in swordsmanship, whereas the captain was an experienced soldier.

"Let me handle this." Axe in hand, Samm took a giant step forward. Instantly dragoons surrounded him, raising and aiming a lethal assortment of arrows, bolts, and spears—any weapon that could be employed from a safe distance.

"Keep out of it, Samm." Describing small circles in the air with the point of his sword, Cezer was prancing threateningly before the captain. "I picked this fight, and I'll finish it."

Covalt nodded once, curtly. "Indeed you will, my friend. I can see that you are extraordinarily quick of hand and foot, with much natural talent. I can also see that you are inexperienced in the arts of war. Though I could cut you to pieces, I won't let you suffer. Your death will be a quick one."

Oskar stepped forward. "Look, isn't there some way we can settle this with further discussion?"

"The time for words is past." Sword fully extended, Covalt widened his stance. "Don't worry—once this one is disposed of and the girl comfortably situated here, there will still be plenty of you left to carry out your quest." Turning his attention back to his opponent, he uttered what might have been a formal challenge—or a local imprecation.

With a wild yowl, Cezer charged. His thrusting sword

was parried with such subtlety that Oskar could not be certain he had seen the captain's blade move. Its point caught Cezer in the left buttock as he rushed past the dragoon, pricking him and bringing blood.

"This is too easy." Bouncing lightly on short legs and feet that Oskar noticed for the first time were slightly webbed, Covalt awaited his opponent's next rush. "I am a soldier, not an assassin of children."

"No: you're a polite would-be rapist—would-be, say I!" Cezer charged again.

This time the captain stood his ground, parrying every swipe and strike Cezer could muster. Eventually bored, Covalt struck back, his sword jabbing at his opponent's exposed chest. Fortunately, the sword point was diverted by a silver pillbox residing in Cezer's breast pocket. The force of the thrust alone, however, was enough to send him stumbling backward. Covalt followed, pressing the attack relentlessly.

"He's going to kill him!" Taj stuttered. "Somebody do something!" His gaze turned up and back. "Samm, you have to stop this!"

The giant's teeth were clenched. "He said not to interfere."

"But you have to!" As Taj fingered the knife he held, he saw several soldiers staring hard in his direction, their own weapons upraised, ready to block any attempt to intervene in the duel. Constrained like his companions, Taj could only stand by and watch.

The remorseless Covalt continued to force Cezer steadily backward. Although his companion's efforts with the sword steadily improved as the fight continued, Oskar saw that his friend remained desperately overmatched against the skilled officer. The dog-man's eyes darted from side to side. No matter the consequences, he knew that he was going to have to intercede. As an upshot they might all die, but despite the surface acrimony that existed between them, he knew he could not let Cezer be killed without at least attempting to save him. They shared too many memories from the times they had slept curled up against one another as puppy and kitten.

Whirling, the embattled Cezer leaped onto a wagon. Covalt followed more slowly, admiring his opponent's gymnastic ability if not his swordsmanship. Now there was nowhere else for Cezer to retreat. The sheer wall of the stockade was at his back. Sweating profusely, muscles trembling, he let out a yowl of anger at the situation circumstances had forced him into.

"Master Evyndd, is this what you intended!"

"I don't know this 'Master Evyndd.'" Sword darting smoothly from side to side like a patrolling dragonfly, Captain Covalt was preparing to climb up into the wagon after his adversary. "But he can't help you. Not now." Choosing his route, he thrust upward with his weapon.

Though still too far away to make contact with the other's blade, Cezer made desperate, wild parrying motions. And then, quite unexpectedly, their blades *did* make contact. But only because Cezer's weapon had suddenly doubled in length. Impossibly, it felt no heavier, though there was clearly twice as much steel protruding from the pommel as a moment before.

It was enough to make Covalt blink. The captain hesitated only briefly, however, before striking again. In response, his opponent's engorged weapon seemed to take on a life of its own, as though drawing strength from some cat part of its holder usually employed in entirely different campaigns of conquest. As he wielded the taut, shining blade that was now some six feet long yet lighter than

ever, an entirely new and fresh expression came over
Cezer's face.

Anticipation.

Stabbing and swinging, it was his turn to press the attack. Unable to slip in a thrust beneath so active and extended a blade, Covalt was forced to give ground. As he
did so, the preternaturally elongated sword began to swing
faster and faster, until it was generating an audible hum
that could be heard everywhere within the Red Dragoons'
post. How he was doing this Cezer did not know, although
every swing of the weapon seemed to be propelled by his
whole body. Not being of as serious a questioning mind as
Oskar or Mamakitty, he was content simply to make use
of the fortuitous phenomenon and worry about explana-
tions later.

Seeing their superior hard-pressed, both of Covalt's aides
abruptly rushed to his aid, as did a pair of foot soldiers
standing nearby. Their intercession was of no consequence.
With the six-foot-long blade humming to itself like a gigantic wasp, Cezer forced them all back while clearing a
circle around himself and his companions.

"How are you doing this?" Oskar shouted as they began
to edge toward the stockade gate.

"How should I know?" Cezer continued to swing and
thrust with zest, enjoying the look of confusion on the faces
of their opponents, and the one of frustrated fury on that
of the captain. When a couple of soldiers let arrows loose
at the retreating visitors, the magically augmented sword
parried them with ease. Thus redirected, one such shaft
pierced the leg of another soldier, with the consequence
that no more projectiles were forthcoming from the assembled, flustered troopers.

"Isn't your arm getting tired?" Sword in hand, Cocoa
had her own potential opponents to worry about.

"Not yet," he yelled back at her. "It's as if an entirely different part of myself is holding it up."

"Through the wonder of the Master's magic we have been given human form." Mamakitty lunged sharply forward, driving back a would-be assailant. "Perhaps we have been given other things as well."

Then why is my sword still of normal length, and my legs already aching? Oskar wondered silently. Did it mean that there was something inherent in Cezer that made him a better swordsman? No matter. He was more than content to retreat under cover of his companion's proprietary enchantment.

By this time, word of what was happening had spread throughout the entire contingent of dragoons. In various stages of uniform and dress, putting aside their daily tasks, they took up arms and trailed the travelers down to the river's edge, waiting for the moment when their bewitched opponents should tire. Several of the uninformed newcomers tried to bring Cezer down from a distance with arrows or spears. His mysteriously elongated and accelerated sword blurring the air like a hummingbird's wing, Cezer once more parried these threats from long range as effortlessly as he did the soldiers' continuing futile sword thrusts.

There were half a dozen boats tied up at the river's edge. One by one, the travelers clambered aboard the nearest. While the miraculously invigorated Cezer held off the entire contingent of dragoons, Samm slipped into the water and pulled the boat off the sandbar on which it was resting, giving it a hearty shove downstream before climbing over the dangerously declining stern to rejoin his companions.

Her own weapon still held at the ready, Mamakitty frowned as the current caught them and they began to pick up speed. "They're not following. As angry as Cezer has made them, I thought surely they would follow. They have the boats to do it."

Oskar gazed back at the shore, which was now lined with gesticulating, jeering dragoons. "It seems they'd rather taunt us."

"Let them taunt all they wish." Emotionally exhausted, Taj lay slumped against a railing. "Easier to parry insults than steel."

Safely away, Cocoa sheathed her own weapon and strode forward. Seeing her approach, Cezer moved automatically to put up his sword. Had he paused to think about it he might not have initiated the gesture, for a six-foot sword would not easily slip into a scabbard designed for one half that size. But as it was turned toward its home, it began to shrink. Oskar blinked, but the phenomenon could not be denied. By the time it had swung around far enough to be scabbarded, the weapon had contracted back to its original length.

"How did you do that?" Cocoa indicated the now sheathed blade.

Cezer shrugged, then grinned. "I have no idea. Some postmortem trick of Master Evyndd's, I should assume. I wonder what other posthumous surprises may await." He straightened, making himself as tall as possible. "I'm quite exhausted from the episode, but the swordsmanship was all mine. No magic in that. After doing battle all my life with two handfuls of smaller versions, it seems to come naturally to me." Holding up a hand, he made a face at the blunt human nails that tipped his fingers. "Miss my naturals, I do."

"Well, *mssst,* thank you, Cezer." She shuddered visibly. "The mere thought of being held as a 'guest' by that loathsome creature is enough to curdle milk."

"My weapon will always be at your disposal, ready to

extend itself to extraordinary lengths at a moment's stimulus." He smiled enigmatically. Trying to read his expression, she considered how to react to this promise, finally deciding to ignore it. Turning, she settled onto a bench to watch the shoreline slip past.

"You know," Oskar mused to Mamakitty as the two sat watching the shore, "keeping in mind what we have learned of the customs of this land, perhaps that soldier was only trying to be very polite."

The woman seated next to him considered. "You could very well be right, Oskar. I didn't think of that. This is a difficult place in which to try and read someone's intentions. Tell me: did you smell the threat in him?"

The dog-man shook his head (that, at least, being a gesture with which he was long familiar). "No, I didn't. There was something else. I think maybe he was coming into heat. And then there was the anger, when Cezer challenged him. Could we have so badly misread his intentions?"

She shrugged. "It doesn't matter. Cocoa wasn't going to stay with him, and we certainly weren't going to leave her behind. I'll be glad if and when we enter country where people touch noses, rub up against one another, and engage in mutual grooming as a way of showing friendship."

Oskar sighed. "You cats are always so touchy-feely."

From near the stern, Cezer had to comment. "More polite than smelling a new acquaintance's butt."

Taj turned toward the river. "You disgust me, the lot of you." Samm had no comment. Snakes usually didn't.

Oskar ignored the swordsman. "That sounds to me like wishful thinking, Mamakitty. I'm afraid the best we can hope to encounter is the human habit of shaking hands."

"So impersonal." Turning away from him, she let eyes and mind relax by concentrating on the slowly changing panorama beyond the boat.

While the near riverbank retained the distinctively red-dish cast of the kingdom it delimited, the low sandbars, high reeds, and rustling palms on the far side had assumed a distinctly orange hue. Very fat birds and puffballs with sunken eyes flitted in profusion among the tropical growths. While it remained warm, the closer they drifted to the far shore, the more the temperature moderated. Humidity in-creased, however, altering without lessening their discom-fort.

"How I long for the cool depths of the Fasna Wyzel." Always fastidious in his personal habits, Taj was suffering from the perspiration that soaked his clothing. Unlike his former feathers, the artificial raiment he was compelled to wear could not be cleansed by simple preening. So it was not surprising that it was he who suggested they take turns washing themselves and their clothing in the river.

Having been the one to advance the proposal, it was he who tentatively slipped first into the water. A couple of ropes secured to the boat had been tossed into the river. These now dangled astern. By clinging to one of these, a bather could enjoy the cleansing action of the current while exerting minimal effort to remain afloat. Come evening, everyone had taken a turn. The river was deep enough so that even Samm's feet did not bump against the bottom. Not that he cared. The snake-man was the best swimmer among them. A few fish nibbled curiously at their toes, but nothing emerged from the deeps to bite or sting the grate-ful bathers. Taj had to remember to hang on to the rope with one hand instead of flapping both simultaneously in the water.

When the stars came out, they were tinged with carmine, and the moon was a pink blot against the blackness.

"Tomorrow we'll pick a place to go ashore on the western bank." Mamakitty was leaning back against the railing, studying the night sky.

"How?" Oskar wondered. "When Master Evyndd took us to Zelevin, we saw boats like this on the Shalouan, and I remember watching them as they were steered. This one has no oars, no sail. Without a way to guide it, we're likely to drift past any suitable spot."

"Don't you remember? It should be enough to just move that wooden thing fastened to the back. I recall that when they were pushed one way, boats turned in the other direction."

Oskar looked back at the rudder that was swinging freely with the current. "That's right, I remember now. People on boats pushed such things in the opposite direction they wanted to go." He relaxed. "I suppose that means we can go ashore anywhere we like."

She nodded. "Let's try to pick a dry place. I don't like getting wet any more often than I have to."

He nodded understandingly. Personally, he loved the water. And for that matter, the mud. "I still wonder why those soldiers didn't come after us?"

Mamakitty shrugged. As performed by her, it was a remarkably liquid gesture. "I suppose they decided being impaled on Cezer's blade wasn't worth capturing a female for their captain."

While this reasoning did not fully satisfy the contemplative Oskar, he could think of no better explanation for what had transpired. Besides, he was tired. Since Mamakitty seemed content to let the boat drift downriver, he saw no point in dwelling on what was past. Finding an empty place on the open deck, he paced in circles, tighter and tighter, until at last he felt comfortable and lay down, curling up as compactly as his new body would allow, before falling into an exhausted and dreamless sleep.

When his eyelids next fluttered, the sun was already up. A mass of orange-red fluff was gazing back at him out of eyes that protruded from the depths of dense down. Whether it was composed of feathers or fur, he could not tell. Taken unawares by its proximity, he snapped awake. Emitting a startled coo, the orange sphere promptly fluttered its feathers (or fur) and rose vertically into the air. Looking up, Oskar saw that it had joined a dozen others of its kind. They hovered above him for another moment before flocking as one for the grove of orange-tinted palms from which they had emerged.

"I wonder what they are." Cocoa was sitting up on the deck.

"I wonder if they're edible." Standing next to her, Cezer rested a hand on his belly. "I'm hungry."

"We should conserve our supplies. How about some fresh fish?" Samm stood contemplating the water.

Cezer's face lit with anticipation, and he all but slobbered on his fine clothes. "Fish! You're asking a cat if it would like some fish?"

"You're not a cat anymore," Taj pointed out.

"I'm not all human, either," Cezer shot back. "Don't tell me you don't feel the urge to flap your arms and take to the sky." Before the other man could reply, the swordsman had turned back to Samm. "Get us some fish, and I'll lick you clean myself."

The giant wore a look of distaste. "Thanks, but I got clean enough in the river."

"How are you going to catch fish?" Oskar wondered. "Master Evynced used to take me fishing with him. There is no fishing equipment on board this boat. Besides, it is a delicate skill. You have to understand how to read the play of swimmer and sand, light and water."

"Then I will be delicate." Leaning over the side, Samm

caused the entire boat to tilt in his direction. While his companions struggled to remain erect, the giant scanned the softly rippling surface of the river intently. Espying motion, he brought his enormous axe down in one swift, arcing movement. Water erupted, cascading over the gunwale and drenching everyone and everything aboard.

Sputtering, Oskar was about to say something disagreeable—until he saw the half dozen stunned fish that now lay twitching on the deck. Water spilling in rivulets from his bald pate, Samm sat back down in the stern, set his axe aside, and patiently began picking at the yard-long specimen nearest his feet. With a cry, Cezer and Cocoa bent to do the same. There was no place to make a fire, but that did nothing to mute the avidity with which those on board tore into the unexpected bounty. Having always consumed it raw, they saw no necessity to cook it now.

Only Taj did not participate. The orgy of consumption, with fish blood and oil staining the deck and pale flesh and bone flying every which way, turned his stomach. He had to satisfy himself with dried fruits and vegetables from those stored in Samm's pack.

Bellies swollen, stomachs packed full, they settled down as cats and snakes will do after eating for a long, contented nap. That left only Oskar—who although he had eaten well was not quite as serious a fish fanatic as his feline companions—and Taj to consider the country through which they were passing. While the boat drifted onward, the others slept off the unexpected feast. Rhythmic digesting sounds issued from somewhere within the somnolent Samm, persuading Oskar that despite what one might think, it was indeed possible for a snake to snore.

"I still can't figure out why those soldiers didn't come after us."

"You heard Mamakitty's explanation." Taj was leaning

over the prow of the boat, contemplating the water. Suddenly he lifted his head. "Maybe that's the reason, up ahead."

Oskar had to squint. Though excellent, his eyesight was not as sharp as the other man's. Then he saw it: the place forward of the bow where the river disappeared into a huge cave. The rim of the yawning opening was dominated by prominent stalactites and stalagmites.

"We'd better wake the others. We have to go ashore before we reach that. No telling what happens to the river once it has entered the cave."

"We'd better wake them quickly." Taj had straightened, and the hair on the back of his neck had stiffened. "That's not a cave. It's a *mouth*. And those things lining its rim aren't cave growths made of dripping stone. They're teeth. . . ."

NINE

$\mathbf{A}$mid frantic yelling and screaming, and not a few accompanying kicks and blows, Taj and Oskar fought to rouse their companions. One by one, as soon as they saw where their free-drifting craft was heading, the others came awake with astonishing alacrity.

"The wooden thing on the end!" Mamakitty led a general rush toward the back of the boat. "Samm—push on the wooden thing affixed to the stern!" As seemed to happen more and more the longer they dwelled in human form, the word suddenly popped into her mind. "The rudder—move the rudder!" The giant obediently leaned a massive hand on the indicated mechanism. "No, no!" Mamakitty yelled. "The other direction! Push it the other way!"

Simultaneously fascinated and horrified, all eyes were now focused on the colossal maw toward which they were helplessly floating. As they picked up speed, Oskar saw that even though they had changed course and were now heading for the eastern bank, their angle of approach would not be acute enough to allow them to beach the boat before they were swallowed up. He began running back and forth the length of the boat until it struck him that such activity was not a suitable expression of concern in his present form.

Two looming ridges high above the dark opening in the mountain that blocked their way suddenly cracked open, exposing a pair of flattened scarlet eyes out of whose depths stared tiny black pupils. From deep within the gaping organic cavern, a voice emerged that was like a sigh of petrified winds.

"I am the Red Dagon, drinker of this river and everything that swims within and upon it! Draw near, and be consumed."

"*Pfssst!*" Cezer yowled back. Leaping up onto the gunwale, he grimaced as he was forced to contemplate the flow below. "By my foreshortened whiskers, how I hate the water!"

Reaching up, Oskar grabbed his friend's pants leg. "It doesn't matter, Cezer! You'd never make it."

Reluctantly, the other man let himself be drawn down. "This boat is doomed. What else can we do but try and swim for it?" He rested a hand on his companion's arm. "You were always a good swimmer, Oskar. You might make it." He looked past him. "So might Samm."

The giant nodded. "I have always been comfortable in the water, but I will not go without the rest of you."

"A sensitive serpent. Who would have believed it?" A downcast Cezer looked away.

"You might have, had you ever been able to talk to me," the giant responded calmly.

"It's a hard thing to communicate in the absence of common speech." Taj was studying the approaching maw disconsolately, lamenting yet again the absence of his wings. "Can we discuss it later?"

"Cezer's right. We have no time to consider alternatives. There's nothing we can do except jump in and swim as strong as we can for the near shore." Mamakitty was readying herself for the desperate leap into pink-tinted water. "It just bothers me so to perhaps perish like this, without even being able to preen one last time my silky black coat with its lovely white spots."

"Black? White?" The gigantic pair of jaws they had mistaken for the entrance to a cave slammed shut with a ponderous thud, then parted less than a foot to allow the onrushing river to continue to drain inward. Oskar marveled that the mountainous spirit could speak and swallow at the same time. "What is this 'black and white' of which you speak?"

Propelled by the current, the borrowed boat of the border guards drifted forward until it bumped up against a truly monstrous set of lips. Water continued to flow into the slightly parted mouth. Oskar knew that should the spirit shape decide to once again fully part its jaws, the clumsy watercraft and all aboard would vanish instantly down that extraordinary gullet.

"Black and white is my normal, natural coloring." Mamakitty gazed apprehensively up at deep-set eyes of sentient vermilion. Having to cross in order to focus on the small boat and its inhabitants, both orbs were squashed between heavy ridges of stone. "White and black." Sensing possible salvation in unexpected curiosity, she hastened to identify the original hues of her anxious companions. "Oskar, here, is mostly a steel gray, while Cezer is normally pale blond. Cocoa is calico, a mix of many colors, while Taj is golden yellow, and Samm—Samm is gray-brown with the most beautiful iridescent maroon and blue and green diamond patterns covering his entire body."

Like biscuits plumping in a pan, the Red Dagon's rocky eyebrows rose. "I see no such colors, though the patterning you describe is visible within the skin of your largest individual."

"I don't like this epidermis either," the giant grunted, "but it's the one Master Evyndd's spell has bequeathed to me." Reaching up, he scratched at a prominent diamond-shaped mole on the side of his neck. "I can't even shed when I'm in the mood."

"You are not citizens of the Kingdom of Red," the Dagon concluded. "Nor the Kingdom of Orange. Why are you on the river that I drink?"

"We just wanted to get across," Cocoa explained plaintively. "We're trying to find some white light to take back to our own home, which lies within a kingdom that encompasses all colors."

"All colors! That would be very tasty. Sometimes I get so tired of eating nothing but red and orange." Water foamed and bubbled around the flinty lips that spanned the river from one bank to the other. "If you were to find such a thing, something that is neither red nor orange, would you bring some back to me? To taste?"

Oskar and Mamakitty exchanged a glance. "I don't see why not," the dog-man agreed. "As long as we can get enough for our purposes, I see no reason why we can't provide you with a taste as well. Where there is white light there have to be many things that are colored other than red and orange."

"But can I trust you?" rumbled the Red Dagon.

"I promise you," Mamakitty replied, "that when we find light that is neither red nor orange, I'll see to it that you are apprised of our find. And as any cat that has hunted in the Fasna Wyzel can tell you, I keep my promises. Ask the mice. One way or another, we will bring to your attention something that is not red or orange." She hesitated. "What would you like? Something green? Or perhaps blue, or yellow?"

"Green, blue—I cannot envision these wonders!" Resonant though it was, the Red Dagon's tone had turned wistful. "What a joy that would be! What a welcome change of flavors!" Eyes of impenetrable crimson met her own. "If you find them, call out to me, and in whatever kingdom of color you are residing, I will come." The vast mouth started to gape. "Now I will let you go, and hold you to your promise."

"Hey, wait!" If it was going to let them go, Oskar thought frantically, then why was it about to swallow them? Cocoa was screaming, and a hissing Samm preparing to dive over the side as their boat slid beneath that stream-spanning upper lip to slip into the yawning maw.

Then he, and everyone else, was clinging to whatever they could reach as the Red Dagon, in a single violent expectoration, spat them toward the eastern shore.

Not only did the powerful spew beach their craft, it sent it careening right through the reeds that grew along the shore and up the sandy bank beyond. Extricating himself from beneath a cussing Cezer and a disheveled Mamakitty, Oskar struggled to his feet and looked back the way they had come. This was relatively easy, since a boatwide path had been mowed right through the line of reeds.

Out in the river, flattened red eyes had shifted to gaze over at him.

"Remember!" boomed the Red Dagon. "Something of color!" With that reminder, the elongated orbs closed tightly, and their owner assumed once more the aspect of a dead, lifeless cave opening in the side of an inanimate mountain. Able to peer behind it from his new vantage point on the riverbank, Oskar saw that the imposing barrier folded gradually into hills that were higher still. No trace of the river escaped the yawning craw to flow over or around it.

"No wonder it wants to imbibe something new." As he straightened his clothing, Taj gave a good approximation of his former self ruffling his feathers. "With a thirst like that, anything different would taste good!"

"We must keep our word." Somehow Mamakitty had managed to retain her dignity despite the tumble she had taken as a consequence of the powerful expectoration.

"In order to do that we have to keep going." With an effortless leap, Oskar was up and over the side of the boat. The ground beneath his feet was sandy, but solid and supportive of his weight. Slowly, he rose from all fours. "Notice the difference here?"

It was true. Everything was changed, even the air they breathed. Warm and moist, it was a definite improvement over the hot, dry air of the Kingdom of Red. The reeds, the palms and other vegetation, right down to the soil beneath their feet, had taken on a fruity orange cast. Whether the color change meant that the land they were about to cross was more hospitable than what they had left behind remained to be seen.

"I don't feel as combative," a puzzled Cezer pointed out. "Could that stem just from a change in the color of our surroundings?"

"I believe it can be so." As they started up the grassy hillock and away from boat and river and talking mountain, Mamakitty took a moment to wax philosophical. "Doesn't the presence of red always heighten your anger, or set your nerves on edge?"

"Not mine. Must be just getting away from that other kingdom." Oskar lengthened his stride, anxious to reach the top of the hill. "Color changes don't affect me much."

"Very little affects you much," Cocoa pointed out. "I

don't think I've ever seen you really upset, Oskar. That part of your personality hasn't changed with your new body." She moved closer to him.

"Carpet dog." Cezer was not pleased to see her walking so close to the other man. "Doormat. Flea hotel." They ignored him.

His irritation faded rapidly, dispelled by the lush attractiveness of their surroundings. It was as if by crossing the river they had entered into not merely another kingdom, but another world. In contrast to the dry and often desolate landscape of the Kingdom of Red, the Kingdom of Orange was lush with a kind of vegetation that was as new to them as it was attractive.

"I think this kind of forest is called *tropical savanna.* I used to sit on Master Evyndd's shoulder and watch while he read through large books containing many pictures." Plucking a thin-skinned, orange-tinted fruit from a nearby bush, Mamakitty took an experimental bite of the firm flesh. "This is delicious! I don't think we will want for food in this place."

Soon they were all feasting on the bounty of the land through which they were trekking. Most selections had distinctive and stable flavors, but all were tasty. In fact, by the time evening arrived the only danger they faced was from upset stomachs due to overeating.

"I think I could live here." Samm was lying on his back, huge hands behind his head, staring up through pale orange leaves at the deepening orange sky. "Pleasant climate, food fairly falling off the foliage."

Oskar regarded him with interest. "You no longer feel the need to eat something alive and wriggling?"

The giant turned his head to look at the other man. "Only occasionally. Strange, isn't it? Some of our tastes and former characteristics remain unchanged, while others have been altered to fit our new bodies and selves. I wonder if such was Master Evyndd's intention?"

"I doubt that we'll ever know. Unless he made plans to return from the dead." Turning, Oskar sought a soft patch of ground on which to spend the night. Enormous leaves plucked from nearby plants provided suitable, if slightly damp, bedding.

Nearby, Cocoa contemplated the orange-white specks of the stars. "While we're lying here safe and with full bellies I can't keep from thinking about the poor people on the other side of these kingdoms of light who must be suffering terribly under the hardships imposed by the Horde and the awful Khaxan Mundurucu."

"I can." With a soft snort, Cezer rolled over, turning his back to the others.

Cocoa snapped at him. "Well, then consider how the animals must be suffering! Your fellow cats, and dogs."

"Not to forget the birds," Taj put in. He glanced in Samm's direction. "And I suppose, the snakes."

Already half-asleep, the giant spoke softly and without opening his eyes. "Mundurucu, Horde, or humans—it doesn't matter. Snakes always suffer. We are condemned to it through rumor, falsehood, and ignorance. I do not believe we would suffer so if others would think of us as quadriplegic lizards. Most folk have no fear of lizards."

"Perhaps in this benign land even the serpents are well regarded," Oskar offered by way of encouragement.

"Perhaps." The giant sighed heavily. "Some of us are born to greater burdens than others. That is just the way of things."

The following morning did not tell them if this was a place where Oskar's hopes for legless reptiles might be fulfilled, but it certainly began in a promising manner. The gnomelike farmer they encountered tilling a thick, ripening field of several different varieties of melon seemed delighted to see them. He was not at all put off by their greater size, or different appearances. Instead, he put his tilling tool aside and rushed to greet them with open arms.

For all the narrow white-orange beard that reached to his belt buckle, he was no older than Oskar. He wore single-piece coveralls, sandals of peculiar but practical design, a short-sleeved shirt that revealed hairy arms, and a wide-brimmed hat to shield his head from the tropical orange sun. His manner of speech was rapid, clipped, and punctuated with laughter.

"Ho my, what a collection, you are! Ho hee oh, never have I seen such a people-bundle! Come in, come! Or rather, tee-hee, come near, for by my foot-socks I don't think you'll the least of you fit comfortablish in my house."

Their exuberant, mirthful host led them around to the back of a sturdy stone farmhouse with a thatched roof. In a neatly fenced yard there was a long bench table with chairs built low to the earth. By seating themselves on the ground, the travelers were able to access the tabletop quite comfortably.

"Myssa!" the swart creature shouted toward the house, "we have company, ho-ho. Bring food, and drinkish!"

Cocoa made a face their host could not see. "As good as it tasted, if I have to eat another bite of orange fruit it's going to cost me one of my hypothetical nine lives."

"We must be polite." Oskar kept his voice down. "Just take a nibble of this and that, and sip of whatever is offered. Would you rather be back in the Kingdom of Red and have this little fellow whacking you across the nose with a stout stick?"

"No," she admitted quietly. "I suppose I should be grateful. There are worse things than being asked to eat too much good food."

"Hee-hee-ha-ha!" Their host's spouse, when she appeared with tray held high on one hand and jug in the other, was a rosy-cheeked little homunculus clad in dress, apron, and spry bonnet—all of varying orange hue, of course. Similarly shaded was the tray of multiple goodies she set before them, each more sprightly garnished than the next. The jug proved to contain a wine that was as tasty as it was cold. Confronted with the unexpected spread, Cocoa decided not to inquire if their hosts had any milk.

"I'm Tilgrick," the farmer chuckled from the head of the table. "What brings an extraordinary hodgepodgey like yourselves to my little farm, ha-ha-ho-hee?"

Do these two ever stop laughing? Mamakitty found herself wondering. Are they always so good-natured in the presence of strangers, or is there something deeper at work here? Without any basis for suspicion, she could only speculate.

"We have come from a far place," she told their mightily condensed host as his wife topped off their happy goblets. "From beyond even the Kingdom of Red."

"So far! But you have, hi-hi-hoo, survived that awful country." Several of the travelers nodded. "Wonderful, that is, hee-hee! The Kingdom of Orange is so much better a place, as you will find-oh."

Samm held forth the bucket that had been provided for him in place of one of the attractive but to him inadequate goblets. Orange liquid sloshed within. "We are already finding it so."

"Good, good!" Tilgrick laughed, his spouse joining in serenely. "What is it you want here? Whatever it is, ho-hoo, I'm sure you will certain find it. You don't have to stare at me like that to get me to answer." Samm immediately lowered his gaze.

"We want nothing here," Oskar told him, "except some

fleeting hospitality." He raised his goblet. "Which we have already found. We still, I fear, have far to go, to find the white light that we need."

"White light?" For once, Tilgrick and his wife did not laugh as they exchanged a look. "This is the Kingdom of Orange. You must truly have, ha-ha-hee, far yet to go. Why trouble yourselves with something so difficult to eye-mag-ine, much less capture? Stay here, in our land, and be al-ways ever always happy like us."

Cezer was intrigued. "You mean, everyone here is as contented as you two?"

"Oh no!" Tilgrick giggled. "Myssa and I are left to our-selves by our neighbors. We are, ha-hee-ho, outcasts of a kind, habitual grouches that we are."

Oskar was unsure he had heard correctly. "You two are considered grouches? If you were cats, now, I could un-derstand." Cezer threw him a look.

"Oh yes, my my me, ho-hee!" Laughing steadily, Myssa refilled Oskar's half-empty goblet.

"Then what," wondered Taj aloud, "is everyone else like?"

"You can see for yourselves, hee-hee-hee." Nodding with his long gnarled nose, Tilgrick gestured toward the north-east. "A delegation is coming to visit. Others must have seen you cross the river, ho-ho-ha, and hurried to spread the joyful word."

"Yeh. Joyful." Though his belly was full, his taste buds sated, and his body warmed by the moist air and mild mid-morning sun, Oskar had to strive to summon up a corre-spondent smile as he leaned to look out the window.

Marching toward the farmhouse across an open, un-plowed field came more than a hundred of the ardent, gnomish locals, every one of them vividly dressed, bouncy with excitement, and laughing hysterically as they walked.

It was a shifting, stumpy, swaying panorama of unrestrained joy, exuberant delight, and runaway giddiness.

Oskar felt the hairs on the back of his neck bristle in all-too-familiar dog fashion.

Out in front of the advancing throng, a slightly taller homunculus raised a hand and waved, his words hard to make out above the communal belly-twittering.

"*Hi-ho-hee* there, Tilgrick! What is this dour company you keep-oh?"

Their host leaned over to whisper to Oskar. "That twisted old graybeard is Nugwot. He's the local farmer's co-op representative. Word of your arrival spread quickly."

"How?" Oskar wondered. "You and your wife are the first folk we've seen since we left the river."

"That *you've* seen, yes, har-har-hi. That don't mean others haven't seen you."

"I don't like the looks of this." Pushing aside her plate full of orange-tinted victuals, Mamakitty had risen from the table and moved to the open space between picnic bench and field fence. "These people aren't very big, but there are an awful lot of them."

"So what?" A blissfully insouciant Cezer continued to munch contentedly on the bounty provided by their hosts. A few tails were all that was lacking to complete the gourmet repast. "They're all cackling and chortling like a giggle of kittens strung out on catnip."

"What about that?" Oskar remained close to their benefactor. "Can you tell what they have in mind?"

"Not sure, ahee-ho." Tilgrick waved his wife back into the farmhouse. "I don't much like Nugwot. He's an officious so-and-so, ho-ho. But we get along well enough when we have to." He started forward. "Come with me, and we'll see what he has to say, and why he's brought so many with him."

"I'll come, too," declared Mamakitty.

"No." Surprising himself, Oskar put out a hand to forestall her. Was this informal "leader" business going to his head? He didn't think so. He would have insisted she stay back in any case. "One of us is enough. If something unforeseen should happen, it's better that one of us be in a position to give advice to the others."

Mouth full of assorted orangey fare, so that his face resembled an exploded melon, Cezer looked up and frowned. "*Hssst,* I can give advice, too, you know!"

"And your point is?" Wearing a smile as wide as he could muster without cramping his jaw muscles, Oskar accompanied Tilgrick out of the yard, through a gate, and down one of the many paths that crisscrossed the farmer's tree-bordered fields.

They met the marchers in the midst of rows of thick, high growths each of which sported at its apex something like a maturing orange coconut. Up close, a relieved Oskar could see that none of the marchers carried anything resembling a weapon. There wasn't even a pitchfork or shovel among them. A few bore long feathers while others wielded large, delicate fans that were no doubt employed to ward off the heat and humidity. All regarded him curiously.

"Good afternoon, Nugwot," Tilgrick began. "As you can see, Myssa and I are having—"

"Woo-hoo-hoo!" the weathered elder interrupted. His chortling was quickly taken up by the rest of the gathering. "They're big ones they are, yo-ho-ha! Especially that one with the axe, who I'll wager is no carpenter." Ardent laughter rolled through the tightly packed throng, buoyant as distant thunder.

"They must be from the humorless Kingdom of Red," snickered someone in the middle of the assembly, not forgetting to punctuate the comment with a tellingly sharp chuckle.

"No, no; not at all." Raising his hands and grinning forcefully, Oskar hastened to reassure them. "My friends and I come from beyond the Kingdom of Red, from a kingdom encompassing all colors. We mean no harm. We're just passing through, actually, on a little quest of our own."

"He doesn't laugh," chortled someone humorlessly.

"His smile seems forced," declared another scornfully.

"They'll bring us down-oh," insisted a third with a dynamic hoot and a holler.

Tilgrick rushed to his guests' defense. "Hi-hi-how, you misjudge these good folk! 'Tis true they don't laugh outright as much as us, but can you blame them? They are to be pitied for not having the boon of being born in the Kingdom of Orange. Ha-ha-hoo, it is not for us to criticize those from other lands, but to help them experience that which we, hi-hi, enjoy as our birthright."

"Har-hardy-hidy, we'll help them, for sure!" Nugwot's long beard jiggled as he spoke. "No way will we let outsiders bring us down, curdle our milk, piss on our peavy, spoil our crops." Turning to gaze at the milling, metronomically tittering mob, he urged them forward with a wave. "We must help the strangers! Give them the marigolding!"

Oskar reached for his sword, but too late, as he was overwhelmed by the unexpected forward surge of the crowd. Going down beneath their raucously guffawing numbers, he felt something strike at his belly and gasped. Anticipating pain, he felt none. Expecting to see blood, he saw only his rippling shirt. Something ephemeral was caressing his stomach.

It was one of the fans, moving lightly back and forth. Something else struck him under an arm as small but field-strengthened hands pulled at him: one of the many long feathers the locals carried. Despite his fright, he found himself starting to giggle, then to chuckle. Within moments, he was laughing out loud, roaring uncontrollably, his body convulsing with unrestrained laughter. His arms jerked and his legs kicked, but he was firmly pinned by weight of numbers.

"The marigolding, the marigolding!" the gathering was chanting—all the while laughing relentlessly among themselves. They were determined to see that he had a good time, that he joined them in full, unrestrained mirth. With feathers and fingers and fans all working skillfully on his helpless body, he twitched and twisted, snared in the grip of unbridled jocularity. His lungs heaved and his throat ached, and still they tickled and prickled him.

Why, if this kept on, he thought through the coagulating haze of hilarity, he might very well laugh himself to death.

Just as he was about to pass out, the feathers and hands fell away, the shadows of compact, chortling bodies parted. Familiar faces gazed anxiously down into his own.

"Are you all right, Oskar?" There was no hint of merriment in Taj's stricken expression.

"Yes, grayfur, how are you doing?" This from Cezer, equally concerned but visibly puzzled. "And what are you laughing about so hard? We thought they were cutting you to ribbons."

Raising his exhausted body to a sitting position, Oskar caught sight of a beaming but concerned Myssa. "Ask her."

The squat woman's smile widened. "Hi-dee-hee, they wanted to make sure your presence was in harmony with your surroundings. Next they would have brung the marigolding to the rest of you." She nodded sagely in Samm's direction. "Hi-yi-hoo, even to you!"

"They were tickling me." Oskar rose shakily to his feet. "Holding me down and tickling me."

"I couldn't do anything." Tilgrick was hard put to do more than grin regretfully. "They wouldn't let me near. I could see what was happening, though-oh. Nugwot didn't care, the old jokester! In those not born to the kingdom, hee-hi-hee, marigolding can end in more than laughter."

"Tell me about it." Oskar clutched at his left side, which was throbbing with pain. "Sometimes laughter hurts—hee-hee-*ha*."

Sword drawn, Mamakitty was scanning the surrounding crops and forest. "When we charged, they all melted into the trees." Her gaze found Tilgrick. "What will happen now?"

"They'll come back for you," their host warned with a somber snicker. "Already, Nugwot's acolytes will be spreading the word that there are strangers in the wood whose smiles are forced and who converse without mirth. They will gather so many farmers and townsfolk that even you, with your weapons of sharp metal, will be overwhelmed. Then," he glanced apologetically at the still aching Oskar, "you will all of you be well and thoroughly marigolded."

"Hey, it's not so bad." The dog-man groaned as he rose to his feet. "For about two minutes. After that, it's a hilarious slice of hell."

"Marigolding does not injure a true citizen of the kingdom," Myssa informed them. "Those who are not born to it, however, can"—she had to fight to mouth the unfamiliar word—"suffer."

"We need to get away from here." Shading her eyes, Cocoa contemplated the dense tropical forest that both blocked and marked the way eastward. "We need to leave this place and exit this kingdom as fast as possible. It may be more overtly friendly than the Kingdom of Red, but it's no less dangerous." To show she meant no ill will, she smiled warmly at Myssa.

"Yes, yes, ho-ho-hi," agreed Tilgrick readily. "You must flee quick quick as you can. I am only a simple farmer, and Myssa and I somewhat a pair of outcasts. But there is one even crankier than us who lives nearby. A hermit who is shunned by all for his un-orangeish temperament. Forced to live alone, he has traveled far and learned many paths and routes we settled folk do not follow." He turned to his wife.

"Myssa, my love, ha-ha-ho, take our guests back to the house." He turned to Oskar. "You must finish your eating and drinking, my friend. You will need your strength for the journey that lies before you. Post a watch, and I will seek out the hermit Wiliam. When I tell him that there are visitors here of a disposition similar to his own, I wager he will gladly guide-oh you."

Oskar put a hand on the farmer's shoulder. "How can we ever thank you, Tilgrick, for your help and hospitality?"

"You already have, hi-hee-har." The stout homunculi's grin grew wider than ever. "The totally absurd and ridiculous sight of you and your friends tickles me to the bottom of my soul, and will provide food for laughter for weeks to come!"

Oskar smiled warningly at Cezer, who looked about to say something. "Vainless folk that we are, we're always pleased when we have the chance to present the gift of our ugliness to our friends."

TEN

The recluse Wiliam, when he finally arrived with a proudly gleeful Tilgrick leading the way, proved to be not the gruff, gloomy dwarf Oskar had expected, but a rather kindly faced, lightly bearded fellow who was noticeably slimmer than the farmer. He reminded Oskar of a gerbil the cats had once chased through the house. Extending a hand, he barely made contact with the dog-man's.

"You're not what I expected," the pleasantly surprised Oskar told the homunculus. "You seem—almost normal."

"Don't be taken in by my attitude, ha." Wiliam put both hands behind his back, interlocking and waggling his hairy fingers. "I'm really a terrible person."

"Yes, I can see that." It was Mamakitty's turn to smile. But not too broadly, lest she frighten their guide away.

"Everyone else thinks I'm mad," Wiliam put in for good measure. "I'm not, you know. I just don't find everything so—funny."

"I'm surprised they haven't tried to marigold you." As he spoke, Oskar was gathering up his small pack and water bag.

"Oh, they have, they have," their guide assured him. "It just doesn't seem to work on me." He almost, but not quite, managed a real frown. "I don't find the world very amusing." Turning, he pointed across the farm's neat fields toward the distant forest. "We need to move fast if we are to avoid Nugwot's followers. It would be best to be deep into the woods before they return on the morrow, when they are likely to bring even greater numbers with them."

He hardly chuckled at all when he spoke, Oskar noted. "Then we'll travel by night and not sleep until morning." Behind him, he heard Cezer sniff.

"Suits me. I'd just as soon be up at night as during the day. Lead on, good Wiliam, and we will follow—amusedly, or not."

The homunculus eyed him speculatively. "Moving at night through thick forest doesn't worry you?"

"Not us." Cocoa exuded confidence. "Nearly all of us see rather better in the dark than you might think. And as Cezer says, we *like* being up at night." Nearby, Taj groaned.

Amid a subdued chorus of chuckles and good wishes, they bade farewell to their uncommonly grumpy benefactors Tilgrick and Myssa, and in the company of their good-natured guide, started off in single file across the tillage. Moments later, they entered the tree line and found themselves walking at a respectable pace through woodland rich in cheerful foliage and giddy, if largely unseen, fauna.

Scanning the upper reaches of the trees, Oskar detected movement but little in the way of discernible shape. "So even the animals"—how strange to employ a term previously used by others to refer to himself, he mused—"hereabouts are riven by laughter?"

Short of stride but effusive of energy, Wiliam glanced back from his position in the lead. "In the Kingdom of Orange, mirth and merriment are the lifeblood of existence. One who laughs large is admired and respected. Those who laugh little are suspect. Anyone like myself, who finds very little in the world worthy of a chuckle, is made to feel an outcast by such as those who are likely to pursue us." He shrugged small, rounded, distinctively hairy shoulders. "I don't mind. I like being by myself. Frankly, I don't see what's so funny."

"Lucky for us you know the ways through the forest." Mamakitty made a conscious attempt to flatter their guide, on whose continued goodwill they were so dependent.

Wiliam looked over at her. "One forced to dwell in the woods soon learns their ways. I'm glad to be able to help. Tell me—in the kingdom you come from, could someone like myself survive? Would I be accepted even though I laugh but rarely?"

Oskar recalled some of the late Master Evyndd's more dour visitors, long-faced men and women for whom sorceral knowledge was the be-all and end-all of existence. Based on what he had seen, looking up from the Master's feet, it would take a magic spell or two just to *make* such people smile.

"I think there are places where you might fit right in, yes. But our 'kingdom' is very different from yours in many ways you can't imagine." He eyed the short, heavily bearded gnome thoughtfully. "I'm sure you would be accepted, but you might not be very comfortable with the manner of acceptance."

"Oh so?" Without breaking stride, their guide passed beneath an orange-blue tree. Everyone else had to duck to clear the stiff branches. As Oskar passed underneath, he could have sworn he heard one branch whispering to another, "Have you heard the one about the redwood and the spruce bush?"

"Then maybe it's better I stay here," Wiliam was saying. "I am tempted, though. You folk seem such good and kind, such normal people."

Cocoa laughed softly. The purring giggle caused flowers

hanging from a nearby tree to bend delightedly in her direction. "Wiliam, you have no idea."

While it was impossible to tell for certain how much ground they had covered, it was not so very many days before they began to notice a definite lightening of the colors surrounding them. Perhaps the Kingdom of Orange was not so great in extent as the Kingdom of Red, Oskar mused. Or maybe it was because, with a local to guide them, they were traveling in a straight line across the breadth of the territory. While the humidity remained oppressive, within the shadow of the forest canopy it was not unbearable. Certainly the subtle shift in colors was as perceptible as it was abrupt.

"We are approaching the Kingdom of Yellow," Wiliam informed them in response to their queries concerning the current chromatic imparity. "Unlike the frontier we share with the crimson kingdom to the west, here there is no river to mark the boundary. By this afternoon you will find yourselves marching through a new color, in a new land."

A perceptible jauntiness had entered Taj's step, notwithstanding the slight jaundice that seemed to have infected everyone's appearance. "I think I should be quite at home in the Kingdom of Yellow." He grinned in anticipation. "I'm looking forward to having my natural coloring back, if only until we pass into the kingdom after that."

"Which, I imagine, would be the Kingdom of Green." Those limbs and branches Samm could not duck beneath, he effortlessly pushed aside. "We are making good progress."

"I don't know what lies beyond the Kingdom of Yellow." Wiliam expressed his regrets. "We all of us cling to our respective homelands. But you will find the yellow lands as different from here as the country of orange is from the aggressive Kingdom of Red."

"In what way?" Oskar inquired.

"Well, for one thing—" Wiliam began.

He did not have an opportunity to finish either the sentence or the explanation. Without warning, several figures emerged from the undergrowth directly ahead to block the travelers' path. Despite the deep orange cast the local light gave to their skin and the curving dark glasses they wore to shield their eyes from the light of the sun, they were immediately recognizable.

Oskar's right hand dropped to the hilt of his sword. Behind him, his companions likewise made ready to draw their weapons. Samm unslung the great axe from his back.

More puzzled than startled, Wiliam looked from the newcomers to his tall friends. "You know these people?"

"We have made each other's acquaintance." There was neither lightness nor levity in the words Oskar directed to those blocking the trail. "Hello, Quoll. What brings you and your tailless puke-pail pals to this part of the world-run?"

Behind the quoll, Ruut and Ratha stiffened but said nothing. Quoll gestured diffidently. "You, of course. Did you think we would give up simply because you managed to stumble into a rainbow? When I explained what had transpired to the Khaxan Mundurucu, they soon determined what had occurred, and through the appropriate incantation made it possible for us to follow you even here. The difference is, we entered the same rainbow as you, but via a different color. *This* color. The Mundurucu said this would be the best place to enter, to confront you. As you see, they were right. The Khaxan Mundurucu are *always* right." He smiled down his rodentlike nose. "Please to understand, there is no escaping them even in these strange lands of color."

Leaning in Oskar's direction, Mamakitty whispered tersely to her friend. "That's interesting: the 'Khaxan Mundurucu' is a 'they,' not an individual."

"Such information is of no use to you," Ruut declared

unpleasantly, overhearing her whisper easily, "since you're going to die anyway."

"I think not." As Oskar drew his sword, the sound was echoed by that of his companions drawing their own weapons. "Or have you forgotten that before we entered the moonbow, we easily kept you three flouncing cadavers at bay?" Beside him, Wiliam's gaze was flicking warily from the travelers he knew to the three menacing strangers he did not.

"Not so easily, as I recall." Ratha made no move to display a blade of her own. "We were diving hard on you when you disappeared."

"Let's rush 'em," Cezer whispered. "We can overpower them before they can pull their weapons."

"Come to think of it," Taj added, "where are their crossbows? I see only long knives slung from their belts."

"We did not bring our crossbows with us." Ruut's smile revealed the narrow, elongated canines through which he and his slightly more attractive cousin extracted the lifeblood of others. "Please to realize that this time we have no need of such clumsy devices."

"Ah," murmured Cezer, "then you won't be surprised when I run you through with this clumsy device of my own." Whereupon he raised his sword and charged.

"Cezer, no!" Mamakitty shouted. As well try to restrain an angry shout as their fellow cat-man. Cursing, Oskar raised his own weapon as the other man rushed past him in a blur of silk and steel.

Blade upraised, Cezer brought it down in a long, sweeping curve aimed directly at Quoll's head. The object of the attack did not attempt to retreat, or use his remarkable quickness to try and evade the blow. Instead, he raised his left hand and uttered a short, sharp bark notable for its peculiar timbre. It was a most peculiar intonation.

From the exposed fangs of his smiling associates there shot forth thin threads of stiffening blood. In the manner of ordinary blood, as soon as they made contact with the open air, they began to coagulate. Like so many slender red-or-ange ropes, they wrapped whiplike around the onrushing Cezer. Before his sword could be brought down to strike the edgy, staring quoll, it was tightly bound by the solidifying, constricting strands. So was the rest of the struggling swords-man, who soon found himself enveloped from head to foot.

Taking a step forward, Quoll reached out and with one hand gave the raging, muffled figure of Cezer a sharp shove. The helpless, bound swordsman promptly toppled over back-ward, hitting the ground hard. He lay there, his sword bound to his side, struggling furiously but futilely.

Oskar's fingers tightened on his own weapon. The fury of his wolf ancestors burned in his eyes. At least, he hoped it did. The fury of Airedale ancestors did not carry quite the same inspirational cachet. "What have you done to him?"

"Restrained him." Quoll turned red-orange eyes on the softly growling Oskar. "Would you have preferred that I killed him? Easy enough to do, you know." Like his animal self, the quoll was in constant motion, willing landlord of a metabolism set permanently on overdrive. "I could simply have directed the gluey expectorations of my companions to seal off his nose and mouth as well as his arms and legs."

"Why didn't you?" Cocoa's own sword dangled ready at her side.

"Because we are commanded by the Khaxan Mundurucu to bring as many of you as possible back alive. For ques-tioning." His jittery smirk returned full strength. "I regret I will probably not be allowed to attend those sessions, which promise to be wonderfully entertaining. You, I think, will not enjoy them as much."

"How did you do that?" Wiliam indicated the now taut strands of organic red-orange that bound Cezer securely.

"One has no need of swords and crossbows when one has access to magic." Ignoring the curious gnome, Quoll kept his attention focused on Oskar. "The Khaxan Mundurucu take no chances. In sending us here, and suspecting that at least one among you may be a transformed disciple of the demised mage Evyndd, they prepared us accordingly. Not wishing to mete out too much power even to those who serve them, they armed us with certain skills that are only reliable when we three act in concert. Does that make you feel more confident? If so, then why not have at me in the manner of your uncomfortably cocooned companion?" Long whiskers twitched in the direction of the prone, bound Cezer. "My companions and I could use the exercise."

Samm hefted his axe, biding his time, watching and waiting for a possible opening. "The Mundurucu must have great confidence in you to send you after us again, since you failed so miserably in your task on the previous occasion."

Quoll's smirk vanished, and he glared at the giant. Of them all, the ferocious former marsupial feared only the ex-serpent. A big snake like Samm would readily and easily have made a quick meal of an incautious quoll, sharp teeth and uncommon energy notwithstanding. No matter how complete, no physical transformation from animal to human could entirely erase such primeval fears.

"Your come-down will be as complete as that of your companions, constrictor. If you don't believe me, please to try it and see." Samm did not move. Instead, he continued to stare in his customary, unblinking fashion directly into the quoll's eyes. Discomfited, their adversary was finally forced to look away. "As for the consequences of the outcome of our previous confrontation, the Mundurucu are as forgiving as they are all-powerful." Holding up his left hand, he exposed his four remaining fingers, the fifth having been recently and violently reduced in length by three-quarters. "In their benevolence and mercy, this was all the punishment they meted out."

From the back of the group, Taj piped up unexpectedly. "I'll bet when you show up again without us, they'll slice off three-quarters of a different part of you. Want to know which part I think that will be?"

"You're next, you sniveling little flesh-strip of a grounded chorister!" Raising his lethal right hand, the quoll took a threatening step forward. As he did so, his two caped companions opened their mouths wide.

"Stop!"

Taken momentarily aback by the source of the interruption, Quoll hesitated, arm still outstretched, lips parted to declaim the incantation with which he had been gifted by the Mundurucu. His furry brows creased as he regarded the undersize inhabitant of Orange.

"What do you want? This doesn't concern you and needn't involve you. Unless," he added after an ominous pause, "you wish it to."

"I just have one thing to say. Then you can get on about your business."

When Quoll hesitated, Oskar appropriated the ensuing silence. "Let him go. As you say, this needn't concern him, and the Mundurucu won't want him for anything."

The rodent-faced assassin's head twitched once. "Speak your say, then, and leave us to the business that is none of yours."

"So I shall." Drawing himself up as much as he could (which was not very much at all) and pulling his beard out of the way, Wiliam began to declaim with utmost solemnity. "There once was a gimp from Doklafa, who noidled his nurse in the patla—"

Oskar and his friends gaped at their thickset guide as he rambled on. For their part, Quoll and his companions likewise stared and listened uncertainly. But as Wiliam approached the conclusion of his crude yet convoluted ditty, a most unusual thing began to happen.

Mamakitty was first to notice the metamorphosis. It began as a hint of a smile on Oskar's face. The hint taken, it quickly matured into a wide grin. Next to her, Cocoa was blushing orange-pink as the rhyming tale jogged serenely to comic fruition. Taj had already begun to snicker, and even the always stolid Samm was smiling broadly. Soon the lot of them were chuckling, then guffawing, and finally roaring with uncontrollable laughter.

Teardrops ran down Mamakitty's face as Wiliam, without pausing or losing semantic stride, segued smoothly into a second story, this one twice as funny as the first. Far more importantly, she noticed through her tears, was that despite their best efforts to resist both the content and consequences of the guide's recitation, Quoll, Ratha, and Ruut were equally overcome with bouts of ungovernable jollity. The bat-folk in particular were unable to shut out the goblinish monologue.

Between snatches of his steady stream of irresistible japery, Wiliam managed to slip a word or two of more serious significance to the belly-clutching Oskar.

"Hurry now! I will hold them as long as I can."

"But how on—ho-ho-har!—how are you—hee-hee-ha!—doing (*gasp*) this?" Sides aching, laughing so hard it took him several tries, he sheathed his sword and beckoned for his companions to follow him. Chortling and crying, they proceeded to cut Cezer free from his bonds. The unavoidable trembling induced by their side-splitting laughter caused some of their sword and knife strikes to slip and slide dangerously as they hacked the red-orange strands from his sides.

Intending to upbraid them for their clumsiness, Cezer instead collapsed in one gale of laughter after another.

Helping him to his feet, the travelers stumbled and tottered past their tormentors. Quoll turned and tried to follow, but by now was laughing so hard he could barely stand erect. Frantically desirous of shutting out the bearded homunculi's hysterically funny and thoroughly incapacitating words, he found that he could not do so. The unrelenting, continuous spate of incorrigible raillery had him and his fanged associates virtually paralyzed with mirth.

"Believe me," Wiliam chuckle-spoke to Oskar as the latter prepared to follow his companions into the depths of the vastly amusing forest, "this isn't easy for me. But just because I don't share the overweening desire of my fellows to see who can outgiggle the next doesn't mean I'm incapable of jocularity myself. In fact, you might almost say that living alone and apart has sharpened my ability to blend harmoniously with a kingdom that rises and falls, lives and dies, on merriment."

"Look—ha-ha-ha!—out!" Oskar shouted warningly.

As Wiliam whirled, Quoll slashed downward. But before his very real and unethereal, unspell-cast knife could strike, the little gnome delivered a punch line that caught the assassin square in his funny bone. The resultant involuntary cackle caused the quoll to clutch at his middle and bend double with laughter while crumpling to the ground. Behind him, Ruut and Ratha were writhing on the moist earth, caught up in paroxysms of unmanageable hysteria.

"Hurry!" Wiliam urged the laughing, weeping man staggering gratefully behind him. "Slight sorcery is no match for strong humor, but there is a limit to what even a really good joke can accomplish."

"How—har-har-hee!—how long can you—ho-ho-har!—keep this up?" Oskar gasped weakly.

"Long enough, I think," Wiliam chortle-assured him. "By the time you have crossed into the Kingdom of Yellow, Nugwot and his followers will be here. When they arrive, I can turn the restraining and joke-telling over to them. Go now, and in a quiet moment, when you are safe and secure, salute me with a drink—and try not to spit all over yourself when you are doing so."

Barely able to nod, Oskar turned and hurried after his companions. As Wiliam's steady singsong of silliness faded behind him, swallowed up by exotic orange-tinted trees and flowers that were all leaning in the gnome's direction to partake of the inspired buffoonery, the dog-man gradually regained control of his emotions. So did his companions, though there were moments in the ensuing hours where Cezer might find himself meeting Taj's glance, or Mamakitty encountered Cocoa's, whereupon all concerned would burst out spontaneously at the recollection of what had just transpired.

"You know," an aching Taj was saying much later, "it occurs to me that if you substituted a cross-eyed cow for the Maid of Milkow in good Wiliam's last soliloquy, then the payoff would be not only twice as funny, but—"

"For Bubastis's sake," Cocoa admonished him, "don't make me laugh any more!" Wincing slightly, she clutched at her left side just below the lowermost rib. "My insides already feel as if they've been taken apart and put back together again with string and spittle."

"Maybe that's what's happened to Quoll and the other two." As he picked his way through the forest, Cezer continued to groom gruesome little bits of red-orange goo out of his hair and clothing. While doing so, he lamented the fact that in his present form he could not reach certain multiple problem areas with his tongue. "With luck, maybe Wiliam made them laugh so hard they exploded."

From time to time they were distracted by a crashing or

thumping in the woods behind them. At such moments they would draw their weapons and assume defensive postures and positions. Each time, it turned out to be nothing more than some eccentric forest dweller, chuckling and chortling its way through the weald. Catching sight of the travelers, it would invariably emit a burst of startled laughter before whirling and sprinting off in the opposite direction.

Even the food here was happy. Prey perished beneath their weapons with nary a scream, inevitably expiring with a smile on its face and a last, gasping giggle. Fruit coughed amusedly when plucked from vines or branches, and berries tittered in squeaky, high-pitched tones when popped between hungry teeth.

Making a face, Cocoa flung one snickering pit from her lips and chewed reluctantly on the sweet pulp that filled her mouth. "The sooner we're out of these woods, the better I'll like it. I prefer my food dead silent, not mocking me as I eat."

"Could be worse." Oskar glanced back over a shoulder. "It could fight back."

"Let it fight," she snapped at him. "I *like* my food to resist a little. What good is a mouse that won't try to escape? Where's the fun in that?" Her expression crinkled. "I don't think I could kill a mouse that giggled at me."

"Hush." Mamakitty raised a hand, and those behind her slowed. "I think the forest is opening up. The light is growing brighter, too."

Conversation ceased as they made their way forward at a more cautious pace. Not knowing what to expect, they had learned in the course of crossing between two kingdoms to be ready for anything. Or so they thought. They were not prepared for the sight that greeted them as they stepped out of the thick foliage.

The daylight had certainly changed. Not only had it grown

brighter, but their surroundings were now tinged with an intense lemony yellow. It was almost normal, and would have been more so had not the tawny tint overwhelmed all else: the brush and high grass that had replaced the forest, the lazy yellowish stream that flowed from north to south in front of them, the translucent flying creatures that soared high overhead in the depths of a saffron sky.

And the gigantic wall of massive cut limestone that paralleled the stream and completely blocked their way eastward.

Oskar had to tilt his head back to squint all the way to the top of the Brobdingnagian barrier. At first glance, it looked as solid as it was high. Closer inspection revealed that it was indeed constructed of impenetrable, immovable, yellowish rock. No facade raised by desperate magic, it had been piled up block by block to discourage intruders. It certainly discouraged Oskar and his companions.

"Can we go around it, do you think?" Mamakitty was gazing down the length of the wall.

"We certainly can't go over it." Standing beside the little stream that ran along the base of the bulwark, Oskar cast an uneasy glance back the way they had come. Were Quoll and his vampiric companions even now being well and thoroughly marigolded by Nugwot and his followers, or had they managed to break free, and were they at this very moment racing through the forest to overtake their fleeing quarry?

"There was a time when I could have." Taj sounded wistful.

"Over here!" Having hiked a little ways downstream from the others, Cezer was beckoning for them to join him.

"What is it?" Oskar called out, cupping his hands in front of his mouth. "A way over?"

"Not over." Cezer was standing up against the wall, nearly

hidden by the oh-so-slight curvature of the barrier. "But maybe through."

The gate was massive. Fashioned of heavy wooden planks embellished with intricately carved whorls and spirals and braced with iron, it loomed over their heads, reaching almost to the top of the smooth-sided stone rampart. Mamakitty was the first to note the similarities among the numerous designs that decorated the wall.

"See?" With a finger she traced one particularly elaborate cochlear shape. "Lines radiate from each corkscrew design, sometimes connecting multiple carvings. I think each one must, in one way or another, represent the sun."

"There are dozens of different kinds." Kneeling, Taj was examining a large disc form near the base of the gate. "Here's one with a multitude of internal coils."

"And here's another that shows some kind of flames spurting from the edge." Cezer laughed. "Whoever carved these didn't know what they were doing. I mean, certainly the sun is hot, but it's not on fire!"

"I suppose it's understandable that the people of this country pay a lot of attention to the sun." Oskar was studying the cast iron hinges and bands that held the enormous doors together. "After all, this *is* the Kingdom of Yellow."

"A kingdom is a kingdom." Retreating to the edge of the glistening rill, Cezer tilted back his head to study the top of the barrier. "If I can climb half as well as I used to, I'm pretty certain I can make it to the top of this gate."

"So am I," concurred Mamakitty, "and likely Cocoa as well. But where does that leave the others?"

"It's too much for me." Oskar stood alongside Cezer. "I never was much of a climber. Somehow I don't think I can dig under this fence, either." As for Samm, the giant's comment on the barrier before them took the form of a single grunt. His thick fingers would never be able to gain a purchase on the grainy grouting between the stones or the thin cracks in the rocks themselves.

"Then we're stuck." Mamakitty was not giving up, but she was clearly discouraged.

"Not necessarily." Cocoa was examining the wall. "If some of us can get over, we can try and open the gate from the other side."

"What if the gatekeepers object to your intentions?" Mamakitty asked her.

She frowned. "What gatekeepers? I don't see or hear any gatekeepers."

"Exactly my point. Why should they have to watch a gate as big and solid and strongly made as this one? But if there's some kind of guard post or station on the *other* side, you can be sure they'll be watching you as you climb down. We don't know how they'll react. We don't even know what they might look like."

"Why don't we just ask them?"

Everyone turned to where Taj was standing next to the gate. "And just how do you propose we go about doing that?" Cezer inquired acerbically.

Turning slightly, Taj pressed both hands against the door behind him and pushed. From within the massive wooden gate there arose a profound creaking as it swung slightly inward. Smiling apologetically, Taj replied to his questioner.

"It's not locked."

ELEVEN

One by one, they approached the narrow opening Taj had accidentally discovered and peered through the gate. Though only a small gap, it was enough to permit them to see clearly within. The panorama that greeted their anxious, impatient gazes was sufficient to banish any fears.

The light within the Kingdom of Yellow was almost normal. Not to the point of allowing other colors to exist, but close enough to what they remembered from home so the travelers felt more comfortable with what they were seeing than at any time since they had entered the rainbow. It was a pleasant, comforting light that imparted a warm glow to everything it touched upon—this although the sky was noticeably overcast, to the point where the visitors cast no shadows upon the yellowish ground.

There was no guard post, no barracks full of angry gatekeepers waiting to challenge those with the temerity to simply walk in. Instead, fields of waving wheatlike grass stretched to the distant horizon, interrupted only by isolated thickets of slender, buttery-yellow trees that rose from the flavescent savanna like stiff whiskers on a cat's face. There was just enough of a breeze to moderate the temperature, which itself was far from unpleasant. The air had a bracing freshness to it that had been lacking in the torpid kingdoms of Red and Orange, and was suffused with a faint perfume Oskar could not identify.

They could not see the color of the sky, hidden as it was by the yellowish gray overcast. The occasional stronger breeze whistling in their ears, they stepped cautiously through the gap and into the kingdom. Having been the one to open the door, Taj thoughtfully closed it behind him. Looking down at himself, he saw that he was once again a delightful yellow.

Stretching his arms high and wide, Cezer inhaled deeply of the pure, delicious air. "What a wonderful place! If we weren't in such a hurry, I'd lie down right here and now and have a nap."

"Have you forgotten that Nugwot and his followers may still be on our trail?" Cocoa reminded him. "Not to mention Quoll and his bloodsucking pair of retainers."

"With any luck, by now Quoll and the others should be thoroughly marigolded. As for Nugwot and his happy-sappy sycophants, even if they are uncompromising enough to continue their pursuit, I don't think they're likely to give us any trouble for a long time, if ever." Shyly, Taj stepped aside to reveal the single large, iron bolt he had thrown. The enormous gate was now locked securely behind them.

"Good for you, featherhead!" Strolling over, Cezer clapped the smaller man hard enough across the shoulders to bruise the skin, following which substantial gesture of affection he yawned and began to inspect the ground. "Now, who else is for that nap?"

"We can't just curl up and go to sleep in the middle of the day," Mamakitty admonished him firmly. "Cats do that. Not people on a mission."

"Grouchy old sardine-head," Cezer muttered.

Deep yellow-green eyes narrowed. "What did you say?"

The swordsman sighed resignedly. "That when night arrives I'll be ready to crouch on my bed. Which way?" Being human, he mused, was far from being all wonderment and delight.

Oskar considered the height of the sun and the balance of the fine day that remained to them. "East, my friend. Always east, until we come to the place where the white light is to be found."

"If there is such a place," Cezer grumbled as he fell into line.

In truth, as the day wore on, Oskar found it harder and harder to keep from seconding Cezer's sleepy-time suggestion. The air, the temperature, the occasional gentle warm breeze, the soft saffron-stained herbage underfoot, combined to induce within him a growing lassitude he had not allowed himself to feel for many days. The thought of lying down and drifting off, of letting himself be lifted gently into the arms of blissful midday sleep, was something he had to fight against with every step.

Where would be the harm? he told himself. With the great gate fastened behind them, their rear was secure. No pursuit, no matter how determined or fanatical, could reach them from the Kingdom of Orange. In all the time they had been traipsing across the golden savanna, no threat had manifested itself. If not an entirely benign land, this Kingdom of Yellow was surely bound to be more obliging than the two they had already traversed.

Unable at last to stand it any longer, with the lure of a nap threatening to drag him bodily down to the inviting earth, he put the proposal before Mamakitty a second time. Perhaps the long walk, he thought, had made her more amenable. Her response surprised him.

"You're our leader, Oskar. If you think this is an appropriate time and place for a nap, then you need to say so."

A quick glance at the rest of his companions was enough to give him the answer he sought. "A rest will do us good. Be a refreshing change. Who knows when we'll have the opportunity again?" He indicated a nearby pond, from which sprouted lemon-tinted reeds with hollow stems that whistled lullabies in the gentle wind. "This place is perfect. We'll set a watch," he concluded.

That was sufficient to satisfy the always wary Mamakitty, who, truth be told, had herself gazed longingly at every potentially soft spot on the ground ever since they had left the great wall behind. With Cocoa volunteering to take the first watch, she curled up against a pile of cushiony fungi and was almost instantly asleep. She was followed by the others, with not one of them having yet bothered to wonder why so seemingly benevolent a country needed so colossal a defensive fortification.

Later, having been wakened from several hours of perfect somnolence, a much refreshed Oskar had been on watch for less than twenty minutes when he detected movement in the tawny grass. No ordinary human would have noticed the slight stirring, but like his companions in trek, Oskar possessed senses far more sensitive than those of his former masters.

He did not draw his sword. Neither did he wake his friends. The stirring bespoke no immediate threat. A wandering animal, perhaps, passing through or simply curious. They had seen precious little wildlife since leaving the Kingdom of Orange. He concentrated on the area of the movement without staring in its direction, ready to pounce or leap aside should the situation require a rapid reaction.

It did not, though some sort of calculated response was surely in order. As the sun finally began to emerge from behind the cloud cover, a line of little people emerged from the high sedge and came toward him. Unlike their former guide Wiliam or the other inhabitants of the Kingdom of Orange, these folk were perfectly proportioned and no hairier than an ordinary human. None stood taller than the dog-man's waist. Had he been standing on all fours, they would have found themselves eye to eye. Men and women walked together, side by side. They were smartly but not lavishly attired. Each carried an unusually large fan or shield fashioned from some woven, yellowish beige plant material. As the setting sun peeked out from beneath the dissipating clouds, these were raised into place to shield them completely from evening rays. So precisely and uniformly did they perform this maneuver that Oskar was reminded of the time he had seen a troop of passing soldiers present their swords in salute to Master Evyndd.

While the body of the line halted, the diminutive woman in the lead continued to advance. Imbued now as he was with human feelings and desires, Oskar decided that she was attractive enough, though mating was not at the forefront of his thoughts. Instead, he found himself focusing on the jeweled knife she wore at her waist. The blade was longer than her short, woven skirt, the tip reaching nearly to her knee. Her companions carried similar finely wrought weapons, though none were drawn. Still, the potential for danger was there.

With a shout, he woke his slumbering companions.

Halting a short distance away as they rose to their feet, she studied the tall strangers. Her gaze lingered slightly longer, as did those of her fellows, on the massive bulk of Samm hovering silently at the rear of the group. When she finally spoke, her words were directed at the nearest traveler, who happened to be Oskar.

"Some of our youths hunting near the great gate saw

you enter. As soon as the village was informed of your coming, we organized this welcoming party." With a supple sweep of one arm she indicated the cortege behind her. "We do not recognize your origin. You are obviously not citizens of the Kingdom of Orange, nor of Green." Leaning to one side, she peered behind Oskar, where there was nothing but weak evening shadow. "Where do you come from? I, the Princess Ourie, entreat the favor of a reply."

Oskar found he was getting used to answering this apparently inevitable question. He proceeded to provide as reasonable an explanation for their presence as he could. While he did so, Taj leaned close to whisper to Cocoa.

"I don't think we have anything to fear from these folk. Not only are they very much smaller than us, from the way their heads keep twisting around and their eyes keep darting constantly from place to place, they look like they're afraid of their own shadows."

The little woman spoke again. "So your intention is not to linger among us, but to move on as swiftly as possible to the Kingdom of Green?"

"That's right," Oskar replied. "Any help or guidance you can give us will be much appreciated."

"Guidance? Help?" She looked at him as if he had taken leave of his senses. "To reach our neighboring Kingdom of Green you must cross the Great Rift. None among us dare try it, but we will not stop you. There is no way around the Rift, and no safe passage through it, though as strangers of unknown origin and powers you may have more success than we." She eyed him thoughtfully, her voice unchanging. "Most probably, you will die."

"That's what I like to hear every time we arrive somewhere new," Cezer remarked dryly. "Encouragement."

"This rift." Mamakitty moved up to stand alongside

Oskar. "Is it a wide canyon, or just a gully with steep sides? There are good climbers among us."

"It is not a question of climbing, but of avoiding the danger that lurks within," the wee royalty informed her. "And as you must know, for you all seem to be of at least moderate intelligence, that which is always with one can never be avoided."

"Petite, beautiful, and vague." Sensing extended conversation, Cezer had assumed a cross-legged sitting position on the invitingly warm ground. There was now enough sunlight for his shadow to join him. "Not how I like my females."

"I wouldn't concern myself about it," observed Cocoa pointedly. "She doesn't exactly seem to be clamoring for your attentions."

"How could you be so sure we were strangers here?" Mamakitty eyed the princess curiously. "Mightn't we have come from some far distant part of the Kingdom of Yellow?"

The highborn shook her head firmly. "Your foreign origins are immediately apparent. Not only are you not Slevish"—she indicated the patiently waiting retinue strung out behind her—"but you carry among you not a single kwavin with which to protect yourselves."

"I guess we don't," confessed Oskar. "Just to satisfy my curiosity, what's a kwavin?"

Her responsive, dewy-eyed gaze was moist with compassion. "That you have no thought or notion of the most vital piece of Slevish attire surely proves your ignorance of this land. It is fortunate for you that you arrived on such a cloudy day." Her gaze swept past him to encompass his waiting, watching companions. "You must come with us, quickly, so that we can make kwavins for you all. Without them you will not live long in this country." She gestured in the direction of the now distant great wall. "Those who arrive kwavinless invariably perish before we can help them." With an air of majesty swirling about her that was most impressive for her size, she turned and moved to rejoin her retinue.

Cezer rose to join Oskar and Mamakitty. There was a twinkle in his eye. "Pretty little thing. I wouldn't mind chasing her tail—if she had one. What was that all about?"

Oskar scratched absently at his left ear. "It seems we're all in great danger unless we allow them to provide us with something called a *kwavin.*" He glanced upward. "Apparently it has something to do with the sky. Whatever the danger she was referring to, the clouds protected us from it."

The swordsman sniffed. "Cats don't get sunburned, if that's what she's talking about. But if they want to give us some kind of talisman or charm for free, that's fine with me. What's a kwavin?"

"I don't know. I asked, but she never got around to telling me. She's very nice, but her manner is a little on the imperious side."

"Well, *ssst,* as long as this kwavin thing doesn't require any tiresome contribution on our part. Something like body modification, say, or the payment of some outrageous fee." Reaching up, he felt of the small notch in his right ear. Mamakitty had taken it out of him when, as a kitten, he was even more generally obnoxious than he was now.

"Until we know what a kwavin *is,* there's no point in assuming the worst." Squinting toward the setting sun, Mamakitty set off in the wake of the princess. For an instant, something seemed to hold her back, but it soon dropped away. Rested and relaxed, her friends followed.

When they turned to retrace their steps, the line of marchers swiftly and as precisely as a coordinated dance team shifted the elaborately decorated sunshades they carried from their left sides to the right, to ward off the last rays of the setting sun. Oskar found his curiosity piqued by the unexpectedly energetic move. Were the Slevish demonstrating their martial efficiency, utilizing shades in place of pikes? Did the balletic gesture have some unknown religious significance? Were they trying to impress the bigger strangers with an unspoken ability to coordinate their actions? Or, bearing in mind Cezer's earlier comment, was their skin simply excessively sensitive to the effects of direct sunlight?

Though certainly a possibility, the latter seemed unlikely. While decidedly pale, the Slevish were not albinos. Even with the lemony cast the ambient light conferred upon everything it touched, he could tell that the flesh of the little folk was not particularly white. Nor did the cloud-muted light that had bathed him and his friends ever since they had entered the Kingdom of Yellow feel in any way unnatural. On the contrary, it was as warm and pleasant as the land it nourished. No, the plethora of carefully deployed sunshades must serve some other, ceremonial purpose beyond simply shielding their holders from ordinary daylight. He would put the question to Princess Ourie when next the opportunity presented itself.

If the much smaller Slevish were intimidated by their visitors, they showed no sign of it—though Oskar caught one or two glancing uncertainly in Samm's direction. The snake-man was so very much larger, they could not help but consider his presence. As the long column crossed several thickly vegetated hills, he noted with approval that even in the company of their new hosts, progress continued to be made eastward. They were sacrificing no time by accompanying the Slevish.

The community situated on the shore of a vast, yellow-tinged lake was more a large village than a small town. Despite the presence of hundreds of dwellings, there was no central square and no structure higher than two stories. Perfectly formed Slevish children, active and bright-eyed as a wizard's toys, congregated in batches to gawk at the towering strangers. They clustered around Oskar and Mamakitty, Cocoa and Cezer and Taj, but shied uneasily away from the perambulating man-mountain that was Samm. Though it was in no wise his fault, he could not entirely escape certain intangible characteristics of his original shape.

Ourie led them through the village and down to the lakeshore. Dozens of willowy, low-slung outriggers rested on the yellow-white sand like beached scarecrows. Fishing nets hung on drying poles, oddly aligned with the setting sun instead of spread against it to take maximum advantage of its drying rays. A few children ran along the beach, laughing and playing, while adults sat and worked at cleaning fish, salamanders, and frogs, or mending nets, or repairing boats. All those not seated in the shade, Oskar noted with bemused interest, carried the by now familiar woven shades to shield them from the sun. Clearly no one went outside, even for a short stroll, without one of the omnipresent shades.

What was it with these otherwise perfectly healthy-looking people that forced them to so assiduously hide from the sun's seemingly beneficent rays? He really must ask the princess the first chance he got, Oskar decided.

That the matter of constant shading involved only sunshine was confirmed when it finally set. When the last direct rays had faded, people immediately began to emerge from the cover of their shelters, and to put down the woven shades they had been carrying. A palpable sense of relief rippled through the community. Cezer, Cocoa, and the others took only casual notice of the change. Only Oskar and Mamakitty, with whom he had been discussing the curious business, wondered at the abrupt transformation.

Ourie beckoned for them to join her, and they soon found themselves seated by the shore of the vast lake. Women of the Slevish, each one more petite and attractive than the next, were seated on the sand or on benches weaving a number of the intricate sunshades that were obviously a vital component of village life. The princess introduced the visitors to these skilled weavers. Those singled out by the greeting smiled ingratiatingly at their guests while practiced fingers flew without pause, effortlessly braiding fronds and leaves into oversize, lightweight sunscreens. So large were the particular examples they were working on that when finished, they would be big enough to shield Oskar or any of his friends from the effects of the sun. Near the back, four women were working together on a most monstrous shade indeed, which Oskar suspected could only be intended for Samm. Interestingly, they worked on into the gathering darkness without benefit of torch or firelight. Drawn in spite of themselves, Cezer and Cocoa sat and began playing with the ends of the bobbing, fluttering fronds.

"Let me guess," Oskar ventured to their royal hostess. "A kwavin is one of these sunshades."

She nodded briskly. "These we make as gifts to you. It is part of our birthright not to allow the ignorant to perish from their ignorance."

"That's kind of them, but not exactly flattering," Taj whispered to Samm.

Stepping forward, Cezer admired both the skilled handiwork and the delicate features of the Slevish women. "I don't want to insult them by refusing a gift, but I happen to enjoy walking in the sunshine. The weather here is de-

lightful, and I'd just as soon not have to bother with lug-
ging around a shade, or kwavin, or whatever."

"But you must!" Princess Ourie turned limpid eyes on
the charmed cat-man. Gazing into them, he was reminded
of a snapper whose head he had once consumed with great
relish. "Without kwavins, you will die even before you
reach the Great Rift. Do you not remember what I said
about being unable to escape that which you carry within
yourselves?"

Cezer responded with a gesture that, had the princess
understood its meaning, might have offended her. "I'm not
romping through beautiful country in perfect weather carrying around some stupid sunscreen. If the rest of you want
to be polite and do so, that's your business." He walked
down to the water's edge and found a comfortable patch
of sand on which to flop. A sliver of silver-yellow moon
was rising in the distance, painting the image of a molten
staircase on the rippling waters.

Kneeling beside the princess to bring his face closer to
hers, Oskar murmured politely. "Please excuse my friend.
He's somewhat headstrong. It's his nature, and he can't
help himself. Tell me; what danger do we face that lies
within ourselves, and in the depths of this great rift, that
requires us to carry sunscreens with us wherever we go? I
confess I don't understand."

"Nor do any of us," added Mamakitty from nearby.

Oskar's contriteness melted a little of the anger Cezer's
intemperate words had engendered in the princess. "Come
in the morning and you will see." She nodded in Cezer's
direction, where the cat-man was lying contentedly on the
warm sand. "Your friend will show you."

Not even Taj, who was the smallest of the visitors, could
fit comfortably within one of the numerous huts, but the
travelers did not suffer from their lack of shelter. Night

proved as benign as day in this marvelous country, and they slept content and confident by the shore of the lake. Samm in particular luxuriated in near-familiar surroundings, digging in until his body was completely covered by the warm sand. Within the village, all seemed equally peaceful and happy. Nary a child cried, and those natives who worked through the night were careful to keep their conversations to a whisper so as not to disturb their neighbors.

It was difficult, Oskar reflected as he lay down among his companions, to envision what danger could so unsettle the princess and her apparently contented people. That they dealt daily with whatever it was he had no doubt. That it was serious in nature he also conceded. He simply could not imagine what it was. If it was as deadly dangerous as Ourie insisted, it seemed unlikely it could be deflected by something as simple as a woven sunscreen. Try as he might, he could not resolve the apparent contradictions.

His head beginning to throb from the effort of trying to envision the unimaginable, he put everything aside in favor of getting some serious rest. In his former body, sleeping was something he had always been good at.

He felt soft skin brush up against his shoulder as a limber shape sat down next to him. Cocoa tried to sit back on her haunches, only to discover, as always, that in her present form she was in possession of too much leg and not enough haunch. She settled for stretching the former out in front of her. Despite the time she had already spent in human form, she found the position unnatural. Afraid of sitting on her tail, she was constantly shifting her seat, even though there was no longer a long, multicolored tail to sit on.

"You know, Oskar, I always liked you. I realize that cats and dogs aren't supposed to get along, but I always admired the way you carried yourself through life."

"Really?" He continued to gaze out across the lake. Meeting a cat's eyes was always dangerous. "How was that?"

"Indifferently. I mean," she hastened to add, "nothing ever seemed to trouble you."

He shrugged, his head resting on his crossed forepaws (hands, he reminded himself angrily—hands!). "As long as I got a table scrap or two, and the occasional bone, I was happy." Now he did turn to face her. In the silver-yellow moonlight, she was as graceful as she had ever been. "I always felt that cats think too much."

Her expression was contemplative. "Maybe you're right," she eventually replied. "Though I never thought of it that way."

"Don't stare at things so long," he suggested helpfully. "And don't worry about your appearance so much. You'll find life is easier to take."

She considered this advice. "I don't know if I can do that. Cats are just—serious. Dogs are—"

A voice interrupted them from behind. "Goofy," Cezer concluded, before rolling over and turning his back to them. Oskar had the feeling the swordsman would have sprayed them then and there, had not his plumbing undergone a preemptive sea change.

"Mister Sarcasm," Cocoa muttered. Her smile returning, she lunged forward and rubbed her nose against a startled Oskar's, then rose and moved off to join Mamakitty. "See you in the morning."

Reaching up, he slowly wiped the tip of his nose with the palm of one hand. Cats, he mused. Who could comprehend them? Their actions and antics had often bemused even Master Evyndd.

All the more reason, he told himself, why he should not try to.

Dawn saw the breaking of a cloudless morning. As Oskar awoke, it was to the bustle of tremendous activity within the village. It was almost as if the inhabitants were striving to accomplish as many of the day's tasks as possible before the sun was fully up. Sure enough, the instant its rays began to cast the first shadows within the community, activity slowed and did not resume until the Slevish had picked up their thickly woven sunscreens.

With appropriate ceremony, the special kwavins that had been finished during the night were presented to the bemused travelers. Oskar and his companions were politely thankful for the gifts, Cezer included. Mamakitty and Cocoa had promised to scratch him severely if he did not respond in a courteous manner. Hiding his disdain, he smiled fatuously while accepting his own screen from two of the little women who had produced it.

"Remember to beware," Princess Ourie warned them, "if you truly intend to try and cross the Great Rift. That which dwells within you also dwells within it." She indicated the kwavin he was balancing on his shoulder. "Keep always the sun off your selves."

"We'll be careful." Though he spoke with assurance, Oskar had not the slightest idea what she was talking about.

Those villagers not presently engaged in purposeful work had assembled to see the strangers on their way. Some smiled, a few wore expressions of concern, and many waved. But only with one hand, for the others were occupied in holding tight to the ingeniously decorated shades that now were everywhere in evidence, shielding them from the rising morning sun.

Admiring the deft pattern that had been woven into it, Oskar toted his own screen effortlessly, balancing it on his left shoulder as he led the way out of the village. Against their own judgment, Princess Ourie's advisers had drawn the foolhardy travelers a map showing the easiest route to the Kingdom of Green. This help notwithstanding, they would still have to find a way safely across the Great Rift.

He could hear Mamakitty and Cocoa chatting behind him. Cezer and Samm discussed what they were likely to find in the next kingdom while Taj happily inspected each new plant or creature they encountered. The songster had developed an inexplicable interest in biology.

As soon as they were out of sight of the village, Cezer promptly tossed his shade into the nearest bush. Mamakitty eyed him disapprovingly. "Useful or not, that was a gift."

"*Fssst,* a useless one." Spreading his arms wide, the swordsman danced a small circle, soaking up the rays of the early morning sun. "Look at me—I'm dying of sunstroke!" He lowered his arms. "*You* lug the ridiculous-looking things around if you want to. I've got better things to do with my hands." Cocoa immediately moved to the other side of Mamakitty.

As the morning wore on, Cezer suffered no apparent ill effects from traveling without one of the Slevish's skillfully woven kwavins. Nor did any harm befall him all the rest of that day or night and on into the following morning. Oskar was beginning to wonder if the undefined danger of which Ourie had spoken so sincerely was a threat only to the Slevish and the other permanent denizens of this land. At that very thought, a sharp yelp from the catman caused him to halt and whirl.

Cezer was lying off to the side of the trail they had been following, writhing and convulsing in the pale yellow grass. A dark rope was wrapped around his neck. His teeth were clenched and his expression distorted. So tight was the black stripe around his throat that he could not even utter a curse.

Being the closest to him, Oskar and Taj arrived simultaneously at his side, only to see that the sooty material clamped around his neck was not a rope but a shadowy arm. This was attached, a stunned Oskar saw, to a shadowy shoulder, which in turn emerged from a shadowy torso topped by a shadowy face utterly devoid of expression, as well as anything with which to give birth to an expression. Cezer was caught in the murderous, unyielding grasp not of a shadowy form, but of a shadow itself.

His shadow.

"Look out!" The two men barely had time to jump aside as Samm arrived. The head of his immense axe preceded him by a second or two, descending in a violent arc that caused the entrapped Cezer's eyes to bulge wider than ever. As the axe head slammed into the earth with a muffled boom, a slight shudder passed through the shadow-shape, as if it were a ripple of pond water racing away from a cast stone. Quickly regaining its discrete outline and former strength, it resumed its lethal pressure on the struggling Cezer's imprisoned windpipe.

Oskar drew his sword, only to find himself pushed aside by Mamakitty. Uttering a primordial growl, she leaped at her friend's traitorous shadow. She never reached it. At the same time she left her feet, she also cast her kwavin aside. Thus liberated, her own shadow (and it was unmistakably hers, Oskar was able to note even in the frenzy of the moment) reached out with both arms and tackled her around the ankles. Hitting the ground short of her objective, she rolled onto her back, clawing at the opaque shape. Not only was she unable to reach Cezer, she now found herself locked in a battle with the spasmodic, twitching attempts of her own shadow to slip its supple, dark fingers around her unprotected neck.

Frantic thoughts rushing to and fro within him, Oskar beckoned for Cocoa and Taj to stay back. "Samm, over

there! Never mind your weapon—just stand over there!"
He pointed to a spot on the ground.

"What?" For a snake, Samm was exceptionally bright.
It was not his fault that all serpents are notoriously slow
on the uptake.

Oskar rushed to the indicated place himself. "Here! Stand
right here, next to me!" While changing his position, Oskar
was careful to keep his own artfully woven kwavin positioned between the sun and himself. As a result, the only
shadow he cast was the one produced by the smooth, oval,
inoffensive shape of the kwavin. His own specter, rebellious or otherwise, remained contained within him.

Taking up a mystified stance alongside the much smaller
man, Samm and his own far larger, custom-made kwavin
blocked not only their owner but also everything that fell
within their oversize shadow from the sun's rays. As artfully
adjusted by Oskar, this shadow fell over and neatly eclipsed
the struggling Cezer and Mamakitty. Swallowed by a shadow
shape greater in extent than their own, the two insurgent individual shades found themselves instantly washed out of
existence.

With the dark arm that had been wrapped so savagely
around his neck expunged, a gasping Cezer was finally able
to sit up. Head turning, eyes darting, he searched in vain
for his assailant. Next to him, Mamakitty had risen to her
feet and was brushing dirt and grass from her pants. Careful to keep her own kwavin properly positioned, Cocoa
handed Mamakitty the one she had just tossed aside.

Hissing an ancient and venerable cat curse, Cezer accepted Taj's offer of a hand up. Vertical once more, slowly
rubbing his neck with one hand, he gazed in confusion at
the ground where he had been lying.

"What was that thing—some kind of local spirit?"

"Not a spirit, and not local." Stepping past him, Oskar

reached out to grab the other man by the arm. "Don't move!"

The swordsman frowned at his friend, but without malice. He was too shaken by the recent attack to protest vigorously. "Why—what's wrong?" He looked around wildly. "It's not coming back, is it?"

"Not unless you step out of Samm's shadow," Oskar informed him seriously.

"Out of—?" Cezer hesitated, glanced at the hulking form of the giant standing nearby, his oversize kwavin resting against his broad shoulder, and then turned back to Oskar. "Why? What's Samm's shadow got to do with it?"

"It's a bigger shadow than your own. Big enough to swamp yours."

"Mine—?" For the second time in a very short while, the cat-man's eyes widened. "Are you saying that it was my own *shadow* that attacked me?"

"No," Oskar replied grimly, "I'm saying that it was your own shadow that tried to *kill* you. And would have, if we hadn't been able to put an even larger shadow in the right position in the nick of time." He nodded to his left. "When Mamakitty tried to help you, she put her own kwavin down. Freed, her shadow immediately went after her. I think it's safe to say that if any of us set our kwavins aside, the same thing will happen to each of us." As he finished, Cocoa self-consciously checked the deportment of her own woven shield.

"But this is such a charming realm," Cezer protested. "It doesn't make any sense."

"Who are we to say what makes sense in kingdoms each lit by a single color?" Sounding uncommonly authoritative, Taj freely but carefully twirled his kwavin on its supporting pole. "Myself, I like this place as much as anyone."

"You would," Cezer muttered. "Your original color fits

right in, and high-flying birds cast no shadows. *You* could live here."

"Not in this form. Just because a country seems benign doesn't mean it is." The songster slowly eased his kwavin off his shoulder. "There, see!" He pointed sharply.

Sure enough, a hand could be seen emerging from the otherwise smooth, curving edge of the kwavin's shadow where it no longer shaded Taj's free hand. The clutching fingers vanished as soon as he readjusted the kwavin's position against his back.

"This is a land of bright yellow sunshine. Except on the occasional cloudy day, such light makes for shadows that are long and strong. Strong enough to want to exist on their own, it seems, free of their original masters. Haven't you ever looked at your shadow and wondered if it had thoughts of its own, or a desire to jump about independent of your movements?"

Cezer kicked irritably at the warm ground, wishing for something to scratch on. "I'm a cat. Of course I've had those thoughts about my shadow. They were just for play, though, as all shadows are."

"Not the shadows here." Chancing a quick peek around the edge of his own kwavin, Oskar saw that while the sun's position in the sky was dropping, it still had a ways to go before it would be safely set. No sun meant no homicidal, independent-minded shadows, he felt. Or would a fuller moon than the one that had illuminated the night sky the previous night also present a problem? If it did, it was one they would not have to worry about for several days, at least. That nocturnal orb was still far from full, and presumably its feebler light would present less of a danger. Shadows cast by moonlight might not even be strong enough to make a break for freedom from those who cast them.

Trying to plan for such a defiance of the natural order of things made his eyes water. Better to concentrate on the problems at hand.

"Perhaps the great wall and gate through which we entered into this land were built to keep strangers, and their shadows, out of the Kingdom of Yellow," Mamakitty theorized. "Perhaps once they have slain their creators, or otherwise liberated themselves, shadows in this country can go wherever they wish, causing havoc and devastation."

"We saw no sign of that at the Slevish village," Cocoa reminded her.

Mamakitty chewed her lower lip. "Obviously, the little folk have learned how to cope with their shadows. I wish we had asked more questions of them."

"Remember how the princess told us that the dangers out here would come from within ourselves?" Taj was watching his own oval, kwavin-shaped shadow spread harmlessly across the ground as the sun continued to set. "She was being entirely truthful."

"But not very informative." Oskar took a deep breath. "It would seem that when we stand or walk within kwavin-caused shadows, or maybe any shadow larger than ourselves, such as that cast by a tree or the inside of a building, that we are in no danger from the hazy executioners we bear within us. Until we are safely out of this kingdom, no one must stand in bright sunlight without such protection." Multiple nods of assent greeted his straightforward warning.

"What about the danger that lurks in this Great Rift?" Samm wondered aloud.

Oskar considered. "A deep canyon or cleft could be home to many unattached shadows. If I were an unattached shadow, it sounds like the sort of place I would try to hide. We will decide when we get there how best to make our way across. If the information provided by the princess's advisers is correct, we still have a fair distance to travel before we arrive." Finding a likely spot, he promptly settled himself on the ground and began to slip free of his small pack, careful first to plant his kwavin in the soft earth in front of him, between himself and the setting sun.

"What about me?" Cezer made no apology for his stubbornness. He didn't have to. It was plain to hear in his voice. "I don't have one of those kwaikdin—one of those woven shades." He murmured a sad sound that was almost a meow. "I—threw mine away."

Sipping from his water bottle, Oskar looked over at the now concerned cat-man. "Well, we're not going back for it. At least until dark, it looks like you're going to have to share the shadow of Samm's kwavin."

TWELVE

They advanced with caution after the attack, everyone careful to always keep their kwavin between themselves and the setting sun. Only after it was well down and the splinter of moon not yet visible on the star-flecked horizon did they at last feel safe in stopping and setting their woven shields aside.

"No wonder the Slevish make sure to always carry their kwavin with them." Mamakitty had planted her own shade in the dirt, jamming the pole firmly into the soil. It would not be sufficient to protect her, she knew, if shadows cast by the moon were as capable of insurgency as their daytime relations. If that proved to be the case, they would have to post a guard whose task it would be to rotate everyone's individual kwavin in tandem with the movements of that nighttime orb. For the time being, however, that thin curl of silver light seemed to pose little threat.

"This is ridiculous." Sitting by himself, Cezer was distinctly unhappy. "I can't cross the rest of this lemon-colored kingdom hugging that upright serpent's side. What if I forget and fall back a few paces, or he trips and stumbles?"

Oskar pondered his friend's concern. "A good point. We're all going to have to watch our step. You can be sure our shadows are just waiting, biding their time, for us to make a mistake and let them loose."

It was a disquieting thought, this notion that each of them might be hosting a patient, ephemeral assassin. Trying to keep watch over one's shadow was not so very different from monitoring a rebellious right hand, he mused. He broke from his thoughts as he moved to stop Cocoa from gathering firewood.

"No fire tonight." He gently placed a restraining hand on her arm. "No fires until we're out of this kingdom and safely into the next—assuming shadows in the Kingdom of Green do as they're told and don't go off and act on their own."

She dropped the several sticks she had already accumulated. "That means a cold dinner."

"Better a cold dinner than a cold corpse," he replied. "Think a moment, Cocoa: fires throw heat, and smoke— and shadows."

"They wouldn't be stable." Taj was considering the possible ramifications. "Any shadows cast by a campfire would flicker unevenly, waxing and waning and dancing like the flames themselves."

The dog-man regarded the speculative songster. "You want to take that chance?"

Taj shrugged amiably. "Doesn't matter to me. I've always preferred my food cold anyway."

"We'll take no chances." Mamakitty's tone brooked no argument. Not that there was a surge of support for a fire anyway. Cocoa had wanted it more for light than heat. Like the days, nights in the Kingdom of Yellow were balmy and comfortable.

Walking over to where the disconsolate Cezer was

seated, Taj clapped the other man on the shoulder. "I was always pretty good at manipulating things with my feet and beak, my friend. Now that I have hands, I should be able to do even better. There's plenty of raw material lying about. I'll take it upon myself to fashion you a kwavin before this night is done. That way you won't be dependent on Samm, or anyone else, for protection from your shadow."

A surprised Cezer looked up appreciatively. "That's right good of you, Taj. Tell me how I can help."

While the others rested, the two men gathered fronds and leaves, coils of vine, and strips of bark. By the time they were preparing to eat a late supper, Taj's quick hands had completed the task. A tired Oskar was still awake enough to be impressed: the songster's fingers had been a blur above his materials.

While undoubtedly functional, the result was less than artistic. Taj had worked quickly and efficiently, but he did not have the experience or the traditional weaving skills of the Slevish. What mattered was that like the rest of them, Cezer would now have a protective shade to shield himself from the sun and keep his own murderous shadow at bay. But he would not win any prizes for artistry.

Rising, the swordsman frowned at the makeshift shade. The cinching vines held everything together, but barely. "Pretty flimsy," he remarked. "Where's the carrying pole?"

"There is no pole." Taj looked apologetic—but not, Oskar thought, eyeing him shrewdly, *too* apologetic. "I couldn't figure out how to tie the shade to a stick. I'm no Slevish weaver. You don't carry it: you have to wear it. It's a hat."

Cezer stared in disbelief at the bulge in the center of the huge shade, at the loose fronds that dangled from the edges. "I'm not putting this ridiculous thing on my head. It doesn't go with my fu—with my chosen attire."

"Then you can hold it," Mamakitty advised him, "and hope we don't have to take shelter from any sudden hailstorms."

"Or wave it at your shadow every time you take a step toward the sun," a grinning Cocoa suggested.

"You're all so very amusing." Walking with his head tilted toward the moon so that the absurd chapeau would shade his entire body, he managed to find a safe place to sit. The shade from the oversize bonnet did not block out his continuous grumbling, however.

"This kingdom could be a real paradise." A seated Oskar was gnawing on a strip of dried fish from their stores, as nutritious as it was uninviting. At least, it was uninviting to him: the cats and Samm loved the stuff. "But one wrong step into the sunshine, and you could be tripped up and killed by your own shadow. From the time you're born here, your very own executioner travels with you."

"Do children's shadows murder children? I wonder." Mamakitty, too, was meditating around her meal.

"If you think this is difficult for you, imagine how I feel." Samm was a looming human hillock shutting out the stars as he chewed reflectively on his own dinner. "I'm far less used to dealing with a shadow than any of you."

They talked a while longer before exhaustion caught up with minds as well as legs. Posted to first watch, Cocoa noted that the scrawny strip of moon continued to cast no shadows upon the ground, whereupon she felt confident enough to indulge in some sleep of her own. Her decision was validated when everyone awoke before dawn feeling refreshed and as eager to be on their way as they were to be out of this kingdom.

The next several days saw them making good time and new discoveries. It was revealed that safe bathing unencumbered by awkward kwavins was possible at any time no matter the position of the sun so long as the bather was careful to keep to running water and stay mostly submerged. Shadows that tried to congeal in a fast-flowing stream shattered helplessly with each ripple and twist of the surface. An impalpable hand might grasp at an arm or leg, only to waver and break apart. A dusky foot attempting to trip its originator would break apart and slip away in pieces in the undulating underwater light. When a more substantial shadow did threaten to form, a quick splash was sufficient to fracture it into gobbets of harmless gloom.

It was also possible to relax unshaded and enjoy a quick lunch at high noon. With the sun directly overhead, no shadows could form. During this brief but welcome window of freedom, cares and kwavins could safely be set aside.

When they finally reached the Great Rift, however, the confidence they had gained over the previous several days evaporated as swiftly as a shadow in the face of the setting sun.

The fissure in the earth was not impossibly wide, but it was both deep and forbiddingly dark. Gaunt trees, fragile bushes, and several varieties of determined grass clung to both rims, spilling over their respective sides and growing as far down into the depths as sunlight would permit. It was easy to see how such an abyss might appear to the diminutive Slevish to constitute an impassable barrier.

Master Evyndd's transformed minions, however, were in no wise ordinary travelers.

"Doesn't look too bad," Cezer ventured as he peered discreetly over the edge. "Plenty of places to rest, and lots of handholds."

"Easy for a cat to say." Oskar viewed the forthcoming transit with undisguised trepidation. "And Taj can take his usual quick, graceful, no-fear-of-heights hops, while despite his exaggerated size I suspect Samm retains all of the ground-hugging abilities of his kind." He glanced in the giant's direction. "Even though he now has to deal with feet. I'm the only one here who doesn't come from a line of good climbers."

"You'll manage," Mamakitty assured him. "We'll help you. It's not your fault dogs aren't as nimble as cats."

The giant was gazing into the unfathomable depths of the crevice. "Master Evyndd could never have made it across. Ordinary humans just aren't very agile. Not like snakes. Or cats or birds," he added after the briefest of pauses.

"*We're* not across yet, either," Mamakitty reminded them all. "We still have to cope with whatever dangers lie below."

Oskar squinted into the darkness, searching for activity or movement and finding none. "If this place is some kind of refuge for unfettered shadows, they're not being obvious about it."

"Maybe they're waiting for when we try to cross," Cocoa suggested. This was not a prospect that sat well with any of them.

"What about trying it at night?" Samm proposed. "Without the sun to cast shadows, maybe they have to sleep, or rest, or do whatever it is shadows do when they're not being shadows."

"I don't know . . ." Mamakitty's always cautious voice trailed away as she contemplated the chasm before them. "If they're able to move around down there in the darkness during the day, what's to prevent them from doing the same at night? And despite the abilities some of us have to see almost as well after sunset as at noontime, traveling at night would still make for a dangerous descent and subsequent climb."

After scouting along the rim of the gorge and settling

on what appeared to be the most likely location for a crossing, they decided to attempt the transit just before noon on the following day. If they could move fast enough, and encountered no unexpected obstacles, they might make it across the place Oskar had named "The Narrows" before the shifting sun could spark shadows long and strong enough to threaten them.

It was determined that Taj, who cast the least shadow of any of them, should lead the way. The others would follow, with Samm bringing up the rear. Of course, the overriding hope was that their kwavins would protect them, and they would encounter no trouble at all. Their principal fear was that, while they were familiar with and had learned how to subdue and monitor their own shadows, they knew nothing of those that might lie in wait, unattached and unencumbered by absent owners, in the chasm below.

Smiling affably both to encourage his companions and to mask his own fears, Taj stepped off the side of the rift and started down, feet held closely together as he hopped from rock to ledge, from inclined surface to flat ground. Several times he and the cat-folk had to slow down and wait for Samm and Oskar to catch up.

The presence in the cleft of so much vegetation helped. Where the rocks were slippery or loose, sturdy trees and well-rooted bushes offered welcome handholds. Making steady progress, they soon found themselves enveloped in the chasm's darkened depths, seeing the sun but rarely. The rocks over which they were clambering emitted an agreeable coolness.

As planned, they reached the bottom when the sun was at its zenith. Directly overhead, it provided plenty of light to illuminate the way, but cast no threatening shadows. Hurrying across the meandering floor of the canyon, they encountered the skeletons and forsaken weapons of less fortunate travelers who had come before. A chill that did not come from the cool air at the bottom of the chasm ran down Oskar's spine. Here was proof that the danger of this place was real, and did not exist only in the minds of the apprehensive Slevish. *Something* in this place killed people. No one spoke as they picked up the pace, their progress followed by empty eye sockets and twisted skulls.

It was with great relief that they completed the most dangerous open portion of the crossing without incident. Soon they were scrambling up the other side, relieved at having traversed the region of greatest potential jeopardy without difficulty. Success lent strength to their efforts. They were a quarter of the way up the eastern wall and beginning to feel almost safe when brilliant sunlight struck their ascent with unexpected force.

Shielding her eyes, Cocoa whirled to seek the source of the bright light. With his less sensitive eyes, Oskar was the first to spot the squadron of shadows. High up near the opposite rim, they clustered together beneath a protective ledge. The scavenged metal shields they were holding had been polished to a high gloss. The resultant mirrorlike finish flawlessly reflected the rays of the afternoon sun all the way across the gap—to illumine the startled knot of travelers.

Unshackled by the reflected light that struck her body at an unexpected angle, Cocoa's shadow promptly leaped onto her shoulders from behind, avoiding the kwavin that she held high to ward off the sun. Owner and shadow crashed to the hard ground. When Oskar turned to help, he found his right arm pinned behind him while murky grasping fingers sought his eyes. Twisting desperately away from those clawing appendages, he was forced to forget all about Cocoa in the struggle to save himself.

Unused as he was to dealing with a shadow in his original form, Samm was having as tough a time as any of them. The monstrous black cloud he threw to the ground was up again in an instant, grappling for its hulking master's throat. All of them were now fully engaged, forced by the shafts of light thrown across the canyon by the shield mirrors to do battle with the most evanescent constituents of their personal selves.

Oskar was flat on his back, with his shadow on top and threatening to smother him, when it was torn bodily away from his torso. Coughing for air, he sat up and saw Mamakitty raking her much reduced but still effective claws across its featureless face. Something in that silent oval emptiness must have been sensitive, for the shadow reached up and clutched at itself. Utilizing the respite to regain his feet, Oskar saw that a rapidly weakening Taj was having a particularly difficult time with his own homicidal shade. Preparing to throw himself into the fray, the dog-man hesitated. Clearly, something more than brute strength was going to be needed to deliver them from this ghostly encounter.

Reaching back behind him, he removed his kwavin from its bindings. Though damaged in the surprise attack, it still retained its oval shape. Positioning it to protect himself, he stepped between the battling Taj and the light reflected from across the canyon. Immediately the songster's shadow vanished, swallowed up by the shade provided by the kwavin. A grateful Taj rolled to his knees and started to rise.

Whereupon another shaft of light struck him, resurrecting his shadow. It promptly wrapped dark, featureless arms around his legs.

Whirling, Oskar peered anxiously around the edge of his kwavin. Another group of shadows on the opposite side of the canyon had brought forth a second set of polished shields. Clustering on a lower ledge slightly to the south of the first troupe, these dusky new arrivals to the battle were reflecting damning sunlight from a location significantly removed from the first.

Feeling pressure on his lower legs, Oskar looked down to see his own restored shadow fighting to pull him off his feet. When he shifted his kwavin to block the reflected light that was giving it renewed life, it promptly vanished— only to reappear again in the bright ray of light cast by the first group.

No wonder the Great Rift proved such a fearful barrier. Equipped with a protective kwavin, a knowledgeable traveler might well think himself safe, only to be ensnared by life-threatening sunlight originating from not one but multiple locations. Making their situation even more desperate was the fact that the longer they remained trapped in combat on the canyon wall, the easier it was for the liberated shadows on the far side of the abyss to aim their shields. What might happen after dark in a place where unfettered shadows ruled was something Oskar did not wish to experience.

He considered wrenching Taj's own kwavin from the smaller man's back. Equipped with two of them, he could block both streams of reflected sunlight. Huddled together beneath the twin shields, both men would be safe.

That was when sunshine from still a third cluster of shadow-manipulated shields struck the spot where the embattled travelers were fighting for their lives. Now imported light was creating shadows from not one, but three different directions. Not only did the tri-pronged assault render the use of kwavins for protection almost impossible, it created an entirely new and unexpected source of danger.

Able to block only one source of light, and therefore of shadow, Oskar found himself under attack from not one but two shades of himself.

His kwavin dragged aside, he felt himself go down beneath three entirely independent shadows. The darkness that covered his face had nothing to do with the setting sun that still rode hazardously high in the sky. He struggled to keep their hands off his mouth and nose and away from his eyes. Though he fought valiantly, there were too many of them.

Then one dusky specter suddenly staggered away, its swarthy hands feeling frantically for the colorless head that had been ripped from its clouded shoulders. A second shadow was ephemerally eviscerated, vaporous guts spilling in a nebulous stream from a ragged cleft that had been ripped in its side. Oskar felt warm hands helping him up. He started to thank his savior—only to have the words catch in his throat.

Staring back at him was a black wraith with bright yellow eyes. Yellow-white teeth flashed in an otherwise ebony countenance. Then the wraith-shape whirled to throw itself onto the shadows that were pinning the rapidly weakening Taj to the ground.

A dazed Oskar thought to recover his kwavin and place it between himself and the malevolent light. Counting, he saw that not one but three of the yellow-eyed black phantoms were now scampering among the rocks, tearing into shadows with gusto, shredding them like the smoke they so nearly resembled. Soon every one of them was down; dismembered, disemboweled, or decapitated. They bled coal-black smudge, and died.

Slightly numb, the dog-man stumbled through the evanescent corpses. It stood to reason, he decided. If a shadow could kill a someone, then could not an appropriately equipped someone also kill a shadow? One by one, the streams of mirror-shield-reflected light winked out as the liberated shadows who had been manipulating them saw the terrible carnage that the raven-hued counterattack-ers had wrought. They were not used to seeing their kind slain, and the shock of it aborted any further attempts to constrain the travelers. In impalpable twos and threes, the shadows on the far side of the canyon slunk back into the depths of abyssal darkness from whence they had come.

One of the avenging wraiths half strode, half flowed up to Oskar and blocked his path. He sensed instinctively that the sword still sheathed at his side would be as useless against this phantom as it had been against the enfolding shadows.

"What do you?" Clenching his fists, he stared at the silent apparition. Slitted yellow eyes and sharp bright teeth were all that were visible in the otherwise featureless face.

Slitted yellow eyes and sharp bright teeth . . . His expression softened to one of bemused but rising astonishment. He *knew* those eyes.

"Mamakitty?" he heard himself inquiring uncertainly.

The blackness seemed to undulate and flow before his gaze. At last it coalesced into a shape that was both solid and human—and something more. A weary but triumphant smile split the sweet dark face of the feline woman he knew so well.

"This is how cats do battle with shadows, Oskar. It is something no one but another cat can descry or comprehend. Humans are ignorant of the manner of it, and though they are more perceptive, so are dogs. It's very much a thing particular-peculiar to cats. Do you wonder why our kind are so often likened to shadows, or said to move like them? Special cat magic it is, but it took the threat of these shadows to allow us to find and make use of it once more." Looking down at her left hand, she rotated it slowly, as if seeing its human shape totally anew.

"This is the work of Master Evyndd." Cocoa had come over to stand alongside her sister feline. "Once more, the essence of our real selves has saved us." Behind her, a jubilant Cezer was going from dead shadow to shadow corpse, whacking each on the head with an open hand, making sure none were faking their unexpected demise. Seeing him at work, Oskar was reminded of a triumphant cat giving the coup de grâce to a row of dead rats.

"First Cezer's elongating sword," Mamakitty observed, "and now, when Death threatens utter and complete disaster, this new and unexpected evolvement. I'm starting to feel a little better about our chances of carrying out the Master's wishes." She eyed her much relieved friend intently. "I wonder what special ability he has allowed to lie dormant within you, Oskar, and when it will manifest itself?"

Not knowing the answer, or even if there was an answer, he could only shrug. "If we ever need any old bones, I'm sure I'll be the one to get hold of them. Other than that, I couldn't say."

"Cats and shadows have done battle since both existed," Mamakitty commented. "It was an enormous relief to once again be able to challenge them on their own terms."

Her explanation was salving, but not entirely satisfying. "Then if Master Evyndd left within you three the ability to transform in this fashion, why didn't it reveal itself when Cezer's shadow first attacked him, soon after we entered into this kingdom?"

Her expression turned serious. "All I can think of is that the situation was not grave enough to spark our latent abilities. It leads one to think that one or more of us is expendable, but not all. To provoke the needed reaction, it seems that an appropriately serious stimulus is required."

It was not a reassuring thought. To break the ensuing uncomfortable silence, she turned and pointed to the eastern rim of the canyon that still lay high above the ledge where they stood.

"Let's get out of this place. We don't know if the shadows here are capable of producing other surprises. I don't want to be caught in this deep, dark tear in the ground if they have any more."

The shadows did not. Or if they did, they were too dispirited by the cat-folk's unexpectedly ferocious counterattack to mount them. Still, everyone kept their kwavins close at hand and properly positioned between themselves and the sun.

In fact, when late that afternoon the tenor of the terrain began to exhibit the first subtle but unmistakable shift from unadulterated yellow to yellowish green, Oskar tried an experiment that left them all with much to ponder.

Pausing by the edge of a stream that flowed down a gentle, grassy hill, he deliberately set his kwavin aside and stood, unshielded and unprotected, in the vivid rays of the setting sun. Taj was aghast, and even Mamakitty wondered if their mustachioed companion had suddenly taken leave of his senses.

For his part, Oskar was not too terribly worried. Not with three lethal felines present to intervene on his behalf in case anything went wrong. But as it developed, the conjecture that had inspired his action was proved correct, and there was no need for Mamakitty or anyone else to leap to his rescue.

All around him, trees and bushes and grass and lemontinged birds cast shadows on the warm ground. Only he, alone and kwavin-less, stood unaccompanied by an elongated, distorted silhouette. Deliberately, he paced off a small circle. It did not matter where he stood or what direction he faced. Nor was there any visible change when he spread his arms wide. His shadow, a permanent fixture of his life, an unshakable companion of both his human and canine forms, was gone.

"Dead." With the lowering sun directly behind him, he stared at the unshadowed ground.

"So it would seem." Having set her kwavin aside in imitation of her bold companion, Cocoa stood next to him, slowly waving her own arms up and down. "Not only yours, but mine as well, and doubtless all of ours."

"Of course they're dead!" A triumphant Cezer saw no point in belaboring the obvious. "We tore 'em to pieces. Why the long faces? A shadow is of no use. It's a parasite, a carbuncle on the spirit. Me, I'm glad to be rid of mine." He examined the human nails that had once again taken the place of sharp claws. "Next time I'm stalking a bird or a mouse, I won't have to worry about the damn thing giving me away."

Oskar looked at Mamakitty. "Is this permanent, do you think?"

She regarded the small yellow-green stream that ran through the little valley at the base of the hill. "Difficult to say, Oskar. It would seem so, but shadows are resilient things. All I know is that in our own country, after they have been gone for a while, they have a way of coming back to haunt you when their presence is least expected."

He weighed this observation, then nodded slowly. "I'll keep that in mind. Just as I'll remember not to take mine for granted should it ever put in an appearance again." Together, they started down the gentle slope. "I don't suppose a restored or resurrected shadow that had been violently slain would have the sense or inclination to seek revenge, would it?"

Mamakitty's shoulders rose and fell ever so slightly. "Who knows what a shadow thinks? Who knows *if* a shadow thinks? Best not to dwell on that which we cannot control." She lengthened her stride a little, ignoring the occasional rock that pimpled the hillside. Tripping was something that did not concern her, Oskar knew. Cats did not trip.

She was right, of course. His shadow, all their shadows, were dead, slain in combat. No longer would the dark outlines familiar from birth provide hazy company on a sunny day. By the same token, no longer would they pose a threat—unless they returned, reconstituted by processes he could never hope to understand, and full of . . .

Full of what? A desire for retribution? Indifference toward what had happened? A sly craving to bide their time? As he loped a little faster to keep up with Mamakitty and the others, he found it hard not to think about the thing she had advised him not to think about. Shadow present or shadow defunct, one thing he did know for certain.

He determined never again, for as long as he lived, to fall asleep in direct sunlight.

◈ THIRTEEN

This time there was no unclimbable wall to mark the boundary between kingdoms, nor a broad and swift river to cross. There was only the small, slow-flowing brook that filled the slight crease in the earth between the kingdom of Yellow and the Kingdom of Green. Their progress through the kingdoms of light continued unabated, Mamakitty noted with satisfaction, and despite their difficulties they had lost not one of their number to hostilities, natural disasters, or magic. She felt confident of their prospects and regretted only the continuing inability to properly clean herself.

Unchallenged and with the way ahead unobstructed, they entered into the Kingdom of Green by the simple expedient of wading across the shallow stream. In the previous traversing of three kingdoms of light, there had always been something of note to observe in the crossing, and this one was no exception. The water on the near side of the stream was distinctively yellow, while halfway across it changed to an unambiguous pale green.

Pausing in the middle of the runnel, a delighted Taj stood with one leg immersed in saffron-hued water while liquid of a distinctly limeish hue eddied around the other. Reaching down, he deliberately swirled some together. They merged briefly before separating out, like paint that refused to amalgamate. As he expected, his slender build cast no shadow upon the rippling surface of the stream. Ceremoniously, he gently set his no-longer-needed kwavin aside. Perhaps some wandering Slevish would find it and be able to make use of it.

"The simplest crossing so far." Raising his great axe, Samm used it to point eastward. "Perhaps for once, we'll have an easy time of it."

"That'd be a nice change." With the water slicking the legs of her pants to her lower body, Cocoa's human, bipedal shape proved more attractive than ever, Oskar noted uncomfortably. He had to remind himself firmly that there was no way she could ever be the bitch of his fantasies.

Even without the expected greenish tint to the air, the territory that lay before them would have cast an emerald glint over everything that lay within. Never had Oskar or any of his companions seen so intense a forest. All manner of trees, straight and twisted, broad of bole and slim of trunk, slender of leaf or smothered by branches, flourished side by side to create the lush landscape. Beneath them clustered hundreds of varieties of flower and bush, all wrapped in shades of green varying from delicate hints of olive to bold assertions of emerald. Despite the obstacle it presented, the forest exuded an air of exuberant life that had not been present in any of the kingdoms of light they had already traversed.

"There's something about green." Cocoa's eyes were darting from side to side, her senses alert, as they climbed the gentle rise that led from the perimeter creek to the first of the outlying trees. "It's soothing to the soul in a way that yellow or red can never be."

Taj was nodding in response to a private thought. "Rest-ful. Less harsh on the eyes. Easier to conjure—thoughts."

"See?" Samm pointed with his free hand. "There's plenty of room to walk between the trees. It's a real forest, like the Wyzel; not a jungle we have to cut through. Walking in shade all the way, we'll reach the Kingdom of Blue in no time."

Only Mamakitty and Oskar were hesitant to join in the general enthusiasm, refusing to be swayed by what were admittedly heartening appearances. They advanced more slowly than their ebullient companions. From his four-legged jaunts in the company of Master Evyndd, Oskar knew that forests were usually home to more than just trees. Still, it was hard not to be hopeful. Maybe, just maybe, here at last was a kingdom they could cross in compara-tive peace, without having to fight their way through some-thing or flee from it.

The first thorns struck Cocoa as soon as she entered the woods. Emitting a series of startled yelps, she was hit by more and more of them as she pulled their predecessors out of her arms and legs. When Cezer hurried to her aid, he soon found himself flinching beneath the same barbed barrage.

With Oskar and Taj's help, they retreated back the way they had come, halting only when the flurry of woody darts began to fall short. The attack ceased entirely soon there-after.

"Now—ouch!—what—ow!" Cocoa's beautiful face squinched tight each time Mamakitty pulled a thorn from her flesh. The projectiles were the size of a thumb; thick, sharp, and sturdy. Examining one, Oskar found himself hoping they contained no poison. If the continuing strength of Cezer's complaints were any indication, they did not.

"I didn't see anyone." Cocoa was studying where the

thorns had pierced her clothing. Perhaps they had been remiss when they had first set out on their search, Oskar reflected, in acquiring human attire but no armor. The latter, however, would surely have slowed them down. "Only the forest."

"There's something hiding in there, *fssst*," Cezer growled. His sharp, alert eyes scrutinized the woods, searching for signs of movement. Nearby, a vigilant Taj and Samm stood with weapons drawn.

"I didn't see anything, either." Mamakitty daubed at Cocoa's punctures with a small cloth she had moistened in the nearby stream. In the shade of fringing growths they probed the forest depths, seeking unseen enemies.

Then, in a response as unexpected as the prickly attack, one of the fringe growths decided it was time to contribute to the conversation.

"You're not overlooking anything. You saw everything. You just don't understand what you're seeing."

The tinny, mildly accusatory voice came from what Oskar took to be a sycamore of subdued dimensions that was struggling to adapt itself to life at the forest's edge. Without straining his vision, he could see where ripples in the bark came together to form a kind of mouth. Above it, slightly slanted eyes gazed back at him. The woody folds did not blink.

"I think I must have been hit in the head." Holding the arm that had suffered the most perforations, Cezer walked over to the young growth and ran his free hand along its bole, just beneath the first branch. "I thought this tree said something."

"That feels good, but harder, and lower down," the sycamore instructed him. Instead of complying, a startled Cezer jerked his hand back. "Shapeist," the tree snapped accusingly. Branches rustling sharply, it promptly dumped a double handful of green-tinged autumn leaves on the swordsman's head. Reflexively, Cezer started batting them aside.

"This is very interesting." A fearless Mamakitty approached the trunk. "I've never had the opportunity to talk to a tree before. Scratch on plenty, but never talk."

"Sadist," the tree shot back. "Carpenter's apprentice."

"I have," Oskar murmured. "Many times. But this is the first time one has ever answered back."

The young oak that had sprouted alongside the sycamore chimed in. "Oppin is more loquacious than the rest of us. It is only fitting that he should be the one to greet you."

" 'He'?" Mamakitty eyed the tree uncertainly.

"I'm feeling rather male today," the sycamore replied. "Tomorrow might be different. It's a pollen thing." Its tone grew solicitous. "Are you all right? The crannocks can be vicious."

Turning, Cezer peered back into the forest. "What are crannocks? I didn't see anything moving."

A couple of unpretentious branches dipped low and pointed. "Over in there. To your right. A little more. See those half dozen especially limber trunks, the ones with the distinctively slim branches? Crannocks," the sycamore declared decisively.

Cezer took a wary step toward the woods, leaning forward and squinting in the indicated direction, ready to retreat at the first sign of a volley of thorns. "There's nothing there but trees."

"Not just trees," explained the greenish oak impatiently. "Crannocks."

Standing close to Cezer, Taj spoke without turning. "Are you saying that those trees are what attacked us?"

"Do you not see the thorns on their branches? Is your

sight worse than ours?" The oak's tone sang of exasperation.

"Just because we're not used to—" Taj broke off wonderingly. "Listen to me: I'm arguing with a tree."

Alongside the oak, willow branches rustled. "And you would lose. We are very adept arguers, having much time to practice such things." In a more tolerant voice it added, with a dip of multiple branches that elegantly simulated a formal bow and which Cocoa could not resist taking a playful swipe at, "I hope none of your injuries are serious."

"No," Cezer mumbled. "Nothing besides a few pinpricks."

"Could be worse." Warming to the conversation, the sycamore cast leaves and words to the wind. "You might have run right past the crannocks and straight into a coppice of spruce. Spruce are particularly irritable and can scratch you to death. Or cocobolo. They'll choke you until you can't breathe."

"Or a grove of sequoias." The oak was grave. "An irritated sequoia will step on you without a second thought."

Step on you? Oskar thought. There was a stand of sequoias not three miles from the home of Master Evyndd. Monstrous trees, rust-red of bark and immense of circumference. The thought of one somehow lifting a portion of its hundreds of tons of solid wood and deliberately coming down on a person brought forth an image unpleasant in the extreme. What was the term Master Evyndd had once used? Oh, yes—road kill.

Not that there wasn't a certain irony to be had in the thought of a tree dumping on a dog.

Ever suspicious, Mamakitty found herself addressing the sycamore. "If there is so much hardwood hostility hereabouts, how come you three are content simply to chat amiably with us?"

"It's that very attitude that we ourselves hate," the young tree informed her. "It seems so futile to bottle up all that latent hostility in a trunk you can never escape. Still, that is how it is. The boughs of this forest are weighted down beneath hundreds, even thousands, of years of accumulated malice and ill will that are just waiting to be released on unsuspecting passers-by."

"On us." A grim-faced Cezer gripped the haft of his sword tightly.

"Not only on you." This from a handsome sapling of indeterminate species that hugged the very periphery of the green-hued woodland. "Have you never stopped to consider the eternal war that exists between trees? A silent fight it is; for space, for sustenance, and for sunlight. One growth's progeny crowding out another, ruthlessly suffocating or shading it to death. Roots wrestling beneath the surface in ceaseless and unseen combat for water. Several trees of the same kind cooperating to shut out the light that might fall on a representative of another species." Agitated branches bestirred themselves. "You mobile creatures fight, yes, but then you stop. Our wars are never won, and are ever ongoing."

Taj ran a hesitant hand along the oak's undulating trunk. "I never thought of it that way. To me, a tree branch was nothing more than a place upon which to sit and rest."

"Typical mobile thought," complained a stunted maple.

Oskar confronted the garrulous sycamore. "Where we come from, and for that matter in any land we have visited, trees do not speak aloud. They don't point with their branches or deliberately fling their thorns at visiting wayfarers."

"This is the Kingdom of Green," the oak reminded him. "Here trees rule, not mobiles. Is it so surprising that those who dominate should have the power to communicate with one another?"

"I suppose not," Oskar replied. From within the forest came rustling sounds that he now knew were not caused by creatures moving through the trees, but by the trees themselves. "Why are these crannocks so aggressive toward us?"

"Mobiles are not welcome in the Kingdom of Green." The maple had, not surprisingly, a sweet, syrupy voice. "They trample roots, break young shoots, snap off branches without a thought. They promote random murder and casual amputation."

"Not to mention chronic cremation." The willow shuddered visibly, its leaves trembling.

"But you feel differently." Mamakitty addressed the oak.

"Yes, we do. We want only to live in peace with all forms of life, and to concentrate on that which we do best." Bark undulated, wooden lips forming woody words of wisdom. "Which is to sit and to think. Hence we of different mind find ourselves banished here, to the perimeter of the kingdom, where our growth is stunted by exposure to wind, storm, and potentially lethal mobiles."

"We have to fight constantly simply to maintain our existence," the maple added. "The forest's more aggressive majority denies us access to the richer soil we need to put on rings and grow. So we remain small, until tree rot or root-bane overcomes us." The words trailed away into sadness.

Oskar was not certain he had heard correctly. "You say you were 'banished' here? How does one tree banish another?"

"Have you never observed a tree whipped by a high wind? Branches can be as flexible as any fingers, and much stronger." By way of demonstration, the oak extended sev-

eral of its own limbs and lifted a startled Cezer right off
the ground. Presentation complete, it put him back down.

"We were all of us uprooted from our places of bud-
ding and passed through the woods from tree to tree, to be
transplanted here—a lingering death for the rebellious instead of a cleaner, quicker demise. We cannot mature properly, nor can we spread our progeny. As soon as any of us
drops seed, other trees see to it that everything we put forth
is crushed too deeply into the earth to germinate successfully." Branches dipped in anguish. "For our beliefs we are
condemned to a life of terminal depression. Several of our
little circle have already died."

The willow sighed. "I still remember the year Ifrim deliberately exfoliated all his bark, allowing borer beetles to
eat into his heartwood."

"We're very sorry for you," Mamakitty finally murmured, "but we have strong convictions of our own that
must be fulfilled. To do that, we have to pass through your
kingdom and on to the next."

The oak could not twist its trunk, but it could shake its
branches back and forth. "You will never make it. The forest of the Kingdom of Green is endlessly and unremittingly
hostile to mobiles such as yourselves. Without the knowledge of where to step and what to avoid, you will all be
reduced to fertilizer within a couple of days. You may enter
the forest, but you will not come out."

Taj voiced the thought that was common among his
friends. "What we need here is a pathfinder, just as we had
good Wiliam to guide us through the Kingdom of Orange."

Cezer responded with a snort of derision. "Wake up, Taj.
There are no guides to be had in this place. We'll just have
to push through on our own, as best we can." Missing the
claws that would have lent the gesture emphasis, he indi-

cated the tall forest blocking their way with a broad sweep of one hand. "There's nothing here but trees."

What they needed, Oskar reflected, thinking hard, was help of a kind only Master Evyndd could provide. That something of the sort might be available had already been shown by Cezer's miraculously elongating sword, and by the ability of his former feline companions to slip into subtle shadow-shifting, shadow-fighting shapes. His attention wandered among them. Who else might possess as yet unsuspected capabilities? Might Taj's singing be capable of projecting magic? Not likely, he decided. Who ever heard of making magic merely with music? Well, what about Samm, then? So far the giant had demonstrated no prowess beyond the physical. If sufficiently provoked or prodded, could he do more?

As for himself, he scarce gave a thought to the possibility that any latent talent might lie dormant within him. Certainly, he felt about as sorceral as the cherished old rug by the back door of the house where he loved to lie in the sun. Remembering the rug and the sheer luxury of doing nothing for an afternoon but lying on his back, feet in the air, tongue lolling, while the warm sun baked him, he was stirred by an unexpectedly strong bout of nostalgia.

Such times had been reduced to naught but memories, he reminded himself firmly. He was a human now, a man, with important responsibilities. As nominal leader of the group, it fell to him to suggest what to do next. Taj was entirely correct, of course. What they needed was a knowledgeable guide to help them penetrate the unknown and demonstrably hostile depths of the forest. A guide who knew the trees—antagonistic, indifferent, and friendly—as well as the trees knew themselves.

He blinked thoughtfully. Who, after all, knew trees better than dogs, with whom there had existed since time immemorial a special and unique relationship? Advancing toward the young sycamore, he walked past carping cat-folk, past a silently staring Samm and an unusually thoughtful Taj, and halted within arm's length of the tree. It was watching him closely, he saw. He tried to remember how Master Evyndd spoke when he was declaiming spells; how he formed the words and emphasized certain phrases. Placing both hands on the smooth trunk, he stared straight into wood-laced eyes and said firmly, "By the brotherhood that exists and has always existed between your kind and mine, I command you to walk!"

At best, he had decided, maybe something would happen. At worst, he would become once more the laugh magnet he had always been. Well, he could deal with that.

Absorbing the impact of this unexpected behest, the tree hesitated. Then branches twitched, leaves rustled, and—nothing.

"I'm sorry," the sycamore murmured. Oak, willow, and maple were watching intently. "Nothing's happening."

"Try again," Oskar urged it. "All of you, try."

This time the collective thrashing of leaves and twigs drew the attention of his companions. Wandering over, Cezer placed a comradely hand on the other man's shoulder. His tone was unexpectedly sympathetic.

"It's okay, Oskar. Having come so far only to be stuck here, we're all frustrated, not knowing which way to jump." His strong fingers slid off the dog-man's arm. "But the Master is dead, pigs don't fly, and trees don't walk. We'll just have to blunder through somehow on our own." Turning to rejoin the conversation with Cocoa and Mamakitty, he could not resist a teasing smile. "Unless, that is, you know some magic words, or are holding on to a pouch of magic powder, or a bottle of magic liquid."

There was nothing more he could do, Oskar realized.

No harm had come from the trying, Taj assured him gently, speaking as one would to the village idiot. As if the songster were some kind of expert in matters mystical. Oskar started to rejoin them, when something Cezer had said struck him with more than a little force.

The bond between dogs and trees could not be denied—though as to the inherent enchanted nature of the fluid involved, he was not qualified to say. If anything lay in favor of trying the thing, it was the fact that such an effort would have met with the approval of their former master. Wherever possible, when preparing his potions, Evyndd had always been in favor of employing natural over artificial ingredients. They were, Oskar had once heard him declare, more potent.

Turning back to the sycamore, he proceeded to unfasten his pants and direct a stream of liquid at the base of the young tree. It was an entirely unforced and natural gesture, one he had performed hundreds of times without thinking. This time it was accompanied by thought, an inescapable raising of his right leg, and a reanimated restatement of the requisite command.

"Walk, dammit!"

Wrenching itself away from the flow, the startled tree leaned backward so forcefully that its fore roots ripped clear of the ground. With a twist, it turned away—only to find itself standing, free of the encumbering earth, for the first time in its young life. Hesitantly, it thrust several roots forward at a speed far greater than normal growth would have ordinarily allowed. The decidedly deciduous trunk followed. More of a slithering than a walking, the awkward action nonetheless advanced the astonished tree across the surface.

"I suffered a shower of starlings once," it declared, "but this development is more shocking by far."

"Keep practicing." Pants still undone, Oskar moved from sycamore to willow and repeated the anointing procedure, complete with command. By the time he reached the expectant maple, the other three trees were rapidly gaining control of their exotic new capability, thromping about with much waving of branches and bowing of crowns. This was fortunate, since his store of surprisingly potent potion was nearly exhausted. Other nearby transplants who could only watch the newly mobile boles were no less stunned by what they were seeing.

"I've got to hand it to you, Oskar," Taj declared. "Metaphorically speaking, of course. I never thought this might be what Master Evyndd had in mind on those many occasions when he spoke of the free flow of enchantment."

Mamakitty was rubbing the back of her neck and grinning. "Does this mean a plentiful supply of water means unlimited access to necromancy?"

"Now, now, let's have a care not to vex our good friend." Taking a moment to shake Oskar's hand, a smiling Cezer was careful of which hand he shook. "I have to admit I never suspected the depths of your innate abilities, old friend."

"Then we have our guide," a delighted Mamakitty observed, "and not just one, but four! You *will* guide us?" she inquired of the trees.

"We would be thrilled to do so, making use of this new skill we could previously only observe and envy." The oak hesitated. "If only what you require was that easy." Extending a branch toward the woods, the oak drew it back peppered with thorns. "Though we can find you a path through the forest, we cannot render the way less hostile."

The willow brought together several dozen branches in a single graceful wave. "We are of the same substance as the forest, and might well survive such a dangerous journey. You, however, are mere flesh, easily pierced and punctured. Drawing the full attention of nearby growths, you would not last but a few hours before your limbs were torn from your trunks or your life-sap was forcibly spilled out upon the ground."

Having accomplished so much, Oskar was not about to be put off by new warnings, however dire. "So long as we have an actual route, and are not reduced to simply stumbling blindly through the maze that is the forest, we have with us the means for making real progress, no matter what spiteful individual trees or thickets may choose to do."

"Ahh!" the sycamore sighed. "More magic!"

"That is a matter of opinion." Eyeing his companions, Oskar accepted their individual nods or words of readiness to press on before turning deliberately and uttering a single word.

"Axe."

Samm was more than ready: the giant was eager for the opportunity to finally put his exceptional strength and stamina to a real test. Taking the lead, he lumbered resolutely into the woods. Almost immediately, he was struck by a barrage of thorns. Ignoring the pain, monumental axe held high, he waded purposefully into the bosk of crannochs. With his first swing he cut down not one but three of the gnarled, spiny-armed boles. The cry of anger and distress that rose from the bosk was as unmistakable as it was surprised.

When the last of the thorn-throwing crannochs had been lopped, Samm sat down on a stump and allowed himself to be dethorned by the solicitous Cocoa and Mamakitty. With more flesh to penetrate, he had been at less risk of serious injury than his smaller companions. Not to mention the fact that his skin was, unsurprisingly, much tougher.

Meanwhile Oskar, Cezer, Taj, and the quartet of giddily

ambulatory hardwoods caucused in the clearing and plot-
ted strategy.

"It won't always be this easy." Having been exiled as a rebellious stripling of a sapling by being passed from branch to
inimical branch, the zealous maple knew whereof it spoke.
"Word of the carnage your hulking friend has wrought will
spread quickly through the woods. Schemes will be devised
to stop you."

"And to return us to our border isolation," the willow
whimpered.

"No one and no thing is going to keep us from reaching the Kingdom of Blue." Mamakitty's resolute words
served to reassure, if not entirely convince, their tetrad of
new guides. "Just show us the path of least resistance."

Oak and sycamore entwined branches. "We store no such
itinerary in our xylem, but we will find a way, sensing a
path from tree to tree."

"Inflexible trees," declared the maple sturdily. "Rooted
trees. Trees incapable of movement unless they are dead
and falling." Half a dozen thick, strong roots rose from
the ground and wiggled their tips. Cezer had to fight back
the urge to jump on them. "Such a wondrous feeling." Bark
lashes fluttered at Oskar. "You had better hope it does not
catch on. From what I can perceive, bipeds such as yourselves would not live so well if all the trees in your land
suddenly took to walking about on their own."

Cocoa nodded. "It would certainly complicate certain
activities. House building, for example. Not to mention the
havoc such mobility would wreak in orchards."

"Verbal cooperation might replace silent coercion," Taj
suggested. "I, for one, wouldn't know how to survive in a
world where trees rejected my presence. Where would I
sleep? Where would I raise a family? I'm speaking as if I

were occupying my normal physique, of course," he hastened to add.

"We would all have difficulties," Cezer agreed. "Or at least, our human companions would."

"You mean owners, don't you?" Oskar corrected him.

Cezer favored him with that look of unalloyed haughtiness only felines can muster. "Speak for yourself. Dogs have owners. Cats have staff." Turning, he started off into the woods, the light continuing to give him, as well as everything around him, a collective greenish cast. "Let's begin. The sooner we reach the Kingdom of Blue, the sooner we'll be rid of this infernal foliage." He nodded in the direction of their guides. "Present timber excepted, of course."

That much could not be denied, Oskar knew. And what awaited them in that next unknown, mysterious kingdom? If the pattern of rainbows held true, beyond it lay the Kingdom of Purple, where, the lecherous soldier-scholar Captain Covalt of the Red Dragoons had told them, they would have the best chance of finding the white light that contained all colors. Assuming they made it that far. As for himself, he was not nearly in so great a hurry to depart from the Kingdom of Green as were his companions.

He quite liked trees, and prior to arriving in this place, had been entirely convinced that they liked him.

FOURTEEN

Its unrelieved hostility to trespassers aside, the amazingly dynamic forest that seemed to comprise the whole of the Kingdom of Green was an impressive place—far more so than its benign otherworld counterparts like the Fasna Wyzel. Instead of trees of a type, all flourished in the verdantly egalitarian domain. Evergreens grew side by side with tropical diderocarps, while the hardy dwarf brush of the near tundra snuggled close to mangroves, cypress, and other tropical water-loving trees. Palms shaded wild roses, while ginkgoes wrapped long, spreading branches around the trunks of exfoliating eucalypti. There was room for all, without rhyme or reason or regard for climate or soil. Aside from the natural competition for sunlight and sustenance, it was truly a magical place, Oskar marveled.

If only it wasn't trying so hard to kill them.

"I don't understand." Ducking a flung, unrecognizable nut somewhere in size and shape between coco and filbert, he and his companions waited while Samm strode forward to chop down the offending growth. "Doesn't this forest understand we mean it no harm?"

Their white maple guide strove to explain while simultaneously shielding Oskar with its trunk from attack by the surrounding vegetation. "Most of the trees in this forest kingdom consider all nongrowing things a threat. Unlike my friends and I, the majority of them are only broad-leafed, not broad-minded. Mobiles dig up our roots, devour our seeds, rip off our bark to eat, or bore through it to lay their parasitic eggs in our heartwood. Those capable of thought like yourselves cut us up and use our bodies for shelter, or burn us to provide the additional heat their own bodies are not capable of producing." Branches leaned in the direction of the perambulating sycamore.

"When but a sapling, Oppin there had a particularly close grove mate. They shared soil and the same access to sunlight. One night the other had a dream, of marching bipeds like yourselves armed with things called saws. Its screams upon awakening unnerved a whole section of forest. Poor thing was never the same after that. All his leaves fell out, he developed a severe scale infestation, and eventually he just withered."

"I'm sorry about that," Oskar responded, "but it's no reason to fear my friends and I."

"Well, not you, perhaps. But your companions are different."

"We're all different. And we're not actually bipeds."

"Ah, an enchantment! Ever since you roused us from our plots, I have been wondering about that. It does not matter. You are bipeds now, and will continue to be perceived as such by the forest."

"It doesn't matter." Cezer started forward as soon as Samm indicated that it was once more safe to proceed. "With our serpentine friend to clear the way, we'll be through in no time."

"His activities are certainly making an impression." Ambling along on its strong, magically emancipated roots, the oak inspected the carcass of the fallen bousoun tree. No longer would it grow, or throw, potentially lethal bousoun nuts at wandering travelers. "Each passing day sees a steady diminution in the frequency of these attacks."

Mamakitty shuffled thick leaf litter with her feet, wishing she had the time and the anatomical structure to scamper through the crunchy, crackling ground cover on all fours. "Hopefully, the trees that lie ahead of us will find out from others what is happening and let us pass without incident." She nodded in the direction of their oversize companion. "I worry that our large friend may be getting tired."

The giant overheard her. "Not at all," he rumbled in response. Resting on his shoulder, the stone blade of the great axe was now stained with sap. "I *like* cutting down trees."

Off to the left, Oskar thought he saw a stand of sugar pines shudder. That was not surprising. Word of Samm's ongoing depredations on behalf of the advancing travelers had surely spread throughout this part of the kingdom by now. What was unsettling was that Oskar thought he could *feel* the trees shudder. No matter how dense their network of roots, they ought not to have been capable of disturbing the earth that forcefully.

There it was again: a distinct and unequivocal trembling underfoot. And then a third tremor, stronger still.

"What do you make of this quaking?" In the olivine-tinted light, Cocoa's striking green eyes appeared almost black.

"You feel it, too?" He shifted his attention to their sycamore. It had edged closer to the willow and the maple. The oak continued to stand off by itself, studying not the route ahead or the surrounding trees but the soil underfoot.

"I don't need a tree to tell me what's happening." Wary and alert, Cezer had come to a halt. Though his sword remained in its scabbard, he scanned the surrounding woods uneasily. "Something's coming."

"Something *big*." Samm unlimbered his implacable axe.

"There!" A startled Taj whistled as loudly as he could.

It came crashing through the dense woodland, its massive crown overawing the surrounding growths. The green-hued light could not entirely obscure the fact that its trunk was an odd grayish hue, with a highly distinctive scale-like bark. Branches grew up rather than out, and many were themselves thicker around than all but the largest trees. It was very simply the biggest ambulatory thing Oskar and his companions had ever seen.

And it was coming straight toward them on short but immensely powerful roots.

"It is the greatest of all trees—a kauri!" The willow fairly threw itself forward, scrabbling across the ground at a speed Oskar would not have believed it capable of mustering. Its three panicked companions followed frantically in its wake.

Having seen how Oskar had liberated four of the iconoclasts among them, the trees of the forest had somehow conspired to set into motion the most monumental of their own kind, an ancient and monstrous member of the pine family. Samm's axe was useless against such a perambulating colossus. It would take the giant weeks, not moments, to make a dent in the gigantic girth. As to the tree's actual intentions, Oskar did not intend to linger to find them out.

"Run!" he heard himself shouting. The warning was unnecessary, as everyone had already taken flight, sprinting to escape the lumbering wooden massif. It was enormous, he noted, but slow, the leafy crown swaying back and forth with each uncertain step. Though he missed the ability to move rapidly on all fours, he soon saw that he and his friends should easily be able to outdistance the oncoming colossus.

He looked back over his shoulder only when Cocoa screamed. What he saw sent his heart leaping into his throat and choked off his next breath.

The kauri was falling. It was sacrificing itself, descending in a dreamy but rapidly accelerating arc of inescapability. It was so broad none could evade its bulk, so tall that Cezer and Mamakitty, running in the lead, did not have room enough to escape its reach. The majestic bole toppled completely in a matter of seconds, smashing into the ground with a thunderous roar that could be heard throughout much of the Kingdom of Green, taking mature trees, dozens of smaller saplings, and a whole thicket of bushes down with it. Impacted dust and dirt rose fifty feet into the air, while splinters flew at lethal velocity in every direction.

Then all was quiet once more. A few woodland dwellers crept from their hiding places to have a look at the fallen giant. Slowly settling dust motes danced in the sunlight that was now able to reach the forest floor in the wake of the colossus's suicide. Of bipedal travelers and their accompanying quaternion of talkative trees, there was no sign save for some splintered branches and a mighty axe that, in the absence of its owner, lay useless and forlorn amid the settling debris.

After some time had passed, it occurred to Oskar that he was not dead. He ought to be, he knew. The last thing he remembered was the falling bulk of the kauri blotting out the light and then, silence.

Opening his eyes, he saw nothing. At that moment even heavily green-tinted darkness would have been welcome, but this was deeper than that. It was as black and solid as a wall. It pressed tightly against his mind as well as his vision. Experimentally, he tried wiggling his right hand. Nothing moved, not even a finger. He could barely flutter his eyelids. But his tongue flicked freely within his mouth, and a strong second effort allowed him to move his jaws slightly up and down. His limbs, however, were trapped in place. He could not even scratch at the confines of his prison.

The rest of his senses proffered only sketchy information. He heard nothing, but his nose brought to him several pungent, distinguishing odors. Primarily of cellulose, but also of sap and dust, of decaying mold and diligent insects. There was around him an overwhelmingness of wood. Extending his teeth as far as he could, he gnawed at the material that held him prisoner. Definitely wood.

Then he heard a voice, sharp and clear in his ears. Mamakitty sounded more positive than she had any right to. "I think we're inside the tree that fell on us."

"That's something of a contradiction, isn't it?" Smothered by the all-encompassing darkness, Cezer was subdued, but still defiant. "If that mother of all splinters landed on us, which certainly fits my last recollection, then it should have squashed us flatter than that old rubber ball we used to play with in front of the Master's house."

"But it didn't." That was Cocoa speaking, Oskar noted. "I can't move a hand to touch myself, and I can't see a thing, but I don't feel flattened. I certainly don't feel dead."

"You don't sound dead, either," Mamakitty observed. "Samm, can you reach your axe?"

The slow, even voice of the giant was reassuring as always, if not on this particular occasion especially encouraging. "I don't even know where it is. When the tree came down, I tried to jump clear of the trunk. Obviously, I failed. When I jumped, I threw my axe aside. Not that it would matter if it had been entombed with me. I can't move my arms or legs."

"So we're trapped inside the fallen tree," Cocoa observed. "We're alive, but unable to move. Breathing, but incapable of freeing ourselves. I'm not sure I wouldn't rather have been flattened. At least that would have been quick."

"This is more of Master Evyndd's magic," Mamakitty murmured knowingly. "It is protection of a sort I would deem peculiar, unless we can somehow free ourselves from these wooden bonds. Samm?"

"I'm sorry, Mamakitty. Even if I could somehow reconstruct my former body, I see not a single hole large enough to slip a worm through, much less my previous self. As for breaking free, I cannot move even a finger. This is no flimsy wooden cage that holds us, but a tree as thick and solid as it is huge. We will not break free by chewing at its interior with our teeth."

Cocoa's voice fell. "Then we are well and truly trapped here, to survive an unknown while longer until we expire from thirst and hunger."

"Maybe our four wooden friends had the easier way out." Straining, Oskar felt that his eyes might be adapting to the absence of light. Another contradiction, he scolded himself firmly. "You'll notice none of them have said anything since the treefall."

"Maybe they managed to escape." Taj was more hopeful than sanguine.

"I don't see how," Samm hissed softly. "The fleetest among them was not as quick as you or I." His ponderous sigh rippled through the dark wood. "I fear they'll be of no further help to us. Kindling makes a poor guide."

"What does that matter?" groused Cezer. "What we need now is a giant drill, operated from the outside, to liberate us. If I could reach my sword, I might be able to at least start to cut us free. But as Samm has pointed out, while our hands are not tied, they are completely immobilized. All we can do is talk. That will open only old wounds, not a way out."

Especially if I have to listen to your interminable bitching and moaning until I expire. Oskar kept the thought to himself. Snapping at one another would only make an already unpleasant situation intolerable.

Silence descended within the imprisoning expanse of the fallen tree as a sense of utter hopelessness came to dominate the thoughts of the entombed. We've failed you, Master Evyndd, Oskar thought glumly. Not Cezer's elongating blade, nor the cats' ability to meld with shadows, not Samm's great strength, nor his own unique talent for inspiring movement in other trees, were of any use to them now. They would be mummified within the kauri, interred out of sight and mind of the rest of the world. No one would find them, no one would know what had happened to them, and no one would care. And why should they? After all, the adventurers were no more than common household pets who had momentarily been raised above their station.

For a little while, that raising had given them dignity and abilities beyond understanding. It appeared now that it was all for naught.

He was not certain when Taj began to whistle. It was a pleasant change from the episodes of deathly silence, and certainly more uplifting than Cezer's sporadic whining. Oskar appreciated the songster's attempt to lighten their mental burden. If nothing else, a little buoyant minstrelsy would help to raise their spirits. He would have thanked Taj, but he was enjoying the tuneful warbling too much to interrupt. Apparently, everyone else felt the same way.

Time passed, until a subtle vibrating in his ears caused Oskar to wonder if the inevitable loss of cognition, with its concurrent mental disturbances, had begun to take hold of his mind. As the noise intensified, however, he came to the conclusion that it was a real sound and not a deranged figment of his lonely imagination.

"Mamakitty?"

"I hear it also." Though careful and qualified, her positive response was heartening. "What it is I do not know."

"Kind of a wild, clucking noise," Cocoa ventured.

Cezer was not one to be easily encouraged. "But of course! We are in the process of being rescued by a giant chicken with an unquenchable taste for pine knots."

"Be quiet," Mamakitty chided him, "and listen. Or have you failed to note that Taj continues with his singing?"

It was true, Oskar realized. Ignoring his companions' increasingly vigorous debate, the songster maintained his steady trilling. Trying to find something in it besides the purely euphonic, Oskar failed completely. But then, except for an occasional howl at the moon more notable for its enthusiasm than any resemblance to actual harmony, he was no connoisseur of music.

The clacking vibration continued to increase in volume, leaving those imprisoned within the body of the fallen tree as apprehensive as they were bemused. What impending event could it portend? Of what significance was Taj's uninterrupted song? Between incessant warble and unceasing vibration, Oskar felt he might go mad. He would have given anything simply to have been able to clap his hands over the sides of his head, but his limbs remained imprisoned at his sides.

Something struck him in the eye with such force that he cried out. Instantly, a flurry of concerned voices reverberated in his ears.

"Oskar—! What is it, what's wrong? What hurt you?"

He swallowed. At least he could do that much. "Light—I see light!"

"Impossible!" growled Cezer. "There's no light inside this damned tree."

"And something else," the dog-man added.

"What?" an anxious Mamakitty demanded to know.

Oskar hesitated only briefly. "I don't know—but *it* sees *me*."

The small figure that was staring back at him querulously cocked its head to one side. Then, apparently satisfied, it resumed its work. So did its several dozen colleagues. The source of both the vibration and the peculiar loud clicking noise was now clear. It was the sound a woodpecker made while searching for the insects that scuttled about beneath a tree's bark.

Only in this instance, it was a sound generated not by one but by hundreds of woodpeckers, all working in unison with a unanimity of purpose otherwise unknown to their kind, summoned hither at the behest of a certain song propounded and somehow successfully put forth by a former master winged warbler named Taj.

"I don't know how I did it."

The songster was sitting on the rim of the great cavity the woodpeckers and flickers and all their multifarious, industrious relatives had made in the flank of the fallen kauri. Oskar relaxed nearby, engaged in the ongoing task of removing a seemingly infinite supply of splinters and sawdust from his skin, hair, and clothing. Mamakitty was helping Cocoa to do the same. Below them, thousands of sharp-beaked birds had exposed the bodies of and were working hard to free Cezer and Samm, who alone among the travelers were still imprisoned within the tree.

"You must have some idea." Oskar extracted a sliver of durable kauri from beneath his right arm.

Hands clasped between his knees, the songster watched his feathery brethren at work and smiled ingenuously. "I really don't. As you know, the Master was always fond of my singing. He used to try to teach me his favorite songs, but I preferred my own. My kind is very good at piling variation on top of variation. Stuck inside the tree, I found myself wondering what could get us out. A human would have thought about a drill, or a saw. A dog, maybe, about digging, and a snake about wriggling out a crack or a hole." He looked away shyly.

"Me, I thought about pecking. But canaries aren't very well equipped for that sort of work, and humans even less so. So I wondered who would be good at it, and what kind of song might bring them to help us." He gestured at the hollow in which woodpeckers swarmed like ants, battering at the kauri heartwood with their beaks. "And here they are."

Oskar's brows creased. "But how could they hear you singing through all that wood, and so many, from so far away?"

Once again the songster could only shrug. "To know that, you would have to ask Master Evyndd. But each of us has been given a little magic that is part and parcel of ourselves. What more natural than that my singing should be similarly so fortified?"

"I wish Evyndd had been more explicit, instead of leaving us to find these things out for ourselves."

Taj flicked wood dust from his boots. "Perhaps he felt it would have frightened us to learn of such abilities before we had spent time getting used to our human forms. Perhaps he feared that, inexperienced and clumsy as we are, we might have done more damage knowing about them than not. Again, you would have to ask him."

"I wish I could." Rising to his feet, Oskar brushed at his pants and peered down into the cavity. Cezer was almost free, while Samm's bulkier frame would require a bit more effort on the part of the diligent birds. "I wish he was here now, to guide us and help us, instead of leaving us to stumble onward by ourselves, suffering and learning as we go."

Taj's tone was unusually contemplative for the normally high-strung singer. "I imagine that the suffering is a component of the learning."

Oskar grunted. "That sounds like something a sorcerer would say. Don't let Cezer hear you say that. Our excitable swordsman is of a different opinion."

"And at the moment, of mouth." Looking down, rhythmically tapping the side of the wood depression with the heels of his boots, Taj could not repress a grin. "It's full of wood dust."

Together they watched and waited as the army of woodpeckers finished freeing the remaining two members of the party. Then, their work done, the ivory-bills and flickers, three-toeds and chestnuts, short-tails and long-tails, rose individually and in groups to disappear back into the depths of the forest. As for those inimical woods, they remained still and silent. Perhaps, Oskar mused, the ill-natured nature of this place was still stunned by the travelers' escape from the entombing gravitas of the sacrificing kauri. If so, then now would be an especially auspicious time to resume their journey, before the denizens of the Kingdom of Green could regain their wits and conjure yet another devilment to place in the visitors' way.

Cezer proved uncharacteristically subdued as he climbed out of the gaping hole in the side of the fallen colossus.

No doubt, Oskar decided, his friend's term of interment had given him ample, if unwanted, time for reflection. In any event, his tone was conciliatory rather than contrary, and his sentences short on (though not entirely devoid of) the expected flurry of expletives. As for Samm, he was his usual stolid self. Used as he was to remaining motionless for extended periods of time, he had been less affected than any of his companions by the potentially traumatizing incident. Brushing chunks of woodpecker-pecked wood from his shoulders, he walked a short distance from the fallen giant to recover his axe, which lay where he had thrown it during his attempt to escape the falling bole.

Freed from their inscrutable wooden prison and gathered together again, they spent the rest of the day searching for their missing forest friends. Of hopeful willow and stoic oak, eager sycamore and unrepentant maple, there was no sign save the millions of splinters that formed a broken and shattered bed beneath the immense bulk of the fallen kauri. By unspoken agreement, no one knelt to examine individual fragments too closely, lest they discover bits and pieces of their former guides. It was not the first time Oskar had wept over the loss of a memorable tree.

Without anyone to lead them, they were forced to continue eastward on their own, using their shared innate sense of direction while trying to keep to the course set by the absent quartet. Oskar's conjecture that the hostile woodland had been left dazed by their woodpecker-aided escape could not be proven, but for whatever reason, they were not attacked as they trekked steadily to the east. No concussion-causing nuts came their way, no flying thorns, no looping vines. Swiftly upthrusting saplings did not arise to form an obstructing palisade in front of them, and roots failed to erupt from the bare earth to clutch at their feet. If the forest had not been left stunned by their unexpected breakout, neither did it act to further hinder their progress. Or perhaps it simply feared the threatening presence of the great cutting axe that rode on Samm's broad shoulder.

Then there came a day when the trees finally began to thin out in front of them. The pale green light ahead darkened slightly, turning a marvelous shade of aquamarine. In the distance they could see clearly the sun setting behind a bright blue sea, above which blue clouds hung in a cerulean sky. After marching for days between oppressive walls of green that might at any moment choose to crumple inward or otherwise assail them, the travelers were mightily grateful to emerge from their soaring company.

Of course, the sea presented an entirely new and, in its own way, potentially far more awkward barrier to their advancement. Oskar didn't care. Anything was better than being trapped among the troublesome trees and their inimical ilk.

"Behold the Kingdom of Blue!" Cezer declared grandly as he spread his arms wide. "For such it must surely be. See where the color change takes place midway between kingdoms?"

Previously, it had been difficult to determine exactly where one kingdom of light ended and another began. No such confusion reigned here. The boundary between the two was clearly delineated by the sandy beach that ran from the outskirts of the forest down to the water's edge. Where sea met land, there lay the border between kingdoms. The fact that it was in a constant, if placid, state of flux determined by the movement of the minuscule waves lapping at the shore did not trouble anyone. Certainly the trees that ruled the Kingdom of Green did not object, and if there were any inhabitants of the Kingdom of Blue who felt contrariwise about the continuously shifting line, they apparently felt no need to comment on the matter.

"We're going to need some kind of boat or raft." Advancing, Mamakitty pushed past an unprotesting young sapling.

Stumbling against a protruding root, Taj looked over at her more sharply than he intended. "I concur, but don't expect me to try and cut any wood for it. Not when the wood in question is liable to object strenuously to the action."

"We've passed many dead trees." Samm hefted his axe. "If we lash them together with vines, I'm sure we can put together a craft capable of carrying all of us."

"*Fssst*, yes—but carrying us to where?" Cezer wondered aloud. "I don't know about the rest of you, but I'm no sailor. In fact, I've never been fond of pond water, much less the ocean." He nodded toward the tranquil sea. "Now that I've actually set eyes on it, I'm even less enthusiastic."

"As am I." Mamakitty's reaction was not unexpected, Oskar knew. Cocoa mentioned her own distaste a moment later.

"Like it or not, we're going to have to cross it." Shading his eyes with one hand, Oskar tried to see across the water and found that he could not. Unlike the cat-folk, he was not troubled by the prospect of an ocean voyage. Like every dog he'd ever met, he loved the water. In this he shared an affinity with Samm. As for Taj, the songster was indifferent. It would be a new experience for him to have to travel on water instead of high above it.

Oskar was pondering whether a suitable dugout could be fashioned from a fallen spruce when the first pale coils exploded from the sand to wrap around him. Yells of alarm and shouts of surprise confirmed that his companions were under similar assault from beneath the surface.

Reaching for his sword, he looked on in horrified fascination as a pair of pallid wooden tentacles promptly punched their way out of a parent trunk to lock themselves around his wrist before he could draw the weapon. Though they might well have belonged to some fantastical sea creature, they did not represent an assault from the Kingdom of Blue. They were not soft, like flesh, but hard, like— wood.

Roots, he thought. Then he noted their smoothness, the absence of tiny cilia or branchlets capable of extracting water and nutrients from the soil. If not roots, then what? he wondered as the rapidly expanding tentacles tightened around him. He could not get loose; neither could he make use of his sharp-edged blade to cut his way free. From nearby, the book-loving Mamakitty (well, she loved curling up and going to sleep on them, anyway) shouted a warning that came too late. It confirmed his fear that the forest of the Kingdom of Green had not done with them yet.

"Strangler fig!" she managed to gasp out.

So that was what had surprised and overwhelmed him and his friends while their attention had been distracted by the newly revealed beach and the sea beyond. They were under attack from trees that even in their normal, natural, nonsentient state, were endowed with the ability to commit murder. Normally, the lethality of the strangler fig was confined to other trees, which it encircled and smothered from the ground up, eventually choking the host growth to death. Now several members of that quietly murderous tribe had been given the task of doing to the intruders what they would normally do to their woody brethren. The abnormal growth spurt the figs at the edge of the forest were demonstrating must have been in preparation for days, as the travelers came closer and closer. The deadly rate of growth was nothing short of phenomenal.

Oskar could feel the multiple wooden shoots swelling

around him. As they expanded, they formed a tighter and tighter cage around his pinioned body. The pressure on his ribs was becoming intense. To one side, he could see Cocoa frantically sawing away with her knife. Though she still had both hands free to wield the blade, she was making little headway toward freedom. The fig that now enclosed her put on new wood faster than she could cut it away.

"Help, somebody, please!" That was Taj. The songster was in obvious pain. What denizens of the sky could he whistle up to aid him? Oskar wondered. It would take a thousand eagles clawing away in unison just to keep up with the stranglers' impossibly rapid growth.

One bulging bole was putting exceptional pressure on the dog-man's right side. When he tried to force it back, he found it was like pushing against a wall. Beyond his line of sight, even the always poised Mamakitty was starting to moan.

Could he influence these trees as he had influenced others? Desperately, he tried to repeat his actions of days before. Unfortunately, he was so terrified that his insides refused to cooperate. As he struggled with his recalcitrant bladder, he found himself wondering if Master Evyndd had ever suffered from a similar problem. He suspected not.

Where, he wondered frantically, was incontinence when you needed it?

Something snapped loudly. He swallowed hard. But if someone's bones had been broken with such audible force, he concluded, surely that individual would have uttered a scream before fainting? And if not bones, then what could make a noise like that?

Another snap and crack inspired him to wrench his head as far around to the left as he could manage within the limiting confines of his rapidly contracting prison. What he saw gave him hope, even though time was running short for all of them.

A massive strangler had sprung up around the largest member of their party. But as it contracted around him, instead of fighting the pressure, Samm had let his torso relax. Demonstrating a flexibility that would have awed a circus acrobat, the giant's unfettered arms and legs had wrapped themselves around the trunk of the fig. Now it was their turn to tighten, as the giant fought his assailant at its own game. What an awestruck Oskar found himself witnessing was a battle between two of the world's most relentless constrictors: one from the kingdom of animals, the other from that of plants. Both killed by contracting, by exerting relentless, unforgiving pressure on their prey, be it motile or fixed in place.

The sharp cracks Oskar had heard had come from the sound of wood snapping.

All those magical abilities the prescient Master Evyndd had bequeathed to his companions sprang ultimately from natural talents they had already possessed in their previous states: Taj's singing to call the squadron of woodpeckers, the cats' ability to blend in with and fight shadows, Oskar's special hereditary bond with trees. Now it was the turn of, not Samm the giant, but Samm the great constrictor, to squeeze back. As his increasingly put-upon companions cheered him on, the giant broke first one limb, and then another, and another, until chunks of shattered wood lay piled at his feet. At last unencumbered, he repeated these mighty efforts to free his friends, breaking apart one at a time the tentacles of the strangler figs that imprisoned them.

It had been a near thing. Mamakitty was in the last stages of asphyxiation by the time Samm managed to reach her, and Taj unconscious. Steady massage applied by a throatily purring Cocoa (massage being another specialty of cats, Oskar knew) helped to revive the songster, leading Cezer to lament aloud the fact that he had not been permitted to pass out himself.

"The axe would have been faster," Samm apologized when the last of them had been freed from the wooden embrace, "but dangerous." He gestured to where the imposing instrument lay resting on the sand. "It's not good for close-in work." Envisioning that massive stone blade chopping away next to his formerly captive flesh, Oskar could only agree.

"Everyone's okay, then?" As she spoke, Mamakitty was rubbing her upper arms where the embrace of the strangler fig had been particularly unforgiving. When the last of her comrades assented or otherwise indicated in the affirmative, she nodded tersely. "All right, then. Enough of the Kingdom of Green. It's time to build a boat! And remember as we work that we have only this last territory to cross to reach the Kingdom of Purple, wherein hopefully lies the white light that contains all colors, which we shall restore to the Gowdlands!"

A few weakened cheers greeted her attempt to inspire them. It was not that her words were lacking in vigor or animation: just that her companions were still too sore from the bruising effects of the strangler figs to respond with more than desultory expansions of sorely afflicted rib cages and lungs.

It was Cezer who was first back into the forest, and therefore first to cry out with dismay.

"There was a big fallen log here." He did not have to identify the exact spot where the bole he spoke of had lain. A long, wide depression marred the earth. "Now it's gone!"

"We can see that." Mamakitty was more puzzled than concerned. "It's all right, Cezer. We'll find another."

But they didn't. And though they braved a resurgence

of flung thorns and whipping vines to probe ever farther back the way they had come, and even did some scouting off to the sides of their previous path, they found nothing suitable for the building of a dugout canoe, or even a raft. Every single fallen log had been removed, or concealed, by the forest. Unable to stop them, it had apparently chosen to deny them even the use of its dead.

"What now?" Taj would have sat down on a log had they been able to find one. In its absence they had to make do with sitting on the beach. "Do we make use of living trees in the absence of dead ones?" He eyed Samm's axe suggestively.

"It appears we have no choice." Mamakitty gazed hopefully at the giant. "Do you think you can do it, Samm? It would take too long and therefore expose you to too many attacks from multiple sources for you to cut down a tree big enough to serve as a dugout. So we'll have to use smaller trees and try to fashion some kind of a raft."

He shrugged broad, powerful shoulders. "I'm willing to try. But if the forest has gone and defended its dead so dynamically, I'm sure it will exert even greater efforts to protect those trees still living. Still"—he rose to his feet, brushing sand from his lower legs—"I've cut down plenty of thorn trees and nut-throwers already. It shouldn't be impossible to manage a few more." His soft smile was as unintentionally mesmerizing as his unblinking stare. "I can deal with a few cuts and bruises."

"Maybe you won't have to," announced a familiar voice. From contemplating the ominous depths of the waiting woods, they all turned to see Cocoa standing in the water. Quite a ways out in the water, in fact. One arm held high, she waved cheerily back at her friends.

"Come on in," she called to them. "Not only is the water fine—it's not even up to my knees!"

◇ FIFTEEN

Feeling a little light-headed, Oskar rushed to join her. The others followed at a more decorous pace: Cezer and Mamakitty because to them entry into even shallow water was a disagreeable business to be embarked upon only after sober consideration, Taj because the experience was wholly new to him, and Samm simply because when given the choice, he tended to do things more deliberately than his companions.

Not Oskar. Knees lifting high with each stride, legs pumping energetically, he made a joyous, splashing dash to catch up with Cocoa. If not precisely in his element, he was for once in their long journey more comfortable in new surroundings than any of his friends. She shut her eyes and turned away from him as his flailing legs threw water in all directions.

"Hey-*ssst!* I'd like to keep as much of me as dry as possible for as long as possible, if you don't mind." Raising her left arm, she began licking away the droplets that clung there.

"Sorry. Guess I got a little carried away." Slightly abashed, he bent at the waist and with cupped hands began to throw water in the opposite direction for the sheer joy of it. The blue-toned liquid felt a little heavier, a little denser, than the ocean water Master Evyndd kept stored in a large jeroboam. "I keep forgetting that certain attitudes carry over, and that your kind finds swimming and soaking unpleasant."

"It's not so much that it's unpleasant." She kept a wary eye on his active, splashing hands. "It's just that it's cosmetically unflattering. Don't you remember spending hours and hours trying to dry and groom yourself after a compulsory bath?" When she drew only a blank look she sighed and turned toward the eastern horizon. "No, come to think of it, I guess you don't."

"What's to dry and groom?" He promptly sat down. Composed almost entirely of particles of what appeared to be very fine quartz, the bottom was eerily translucent. He let the warm water swirl around his legs and partially submerged lower body. At that point his previously uncooperative bladder relaxed. Even though the shore was lined with trees aplenty, there was no way he was going back into the Kingdom of Green. "You lie out in the sun until you're dry. As for grooming, the wind takes care of that."

"You ought to know that that's not how cats do it. We're a little more proper where our appearance is concerned." Shading her eyes with one hand, she pointed across the water as Mamakitty trudged to a prudent halt nearby. "I don't see any landmarks. No distant shore, no bump of an island, no trees: nothing."

"Perhaps the whole Kingdom of Blue is like this," the older woman speculated. "Maybe we won't need a boat after all."

Taj tiptoed up behind them. "Surely it can't be all ocean. And if it is, there must be places that are much deeper than here." He looked down at his booted feet, clearly visible through the warm, pellucid salt water. "It defies everything I've ever heard about such bodies of water. Anything this shallow should quickly evaporate away."

Mamakitty eyed him thoughtfully. "How comes a canary to know so much about oceans?"

He looked away. "I didn't spend all that time in the Master's study singing. With my cage hanging over his desk, I couldn't help but look down at some of the books he read."

"You're thinking of the oceans of our world; the ones Master Evyndd spoke of often." As Samm joined them, the others moved to stand discreetly in his cooling shadow. "Couldn't it be that the water here, where everything is so saturated with blue, blue, blue, acts differently? Obviously it doesn't evaporate as fast, or under the same rules. Or perhaps there are forces at work we don't understand."

"Coming from a snake, that qualifies as almost an insight." Crouching but making sure his backside stayed dry, Cezer scooped up a palmful of liquid and brought it to his lips. They promptly curled back on contact. "Tastes like thick salt water, looks like thick salt water, but that doesn't mean it has to behave like thick salt water."

"There goes lunch!" Turning and leaping into the air, Cocoa came down with all four hands and feet on a tranquil patch of sparkling clarity. The rivulets that subsequently ran down her cheeks and chin were indicative of a good effort but lack of success. "Missed, *ssst!*"

"What was it?" A curious Mamakitty waded over.

"Some funny-looking kind of flatfish. The only kind that would be comfortable in these long shallows. Not a flounder, or a small halibut. Something different."

Cezer licked his lips, and would have licked his whiskers had they grown long enough. "A nice change from trail food. This traverse might not be so uninteresting after all."

Bending low, he began scanning the nearby shallows and the crystalline sands beneath.

"Provided the water doesn't get up over our necks," Taj reminded him as he joined in the hunt. Canaries liked fish, too, but only in the form of minuscule flakes. With the addition of teeth, the songster had been experiencing and enjoying a whole new universe of taste sensations ever since the first day of their transformation. This was just as well, there being a decided dearth of fruits and vegetables, not to mention seed, in evidence on the route that lay ahead of them.

With three cat-folk on the prowl, locating and catching the fishlike denizens of the shallows was a problem soon solved. Consumption, however, was another matter entirely. In their human guises the travelers had grown used to cooked food. Even if they had been able to locate any drifting wood, it would first have to be dried. Assuming they managed to do that, they then faced the dilemma of how to construct a fire in the midst of open ocean.

Returning cautiously to the beach, they managed to snatch some dead chips and branches from beneath the disapproving gazes of the denizens of the Kingdom of Green. The resultant humble blaze the travelers then managed to kindle on the sand caused the nearest trees to bend away in horror.

"This is all very well and good for now," Taj pointed out, "but what are we going to do when we start across the sea?"

Oskar shrugged indifferently. "I don't mind raw fish. How about you, Cez'?"

The swordsman was amenable. "Same here. We'll manage without human cooking until we walk out on the far side." Mamakitty and Cocoa nodded agreement, while Samm simply ignored the question. Everyone knew that not only did the giant not require his meals to be cooked, it was not even necessary for his food to be cut up.

"I think I saw some shell-wearing bottom dwellers moving about, too." Cocoa spat out a cluster of limp, pale white lumps of cartilaginous material from which her teeth had efficiently stripped the flesh. Conveniently, the fish-things had no bones. "Scallops would make a nice addition to our diet, or clams."

"We'll be fine." His belly stuffed with food the more agile cat-folk had caught for him, the giant leaned back against his folded hands and stared out to sea. "So long as it doesn't deepen I don't see any reason why we can't just walk across." He gestured casually. "How big and dangerous can a creature get that only has a foot of water in which to grow?"

"Beware overconfidence," Mamakitty warned him. "Deadly poisons often come in small packages."

He turned to look at where she was seated near the cooking fire. "I don't plan on doing anything stupid, but after all we've been through to get to this point, I don't think I'm going to be afraid of anything I can step on."

"Or jump over," added Cezer.

"We can catch fresh food along the way," a confident Cocoa insisted. "All we have to do is carry enough drinking water, and we can use the big leaves of some of these trees for shade umbrellas." She sat back on her heels, looking very pert and alert indeed, not unlike the cat that ate the cana— in deference to their songster, she banished the aphorism from her mind. "And by the time we reach the shores of the Kingdom of Purple, we will all have exceedingly clean feet and ankles."

Certainly nothing happened the following day to diminish her optimism. Mile after mile, the water varied in depth from place to place by no more than a few inches.

The cat-folk advanced with deliberate, easy strides; Taj with unconsciously mincing precision; and Oskar with unfettered exuberance. As for Samm, the giant trudged effortlessly forward, shouldering the bulk of their supplies while suffering little more than the moistening of his feet and ankles.

Everyone else had slung their boots and socks over their packs and rolled up their pants legs to keep them as dry as possible. As suggested by Cocoa, scavenged shade leaves kept them cool as the cantankerous Kingdom of Green receded farther and farther behind them. Around them now, all was flat, teal glare—blue sky, blue water, blue-tinged sand, azure-shelled bottom dwellers, and the occasional wandering, sapphire-tinted invertebrate.

A week out from land marching steadily along beneath an unforgiving sun saw their water supplies significantly reduced, but not yet dangerously so. Everyone was still in good spirits, no one had stepped on anything deadly, and supplemental food remained plentiful and easy to catch. When he lay down for the night, the cat-folk took turns sleeping on Samm's back, that being the only dry land within view. The giant could accommodate two of them at a time. This did not always guarantee either sleeper a dry or restful nap, however, since from time to time something in his pythonic dreams would bestir the serpent-man, causing him to turn over in his slumber and dump his dozing companions unceremoniously into the drink.

It was not dog heaven, Oskar reflected. Dogs were not fish, and like his feline friends he preferred dry land to damp. But there was no question that he was more at ease in the wet blue surroundings than all of his companions save Samm. About time, too, he mused with gentle indignation. Come the Kingdom of Purple, their situation might be reversed. With the Kingdom of Blue imparting only dank distance as an obstacle, he found himself wondering what the Kingdom of Purple might be like, and how they would go about locating and securing a bundle of white light to take back with them to the Gowdlands. Voicing the thought aloud, he was not surprised to receive a response. The source, however, when he finally identified it, was something more than a surprise: it was an unadulterated shock.

It was the ocean, shallow and warm and blue of hue, that had answered him, and not one of his companions.

Shooting from his resting place to a standing position, he stared wide-eyed at the water rippling quietly around him. Surely he had imagined it. Surely the heat had affected his concentration. One way, he knew, to find out.

Gazing down at the undulating water, he reiterated the thought. Sure enough, for a second time, a sympathetic response was unhesitatingly forthcoming. "Nothing know we about white light, sand treader, and no help can we give thee."

It was truly the ocean that was replying, Oskar observed. One might dispute the exact direction of the sound, but not the fact that it arose from somewhere beneath the surface. He had felt the slight vibrations in the water from the speech. Cocoa had come over to stand next to him, her shade leaf parasol hovering above her normally calico-colored but presently blue-tinted hair.

"There's something in the water, Oskar, and it's talking to you!"

"How can there be something in the water, Cocoa?" He had not taken his eyes from the gently rippling surface that had emitted the sounds. "I don't see anything moving, it's too shallow for something to disappear against the bottom, and there's nowhere to hide." He bent lower. "Maybe something's living under the sand?"

"Near the top the sand layer is transparent." She was

bent over at the hips so that her pert nose was less than an inch from the water. For once, her enchanting personal perfume was overwhelmed by the odor of salt. "I think we'd be able to see anything hiding within it."

"We are not living beneath the granules, but just under the surface," explained the speaker. "Come over this way. We know that we are difficult to see. That is intentional."

Side by side, Oskar and Cocoa searched for the source of the tiny but emphatic voice. Mamakitty was gazing curiously in their direction, while the other members of the group were finishing their lunch.

"There!" Her feline vision better attuned to the movement of quick, small objects, it was Cocoa who spotted the speaker first. With her help, Cezer soon found himself staring at the same spot in the water. One by one, the others joined them, and one by one, they found themselves alternately transfixed and delighted by what they had discovered.

Drifting just beneath the limpid surface were dozens of tiny finned shapes, human in outline and form save for their exceptionally broad nostrils and mouths and slightly bulging eyes. Naked and perfectly formed, they either darted to and fro at astonishing speeds or remained perfectly still. There was no in-between motion; no languorous swimming or casual treading of water, no measured acceleration. Movement was accomplished at maximum velocity or not at all. The largest of the creatures was no bigger than Oskar's little finger. Easy enough to espy, one might think, especially when clustered together by the dozen. Except for one thing.

They were all of them, male and female alike, almost perfectly transparent.

The pale azure light of the Kingdom of Blue shone straight through them. Only a faint hint of cobalt blue signifying the presence of tiny internal organs had allowed Cocoa to pick them out from the surrounding liquid. That, and the flash of light off their diaphanous skins when they moved. The minuscule flaps of flesh that transformed hands into flippers and feet into fins were virtually invisible.

"Why do thee seek white light?" The diminutive speaker was floating on its back directly beneath Oskar's face. "Blue be best! There be no need for another."

"Just so!" added a female of the species. Appearing as if from nowhere, she came to a sudden stop alongside the speaker. "Blue be calm, blue be soothing, blue be a color beyond reproving!"

"We need the white light to return color to our own homeland," Cocoa explained obligingly, "where only a somber and depressing gray now rules."

"Oh, that's terrible, terrible!" The two tiny figures squealed simultaneously, whirling about a common center until by their frenetic swimming they had generated a miniature whirlpool between them. It faded quickly when they slowed to an abrupt stop. "What be 'gray'?" the male inquired curiously.

"It doesn't matter. It's our problem, not yours," Oskar told him. To Cocoa he added, visibly relieved, "Even in the depths of a rainbow, I'm glad to see that water doesn't possess the power of speech. For me, at least, such an ability would make it hard to swallow."

Cocoa nodded knowingly. "It would surely give new meaning to the idea of soaking up a conversation." Of the diminutive creatures bobbing below them she inquired, "What are you called?"

The pair glanced at one another before replying. "Why, we are thweens, of course. We live just beneath the surface. That is why it is hard for such as thyselves to see us. The surface refracts the light around our bodies. When we lie still, which is most of the time, or move rapidly about, which is the rest of the time, we are very well concealed."

"You certainly are." His back beginning to protest at his crooked posture, Oskar straightened slightly. Being cat, Cocoa could hold the pose for hours. "If you hadn't spoken, I don't think we ever would have noticed you."

"That's right," a curious Cocoa agreed. "Why *did* you speak?"

"Because not many creatures *can*, besides the thweens. Despite thy size, thy speech intrigued us. Thee are almost interesting."

Nearby, the heretofore silent Taj spoke up. "And thee are almost thanked. What do you eat?"

With a perfectly formed little arm, the female made a sweeping gesture. "Our world is full of food. You have eaten some yourself, for which we are grateful. Unfortunately, the negwen you find so tasty are equally fond of us."

Oskar envisioned the flat, boneless bottom dwellers he and his companions had been feasting upon since they had started wading through the shallow sea ingesting and masticating the delicate little thweens. The disturbing image left him feeling thrice thankful for his own hearty appetite.

"Much of the life that surrounds us," the male added, "is, like ourselves, quite transparent. We can also live for quite some time outside the water. We simply have difficulty breaking through to the place of air. Surface tension, you know."

Mamakitty and Oskar exchanged a glance. "Surface what?" she inquired.

"Never mind." The female extended both tiny arms upward. "Pull me through. Up and through."

Tentatively, careful not to strike the speaker, Oskar pushed his index finger down into the water. When he lifted

his hand, both the male and female thweens were clinging
to his finger. He positioned them over the open palm of
his other hand, intending to give them a soft place to land.
They did not need one.

Spreading hitherto unseen wings, both promptly took to
the air, buzzing back and forth in front of the captivated
dog-man like translucent dragonflies.

"How wonderful to be airborne again!" The female executed a series of aerial pirouettes as notable for their swiftness as for their grace. Descending until her perfect little
webbed feet hovered just above the water, she gestured excitedly. "Help Lis out, too. And Maygyn, and Plel, and
don't forget Bou, and Geil, and Evave."

With everyone pitching in, the travelers soon found
themselves enveloped in a cloud of soaring, darting
thweens. The amphibious little sprites filled the warm blue
air with a confusion of delighted giggles and captivating
cooing. They danced around Mamakitty's face and rested
on Taj's ears, scaled the heights of Samm's bald pate and
plumbed the folds of Cezer's pants. They were altogether
charming.

And then, quite unexpectedly and without warning, they
embarked on an ardent and passionate variation of their
aerial ballet. In a word, they began to mate.

"Amorous little pixies, aren't they?" observed Cezer admiringly. Next to him, Mamakitty looked on with academic
interest. Cats did not blush, and neither did she.

The female they had first encountered zipped over to
hover in front of Oskar's face. Her gossamer skin was
flushed turquoise and her jewel-like eyes bulged even more
than usual. "We can only mate and reproduce when we are
out of the water."

"No wonder they were so anxious to have us help them
out of the sea." Taj watched while an octet of thweens

swirling near him executed a byzantine sequence of aerial acrobatics that would have struck a host of hummingbirds dumb with admiration. "This is undeniably entertaining—but it's not getting us any closer to a purpling shore."

"We are glad we could be of assistance," Mamakitty informed the female. Rather primly, Oskar thought. "But we have to move on. We have our own agenda to fulfill."

As she turned to go, the male and two companions materialized in front of her. "Oh no, don't leave! Must thee be on thy way so soon? Thy company is so very welcome to us."

"I'm sorry." Advancing, she forced them to move aside. "We have to follow the path that has been set before us. But if you enjoy our conversation so much, why not accompany us? As long as we keep making progress, we'll be happy to keep you company."

Three thweens put their heads together. When they separated, it was another male who spoke. "Some will choose to remain here, where there are known dangers and familiar food. But many will come with you. All the Bluesome is our home, and we do need to spread our seed as far and wide as we can."

"Come along then." Cocoa was pleased by the decision. Even when they weren't mating, the thweens were fun to watch. "We'll protect you from the negwen, and you can help us find food."

"Done, done—done it be!" Tiny webbed hands clapped wetly.

The thweens proved not only good company but avid guides, helping to ensure that the travelers stayed on course in their trek across the featureless, shallow sea. When not airborne, they rested on the shoulders and heads of the travelers, luxuriating in the unique opportunity to see their world without having to expend a constant flow of energy.

They piped tiny curses whenever a school of negwen or other predators was spotted, and cheered as the agile, active cat-folk snatched up the hated archenemies one by one.

They restricted their own mealtimes to coincide with those of their new, much larger friends. Darting and diving beneath the water, they gathered up armfuls of food for their own consumption. Most of it was of such small size that even the sharpest-eyed of the travelers could barely descry it. The thweens assured them that it was all delicious, even if largely invisible to the naked eye. Meanwhile, drawn by the commotion and the calling of their fellows, more and more of the amphibious pixies arrived in a steady stream to join the procession—and to mate. Watching them, unable to avoid their ardent aerial couplings, Oskar found himself glancing more often in Cocoa's direction than would otherwise have been the case.

In this fashion travelers and thweens progressed eastward for several weeks, taking much mutual pleasure in each other's company. "What is this briny basin we are crossing called?" Mamakitty asked one morning.

"Thee really know not?" The thween fluttering beside her sweating face seemed genuinely startled. "Why, it be the Eye of the Beholder, of course."

"Evocative," observed Samm in his usual laconic manner.

"There is nothing else in the Kingdom of Blue? No land?" Cezer inquired curiously.

"Land?" The female thween sounded puzzled. "Why should there be land? There be only the Eye of the Beholder, blue and omnipresent."

"Something I've been wondering about." Oskar stepped over the siliceous skeleton of a long-dead vrorvel that was lying on the bottom. "What is it that you thweens *do?* Do you just swim around and eat and reproduce? Is that your only purpose?"

"Sounds very like the life of a certain dog I know," Cezer gibed.

Oskar made a face. "I wasn't criticizing. I'm just curious. Dogs do other things," he added, a bit defensively. "We hunt, and provide companionship, and dig things up, and bury them again. Occasionally, we sing."

"That's a matter of opinion," put in Taj, who ought to know.

"Well, not compared to your kind, of course," Oskar admitted. "But to us, it's singing."

"We do not sing," the thweens declared, "though we occasionally burble. And out of the water, we hum. It is a way of calling to one another. Mostly, we try to eat and reproduce as much as we can without disturbing the Eye."

Mamakitty frowned. "Disturbing? How can creatures as small as yourselves possibly disturb all this?" She indicated the horizonless surface through which they were traipsing.

"There can be quite a lot of us. There are now especially, thanks to thy help."

"Our help?" The conversation was leaving Oskar more confused than enlightened.

"Yes." The thween zipped over to hover before the dogman's face. "Thee consume the negwen and others that eat the thweens. In their absence, we can propagate further. We must, however, have a care not to upset the balance, or it will disturb the Eye." Bulging orbs fell slightly. "Perhaps we have not been sufficiently forthcoming with you. We be parasites on the Eye, you see."

Mamakitty shook her head. "I'm afraid we don't understand."

Flitting up and down in front of her, the thween tried to explain. "All those delicious little bits you see us eating are important to the continued health and function of the Eye. If we eat too many, it will become irritated and not function as well. By preying upon the thweens, the negwen and vrorvels and such maintain a balance. It is not a balance that be to our liking, but there be nothing we can do about it." Tiny glistening oculi looked up at her afresh. "Unless we have the assistance of bold outsiders such as thyselves."

"Well, we're glad to help." Cezer sloshed steadily onward. "But I still don't see how you wee folk can irritate an entire sea, no matter how many of you there are. How do you upset an ocean, anyway?"

The thween was about to reply when a sudden shaking commenced underfoot. The myriad little creatures darting through the water felt it first. They began swimming faster and faster, occasionally bumping into one another or into the legs of the travelers, until the last of them had vanished off to the west. The airborne multitude immediately ceased mating and bolted in the same direction.

Looking down, Oskar could see that the water was frothing around his ankles. The hitherto stable bottom of translucent granules had begun to shudder. "Is this what you meant by 'disturbing' the ocean?" He addressed the one thween that remained. "If it doesn't get any worse than this, then what's to be concerned about?"

"Ocean?" The clearly agitated thween zipped nervously back and forth in front of the scruffy mustache. "What ocean?"

"The one we've been walking across for the past several weeks," Cocoa reminded it impatiently.

The thween spun around to look at her. "There be no ocean here. There be only the Eye of the Beholder."

"Yes, of course," Mamakitty commented irritably. "That's what you call it."

"That be what we call it," the thween explained, "because that be what it is. The Eye of the Beholder. Or if thee prefer, an Eye of the Beholder. It dwells within the kingdoms of light and sees all, observes all, memorizes all. When thee see the kingdoms from without, as only visitors such as thyselves can do, do not most of thee focus on the Kingdom of Blue? It be because that kingdom, which be all the Eye, be looking back at and contemplating thee. Not all eyes be round, thee know. There be many ways of seeing. But there be only one Eye of the Beholder."

The trembling underfoot intensified. "You're not making any sense," Oskar insisted. "We're standing in a sea, not an eye."

"If this was an eye, even a very big eye," Cezer added, pointing to one of his own oculars, "where's the pupil?"

"Below thee." Now the thween was looking around anxiously, as if expecting the arrival of something unspecified and unpleasant. "It be the dark area beneath the transparent cornea. These past weeks thee have been wading through the protective optic fluid that forms a film atop the cornea. And now I really must go. I am sorry for thee, for thee have been good friends to the thweens." It waved once before dashing off in the wake of its fellows.

"Hey, *ssst,* wait a minute!" Cezer yelled. To no avail. In the absence of the thweens, there was now only the increasingly intense undulating underfoot. It was not severe enough to knock them off their feet, and the ground beneath the water did not crack or shift, but the sensation was unsettling, to say the least.

"That's just swell," Taj muttered. "By helping the adorable little creatures, we've gone and upset some kind of territorial balance. But *what* kind?"

Mamakitty held her ground, watching the water foam

around her legs. "Maybe now that they've left, whatever they've disturbed will settle down."

Bending low, Cezer was staring at the crystalline layer beneath the surface. "Did you ever notice the funny shapes that kind of lie under the ground here? Maybe we should try and dig down a little ways and see what we find."

Oskar was gazing anxiously southward. "I don't think that would be a good idea. We might aggravate this Eye further. Not that it's going to matter. Not at this point."

"What are you talking about?" Straightening, Cezer saw that everyone else was staring in the same direction. As he joined them in looking, his mouth gaped involuntarily.

A tsunami was rushing toward them, rising higher and higher above the hitherto featureless southern horizon. Though tinted with the same ubiquitous blueness that suffused everything in this kingdom, it was noticeably darker than the water in which they stood or the sky above their heads. At its forefront, riding the crest of the wave, was an entire uprooted forest of crooked trees from which the branches and leaves had already been stripped.

Then the swordsman's jaw dropped still farther. The dark, twisted growths were not trees, and the wave rushing toward them was composed of something other than water. He identified both well before his brain would countenance and accept the inescapable conclusion.

What he thought were trees were in fact lashes, lining the leading edge of a most monstrous eyelid, embarked upon a single gargantuan blink.

SIXTEEN

This is it," whispered Taj. "So close to our destination, only to be crushed like ants." The Eyelid of the Beholder stretched from horizon to horizon, from east to west as far as they could see. There was no imaginable path of escape, and the songster did not hesitate to say so.

Only Oskar, possessed as he was of an indefatigable optimism, refused to bow down before the oncoming darkness. "Then we'll just have to find an unimaginable one."

"Oh, well-spoken, master of barking orations!" snarled Cezer sarcastically. "My guess is you have less than a minute to think of something before we are blinked out of existence." Standing firmly, agitated optic fluid swirling around his legs, the swordsman shut his eyes and prepared himself as best he could for what appeared to be an inescapable demise.

Mamakitty stayed calm and composed, even though devoid of hope. "And to think that we brought this upon ourselves. If we hadn't killed so many negwen and vrorvels, if we hadn't helped the thweens and allowed them to multiply so freely . . ." Her voice trailed away, lost in the eerily sonorous hiss of the onrushing eyelid.

As it drew ever nearer, it seemed to accelerate, though this was only an illusion caused by its increasing proximity. Cocoa closed her eyes, and Mamakitty turned stolidly away, but Oskar found he could not tear his gaze from the onrushing phenomenon. Then it was next to them, on top of them, and—over them. Despite his determination to meet his fate boldly, he flinched. The eyelid reached his head.

And passed over it.

Still crouched, he turned to follow the edge of the immense fleshy flap as it continued on its northward rush, blotting out sky and clouds. The illusion of all-pervasive size had been complete, so much so that the eyelid had appeared to be much closer to the surface than it actually was. There existed, at least in the place where they were standing, an air space between optic fluid and the underside of the lid some six feet in height. While this caused problems for Samm, who practically had to lie down to avoid bumping up against the fleshy barrier, everyone else was able to remain standing.

"What do you know?" Having opened her eyes to pitch darkness, Cocoa was gently jabbing upward with a hand, prodding the underside of the eyelid. The rubbery tissue flexed slightly beneath her fingers but did not otherwise react. "We're not dead."

"Maybe," posited Taj hopefully, "the eyelid will retract again once it has responded to the irritation caused by the thweens."

While easy to utilize, time is an expensive weapon. Unable in the absence of daylight to know the true passage of time, they were reduced to making crude estimates. Certainly, Mamakitty determined, a goodly number of hours had passed when she finally rose from where she had been sitting in the optic fluid and pointed, forgetting that in the darkness her companions were unable to follow the gesture.

"Our destination lies eastward. I took care to mark it well before the light was taken from us. By putting one foot carefully in front of the other, we should be able to continue, albeit slowly, on our chosen path. We have food and drinking water in the packs Samm carries, firm footing beneath our feet, and if necessary we can hunt for negwens by feel."

Cezer voiced his doubts about this proposed course of action. "I pride myself on my sense of direction, but I can't see a damn thing. A hamster could be making faces at me and I wouldn't know it. Sure, we could continue on the way we're supposed to go. But we could also become disoriented and wander around in circles until we drop."

"Have you a better suggestion?" she asked him bluntly.

"No," he grumbled. "According to the rest of you, it seems I never have a better suggestion."

Careful to stay within earshot of one another, they began to move, forming a line behind Mamakitty. Everyone periodically announced their presence to ensure that no one wandered off. In this manner they made progress, pausing only to eat, drink, and rest. But it was progress that, without any real means of orienting themselves, remained dubious at best.

"Light!" Cocoa's exclamation caught everyone off guard. "I see light!"

Oskar kept moving until he bumped up against her. Whether out of excitement or indifference, she did not object to the contact. "Where? I don't see anything."

"You wouldn't, lover of carrion." Judging from the sound of his voice, Cezer was standing slightly to the right and in front of him. "It's directly ahead of us, right in our path."

Taj strained to see. "Is it the eyelid finally blinking back?"

"Use your bird brain," Samm admonished his friend. "The light is appearing in front of us. Unless we have become badly turned around, that means it's coming from the east. Since it emerged from the south and blinked its way northward, if the eyelid was retracting, then any first light we detect should appear to our north."

"It's blue," Mamakitty announced encouragingly. "Naturally it would be blue."

"That's strange." Cezer had to squint, even cat-sharp vision needing a moment to readjust from the total darkness. "There seem to be multiple sources."

The pale blue phosphorescence advancing to meet them was not a consequence of any gargantuan blink. Instead, it revealed itself on a much more modest scale. It wiggled and writhed and was streaked with dark patches that did not glow. Though faint by comparison with daylight, or even the reflection of the moon, in the otherwise complete blackness it produced enough illumination to reveal the absence of eyes and the presence of teeth: short, ugly, serrated triangular teeth that lined the rim of a circular mouth equipped for gripping and sucking.

"Not negwens," Oskar whispered unnecessarily, "or vrorvels, or like anything else we've seen."

The nearest of the blue worm-shapes suddenly lunged in his direction. He had barely enough time to draw his sword and swing wildly, striking the serpentine blueness just behind a gaping fist-size maw of a mouth. Phosphorescent blue liquid fountained from the gash. Some of it landed on Oskar's thighs and feet. It dripped down his legs, flickering as if blue fireflies had been glued to his clothing. Gradually it faded away to become one again with the darkness.

Wounded, the surprised worm had drawn back. As it did so, another and then another, each equally lambent, equally grotesque, emerged from the granular surface underlying the warm optic fluid, corkscrewing their way upward from below.

"It's another kind of parasite that lives in the Eye. But this one lives in the body of it, in the flesh. Or in whatever it is we're walking on that passes for flesh. Our presence must be drawing them out. They must emerge only in darkness, when the Eye is shut." Having observed the attack on his companion, a tense Cezer had drawn his own weapon. "By the look of those fangs, I'll bet it usually preys upon other parasites."

"We're not parasites." Watching the approach of the ghostly phosphorescent blue shapes, Oskar held his sword at the ready. The blade pulsed with fading blue light from the blood of whatever it was he had cut. "Maybe they'll see that we're not their usual prey and leave us alone."

"Oh, let's bet our lives on that assumption, shall we?" An apprehensive Taj held one of his knives loosely out in front of him. "You march up to the nearest one, Oskar, and identify yourself. The rest of us will wait here so we can properly gauge its confused response."

One of the huge worms raised its forward half out of the optic fluid and began swaying from side to side, examining them with sensory organs that were not eyes. When it dropped back down into the supportive liquid, a second worm promptly repeated the scrutiny. Mamakitty counted half a dozen of them, each bigger and thicker through the middle than Samm had been in his original body. *Much* bigger.

"We've killed negwen and other parasites." Silhouetted against the wriggling inimical bluishness, she held her sword out in front of her. "We can kill these as well."

"Uh-huh," Cezer murmured skeptically, "sure we can."

Cocoa whirled on him. "Must you always be so cursed negative!"

"I'll be as negative as I please when it pleases me to be so," he shot back.

Goosed by a mixture of fear and anger, her voice rose precipitately. "Well, I'm sick of it! Stand and fight or shut up and run, but show some faith!"

His expression thoughtful, Oskar said sharply, "Do that again."

Taken aback, both curser and cursed glanced uncomprehendingly in his direction. "Do what again?" Cocoa asked him.

"Jump up and down violently," he told her. "Yell if you want to also, but jump up and down."

"Look here," muttered the swordsman, "she already curses me plenty. She doesn't need any encouragement from you."

"And you," Oskar replied calmly while keeping an eye on the advancing blue worms, "do the same. Mamakitty, you too."

The three cat-folk exchanged looks of bewilderment. "We're missing something here, aren't we?" Cocoa finally asked the dog-man.

"When you were shouting your angriest at Cezer," Oskar explained, "your hair was flying all over the place. When cats do that, hair invariably goes everywhere. Don't you remember? A number of Master Evyndd's visitors had to do their business with him outside, on the front landing— because of you three." Cezer eyed Cocoa uncomprehendingly, but a look of understanding was beginning to dawn on Mamakitty's face.

"That's right!" Taj chirped. "Oskar's right. I once heard a visitor say that there was nothing in the world so irritating and upsetting as cat hair." He waved his hands at the verbal combatants. "Jump up and down, like Oskar says. Move around, shake your heads, fluff your fur—what's left of it."

Though still uncertain, Mamakitty and Cocoa complied as best they could; running their hands through their long locks and shaking their heads. Reluctantly, Cezer joined them.

"A fine state of affairs for a first-rate swordsman: reduced to fighting with curls." Head bent forward, he pushed his fingers through his blue-gold locks again and again. In the phosphorescence cast by the worms, Oskar could see individual strands flying from all three of his feline companions.

A second worm struck at his legs, and he used his sword to repel it. The circular fanged mouth recoiled, then advanced anew; searching for an opening, for a route around the sharp object that was obstructing its path, for a way to sink its tenacious teeth into the soft meat it sensed close at hand.

Then the mouth contracted violently, closing like a sphincter. Drawing back, the worm appeared to hesitate, hovering before the tense dog-man.

And then it sneezed.

It sneezed so violently it blew blue goo all over Oskar's legs and feet. It continued to sneeze until it lay twitching and convulsing in the water, vomiting blue froth. Watching it, Oskar felt a tickle in his nostrils himself. He fought it down, successfully. After all, he had been forced to coexist with three cats ever since he was a pup. But having seen the violent reaction and consequent misery suffered by some of the Master's more sensitive visitors, he found himself almost feeling sorry for the carnivorous worms.

Excitement lent energy to the travelers' efforts once they

saw that the limited amount of cat fur was having an effect on their attackers. How it was affecting the creatures they did not know, nor did they particularly care. It need not make sense to be effective. As he brushed out his long hair, Cezer marveled at the results. He breathed cat hair every day, and it had never bothered *him*.

It was certainly disconcerting the worms. In their aqueous environment, Oskar mused, the poor creatures had probably never encountered anything half so irritating. One by one they twisted their murderous foreparts around, thrust them forward and down in a powerful burrowing motion, and sneezed their way back to the depths from which they had emerged. Blue coils vanished, vanquished by something as simple as the tiny strands that caught in their throats and tickled, and itched, and scratched, and prickled . . .

Oskar hurriedly took a long swallow of soothing water from the small bag he carried on his back.

"Look!" Now it was Taj's turn to point: not because his vision had grown suddenly more acute than that of his companions, but because he happened to be gazing in the right direction when the phenomenon manifested itself.

Off to the north, light had begun to reappear. It swept toward them as if an invisible hand had impishly accelerated the clock that governed the world. It was, in fact, caused by a retraction of the Eyelid of the Beholder that was both abrupt and unexpected.

But not necessarily, as Mamakitty was quick to point out, mysterious.

"It's the fur we've been shedding! Not only did it drive off the worms, it's irritating the Eye!" Whirling on Cezer, she suddenly grabbed his hair and pulled as hard as she could. His eyes blazed with anger.

"You stupid, mindless sack of rodent guts! What do you

think you're doing?" He broke off. A grimly grinning Mamakitty had one hand thrust skyward, pointing.

"Oh," Cezer mumbled. "Oh yeah, right." Reaching out, he began tugging at her hair, tugging loose strands that would not otherwise have come loose by themselves. Nearby, Cocoa pulled at her own head. Oskar considered offering to help, but was not entirely sure his offer would be taken in the proper spirit. Instead, he stood back and watched as the three cat-folk plucked fur from their own heads and flung it skyward.

Their fur-flinging efforts seemed to be bearing fruit. The Eyelid continued to retract. Not wishing to appear standoffish, he pulled out a few clutches of his own hair and added it to the mix. Samm had no fur to fling, and Taj's would in all likelihood prove no more irritating than a handful of feathers.

They kept at it until the Eyelid had withdrawn, insofar as they could see to the south, completely. Once again, blue sky splotched with blue clouds shone overhead. Once more, the way eastward was open not only to access but to view.

"Let's not waste time here." Mamakitty started forward at a quick trot. "We don't know when the Eye will become irritated again and return to blink back blackness over this kingdom. We need to make the best time we can and the best use possible of the light that's been returned to us!"

"Everyone, eastward at the gallop!" Cezer tried to follow in Mamakitty's wake. "You can stop pulling my fur now, Cocoa."

She slowly released him. "So I can. What a pity."

The swordsman blinked. "What did you say?"

"I said, it's a pity that I don't have four legs anymore. I could scout on ahead and search out the best route."

"There is no best route. This kingdom is all flat and wet and shallow, like it is right here." Arms swinging loosely at his sides, he eyed his friend uncertainly. "Are you sure that's what you said?"

"Certainly." In lieu of four legs, Cocoa had been granted a certain suave volubility that complemented her conspicuous beauty.

"If the Eyelid comes back, we'll just fling some more hair." Oskar was exulting both in the discovery of their new collective power (such as it was) and the return to open skies and freedom. His strong legs strode easily through the shallows, carrying him forward.

"I'm not sure we can rely on that to save us again." As always, Mamakitty had second thoughts even about proven triumphs. "The next time we irritate it, instead of blinking away the annoyance, the Eye might try to scratch it."

"Scratch it?" A querulous Cezer gestured at the flat shallow sea of optic fluid through which they were jogging. "With what?"

"Do you want to find out?" she responded pointedly.

After giving this due thought, the swordsman made a conscious effort to lengthen his stride.

The Eye did not blink again. Nor were they further troubled by sinuous blue worms taut of body and sharp of tooth. Such was the inherent power of unchained cat hair. No negwens manifested themselves, nor any vrorvels, and certainly not any thweens. That was just as well. None of the travelers were very happy with the thweens at that moment, and might well have made a quick meal of any who had presented themselves.

They set (unirritated) eyes on their long-sought-after final destination well before they reached it. After the comparatively flat lands they had fought so hard to cross, the towers of the Kingdom of Purple were first a ragged dark line on the horizon. As they drew steadily nearer, these uneven outlines resolved themselves into a breathtaking vista of amethystine spires, weblike walkways, lofty buttresses, and soaring crenellated structures that sparkled like crystal in glorious lavender sunshine.

"At last." Mamakitty's pace slowed as much from exhaustion as wonder. "There were times when I wondered if we would ever set eyes on it—the Kingdom of Purple!"

"It's magnificent." Cocoa's gaze scanned the extensive skyline of the vast metropolis. "Prettier and much more developed than anyplace we've visited so far."

"Don't be so quick to bestow admiration." The long run through the water had been especially hard on Taj's slender frame. Despite his wary admonition, the realization that their goal was now in sight restored some of his spent strength. "It may look appealing from out here, but who knows what awaits within? It might be ruled by a murderous despot, or beset by a plague, or off limits to outsiders."

"And you might try keeping your mouth shut once in a while." Cezer was high-stepping tiredly through the water. "But you won't."

Taj shrugged apologetically. "It's my way. Birds chatter constantly, and canaries more so than most. Being recast in human form doesn't change my nature."

Oskar was not as ardent as his companions in expressing admiration for the looming wonders of the next kingdom. For one thing, he was too tired. His legs throbbed, and he was sick of being wet all the time. It would require an effort of will to avoid lying down and rolling luxuriously in the first patch of dry dirt they encountered upon leaving the water. For another, he could not make himself relax: not until they were completely clear of the salty, viscous, shallow sea that covered the Eye.

That blessed moment arrived soon enough. Ahead of them, a beach beckoned, teasing the expectant travelers into a final wild sprint. When at last they collapsed on the sun-warmed sands, out of the Eye and thus also of its multitude of parasites and threatening lid, they could finally rest. Even Taj, flanked by low purplish scrub, found himself overcome by the realization of what they had accomplished. They had traversed the entire rainbow, crossed every kingdom of light, and now found themselves on the periphery of the last one, within reach of their ultimate objective.

Provided that the lecherous Captain Covalt had known what he was talking about.

The indomitable Mamakitty was all for pressing on into the city, from which the muted cacophony of urban life echoed down to the beach. She was outvoted by her companions. Everyone was worn out from their long run. Even Samm had stretched out as far as his present form would allow in order to soak up the rejuvenating sun.

"This evening," Cezer told her as he lay on his back between two oddly entwined purple bushes. "We'll enter the city this evening. Don't you think we've earned a few hours of rest?"

Hands on hips, she stared sternly down at him. Cocoa reposed nearby, and Oskar not far from her. From time to time his body would twitch, and one foot would kick lavender sand high in the air for no other reason than that it could.

"Back in the Gowdlands, people and animals are dying," she reminded the swordsman.

The look of utter contentment he wore faded slightly. "I know that as well as you, stiff-tail, and am as sorry for it. But we can only do what we can do. If we push ourselves too hard, we run the risk of injuring ourselves, of damaging these human bodies we have been granted, or of making a fatal mistake not out of ignorance but from weariness. There are times, Mamakitty-cat, when rest is as important as food." He patted the sand next to him, on the side away from where Cocoa was lying.

"Lie down, why don't you, and for a little while at least, put your mind at ease—if you can."

Still anxious to be on their way, she hesitated. Then she sat down, reluctantly, and stretched out. The sensation of the fine, warm granules against her overstressed back and legs was not simply relaxing: it was positively sensuous. Against her better judgment, she allowed herself to be seduced by sun and sand.

Come evening, there was not one among them who did not feel better, indeed revitalized, from the afternoon spent lazing on the beach. There on the sand, they shared a meal that for the first time in days did not involve holding food and water clear of the shallow saltiness that was the Eye. Oskar didn't even mind the occasional grain of sand that crept into his makeshift sandwich of dry flatbread and jerked fish. How he longed for a bone, any kind of bone, to chew on!

The temptation, following the meal and given the sun's downward path, was to remain where they were and sleep the sleep of the just until the morrow. But Mamakitty would have none of it. She had struck a bargain and held her silence on the matter until evening. That time was nigh, and they would use it to make an entry into the city.

"Besides," she encouraged her companions, "if there are any guards on duty, we will catch them at the end of their shift, when their attention is wavering and their principal interest lies in relinquishing their posts."

But there were no guards. Every couple of hundred yards, a vaulted purple archway granted unimpeded ingress to the metropolis. Beneath the ceremonial arches there were no tall gates of wood or metal; nothing to bar travelers from entering or restrain citizens from leaving. For that matter, the splendidly decorated wall the arches connected, with its ornate bas-reliefs of contented folk of many kinds, was low enough for a determined visitor to scale.

Several much taller structures rose on the other side of the wall, overlooking both the city proper and the beach that marked the line where the Kingdom of Purple met the Kingdom of Blue. As the silent travelers wandered in through the nearest arch, they saw that these structures boasted porches that overhung the street. Strands of fine linen and embroidered clothing hung from lines that stretched from building to building like so many very personal pennants from the rigging of a ship. The cobbled paving they soon encountered was pleasantly dry underfoot. For this Oskar was inordinately grateful. He had seen enough of water, even shallow water, to last him a lifetime.

Or at least, he reminded himself, until they had to recross the sea of optic fluid that covered the Eye on their way back.

They had advanced only a short distance into the conurbation when he felt the hair beginning to stiffen on the back of his neck. The cause of this follicular erectation was twofold: first, because of what he was seeing around him, and second, because he no longer had that many hairs on the back of his neck.

Mamakitty was staring back at him. Staring back at him out of the eyes of a deceptively muscular, mature, female black cat. Prominent as ever was the white patch that ran from her nose back toward her left eye. Her ears twitched as she spoke. The hair on top of her head had been noticeably thinned.

"By the tail of the all-consuming Great Tiger, you're a *dog* again!"

"Look down at yourself," he advised her. "If it's a re-transmogrification you're referring to, I'm not alone."

Murmurs of astonishment, agitation, and not a little fear rose from the group. They stood there in the street, all of them except Samm (who had nothing to stand with) and examined themselves. Without warning, without sign or sorceral signification, without dazzle of light or thunder of word, they had reverted to their antecedent animal forms. Their bulky human attire lay in limp piles around them. All that remained of the miraculous transformation that had been elicited by the Master Evyndd's passing was the power of speech. Unsurprisingly, it was Cezer who was first to employ it in his restored feline form. His familiar voice summarized the confused emotions that were racing through them one and all.

"What," the handsome, thickly furred, reddish blond cat ventured through jaws that had broken the back of many an unlucky rodent, "the hell are we going to do now?"

SEVENTEEN

This time, not even Mamakitty had an answer. One thing they could not do, it was generally agreed, was allow themselves to be confronted in their present animal form by the still unseen inhabitants of this kingdom. At least, not until they had become more acquainted with those as yet unseen inhabitants, and had learned something of the lay of the land. There were places, Oskar recalled Master Evyndd saying during their visit to the city of Zelevin, where animals unassociated with humans were rounded up and disposed of without a thought, like trash. While the attitude toward strays might be quite different in the city that dominated the Kingdom of Purple, they could take no chances.

Needing time to collect their thoughts, they decided to return to the beach. Oskar and his feline companions were glad to be back on all fours, and Samm could slither forward at a surprising speed. But of them all, diminutive Taj was the most relieved. In the course of the bewildering shape reversion he had gone from being the weakest and slowest among them to the fastest.

Skimming along overhead, he scouted the route back

the way they had come. It was still devoid of citizens, still deserted. Here on the edge of the great city, it appeared, evening was not a time for visiting the border between kingdoms. Or perhaps they had simply been lucky enough to come ashore at a location that was little frequented by the inhabitants.

They raced back through the same arch that had admitted them. Back on the sand, the usually surefooted Oskar unaccountably tripped. He went down in an unceremonious tumble, head over heels. So did every one of his four-legged companions.

They were human again.

Spitting sand, Oskar looked up in response to a pained moan from nearby. Taj was sitting up and holding his head. It was fortunate for the canary, Oskar realized, that he had not been flying too high at the moment of remetamorphosis. The soft sand had cushioned the impact of his fall from the sky, and the songster was only bruised.

"If this kind of rapid transformation is to occur periodically," Samm surmised gravely as he brushed sand from his massive form, "life could become exceedingly confusing."

Cocoa's nude female shape stood silhouetted against the setting sun as she straightened and looked back into the Kingdom of Purple. "Something acted upon us as soon as we entered the city. Some kind of permanent enchantment that is attached to this place. If we go back inside, we might change back all over again."

"Then we have a new problem." Wincing, Taj rose. "I don't see how as our animal selves we can hope to obtain the white light. No one will pay any attention to the demands of a bunch of animals, even if we can make ourselves and our wants understood."

"The magic that returned us to our natural forms left us

with the power of speech," Mamakitty observed solemnly. "If that is a constant, then we will be able to explain to the citizens of this place what it is that we want. No matter our appearance, we have to go and find what we have come for. Don't be so disparaging of your natural selves." Seeing the discouragement in their faces, she tried to cheer them. "There are times when cats and dogs can go where humans cannot." She nodded in Samm's direction. "A snake can explore small places, and a bird can give us an overview no human could hope to match. Two legs or four, we'll get what we came for—and leave with it. I've not come all this way to be dissuaded by something as simple as a little change of shape."

Taj stared at her. "You have a way, Mamakitty, of rendering the most profound developments as plain and uncomplicated as a morning's bath. It so happens that I hate that."

"But she's right." Burly and hirsute, a naked Oskar stood gazing at the arch beneath which they had so recently passed in haste. "If we can find friendly scholars within the kingdom, maybe they can revive our human forms permanently."

A naked Cezer eyed his friend thoughtfully. "Is that what you want, Oskar? To have this body type made permanent? To be a human for all time?"

It was a question Oskar, along with every one of his companions, had been forced to contemplate ever since the miraculous transformation that had taken place in Master Evyndd's dwelling. He thought of lazy summer days spent doing nothing but lolling in the sun, of burying bones only to extract them later, at leisure, when they had been properly aged. Of rolling in piles of leaves, or inhaling the scent of a wandering bitch in heat. He thought of all that, and none of it accompanied by a care in the world.

"No," he replied finally. "I'd rather be a dog."

"Even though," Cocoa asked him in a voice he could not quite place, "it would mean that we couldn't talk to one another again, and would have to communicate once more only through touches and smells, barks and meows?"

Maybe he replied without thinking. Or maybe he was simply voicing the truth of how he felt without considering other, previously inconceivable, possibilities.

"I would miss being able to communicate with the rest of you this way. I would miss the ability to talk. But dammit, I'm a *dog*, not a human. I *like* walking on four legs instead of having to balance on two. I miss my full sense of smell, and sight, and—other things. Maybe one day I'll have the chance to be one again. But not here. Not in this place. My home, our home, is the Fasna Wyzel, in the Gowdlands. If the Fates decree it, I'll be a dog there, and a contented one, but not until the evil of the Khaxan Mundurucu has been snuffed out and the color they have stolen is returned to the land. That much the Master Evyndd charged us with, and that much will I do before I worry about the matter of what kind of body I really want for myself."

It was quiet on the beach. Embarrassed, Oskar realized he had been pontificating. It was most unlike him. He would have wagged his tail reassuringly, but the one possessed by humans was not well designed for such animated demonstrations.

Mamakitty finally broke the hushed silence. "If we're going to do this thing, we'd best be about it. If we don't hide the clothes that we left behind on the street when we changed back, some enterprising citizens are sure to help themselves to the unclaimed booty. We might have need of those garments again."

A wary Oskar headed slowly in the direction of the arch.

"Funny how quickly you become used to something like hands." He peered down at his fingers. "On the other hand, so to speak, I surely do miss having four feet to run upon. Having now spent some time in this form, it's a wonderment to me how human people keep from always running into one another."

Cezer paced alongside him, neither insulting nor joking now. "I never cease to wonder, my friend, how it is that humans can even stand, let alone keep from falling over."

"And without a tail to help balance them," Cocoa added, unaware as ever of the transmogrified attractiveness of her own.

This time they were not taken by surprise when, upon entering a short distance into the city, they once again reverted to their animal selves. Much to everyone's relief their human garb, which they would need again when they left the Kingdom of Purple, remained undisturbed in the same scattered piles where it had been abandoned on the empty street. As he watched his friends drag and push the clothing into a small opening beneath one structure, Taj reflected from on high that they were fortunate they had not entered the metropolis via a main thoroughfare, where their brazenly unclothed appearance might have attracted more than mere comment. It took all of them, working together, to move Samm's great axe into an open culvert.

Taking care to memorize the location so they could be certain to find it again, they gathered together in a darkening purple-stained alley to consider how best to proceed. Beautiful strange though it was, as they continued to advance deeper into the metropolis Oskar was leery of the towering purple structures and the distant sounds that reached them. Completely at ease in the gathering darkness, the cats and Samm the snake were less intimidated.

Only the sunlight-loving Taj shared his canine companion's growing anxiety.

"Relax, Oskar." How strange, Cezer felt, to be walking once again on four legs instead of two. How effortlessly it all came back. "This is a place of beauty, not danger. I can feel it." He grinned, showing sharp teeth. "Cat-sense, you know. We're overdue to explore a kingdom that's not over-run with dangers." He halted suddenly, every muscle alert, yellow eyes fixed on a pile of wooden crates stacked neatly against one wall.

"What is it?" Taj whispered uneasily from above. "The danger you say you didn't sense?"

"No." With Cezer advancing in stealthy cat-fashion to-ward the crates, it was a barely audible Cocoa who replied. "Dinner."

The swordsman-cat leaped in perfect silence, his forepaws coming down on a small purple-gray shape that tried, unsuccessfully, to avoid the lethal furry pounce. There was a short, sharp squeak, a soft yowl of elation from Cezer, followed by a stream of invective that was as tren-chant as it was unexpected.

"You blithering idiot!" the tiny voice protested accus-ingly. "You couthless furry imbecile! What do you think you're doing?"

"I—" The astonishment in Cezer's voice was plain.

A flurry of diminutive protests joined the first, shaping a miniature chorus of outrage. "Let go of him! . . . Are you out of your kitty-catty mind? . . . Who do you think you are? . . . Release him this *instant!*"

Oskar and the others approached tentatively. The source of the combustible complaining was immediately apparent, as was the source of Cezer's incredulity.

Trapped between his front paws was a mouse. It was a perfectly ordinary-looking mouse—if one discounted its cultivated gestures, scandalized expression, and the way it was furiously shaking one finger in its captor's face. Surrounding it were half a dozen other mice, a pair of enraged rats, and one slightly somnolent but obviously irked vole. Tiny fists and feet hammered on Cezer's forelegs and flanks in an attempt to get him to release his captive.

"I think," murmured Mamakitty, "that all is not what it seems in this place, and that you had best let him go, Cezer."

"Let him go?" Though more than a little stunned by the nature of his prey's resistance, not to mention that of its friends, he was reluctant. "I don't care if he *does* talk. Dinner is dinner."

"I'm nobody's dinner, hairball-for-brains!" Despite Cezer's words, the mouse remained defiant rather than fearful. "Do you want my friends to call the Night Guard? Where are you from, anyway? You act like you just wandered in off the beach."

"As a matter of fact . . . ," Samm began slowly, slightly slurring his ess.

"I might've guessed." Folding both forelegs across its tiny chest, the mouse glared at Cezer while tapping one hind foot impatiently against the pavement.

"'Night Guard.'" Oskar put a cautioning forepaw on Cezer's leg. "I don't care for the sound of that."

"Let it go." Cocoa had come up on the tomcat's other side. "We can always catch more later."

"You'll do nothing of the sort," the mouse declared firmly. "You really are new here, aren't you?" In response to Mamakitty's nod, the rodent sighed. "All right. I was looking forward to a nice, relaxing evening, but I can see that I'm going to spend it rebutting ignorance instead. Not that I have any choice. It's every citizen of the kingdom's responsibility to take new arrivals in hand and explain the realities of life to them."

Reluctantly, Cezer separated his paws. The mouse took a moment to preen and straighten his fur before dismissing his friends. "It's all right now," he assured them. "They're barbarians, but some of them, at least, have enough sense to listen to reason." As he said this, he glared accusingly at Cezer. The big cat growled menacingly but kept his paws to himself.

Slowly the gang of small rodents scurried or hopped away, vanishing back into the complex of crates. Squinting at them, Oskar now saw that these were riddled with neatly incised doorways and windows. Reasonably content with his appearance once more, the mouse sat down and considered the assemblage of cats, dog, bird, and snake arraigned before him.

"I'm Smegden. I was out for a breath of fresh evening air when my walk was so *rudely* interrupted." Again he scowled at Cezer, and again the cat ground his teeth and remained where he was. It was something, Oskar mused, to see a mouse scowl.

"This is the Kingdom of Purple."

"We already knew that," growled Cezer.

"How clever of you," Smegden responded without hesitation. "This kingdom is unique in that it is home to intelligence of every kind. All are welcome here, no matter how simple or low." It was fortunate he did not glance at Cezer as he said this, as the cat was just about at the end of his patience with this mouse, his companions' equivocation notwithstanding.

"All animals who arrive in the kingdom gain the power of unified speech. Humans who wash up on the beach or otherwise make their way here are reduced to their animal natures. This is the consequence of a protective enchantment enjoined by the kingdom's original inhabitants, the Folk of Faerie and Fancy. Ogres, imps, elves, gnomes, trolls, gremlins, faeries fine and foul, hobgoblins, sprites— whereas elsewhere they exist in intermittent conflict with one another, and under the burden of much disbelief in their corporeal selves—here they thrive together in peace and contentment. The Kingdom of Purple is a utopia for all who have been displaced, be they animal, human, or enchanted. So it is for my kind as well as for you and yours."

Oskar looked thoughtful. "If it's such a paradise, then why the need for something called a *Night Guard?*"

Preceded by his whiskers, Smegden turned in the dog's direction. "There are always one or two malcontents, even in Purple. Anyone can have a bad day. Even an elf. Even," he added, this time looking but not glaring in Cezer's direction, "a cat."

"A cat who's still mighty hungry." Having come to see the obstreperous rodent in a different light, Cezer refrained from licking his chops. It could have been considered impolite.

"Cezer's not alone." It still took an effort for Cocoa to see the loquacious mouse as a friend and guide instead of a quick, crunchy snack. "How do you get along here with other cats? Not to mention hawks and owls, and wolves, and buck-toothed goblins. Does everyone become a vegetarian?"

"That would be no paradise," Samm hissed. "Snakes can't eat fruit. It's the pits."

"Obviously," Smegden informed them, "none of you has ever heard of, much less encountered, meatfruit."

Oskar gawked at the diminutive elucidator. "We've seen and encountered much in our travels, but don't count anything called *meatfruit* among the marvels we've come upon."

The mouse nodded understandingly, his minuscule black nose bobbing up and down. "Then it's time that omission was remedied. Follow me."

They had walked perhaps half a block, and traveled deeper into both the city and the night, when Cezer extended a paw. "Come on, come on—up on my back. Otherwise, unless this place you're taking us to lies right around the next corner, I'll starve to death before we get there. And if you say 'giddyap' even one time, I'll bite your greasy, naked tail off at the butt."

With a curt nod, Smegden allowed himself to be lifted up and placed on Cezer's neck. The blond ruff there was so thick the mouse had to use both tiny forefeet to part it so that he could see where they were going. Tongue lolling, a panting Oskar would have offered their guide the ride had not the impatient Cezer beat him to it.

"Turn right here." Smegden pointed confidently. Beneath him, Cezer remained a cooperative but truculent steed. Noticing Cocoa smirking in his direction, he growled warningly.

"If you ever tell anyone in the woods when we get back to the Fasna Wyzel that I was a mount for a mouse, I'll personally take an inch off your left ear."

She nodded gravely in response to this threat, even as her smirk grew wider still.

"If many of the animals here were people elsewhere," Mamakitty inquired curiously of their diminutive pathfinder, "what were you?"

Smegden shrugged very small shoulders. "Does it matter?"

"No," Mamakitty admitted. "I was just curious."

"Of course you are. How else could you be?" Without

answering her question, he launched into a description of the building they were passing.

When the last lavender rays of the setting sun finally vanished, it was the turn of the nocturnal inhabitants of the city to emerge from their daybeds. Meows and whistles and hisses of delight arose from the impressed visitors as the ethereal beauty of the mystical metropolis's citizens began to manifest itself.

By their nature favoring the darkness, those denizens who now variously strolled or flew forth from their dwellings generated their own light. There were glowing faerie-folk who zipped to and fro on wings of membranous luminescence, heavyset hunched-over throgs and ogres who pulsed with the intensity of their respective gruntings. Effulgent gnomes soared high on the backs of cooperative griffins whose wingbeats flung loose sparks with every powerful downbeat, and sprites communed in clusters like bunches of prattling phosphorescent grapes. Within the omnipresent purple hue, the variety and intensity of color was startling, varying from the lightest and most delicate shade of lavender to a deep Tyrolean tint that was almost black.

The temptation on the part of Cezer, Cocoa, and Mamakitty to take energetic swipes at the vast plethora of darting, plunging shapes verged on the irresistible. They restrained their natural instincts, as one must in such a place. Indiscriminately swatting down commuting residents as if they were so many mindless fireflies would be a poor way to endear themselves to a citizenry whose help they might need.

A pageant of pixies puttered past them, all hummingbird wings and uppity attitude, one adult and a couple of dozen youngsters. One of the latter flew teasingly into Cezer's ear, causing him to emit a yowl of surprise. Before he could raise a paw to scratch at the offended organ, the adolescent flier had backed out to rejoin her troupe. The cat was not amused.

"Pay no attention," his Lilliputian rider advised him. "What else can you expect from a pixie?"

"I'd like to see her laugh like that after I'd torn her wings off." Cezer reluctantly contented himself with a snarl in the direction of the rapidly retreating aerial troupe. From between his ears, Smegden leaned forward to gaze disapprovingly down into one yellow eye.

"*That'll* endear you to the locals."

"How much farther?" Cocoa asked. Though she was as entranced as her companions by the nocturnal beauty of the city, the scenery had done nothing to assuage the emptiness in her belly. It did not help that their guide was looking more and more like the tip of a furry brochette with ears.

"Just ahead," Smegden assured her, entirely innocent of her envisionings. "Around this block."

"What do all these enchanted folk do?" Oskar wondered. "Being enchanted, I wouldn't think there's all that much to occupy them."

"Oh, but there is," their diminutive guide informed him. "There are old spells to maintain and new ones to propound, transcendental interstices to be filled and otherworldly gates to be oiled. Interdimensional portals need regular upkeep lest shards of the discarnate flake off, and the dry cleaners hereabouts are kept busy around the clock. All that ephemera and evanescence can't be kept immaculate by charm alone, you know. Everyone here has a job."

"Even you and your squeaky friends?" Taj asked from above.

"Especially me and my friends." Smegden strained to see over and through Cezer's miniature mane. "For one thing, spells alone aren't very effective against bugs. Even at their most cultivated, cockroaches are never enchanting. Tasty, though."

Oskar wrinkled his whiskers. "No, thanks. I'll take a bowl of nice, fresh carrion any day."

"You won't have to." The mouse gestured. "There's the Commons, just ahead."

Oskar had thought the vast forest of Fasna Wyzel the most beautiful place he had ever seen, and not just because it was his home. But the Grand Commons of the Kingdom of Purple surpassed in every way the ancient woods through which he had roamed as both pup and adult.

An implausible diversity of trees shimmered before them—not in the moonlight that was rising, but by their own internal lights. Though every tree-glow and leaf-light was a variation on the all-pervasive purple, they nonetheless managed to give the impression of being kissed here with gold, there with silver, and elsewhere with a multiplicity of shades the travelers had not seen gathered together in one place since they had left their home and fallen into the rainbow.

Within the trees played the nocturnal animals of the kingdom. No enchanted folk here; only possums and sugar gliders, bats and big-eared lemurs, a variety of snakes and frogs, and all manner of night-loving creatures.

Their guide directed them to an eccentric hardwood with three conjoined trunks. In addition to enormous flaring flowers, it bore on its branches long, thin, tubular fruit. Piles of this lay on the ground, tempting the travelers. Hopping down from Cezer's neck, Smegden implored them to restrain their hunger for one more moment.

"Don't eat that stuff. It's last week's droppings. Let me get you some fresh." Turning and craning his neck, he called up into the tree. For so small a voice, it carried surprisingly far.

A couple of sleepy squirrels appeared. Though roused from their hollow, they grudgingly complied with Smegden's request. Apparently, the mouse was a person of local importance out of all proportion to his size. Oskar remembered how quickly a host of the rodent's comrades had hopped to his aid.

Working rapidly and efficiently, the two squirrels chewed through the stems that secured several mature fruits to the branches of three adjoining trees. These plunged to the neatly manicured grass below and bounced a couple of times before stopping. Hopping over to the nearest, Smegden took a bite out of one end and chewed reflectively, a minuscule gourmet sampling the latest product of an entirely natural kitchen.

"Not bad tonight." He gestured at Cezer. "Have a taste."

The cat was reluctant. "Rodents are like dogs; they'll eat anything."

"Hey!" Oskar protested.

The swordsman-cat ignored him. "It doesn't look very appetizing. It looks like a vegetable. I hate vegetables."

"I'll make you a deal." A confident Smegden helped himself to another bite and continued speaking with his mouth full. "If you don't like it, you can take a bite out of *me*."

"Now that's a proposition I can wholeheartedly embrace." Padding forward, Cezer put one paw on the fallen fruit to steady it and bit down tentatively with his strong jaws. As his friends looked on expectantly, he chewed a moment, then swallowed. When he looked back at them, he was smiling as broadly as his cat face would allow.

"Tastes like chicken!" he chortled delightedly, and dove without hesitation back into the elongated pod.

Soon they were all gorging themselves, quest and questions temporarily set aside as they wallowed in the unexpected flavors of the miraculous fruit. The one Cezer handily devoured without assistance did indeed taste like chicken. So did several of the other fruits from the same tree. But those from its neighbor possessed the flavor of fresh beef, while the fruit of the third had a distinctive whiff of fresh fish. By the time they decided they had had enough, not one among them retained a flat belly—Samm being the most prominently engorged of all. Though he had fought to restrain himself, it was in the nature of serpents to eat until they could hardly slither. As for the decidedly uncarnivorous Taj, he had ignored the meat-flavored fruit in favor of the many seeds readily available in the surrounding grass.

Thus most excellently stuffed, they left it to Oskar to consider what they should do next. "We must take some seeds of these trees home with us," he declared, following a resonant canine belch, "and plant them in the yard of Master Evyndd's house. But that's for later. For now, for tonight, where can we sleep?"

Smegden gestured expansively—or as expansively as his diminutive arms would allow. "Why not spend the night here, in the Grand Commons? It's what many animal folk do." Turning, he indicated the lacy towers and spiraling buildings nearby. "Though seemingly capacious, many of these structures are honeycombed with small rooms and chambers fit only for enchanted folk—and sometimes the likes of me. You lot would not be comfortable, squeezing your way through narrow corridors while enveloped in thick odors most strange and peculiar." He trotted away from the base of the fresh fish tree.

"Here you can stretch out and be comfortable. There is plenty of room, the climate is ever amenable, and there is lots to eat. Your fellow animal folk will not bother you." His tiny face wrinkled up in a grimace at the memory of an unpleasant smell. "Who wants to sleep in a troll tenement, anyway?"

Cocoa eyed the florid paths, paved with flat-faceted purple gems. Overhead, a wry and tasteful assortment of branches scattered the stars while the energetic chatter of tree-dwelling animal folk began to fade with the deepening of night. The temperature had not changed since they had arrived on the beach outside the city wall. It all seemed so benign, so accommodating, that it made her nervous. She told their guide as much.

"Oh, piffle!" Putting tiny hands on bulging hips, Smegden let out a squeak of a sigh. "Very well, then. I'll stay one night with you." He did not try to hide his irritation. "Will *that* put you at ease?"

"Substantially," a relieved Cocoa agreed. Though he had said nothing, she could see that Cezer was silently pleased with the mouse's offer. Nor did any of her other companions offer an objection to their guide's continued presence among them.

It was something to see Smegden curl up, utterly unafraid, next to the coiled bulk of Samm, a traditional predator. But the powerful constrictor was stuffed like a striped sausage with pounds of meatfruit and was already asleep, digesting silently. Given the quantity of food the serpent had just ingested, Oskar was grateful that snakes did not snore. Choosing a suitable tree, he paced half a dozen circles before settling down at its base, nose to tail. Cezer went off a little by himself, as did Cocoa, while Taj sought a suitably cozy branch on which to spend the night.

Mamakitty settled herself down next to the disheveled dog who was their nominal leader. Oskar tried to ignore her unblinking gaze, but one might as well hope to slip-slide into another dimension as avoid the stare of a determined cat.

"All right." He yawned, suddenly aware of how tired he really was. "What is it now, Miss Worry-whiskers?"

"This Kingdom of Purple is a beautiful and benign place."

"And that upsets you?" Dog or no, he could still raise a querulous eyebrow. Given the amount of gray fur attached to the flap of flesh in question, it was a gesture of some substance.

"No. If we're ever going to find the white light that we need to take back with us, this certainly does seem like the place—just as we were told long ago by that otherwise disagreeable Captain Covalt."

"Then what's your problem?" He yawned impressively, the yawn passing as a quiver down the entire length of his body to finally conclude with a twitch of his short tail.

"There are questions we avoided in the course of our journey that we can no longer put off. Suppose we find it? How do we acquire it? We have no money, and if we did, it most likely wouldn't be good here. Assuming that we do manage to obtain it, how do we transport it home? How do you package light?"

"With a pouch made of moonbeams, maybe. How should I know?" Trying not to sound too cross, he let his head flop back down on his crossed forepaws. "Can't we worry about it tomorrow?"

"That's what we've been doing for weeks. But I guess it will have to wait one day longer. Everyone else is already asleep." Raising her head slightly, she searched out each remaining member of their exhausted little party. "It's just that, so near to the goal we've fought so hard to reach, I find myself more fretful than ever."

"Fine," he told her. "Fret all you want. But I'm not worrying about anything, including the future of the world, until tomorrow." He managed a canine smile. "That's an advantage we dogs have over cats *and* humans. We don't suffer overmuch from stress. Except for purebreds, and I've always pitied them." Turning his head slightly and closing his eyes, he shut her out of his thoughts. If all her kind worried half as much as Mamakitty, he reflected sleepily, it was no wonder felines had so many internal problems.

His last glimpse was of the affable Smegden, comfortably curled up in one of Samm's brawny coils, indifferent to the proximity of powerful, fanged jaws that on another occasion might have devoured him as easily as a whale would swallow an eel.

EIGHTEEN

Oskar felt as if he awoke only moments later. But though he did not know the duration of the local night, it seemed unlikely that it should vary much from what they had encountered in other kingdoms. Overhead, the amethyst-hued sun was shining with a clarity born of crystal. It was not the shimmering sunshine that had awakened him, however, nor any prodding or chiding from his companions.

It was the music.

And such music! It spilled forth from thousands of throats, all chorusing together, not one out of tune—throats capable not only of imitating and surpassing the songs of humankind but of reproducing almost any harmony imaginable.

There must have been ten thousand bird-folk awakening in the trees of the Grand Commons, and their joyous hymn to the morning was truly something to behold.

Birds of paradise trilled sensuously alongside dozens of smaller songbird-folk. Cranes and crows supplied percussion, while macaws and parrots counterfeited human voices as perfectly as if they had possessed hands instead of wings.

The smaller birds provided woodwindlike accompaniment, while a rustling of raptors surged in counterpoint to the elegiac central motif.

Rolling onto his back on the soft grass and crunchy leaves, all four legs waving in the air, Oskar stretched and delighted in the majestic swell of music. Only after the magnificent overture to the sun had crescendoed and begun to fade, drifting away into the distance as soft as down from a newly fledged chick, did an exultant Taj glide down from his branch to greet his friends. He had been participating wholeheartedly in the concert.

"Did you hear it? Oh, did you hear, Oskar?" The jubilant canary hopped an ecstatic circle around an imaginary axis. "Wasn't it splendid? Wasn't it glorious?"

A familiar voice interrupted from nearby. "Doesn't this town let a visitor sleep?" Rising, a rested but exasperated Cezer stretched, digging his front claws purposefully into the ground, his chin scraping the grass between them.

"Always the complainer." Nearby, Cocoa had risen and was using her right paw to inspect a freshly fallen meatfruit. "Who's for breakfast?"

Gathering around a pile of suitable eats, they fell to discoursing freely among themselves while dining at their leisure. Smegden joined them, in no hurry to rush off before eating. Indeed, Oskar mused, there seemed to be no reason for animal folk to hurry anywhere in this relative paradise. What real work there was to be done fell within the province of the much more active enchanted ones.

"You know," mouthed Cezer, his cheeks bulging with the meatfruit of the moment as he ruminated reflectively, "this is a pretty nice place."

"Very nice," agreed Samm from somewhere within his coils.

"Exceedingly nice," Cocoa added unnecessarily.

"It's so nice," Cezer continued, "that we might consider staying here."

Oskar eyed his companion narrowly. "You mean, you might consider returning after we've carried the white light back to the Gowdlands."

Instead of meeting the dog's eyes, the golden feline contemplated the sky through branches heavy with lavender-tinged leaves and fruit. "Not exactly. I was thinking that this might be the most propitious possible ending to our journey."

"What about the inhabitants of the Gowdlands?" Mama-kitty's tone was accusing, but Cezer refused to back down.

"What about them? I know all of this was discussed earlier, but that was before we had risked our lives ten times over, and long before we knew a land such as the Kingdom of Purple existed outside the country of wishful thinking. What if our luck is running out? How many narrow escapes can we reasonably be expected to survive? This place has everything we could want: free food that falls from trees, clean air, pure water, and industrious enchanted folk to keep everything running smoothly. It's more than a refuge; it's a kind of heaven. A singularly purple heaven, to be sure, but a heaven nonetheless.

"As for the people of the Gowdlands, what did they ever do for us? I'm sorry they're suffering—I don't like to see anyone suffer. But to tell the truth, I feel no especial affection for them. They're humans; we're not."

"You were once," Oskar reminded him, "and can be again."

"Why?" This time Cezer raised his gaze to meet those of his friends. "From everything we've experienced and everything I remember from my life as a cat, humans have a tough time of it." He spread both forelegs as wide as his quadrupedal shape would allow. "I'm more used to being a cat than I am to being a man. This isn't such a bad way to spend one's life. Of course," he added thoughtfully, "if I was forced to spend it as a dog . . ."

Mamakitty stepped between them. "That isn't the point. We swore to carry out Master Evyndd's last wish, which was to aid those in need. What about *that*, Cezer?"

The tomcat looked uncomfortable. "Master Evyndd was a good person, even if he wasn't cat. But Master Evyndd is dead. We're not."

"So you think that cancels out the debt?" Oskar challenged him.

Cezer held his ground. "Spoken like a true dog. A fawning, slavishly affectionate, drool-dripping dog who'll cut off his left ear in return for a pat on the head."

Mamakitty spoke before an increasingly angry Oskar could reply. "There are among cats those for whom the word *loyalty* is not only for dogs."

Cocoa joined the discussion. "By my count, you owe Master Evyndd for about two thousand bowls of milk, a hundred and fifty pounds of meat, uncounted table scraps, assorted chunks of cheese, and enough catnip to stun a cougar. Have you no gratitude, no sense of honor?"

"*I* couldn't turn my back on the Master's last wish," Samm announced with finality.

Cezer glared at the python. "Do you even *have* a back? Oh, all right!" he hissed. "I refuse to have my honor as a cat impugned by a snake. But I think you're all mad." Turning, he trotted off toward a tree where some wallabies were playing ball with a coterie of meerkats and bonobos.

Oskar remembered the smallest member of their party. "Well," he asked the songster, "we haven't heard from you, Taj. What's your opinion?"

The canary pushed out his purplish yellow chest. "I owe Master Evyndd everything. If not for him I would be nothing more than a bird in a cage. I mean," he added quickly, "I would not have been given the opportunity to partici- pate in so important a journey."

Oskar nodded, then looked seriously at Cocoa. "Do you think maybe Cezer's right? That we should put aside our task and remain here?"

She shook her head, as pert in feline form as it had been in human guise. "What kind of animals would we be if we abandoned the one important undertaking we had ever been given? Not by a master: that's only a word. Myself, I al- ways thought of good Evyndd as a friend. A large, clumsy, ungraceful, but well-meaning friend." She nodded once. "I'll see this undertaking through to the end—for my friend."

"Spoken like a true cat," Mamakitty murmured admir- ingly. Pivoting, she presented her tail. Held high, the tip provided a comfortable perch for the smallest member of their expedition. "I'm sure that once we've located the white light, Cezer will realize where his loyalties lie and come to his senses."

"What 'senses'?" Cocoa growled. "The word doesn't apply to Cezer. *Pfft!* The only senses that cat possesses are base ones."

"Don't be too harsh on him," Taj told her. "This place calls strongly even to me." He punctuated his point with a brief but joyful burst of song. "The temptations are many."

She sniffed grudgingly, whiskers bobbing. "Then we'd best gather him up and be about our business, before he takes off after some flying scrap of paper or loose piece of string and we have to waste time running him down."

They found Smegden cloistered with a cluster of chip- munks, squirrels, and tree rats. Demonstrating that human hands were not required to carry out higher manipulative functions, they were playing a complicated board game with leaves substituting for squares and different-shaped seeds for markers. Those onlookers not actively engaged in play chattered incessantly—which, considering the characteristic speciation of those present, was to be expected.

As he moved a small oblong seed three leaves forward and one sideways, the aggravated mouse caught sight of his former charges. "Botheration!" he snapped. "Now what? Didn't you get any sleep?"

"Plenty of sleep," Mamakitty assured him. "In fact, we're so well rested that we'd like to see some more of the wonders of the Kingdom of Purple."

"What, do I look like a tour guide to you?" he squeaked in exasperation.

"No," she replied. "You look like breakfast. But I've already eaten. Can't you show us around for a little while? Just enough so that we can get ourselves oriented?"

Shaking his head sadly, Smegden turned his portion of the game over to the chipmunk squatting next to him and hopped over to confront his tormentors. "Babysitter to cats and dogs," he muttered irritably. "Snakes and canary birds." He sighed. "Maybe after one quick tour you'll be ready to settle down. And to leave me alone!"

"Maybe," Oskar agreed enticingly.

"Very well then." Impatiently, Smegden tapped the ground with one foot. Since Mamakitty already was serving as a mobile roost for Taj and since Cezer was not in the best of moods to serve as mount for a mouse, Oskar kneeled down so the mouse could scamper up onto the top of his head.

"Fagh!" Even though his scruffy steed could not see the gesture, Smegden made a production of waving both tiny hands in front of him as if to clear the air from in front of his face. "Cats may be more inherently wicked, but at least they smell better! Oh, well—come on, then. Straight ahead, and take the first right once we're out of the Commons."

For all his confirmed irritability, the acerbic Smegden proved to be as congenial a guide during the day as he had been the previous night. He showed them the Council Hall, afire with purple gems, where the Chosen of Faerie and other enchanted electors met to discuss matters of importance affecting the entire kingdom. They visited the stablelands, home to cloven-footed animal folk, where giraffes raced griffins and antelope streaked with makeup competed in high jumping against gravel-voiced jackaroos. There were well-organized facilities for storing food and water against the rare times of drought, schools where lectures in the fine art of thud-dunning were attended by gangs of aspiring adolescent ogres and trolls, and high-speed flying academies for the effervescent offspring of pixies and sprites, where pedantic dragonflies served as instructors.

And then there was the museum.

A structure grand even by the exalted standards of the illustrious Kingdom of Purple, it rambled off in all directions, adding rooms and displays, corridors and exhibits, according to Smegden, whenever it felt like it.

"You mean," Oskar remarked, "whenever the enchanted folk feel like adding to it."

Reaching down, the mouse gripped the hair above Oskar's eyes to balance himself as he leaned forward to peer into one eye from a distance of little more than an inch. "Did I say anything about the enchanted folk, bonebrain? When the museum is ready to grow, it grows. Do you think only flesh can grow? The museum is quite capable of supervising its own expansion."

Indeed, the edifice they entered breathed and exhaled uncomfortably like a live thing, the tepid air rushing systematically in and out as if it were wheezing softly, the walls quivering in response to unseen stimuli. For all that, it looked like an ordinary building. Oskar resolved not to pee on the floor to test the resemblance further.

There were hundreds, thousands, of displays, all neatly mounted and labeled. None of them, he noted as they explored the myriad rooms and trotted past other visitors, were particularly well protected. As near as he and Mamakitty and Taj could tell, there were no guards. There was no need for any. In paradise, there was no reason to steal.

"This is a wonderful place," Taj commented to their guide. "Is it, perhaps, some kind of temple? A temple that contains examples of everything that is, and everything that can be imagined? Perhaps even such a rarity as—white light?" Recalling the words of the unlamented but knowledgeable Captain Covalt of the Kingdom of Red, the songster's friends held their collective breath.

"Not at all," Smegden replied. "Are you crazy? This is no temple!" Behind him, Mamakitty sighed heavily, Samm let out an attenuated hiss of disappointment, and Cezer, sensing among his companions an emotional line it was better not to cross, bit back the sarcastic observation that begged to be liberated from his lips.

Smegden drew himself up. "Every citizen knows this place. It is not a temple but a museum. The Celebrated Grand Mystic Museum of the Exalted Faerie Kingdom of Purple. Wherein," he concluded importantly, "may be found examples of everything that is, or ever was, or can be imagined."

Unable to stand it any longer, Cezer stepped forward to say something. Before the first word could escape from his lips, Cocoa reached over with her mouth, caught one of his long white whiskers in her teeth, and pulled. The resulting look of shock and pain on his face was more than sufficient to forestall his incipient comment.

"When does it close?" Mamakitty inquired quickly of their guide, adding thoughtfully, "We'd like to get back to the Commons before dark."

"The Celebrated Grand Mystic Museum never closes," Smegden informed her. "Nothing in the kingdom ever does. It wouldn't be fair, or appropriate. There are too many citizens of this land who sleep by day and live by night."

"But the kingdom, the city, is not as busy at night," Oskar speculated innocently.

"I don't believe so, no." Smegden was not in the least suspicious. "You asked about white light. As I said, the museum contains examples of everything that is or was or can be imagined. Compared to some of the exhibits here, white light is of comparative insignificance." He sank deep in thought for a moment, then raised a diminutive foreleg and pointed. "That way. Second left at the first long corridor, right after the special exhibition of embalmed censors and petrified lawyers."

They followed the rodent's directions, trying not to hurry, fighting down their rising excitement. A few turns and twists past cases full of the inexplicable and on beyond the impossible—and there it was. After all they had endured, all they had survived, after the arduous crossing of multiple kingdoms of color, their goal gleamed brightly before them.

In an unremarkable room that was home to several dozen exhibits, there stood a tall cabinet of clear crystal containing nothing but glowing balls of color. All the colors were there, including many distinctive shades unfamiliar to the travelers. At the far end of the cabinet, almost as an afterthought, drifted a small globe of pure, unadulterated white light. Each of the diffuse, drifting orbs was clearly labeled as to its nature, pierced and fixed in place by a display rod that had been suitably ensorcelled.

Hopping from upcurled tail tip to head, Taj leaned forward between Mamakitty's ears and whispered, "The problem of how to transport the light is solved. We simply lift up the stick to which it is fastened, and bring both with us."

Mamakitty nodded, inadvertently forcing Taj to take to the air with a temporary fluttering of wings. "I wonder why the individual lights are not all tinted with purple. It's quite unlike anything we've encountered before on our journey, where every object and creature in a specific kingdom of color takes on the tint of that land."

"This is an enchanted museum run for the edification of enchanted folk," the canary pointed out. "What is the wonder in one more enchantment?"

"We have found what we came for," Mamakitty hissed softly, as much to herself as to her diminutive passenger. Beside her, Cocoa was staring silently at the cabinet of wonders. Even Cezer, confronted at last by the object of their quest, was subdued. Louder, she said, "We've taken up enough of your time, Smegden."

"Indeed you have," the mouse agreed readily. Once more the tiny paw indicated the way. "The quickest exit is back that direction, then down a ramp."

Mamakitty and Oskar exchanged a meaningful glance. "If you don't mind," Oskar responded, "there are so many wonderful things to see here. We'll just wander around for a while. We can always ask others the way out."

"That means a long run for me on these short legs, to get out of these endless corridors," Smegden groused, "but better, I suppose, than having to suffer any longer the abiding banalities of your clichéd conversation. If I hurry, I can still make the weekly hunt scheduled for this evening." He drew himself up to his full five-inch height. "Riding to cockroaches, you know." Effortlessly, he leaped down from Oskar's head. From the floor, he turned to confront the trio.

"I wish you a pleasant afternoon of edification, with the added hope that we may never meet again—at least until you have shed your provincial demeanor and developed some sophistication. Fare thee well, O bearers of a benign befuddlement." With that he spun round and, at high speed, scampered off down the corridor he had previously identified as leading to the quickest way out.

"What now?" wondered Cezer, reluctantly reconciled to pursuing their quest to its conclusion.

"We wait," Mamakitty whispered. "Mark this room well." When Oskar raised his right hind leg, she hastened to forestall him. "No, no—that's not what I meant, you idiot! Mentally, mentally! Use your human-augmented mind. At least, I think yours has been augmented."

"Sorry." Abashed, Oskar lowered his leg. "Old habits, you know."

She took a deep breath. "I believe the best time to make our attempt will be at eventide, when the daytime inhabitants of this kingdom begin to retire and before the awakening night dwellers arrive. That time of day should find this measureless structure at its most deserted. We will take the white light from its resting place and slip quietly out of the city. Having once passed that way, the return journey will be easier and less dangerous for us at night."

"You make it sound so easy," Cezer grumbled.

"Every one of those globes of light is pretty bright." Oskar kept his voice down lest he be overheard by a group of female faeries fluttering through the exhibition room. Stylish tiny purses dangled from their hands like pollen from the legs of bees. "If only we had some magical means of temporarily muting their glow."

Wings beating, Taj rose from between Mamakitty's ears. "No sooner said than done. I'll be right back with something I recall seeing several rooms away."

Risking the attention of other museumgoers, Oskar called out to the receding songster. "You saw suitable sorcery just lying around?"

"Not exactly." Taj called back to them just prior to banking a hard right. "It was a very nice paper bag."

And so it was. Retreating to a corner to examine the crumpled container without being observed, Oskar and Mamakitty determined that the sack would indeed fit snugly over the globe of white light. What effect the steady radiance would have on the opaque paper remained to be seen. Perhaps, Taj suggested, like so much else in this kingdom, the sack itself would be adequately enchanted for their purpose.

Feigning interest in every exhibit they passed, no matter how boring, they wandered through the labyrinthine structure, pausing occasionally to discuss this sculpture or that artifact with mock erudition. As the daylight began to ebb, so did the increasingly scanty crowd, until the corridors that sparkled with crushed gemstone spackle no longer echoed to the chatter of elves, the giggling of pixies, or the appreciative grunts of aesthetically discriminating goblins.

Taking a roundabout route, they worked their way back to the room that contained the samples of illumination from other kingdoms. Throughout the museum complex, faerie light was winking to life. As might be expected, it was soft and diffuse so as not to hurt the eyes of the nocturnal visitors, who had not yet begun to arrive in any numbers worth worrying about. As Cezer trotted out to the nearest main corridor to keep watch, and Samm spread himself the length of the room's entrance to trip up any unobserved arrivals, the others considered how best to go about expropriating the precious globe of whiteness.

"Back here." From behind the cabinet, Oskar's voice was an urgent whisper. "There's a latch."

It was a very simple, straightforward latch, quite uncomplicated and devoid of charm. There was no reason for anything more elaborate, they decided. Who would want to steal light? What possible use could anyone abiding in the Kingdom of Purple have for nonpurple numinous luminosity? Lifting the latch with his nose, Oskar put his shoulder against the edge of the compartment's rear door. With Mamakitty and Cocoa's help, he was able to push it aside. Lamenting the dearth of hands, but determined as ever, he cocked his head sideways and reached in to seize with his strong jaws the pole that pierced and supported the pure white globe. When he lifted the rod carefully out of its slot, the crystal display case caught the moving light and scattered small rainbows about the room as casually as a rich man casting alms to the poor.

"Look at the colors!" Beneath calico fur, Cocoa's chest swelled elatedly. "It really *is* white light, and it really does contain within it all the colors of the rainbow!" She retraced her steps as Oskar backed carefully out of the case. "It's everything we've come for. We'll take it back to the Gowdlands and turn it over to the wizards who still roam free. They'll know what to do with it, how to use it to break the curse of the Khaxan Mundurucu."

"I don't think so," an all-too-familiar voice declared.

Oskar spun around on his hind legs so fast he almost dropped the rod and the shining sphere it transfixed. Beside him, Mamakitty let out a furious hiss and Cocoa dropped into a fighting stance, ears flared back and teeth bared. He considered making a mad dash for the exit, only to see that that route, too, was blocked. The axe-wielding trolls who stood there might be slow of foot, but they would only have to hit him once to end forever any hopes of returning to the Fasna Wyzel—or any other part of the land of the living. One stood with a foot on Samm's neck, its sharp axe poised over the serpent's skull. Samm hissed in frustration, wishing for the great stone adze he had been forced to leave behind in the culvert at the edge of the city—and for hands to swing it with.

A grim-visaged ogre (was there any other kind, Oskar wondered?) lumbered forward. With a disapproving oink, it took the shaft from the dog-man's jaws. It hurt Oskar more to let go of it than it had to keep it gripped between his teeth. Exhibiting an unexpectedly light touch, the strapping sentry placed rod and globe back in the display case and slid the door shut behind them, nudging the latch back into place with a blunt forefinger as thick around as Oskar's leg.

Other armed and armored enchanted folk proceeded to place heavy hands on the intruders. As they did so, the voice that had interrupted the attempted theft, which had come so near succeeding, spoke again. It arose from a decidedly charmless ratlike individual who stood quivering with delight and repressed ferocity between a pair of dark-winged, gargoyle-faced night fliers. The speaker had a pointed snout, quivering whiskers, rust-red fur splotched with white spots, alert ears, blazing homicidal eyes, and teeth like needles.

"You'll break no spells, dead meat," snarled the quoll Quoll. "Neither light nor color will you return to the Gowdlands. You'll spend your time in gaol purple, you will, and by the time you get out—if they let you out—there'll be nothing left of the Gowdlands to save. All resistance will have been crushed, the last wizard expunged, and all rebels fled, dead, or missing their heads." Cackling gleefully, he pronked about in delighted, triumphant circles.

"After our last encounter, it was decided we should follow and watch, watch and follow, and bide our time. Please to understand, that's not my style. I like to tear straight-away into quarry every chance I get. But my colleagues"— and he indicated the two softly squeaking bats that flanked him— "managed to persuade me to be patient. So wait we did, until you reached your goal. Only when you were on the verge of winning it did we act."

Ruut stepped awkwardly forward, membranous wings luffing about him like wrinkled black sails. "We had been waiting for a good time to strike. Thanks to your actions, we did not have to decide. This is better—much better. Once informed of a burglary in progress, the local law came shambling with admirable speed."

Raising up on his hind legs, Quoll thrust a quivering forefoot in their direction. "All this time, all this follow-ing and waiting, and we didn't even have to fight! By your own actions, you've done yourselves in. All *we* have to do is sit back and take pleasure in the consequences."

That is what the trio of duplicitous devils proceeded to do, smirking as an elf of scowling mien pushed his way past the guards, stepped over the pinioned Samm, and con-fronted the rest of the accused. Resigned dog and choleric cats he eyed gravely. Noting the several large nets held by a number of the guards, Taj stayed perched on Oskar's head and prayed for an opening.

"You are charged under Articles XXVIII through XXXII of the Code of the Kingdom with multiple counts of at-tempted theft of public property, use of a public facility for nefarious purpose, conduct unbecoming guests of the Purple, and general felonious naughtiness. You are to be bound over to the Court of Proscribed Enchantments for trial and sentencing."

Mamakitty frowned. "How can we be bound for sen-tencing if there hasn't yet been a trial?"

"Procedures must be followed." Stepping back, the imperious elf gestured to the ogres. "Take them and see that they're properly secured. Make sure the bird doesn't get past you. I'll see to the necessary paperwork."

"Your pardon, meritorious sir," husked Ratha as the downcast travelers were escorted from the room, "but can we drink their blood?"

"Sorry," the elf replied. "Against city ordinances. But I'll speak to the presiding magistrate. Considering the help you and your friends have provided in this matter, perhaps something can be worked out."

Greatly pleased with themselves and the evening's evil they had wrought, the twosome of vampire bats alternately walked and fluttered at the head of the somber procession. In a fever of triumphant excitement, Quoll danced and darted back and forth in front of the crestfallen captives. The taunting of prisoners, evidently, was not against the regulations of the kingdom.

Only when all was once again silent within the exhibition room of multicolored lights of other kingdoms in the Celebrated Grand Mystic Museum of the Exalted Kingdom of Purple, save for the gossiping voices of distant strollers, did a small, compact figure emerge from the depths of the ornate Havetra'ng vase of spun spidersilk and regurgitated moonbeam where it had been hiding. Checking repeatedly to make certain that the way out was clear, a grateful Cezer fled as fast as he could for the pastoral, treed sanctuary of the Grand Commons.

❖ NINETEEN

If they had not been under arrest, Oskar and his companions would have marveled at their surroundings. The interior of the Justice Building was fashioned of twinkling spun glass and limpid crystal, all of it vibrant with purple and lavender light. Preoccupied pixies darted down corridors while mercurial sprites delivered missives from one chamber to the next. Trolls conferenced in the darkest corners, elves engaged in slavish banter, and something like a squashed sphinx limped slowly past on all four legs, complaining mightily to an attentive retinue of sylphs whose sleek flesh jiggled like tapioca pudding.

The courtroom was small; barely large enough to hold the prisoners, their ogrish guards, a modest audience, and a goggle-eyed, multiarmed court reporter. Oskar, Mamakitty, and Cocoa were seated in the front rank of a triple row of bloated toadstools that sparkled with petrified dew. Next to them, Samm lay stretched out and splinted to keep him from making use of his powerful coils, while a dispirited Taj found himself, for the first time since their original transformation, back in a locked cage.

To make things infinitely worse, the object of their long,

grueling journey sat glowing whitely on its rod in the evidence box at the front of the courtroom, within easy reach of the prisoners—if one discounted the presence of the brace of heavily armed trolls that flanked it on either side.

On a back bench, a quietly triumphant Quoll sat flanked by a silent Ruut and Ratha. Oskar growled in their direction, only to have their gleeful foe respond with a taunting, infuriating smile.

The nearest guard cuffed Oskar smartly upside the head and grunted. "No snarling in the courtroom. Show some respect."

Shortly thereafter, a door opened behind a toadstool of truly prodigious dimensions, and a figure appeared within. As it tottered up to the oversize fungi, a sprite clad in flowing frillwork appeared from nowhere to tootle on a small, cochlear horn.

"Hear ye, hear ye! The City Court of the Kingdom of Purple is now in session. His honorable and mystic magisterial elf self Judge Cooble Pilk presiding." A second, slightly less elaborate tootle from the tinny trumpet, and the sprite vanished.

Ascending all of two feet to the high chair located behind the commanding toadstool, the judge had extraordinarily large, pointed ears, a shiny forehead from which a few determined, scraggly hairs emerged, narrow, intense dark eyes, and the long, supple fingers of a courtesan. The lavender-whitish wig he wore spilled in carefully powdered curls down his back, onto the floor, and beyond, stretching several feet in two directions. No book lay open before him, nor was a gavel of any kind close at hand. Pushing out his hairy lower lip and glaring importunately at the unhappy prisoners, he folded his hands and leaned forward, his elbows resting on the curved, slightly flexible surface of the toadstool.

"Well? Do you have anything to say before I pronounce sentence?" From the back of the room, one of the bats snickered loudly.

"Now wait a minute!" Mamakitty would have sprung forward had not she been yanked back onto the bench by the ogre that stood behind her. She struggled to remain calm. "What kind of a trial is this? You haven't even heard any evidence yet!"

"Don't need to," the Honorable Cooble Pilk snorted. "Waste of time, evidence. You lot were caught trying to steal an exhibit from the museum of the kingdom." With a hirsute hand he indicated the silently pulsating globe of white light posted in the nearby evidence box. "*That* exhibit. Terrible business, terrible. Why, if everyone started helping themselves to exhibits, pretty soon all the kingdom would have left is an empty, unhappy building. Have you ever seen a building cry? Especially one the size of the Grand Glorious Multitudinous . . . uh, the Gigantic Inconceivable Miraculous . . . clerk?" he snapped irritably.

"The Celebrated Grand Mystic Museum of the Exalted Kingdom of Purple, your honored necromancy, sir." The multiarmed court reporter goggled its eyes a little more than usual.

Wagging his tail anxiously, Oskar slipped off the bench to which the defendants were confined. The guard behind him tensed, but let him stand on all fours. "Aren't you even curious to know why we tried to take the globe of white light?"

Hacking up something decidedly unenchanted, the judge spat into an unseen but resonant spittoon. "Not particularly. But I have this sinking feeling that you're going to tell me anyway."

Aided in emphasis and detail by Mamakitty, Oskar proceeded to relate the history of their travels, beginning with the assault on the Gowdlands by the Totumakk Horde, the curse that had subsequently been laid by the horrific Khaxan Mundurucu, and their own efforts, following their transformation by a posthumous spell of the wizard Susnam Evyndd, to find and acquire some light containing all colors to bring back home.

The Honorable Cooble Pilk listened tolerantly to every word. When Oskar finally concluded with a deferential, "That's all, Your Honor," and sat back on his woolly haunches, the magistrate appeared to have fallen into deep contemplation.

Appearances can be deceiving, however.

"If you've finished, we can get on with this. I have a game at three. I'm playing with two nymphs and a senior gremlin. Nymphs don't like to be kept waiting." He smiled tersely. "*I* don't like to keep nymphs waiting."

This time, Mamakitty slid slowly off the bench, mindful of the massive ogre standing behind her. When she tried to approach the judicial toadstool, however, it reached out to grip her upcurving tail in massive fingers, holding her back.

"Your Honor," she pleaded, "everything we've done has been on behalf of others. I know we were wrong to try and take the white light, but we weren't doing it for ourselves. It was only for all those whose lives have been made unbearable by the Mundurucu!"

"Not all lives have been made miserable!" a gleeful Quoll called out from the back of the chamber.

Mildly annoyed, the presiding elf focused his gaze in the direction of the outburst. "Silence in the court! I'll tolerate no unsolicited comments from spectators." Returning his attention to the attentive prisoners, his thick eyebrows lowered until they cast perceptible shade across his prominent nose.

"Theft is theft and the law is the law. Why, without the law we'd be no better than mortals, subject to the whims of ordinary existence. Benign motive is no excuse." Bringing both hands together sharply, he demonstrated why the presence of a gavel was unnecessary in the courtroom. A petite sonic boom rattled the chamber, ruffling the cats' fur, lifting Taj's feathers, and even knocking the hulking ogre and troll guards back a step or two.

"The sentence is death, to be carried out at a place of execution three days hence." Rising, his curly wig of office swirling about him like a pair of permed serpents, he turned to exit the courtroom. The trial was at an end.

From the back of the chamber rose a vile, cackling whoop of quollish satisfaction. Leaning toward her mate, Ratha whispered delightedly, "The Khaxan Mundurucu will be pleased." Mamakitty, Cocoa, Taj, and Samm were too stunned to speak.

Not Oskar. Advancing on the toadstool, he dodged the grasping hand of the troll stationed on his left. "Sir, Your Honor! You can't— I mean, this isn't about us! It's about our purpose, our mission to save others! No matter what you think of us and our actions, surely you can't just dismiss the misery of thousands of other suffering beings with a wave of your hand?"

The Honorable Cooble Pilk paused and looked back. "I didn't wave. I distinctly remember not waving. There being no one to speak on your behalf save yourselves, who are already condemned by your actions, I see no reason to reconsider my decision."

"But there are others!" a voice cried.

Everyone in the chamber turned toward the entrance, prisoners, guards, and momentarily victorious allies of the Mundurucu alike. Striding boldly through the diaphanous doorway was an agitated cat wearing a mouse on its head.

They were accompanied by a troika of exceedingly well-turned-out gnomes.

Mamakitty's whiskers curved so far upward they almost pointed at the ceiling. Nearby, Oskar had begun to bark uncontrollably. Cocoa's eyes shone with a new inner light, Taj was bouncing excitedly up and down on the perch within his cage, and Samm's flicking, sensitive, unsplinted tongue caught the scent of something welcome and familiar in the air of the courtroom. Leaning to her left, Mamakitty whispered softly to Oskar, her quivering whiskers almost touching his muzzle.

"I *knew* the selfish little show-off wouldn't abandon us! No matter how much he rambled on about liking this place."

Oskar looked down over his nose at her. "You knew? Hey, what's that in your eye?"

"Nothing, dog-breath. Mind your own business." She turned back to the front of the courtroom. "Anyway, don't you know cats can't cry?"

Each gnome carried beneath his left arm a small briefcase, sewn from tanned snowflake. There was nothing in them, but in the kingdom of enchantment, appearances are important. Approaching the bench, the middle gnome spoke for his colleagues as well as for himself.

"Horglum, Grugle, and Migwig, Your Honor. Counselors for the defense."

Folding his enormous ears forward so that they momentarily covered his face, the judge let out a high-pitched gargle of resignation. By the time these impressive organs of hearing had relaxed back into their normal positions, he had reluctantly resumed his seat behind the imposing toadstool.

"What is this?" Whiskers quivering violently, a furious Quoll rose on hind legs at the back of the chamber. "You've already pronounced sentence! The trial is over!"

"No trial is over until I say it's over!" Leaping to the top of the toadstool rostrum, the Honorable Cooble Pilk clapped his hands in Quoll's direction. The resultant sonic boom blew quoll and bats up against the back wall, where they remained flattened and motionless, as if glued in place. "You'll stay like that until this is over with. By Titania's tush, I'll have order in this courtroom!" Muttering to himself, he hopped back down into his chair, straightening his imposing wig as he resumed his seat. "Vex and hex the general public, anyway! Always interrupting. Especially when an elf has a game upcoming." Settling himself, he glowered unhappily at the trio of gnomish attorneys.

"Snap to it, gentlebeings. This court is in a hurry."

Though thoroughly bewildered and able to understand nary a word of the esoteric enchanted legalese articulated by the three gnomes, Oskar allowed himself to feel a surge of hope. Whatever the meaning of the gibberish they were spouting, the impish advocates were certainly pouring it on with enthusiasm. Even the guards were impressed—or as impressed as dim-witted ogres and trolls could be. Almost as important to Oskar as this formal defense was the kittenish grin of his friend Cezer. The tomcat had strode forward to rejoin them, his four-legged stride more strut than saunter. Once more, the dedicated band of travelers was together. As for their minuscule savior Smegden, he appeared to find the entire proceedings almost as much a waste of time as did the judge.

"Hi, rat-breath," Oskar murmured to Cezer as the male cat sat down beside him on his blond haunches.

"Hello, piddle-pants. How's it going?"

"Better, now. What brings you here? Miss me?"

The tomcat spat derisively. "Like I'd miss being locked in a bath."

"I thought you'd run off to stuff your feline face full of meatfruit in the oh-so-accommodating Commons."

Daintily, Cezer raised his left foreleg and began to lick the underside of his paw. "No, thanks. I had my fill of paradise."

Oskar was panting softly. "And what did you decide about it?"

Deigning to glance in the dog's direction, Cezer replied curtly, "It's boring," and resumed cleaning his other forefoot.

It was growing late when the Honorable Cooble Pilk finally threw up his hairy hands and part of his lunch in frustration.

"Enough already! At this rate we'll be here till the End of Faerie. Not to mention that I'll miss the second half of my game. Noble but long-winded barristers, I implore you—step back, if you please." Clutching their briefcases to their chests like shields, Horglum, Grugle, and Migwig were quick to comply.

"Theft is theft. The conviction stands," the judge declaimed. From the rear wall of the chamber, a spread-eagled Quoll snarled satisfaction while the pair of vampire bats flanking him like mounted butterflies squeaked delightedly. "However, bearing in mind the energetic defense mounted by this most distinguished team of nit-picking obfuscators"—the legal trio bowed appreciatively—"I have determined to reduce the sentence."

From where he was seated, Oskar looked up hopefully. Beside him, Mamakitty leaned forward, the twitching of her tail stilled. Everyone eyed the judge in expectant silence.

"I, the Right Honorable Judge Cooble Pilk, senior magistrate of the exceedingly superior court of the Kingdom of Purple, do hereby order that the prisoners be banished forever from the Kingdom of Purple and the Realms of Faerie back to their revoltingly commonplace place of residence, there to be released into exile with the promise never to return."

The courtroom dissolved into chaos.

A joyful Mamakitty rose to wrap her legs around a wide-eyed, disbelieving Cocoa. Taj let out a piercing whistle of delight. An excited Oskar began barking wildly. Disputatious spectators leaped from their seats to exchange harsh words and energetic blows. Peeling himself off the back wall with a tremendous effort of will, the outraged Quoll snatched a knife from a startled troll. Holding it firmly in his mouth, he darted forward, heading straight for Mamakitty. The incredible energy and natural agility of his kind saw him sprint through the flailing grasp of several massive but sluggish guards.

Raising both hands, Judge Cooble Pilk proceeded to execute the sentence he had just pronounced. Faerie lightning crackled around his wrinkled brow and hovered above the tips of his prominent ears. Rising from the floor, the two lengths of his gargantuan powdered wig hovered above and behind him like a pair of gigantic lavender antennae. A roaring filled Oskar's ears, and a singular pressure blocked his sinuses, as if he had suddenly become trapped underwater. Out of the corner of an eye he saw the snarling Quoll leap, the tip of the knife held between his jaws aimed at Mamakitty's throat. Smegden let out a warning squeak as Cocoa had the presence of mind to take up the handle of Taj's cage between her teeth.

At the same time, Samm struck. Having quietly bided his time, the great serpent burst his constraining splints with a show of power only a fully grown python could muster. His jaws parted wide as his blunt head shot through the air toward the flying Quoll—and past the raging, apoplectic animal, to snatch up in his teeth the rod in the evidence box on which was transfixed a softly pulsing sphere of concentrated white light. Dazed and benumbed, Oskar thought he heard both bats squeal out a startled *"No!"* from the back of the courtroom.

Then the numbness overwhelmed him, nausea curdled the contents of his stomach, and something cold washed over his face. Suddenly, he couldn't breathe.

Kicking frantically, he burst free of the smothering dampness, his head exploding through the surface of the swirling pool of clear, cold water that lay at the base of the Shalouan Falls. Spitting out water, sputtering at the unexpected icy contact, he began to dog-paddle toward the rocky shore, shaking his head and sending sparkling droplets flying from the ends of his long hair. He was back home and alive, but something had changed. When he reached, exhausted, for the first projecting rocks of the shoreline, he realized immediately what had happened.

In the instant of being banished by the Really Impressively Irritable Honorable Judge Cooble Pilk from the Kingdom of Purple to their homeland, they had reverted back to the exact same enchanted forms they had inhabited on the day they had left it.

Like it or not, he was human again.

He was also naked, and seriously waterlogged. Searching his immediate surroundings, he saw his companions pulling themselves out of the river onto the damp, mist-slickened rocks to the left of the falls. Ravishingly long-legged Cocoa was wringing water out of her hair. Taj stood nearby, shouting and gesturing to him as the songster picked pieces of broken metal cage off his shoulders. Oskar waved back and called out that he was okay, even though he was not sure he could be heard above the roaring of the falls.

"That worked out very well, I think," Taj told him when the latter joined the rest of the group. "Everything happened so fast, I was worried that one or two of us might have been overlooked. But the judge was very thorough."

"Didn't want to be late for his game," Cezer remarked from nearby. "I don't think I'd like to play with him."

Tilting back his head, Oskar looked upward, squinting against the leaden but welcome sunshine. Though dominated by the omnipresent drabness that had been imposed by the Mundurucu, the daylight in which they now found themselves was a welcome change from all the monocolored alien skies they had trekked beneath during the past weeks. Before them, the permanent rainbow born of the falls still bloomed with vibrant color, a beacon of normality shining forth in the midst of an otherwise all-pervasive grayness.

A sudden thought made him look around sharply. "Where's Samm?"

"Over here!" Emerging from the woods that filled the canyon, the dour giant waved encouragingly. In his huge right hand rested the radiant orb of white light from the Celebrated Grand Mystic Museum of the Exalted Kingdom of Purple. Oskar's heart leaped.

"You got away with it!"

Joining them, the giant nodded slowly, looking slightly abashed. "I fixated on it the instant we entered the courtroom. I was waiting for the right moment to strike, hoping I might be able to slip into a drain hole or a gutter with it. Then the judge changed our sentence, and everything went crazy at once." Holding the globe high, he squinted at the precious luminosity. "I was afraid I might swallow it. The instant I changed back to this shape, I spit it out into a hand. Handy things to have, hands."

They gazed in silence at the lambent sphere. Now that they were back home, or nearly so, each of the travelers was more than a little awed at what they had accomplished. It was Cezer who, a little self-consciously, broke the reverie.

"All right—we've done the thing. What do we do now?"

Cocoa frowned at him. "What do you mean? We've gone through the rainbow, crossed all the kingdoms of light, and brought back the essence of white light the Master enjoined us to find."

He nodded agreeably. "So we have. And now that we have, what do we do with it? Does it go into a stew, or some kind of potion? Are there special words that need to be pronounced over it before anything happens?" He indicated the enveloping grayness that surrounded them. "Clearly, it doesn't do anything by itself. Just bringing it back here isn't enough. Something more has to be done. Something's lacking."

A slight but mellifluous whistle turned them all in the same direction. It was a very familiar whistle, even though they were used to hearing it emerge from an avian throat.

Taj looked embarrassed as he gazed back at his friends and companions. His voice was characteristically subdued, yet somehow confident. He met their curious stares without flinching. "I'm afraid—there's something I haven't told you. It is a matter of some significance."

Cezer's eyes rolled upward. Cocoa looked puzzled, while Mamakitty's curiosity lent an unforced stiffness to her words.

"What is it now, Taj?"

"It's just that—well, I'm not exactly entirely who I appear to be." Though strengthening, his voice remained low-key as ever. "My full name is Tajek of the Gold Flame. I am also known as Tajekafen ben-Arubar, Associate of the Faith Necromantic, Anointed Assistant Alchemical, Odosa— officially designated ordained sortilege affiliate. In more everyday terms, in other words, the Master Susnam Evyndd's canonical, dedicated, and long-time familiar."

"Oohhh," whispered a reverential Cocoa.

Cezer was rather less impressed. "That's an awful lot of title to carry for someone who spends his normal existence as a very small and conspicuously inconsequential songbird."

Taj shifted his attention to the naked swordsman. It appeared to Cezer that something flickered in the back of the smaller man's eyes—no doubt a trick of the shifting, deceptive light that prevailed near the falls.

"Consider, friend Cezer, my condition and position a credit to Master Evyndd's limitless forethought. When he received visitors and wished to know what they were saying outside his presence, I was there to listen and record—between songs, of course. When he was executing a spell and needed help, but desired to appear as if he alone was performing the necessary machinations, I was present in the background to provide the required assistance." He looked over at a thoroughly dumbfounded Oskar.

"When he needed a second pair of eyes, or someone to watch over his belongings when he was not present, I was there. Why else, Oskar, do you think he sometimes took me with him on his journeys and not you or Mamakitty? Whether at home or away, others would assume I was present to provide my gift of song. When striving to identify a sorcerer's possible familiar, with three cats and a snake in house, what enemy would give a thought to a canary?"

"Not I, certainly," Cezer sniffed. Sniffing disdainfully was more effective with a cat nose, the swordsman lamented.

"None of us would." Mamakitty was wary, but impressed. "I often wondered why Master Evyndd did not anoint one of us his familiar. That is a question now answered: he already had one."

Taj nodded solemnly. "I regret to say that you three cats, together with you, Samm, were present in the Master's household not merely for company but also to serve as decoys. Anyone wishing to destroy the knowledge and wisdom of Susnam Evyndd would also take care to eliminate any familiars. As I have pointed out, the Master thought it doubtful any angry adversary would take the time or trouble to bother with a small, inoffensive bird."

"A decoy." Cezer's expression changed from vexed to unhappy. "The callous son of a bitch—no disrespect intended, you understand. To you, either, Oskar," he added after a moment's thought.

"Master Evyndd did what he thought was necessary for him to do to preserve himself and his legacy." In the absence of that deceased worthy, Taj took it upon himself to offer the modest apologia. "I'm sure he meant no harm by it, and I know for a fact that he loved you all."

There was silence for several minutes while each of them reconsidered anew their relationship with their now departed master; a relationship they thought they had understood, both as animals and as humans. Now it appeared that emotional tie, along with everything else, had been very different from what they had supposed all along.

Oskar confronted Taj, but not for the reason the latter suspected. "You said that you recorded and remembered for him. So that—what was it you said?—so that his knowledge and wisdom would be preserved." He thrust his mustachioed face closer to that of the other man. "Does that mean *you* now possess his knowledge and wisdom?"

Mamakitty held her breath. The songster's expression was unreadable. "I have none of his wisdom. Wisdom dies with the wise. But a little knowledge, that I retain." He shrugged modestly. "It was my job."

Oskar's eyes widened. "You! You were the first one

through. You were the one who found the opening in the rainbow and summoned us to follow."

Taj nodded, and this time allowed himself a slight smile. "I had to risk exposing myself. It was the only way to save us all. Fortunately, our stalkers did not descry the use of magic on my part. Had they done so, I fear we would have been forced to deal much sooner with the Khaxan Mundurucu. And there were other times, other occasions these past difficult days, when I surreptitiously made use of what small learning I had acquired in the service of the Master." He saw Cocoa staring at him. "Do you remember when we entered the Kingdom of Yellow?"

She nodded. "The great gate. You were the one who discovered that it was unlocked."

A ghost of a grin creased his face. "It wasn't exactly 'unlocked.' A small magic, that. And of course there was the time when we were trapped within the fallen kauri tree in the Kingdom of Green. Did several of you not wonder how all those fellow avians who finally freed us could hear my whistling calls through all that wood? To avoid the details of an explanation, I had to several times change the subject in haste."

"When else?" Cezer could not keep from asking. He was remembering now: little comments, small observations that at the time had not jibed with their view of Taj as a simple songster, but which they had been too busy or too tired to pursue.

"I'll remind you another time, another time, my furry friend. When we sit again by a warm fire in a safe country, and you decide to show an interest in what I have to say instead of wondering how I might taste."

"We have the white light. Do we begin here?" Eagerness glistened in Cocoa's eyes. "This is as good a place as any to start overturning the Mundurucu's baneful spell."

"No, it isn't." Taj was firm in his objection. "We must return home, to the Master's house. Not only will we all be more at ease once we are back home, but there are active at that place certain evanescent forces that will aid and abet our efforts. It is why Evyndd caused his abode to be raised in that spot in the first place—or so I was once told."

Oskar looked closely at his friend. "You didn't say 'Master.'"

"What?" Taj blinked at him.

"When you mentioned him just then. You didn't call him Master Evyndd."

The familiar started, then nodded soberly. "It signifies a change. In our status as well as his. We must be our own masters now, and act like it if we are going to do battle with thaumaturgy as powerful as that cultivated by the Khaxan Mundurucu."

Samm's massive fingers opened and closed. "I wish I hadn't left my axe behind."

"We'll take new weapons from the armory at the house. Sorcery notwithstanding, it's always good to have a sharp blade close at hand." Taj started past the two men, heading for the steep slope that led upward toward the road they had wandered down not so very long ago.

"Maybe that person can help us secure some for the journey back to the forest." Starting up the base of the hill, Cezer had noticed a woman standing in the shallows downstream from the falls. Now he headed toward her, waving one hand and calling out a cheerful greeting.

Hearing his shout, she turned and saw his approach, whereupon she flung aside the bucket half full of crayfish she had collected, gathered up her skirts in both hands, and ran screaming from the water to the nearby path. Once she reached dry land, her speed increased markedly, so much so that a baffled Cezer slowed to a halt. He could have caught up to her easily. Dropping his arm, he followed her frantic flight until her feet had carried her out of sight. Returning to the waiting group, he cast a bemused glance at his friends.

"I don't understand. I was smiling, and my voice was full of friendship and reassurance. Why did she run from me? Have we in our journeying undergone some awful transformation that is now to make others flee in terror from the sight of us?" He paused to shake his head, more baffled than ever. "Say—why are you all grinning at me?"

Oskar was fighting back the laughter that threatened to overwhelm him. "I'm no dog today, Cezer. And you're no cat. Had you presented yourself before the unfortunate lady as the cat you usually are, I'm sure she would have greeted you fondly. In your present condition, however, you were bound to provoke a somewhat different reaction."

The swordsman looked down at himself. "What's wrong with—oh. I forgot. Humans have this thing about clothing, don't they?"

"Indeed they do." Glistening and nude, Mamakitty grabbed on to an overhanging tree branch to help pull herself up the damp slope.

The disconcerted swordsman sidled up to Taj. "You're a sorcerer. Why don't you just conjure us back some clothes?"

"I am not, by any stretch of the imagination, a sorcerer." The lean-muscled songster was contemplating with distaste the long climb from water's edge back up to the river road. "I am only a familiar, and a very lowly familiar at that. And I miss my wings." Stepping past his companion, he began to ascend in Mamakitty's wake—which, under the circumstances, was not so very bad a place to be.

TWENTY

In those dismal days of depression and misery, the road that led from Zelevin was not nearly as busy as it had been before the arrival of the Horde and the Khaxan Mundurucu. Like every other aspect of daily life, commerce, too, lay under a cloud. Because of this, the travelers managed to avoid drawing attention to themselves. The first village they encountered was too busy for them to enter, but with nearly the entire population of the second in attendance at a pitifully bleak marriage ceremony, they managed to sneak in and back out again with a ragtag assortment of appropriated attire Mamakitty insisted must be returned later, and enough food with which to stuff their borrowed pockets.

When eventually they reentered the Fasna Wyzel, more than memories came flooding back. They journeyed onward in silence, each lost in his or her own thoughts and emotions, no longer certain whether they were animal, human, or some enigmatic melding of both. As they left the marked trails behind and moved into the silent depths of the great forest they were confronted with places, sights, smells, and sounds they had known intimately in animal form. As humans, they perceived everything differently. When they had left the forest before, their human bodies had been new to them and their attention and interests directed elsewhere. Now they had time to reflect on the striking transformation they had undergone. It left each of them feeling very humble—except perhaps Cezer, who alone among them probably could not count that particular sentiment in his emotional vocabulary.

When the house of the good wizard Susnam Evyndd at last came again into view, however, even the flint-hearted swordsman was overcome by emotion.

It stood much as they had left it. The spiders had been busy, and a profusion of webs decorated the sheltered places under the eaves, in the doorway, and in some of the windows. But the sturdy structure had not burned or fallen down. It hunkered up against the bracing rocks against which it had been built, facing the forest and the rest of the world with thatched defiance—the only real home any of them had ever known. It at once drew them on and repelled them.

It was fitting that Oskar, having watched over the front door all his adult life, should be the one to push it open. How much easier, he reflected, to do so with hands than with nose or paw. But not necessarily as satisfying. Considering how long the house had been empty, they found the interior in surprisingly good condition. Plenty of dry food remained in the pantry, undisturbed and unfouled by weevils. But the small crunchy bits of dried and processed protein no longer appealed to Oskar and his feline friends, nor the barrel of assorted seeds to Taj. As for Samm, having gorged recently on meatfruit in the Kingdom of Purple, he felt no urge to eat again so soon. In that respect he was alone.

For years they had watched Master Evyndd prepare

meals for himself. They had eaten human food during their arduous trek through the kingdoms of light. Now they set about improvising what they could from the available stores. The result would have appalled a genteel gourmet, but it filled their bellies and assuaged the ache that had begun to grow there.

It was very late on the morning of the following day when they finally awoke from a long-overdue sleep. Samm would have dozed on had Oskar and Mamakitty not pounded on his shoulders and slapped his face until he finally opened his eyes.

"Sssorry," he mumbled as he rose to his feet. All night long, he had slept with the white radiance held close to his stomach to ensure its safety. "It's easier to shed one's skin than an old lifestyle."

They cleaned themselves, using the rainwater shower and towels instead of tongues and paws. Then, with Samm carefully carrying the lambent white orb, they went looking for Taj. They found him standing and waiting for them on the front lawn.

"How many times I sat in my cage, gazing out at this vista"—he turned to his refreshed and ready companions—"watching you play on this lawn, Oskar, while Mamakitty and Cezer and Cocoa chased bugs and chipmunks and the occasional ball of discarded wizard shine, while I was stuck in my cage, singing. Or studying."

"I can sympathize." For a snake, Samm was unusually compassionate. Except when he was swallowing someone. "Apart from the singing part, of course. Not that I couldn't sing," he added in response to their disbelieving stares, "but no one wanted to hear me. My kind aren't celebrated for harmony."

Apprehensive but game, Cocoa eyed the familiar. "There's no use in putting it off, Taj. What do we do now?"

This morning, the songster looked older than his years. Try as he might, he could not escape the feeling that the ultimate responsibility for the success or failure of what they were about to attempt was his. With a deep sigh, he extended a hand to Samm.

"Give me the white light."

The giant passed it over. Taj held it lightly in his open palm. It was warm, but not unpleasantly so, and weighed, according to his best estimate, less than nothing.

"Gather around."

Cezer frowned at him. "What for? You're the wise and powerful familiar, not us."

The songster smiled at him. "Did you think the Master set you all on this quest to keep me company? Just as we were all part and parcel of his life, so, too, are we parcel and part of his magic, even though he has gone from us. For an enchantment this profound to work, it requires input from every one of us."

The swordsman shrugged and stepped forward. "If you say so." He eyed the shaggy-haired dog-man standing next to him. "Just don't ask Oskar to pee on me, okay?"

"That's close enough. Now join paws—I mean, hands." Self-consciously, the members of the little company complied. Taking a last look at the clouds (and hoping it was indeed not his last), Taj began—not to speak, which skill had never been his forte, but to sing.

"Strength of serpent, circle round this space." Next to Mamakitty, Samm stiffened. A cold breeze sprang up around them; a small wall of conjoined atmosphere.

"Swiftness of cat, bar evil's trace." The breeze grew stronger. A strange tickling sensation prickled Cocoa's skin. Blinking against the rising wind, she saw that everyone's hair was standing vertical, as if the current of air were blowing straight up out of the ground under their feet. She gripped Mamakitty's and Cezer's hands tighter in her own.

Taj sang to the sky for all he was worth, a song less melodious than it might have been had he been inhabiting his original form, but infinitely more powerful.

"Devotion of dog, hold all in place! *Now spread the light, and color everywhere race!*"

Oskar felt himself shaking. Or maybe it was the ground underfoot. It was a wholly eerie sensation because it was utterly quiet. Even the animals of the forest had gone silent. With the now gale-force wind rushing up from his feet to his ears, he had to squint to see through the rising column of dust and litter that was shooting skyward.

The globe of white light began to rise. Caught in something much more significant than the howling pillar of wind, it rose skyward, accelerating as it ascended. As it climbed, it began to expand. It was very bright, very intense, and perfectly, dazzlingly, white. Soon it was four times the size of the sphere Taj had held so effortlessly. Then it doubled in volume, and doubled again. By the time it neared the underside of the lowest cloud, it had expanded to the size of a small ship.

Whereupon the swaying, hand-holding group of transmogrified friends gathered below had to avert their eyes and cover their faces, as the refulgent sphere unexpectedly and violently exploded.

It detonated not with a percussive bang but with an infinitely vast rush of air, as if the heavens themselves had suddenly released a single vast, thankful sigh. From the ultimate depths of the explosion a wave of solid swirling color emerged, to boil away in all directions like an expanding wave. It washed over the roof of the sky, the clouds, the land, and everything above and below.

Straightening cautiously, Cocoa gazed down at herself

in wonderment. The column of wind had vanished, and her long bright tresses lay gracefully against her neck and shoulders. "Look. Everybody, look! It's back. The color of light is back!"

As indeed it was. Her heretofore dull-as-dishwater village raiment now flaunted the startling crimson and jade green with which the material had been dyed. A dazed Cezer sat down on the grass, resplendent in simple clothing that was dark blue trimmed with touches of tangerine. Samm's temporary, too-tight body wrappings of hastily scavenged cloth were once more off-white and beige. Everywhere about them, color had returned wherever the miraculous pigmented swell had washed over them. Certainly the rush of blood that now suffused Taj's countenance was bright pink.

Samm walked over and put a comforting arm around the somewhat stunned songster's shoulders. "I have to hand it to you," the giant declared admiringly, "now that I once again have hands to hand it to you with. You did it. *What* you did, I'm not sure, but it worked!"

Cocoa leaned forward and pressed her lips firmly against the songster's. "You had us all well and truly fooled, Taj. It's a right good familiar you are!"

The pink rush to the slender singer's cheeks deepened as she drew back. "Thank you, both. Thank you all. I couldn't have done it without you. Without all of you. In that sense, in that way, we are one."

"Hell's kittens," Cezer remarked, "we were always one. At odds with each other, sometimes. Quarrelsome and bitchy. Nasty and mean-spirited. Argumentative and—"

"We get the picture, Cezer," Mamakitty declared, interrupting him.

"You know what I mean," the uncharacteristically solemn swordsman muttered. "A household."

No one said anything, but Cocoa quietly hugged Samm. Mamakitty smiled and nodded knowingly at Taj, while a newly ebullient Oskar spread his arms wide to embrace Cezer.

Holding his nose and wrinkling up his face, the swordsman hurried to duck away from the dog-man's effusive reach.

Friends they might be, companions in peril and comrades in arms—but a cat had its limits.

As the surge of color exploded from above the little house in the deep forest, it expanded and grew, piling up higher and higher upon itself in great frothy curls of azure and gold, scarlet and saffron, ocher and maroon. It gushed across the Gowdlands in a spreading prismatic wave so vivid it bordered on iridescence. And wherever it passed, color returned to the world.

Redbirds and cardinals again became worthy of their names. Pigs turned a healthy pink, goldfish gleamed in their bowls, and children inspired to resume their laughing and playing no longer wore expressions gray-washed by despair. The return of color brought forth laughter, laughter brought forth joy, and joy a lifting of the curse of depression that was worse than the absence of color itself. Hue and tint returned to conversation as well as complexions. Buildings brightly painted suddenly glowed anew with fresh life. From worm to washerwoman, the world was reinvigorated, as everyone and everything that had slumbered beneath the curse of the Mundurucu began to reawaken to the thrill of a colorful existence.

With the return of the glorious tints of natural life, musicians were inspired once more to make music. Hope returned to disconsolate painters in concert with their pigments. Accountants again took pleasure in the compiling of figures. The absence of color had not been a small thing in people's lives, and its sudden and unexpected return was the occasion for great rejoicing. Many were the children born that day who were joyously christened with the forename "Rainbow" or "Red" or some other descriptive reminder of the unexpected miracle.

Coloration returned to the rivers, to the fish and frogs that dwelled within them, to the trees and flowers that lined their banks, and even to the somber fortress of Malostranka that loomed above them. It flooded back into the faces of the melancholy refugees huddled within its sheer stone walls, reanimated the arms and armor of its defenders, and struck with unwholesome spots of mottled brown and green the gargoylish faces of those who besieged it.

No one, from the lowliest kitchen drudge sorting through the fortress's dwindling supplies to the most toadlike spear-carrier farting his way through the front ranks of the blockading Horde, escaped the import of the atmospheric transmutation. The latter drew much of their strength and determination from the knowledge that none could stand against the might of the Khaxan Mundurucu. When they were confronted with undeniable evidence to the contrary, a disorderly and disturbed murmuring arose among them that their officers were unable to suppress with fulminations and whips.

Within the castle Malostranka, Valkounin the Strong, resplendent in battle gear to which every glaze and patina had been restored, appeared before Princess Petrine, his face flushed with excitement and barely repressed zeal.

"Your Highness, something—we know not what—has broken the hex laid upon the Gowdlands by the Khaxan Mundurucu. Those of us who have survived to defend this fortress are the best, the toughest, and the most determined warriors remaining." Helmet tucked firmly in the crook of his left arm, he drew himself up to his full height. Around him and hanging from the rafters were myriad banners to which full glory had been restored. "I have been deputed to request your permission to mount a sortie, in an attempt to drive from our doorstep an enemy that is at present clearly flustered. If it should prove successful, we propose to move against the Horde in strength and push them out of the province. As word of our victories spreads, the dispirited folk of the Gowdlands will flock to join us."

Princess Petrine, who was wise beyond her youth and beauty, rubbed her fine, pale chin with one delicate finger. "What if this is a trick of the Mundurucu, to draw us out of the castle so they can destroy us?"

Terwell Dhradvin of the Barony of Umbersaar stepped forward to stand alongside Valkounin. "Reports are already flooding in to those few masters of magic who have survived among us, Your Highness. Everywhere throughout the Gowdlands, the curse is broken. If this is simply a ruse meant to draw us forth, why risk rebellion throughout the civilized countries by lifting the curse everywhere? Why not simply do it here, since we are the only fighters left who need be deceived?"

From behind the two general officers, a rejuvenated Captain Slale spoke up. For the first time in a very long while, he had something to live for. Why he spoke out of turn, and out of rank, he later could not say—only that his outburst seemed to have been prompted by memories of a silver box, and a handful of dust.

"Your Highness, I have looked through far-seeing glasses from atop the fortress walls. The enemy's confusion is too widespread to be faked. Some of them can even be seen to be deserting in the direction of distant Kyll-Bar-Bennid."

Muscles taut, Valkounin took a step forward. "Strike now, your Highness! Before they have a chance to regroup. Before the Khaxan Mundurucu themselves arrive to take charge of the siege and endeavor to resuscitate their hex."

Princess Petrine rose slowly, her pale embroidered robes, to which full brilliance had been restored, trailing about her. "Take charge of the brave fighters who still stand, and drive the heinous besiegers from our walls, bold warriors of the Gowdlands. I grant permission—on one condition."

Valkounin the Strong eyed the princess uncertainly. "Your Highness?"

Eyes glistening, she extended her right hand. "My backside is sore and blistered from doing nothing but sitting on this damned unyielding throne. Find me a sword!"

Within the crenellated tower rooms that occupied the highest point of the fabled castle Burgoylod, atop the central hill that dominates the great trading city of Kyll-Bar-Bennid, the Khaxan Mundurucu were taking their detestable ease when pint-size Klegl came running in from outside, his expression all wheeze and spittle.

"Brethren, my brethren! Kobkale and Kmeliog, Kwort and Kmotho—all of you, come quick, quick come!"

Displeased by the manic interruption, no less so because it came from one of his own, Kobbod rose from the backs of the whimpering young human children on whose ribs he had been composing a musical interlude and followed the squat, distraught Klegl outside. Kobkale and the others of the Clan who were present joined him, muttering various and inventive calumnies under their collective fetid breath. Their intention to pummel the obstreperous Klegl severely was forgotten as soon as they saw what had so unsettled him.

Approaching from the southeast, a veritable tsunami of roiling, coruscating color was rushing in all directions—including straight toward the castle. The fantastical phenomenon filled the sky, transfiguring the gray clouds as it embraced them, washing over and transforming any birds or treetops in its path. His heavy lower jaw dropping, Kobkale stared in disbelief as the onrushing chromatic juggernaut came screaming toward him. At the last instant he threw up his thick, short arms to protect his face. Around him, other clan members gasped or squealed in alarm.

The spectral surge passed over the castle with a great sigh and continued on its way toward the most distant reaches of the Gowdlands. When Kobkale lowered his arms and opened his eyes, he saw to his shock that the massive stone fortifications once more glittered with colorful crystalline inclusions. Color had returned to the pennants that hung limply from staffs, to the noisome liquids that stained the harsh stone underfoot, to the wood that framed certain of the windows—even to his own clothing.

A hand pawed urgently at his shoulder. Kesbroch was next to him, babbling incoherently. Drawing back his left hand, Kobkale dealt his relative a furious blow across the face that knocked him into a complete back flip. By the time he landed on his belly, the stunned but unharmed Mundurucu had managed to regain some control.

"But what are we to do? No one is powerful enough to break a curse of the Khaxan!"

"No *one*." Eyes narrowed, Kobkale was gazing speculatively into the distance from whence the prismatic storm had arisen. "Assemble the Clan. It appears that our work here is not quite finished. There remains one more overlooked detail that demands our attention."

He remained by the parapet, brooding into the southeast, as the bewildered Kesbroch waddled hastily back into the castle, bleating at the top of his considerable lungs.

It did not take long to gather the two-and-twenty. The return of color had left every one of them alternately appalled and confused, agitated and enraged. Several fights broke out among the assembled as they waited to listen to Kobkale: not because the respective combatants were particularly angry at one another, but because among themselves brawling and scuffling were a traditional means of releasing frustration.

Even those with teeth buried in a kinfolk's arm or leg, however, desisted when Kobkale demanded their attention.

"Our hex has been overturned," he declared, utilizing his toadlike mouth to the fullest.

"We know that," croaked Kushmouth. "What are we going to do about it?"

"*Grork,* that's right," added Korpbone. "If we don't put things back the way they were, some of these treacherous humans might start to get ideas." He ground one warty, pustulant fist into a leathery open palm. "Best to keep them crushed underfoot with their faces in the dirt."

Turning his head slightly, Kobkale spat something vile over the wall. "While you were all running around with loose heads, I have taken care to mark the nexus of the countervailing conjuration. Calculating backward from the place where the ripples of color first were seen, I believe I know the place where it originated as well as the possible identity of those who perpetrated it." His eyes blazed. "The Clan will go there, and we will put an end once and for all to those who dare defy our mandate."

The bloodthirsty cries and shrieks of support that greeted Kobkale's avowal sent shudders through those humans in the castle unfortunate enough to have been conscripted to serve them. Fear was visible even on the faces of the members of the Horde who arrived shortly thereafter with a trio of recently transformed individuals in tow. But the expressions of the soldiers were tranquil compared to the looks on the faces of Quoll and his companions.

As the members of the Clan pushed and shoved, clustering tighter and tighter together on the high open platform that overlooked enslaved Kyll-Bar-Bennid below, Kobkale greeted the new arrivals. Halting in front of Quoll, the squat Mundurucu looked up at him and the two former vampire bats. Too much the berserker to be really afraid, Quoll glared defiantly back at him. Ruut and Ratha, on the other hand, were quaking with unashamed terror.

"What's the meaning of this?" The tightly bound Quoll glared at the silently seething Mundurucu. "Why have we been brought here like this?"

Kobkale's voice was dangerously calm. "It would appear, friend Quoll, that you have not been entirely truthful with your friends the Khaxan Mundurucu."

More mystified than frightened, Quoll stammered with repressed energy, "What are you talking about?"

"I have only just now been given reason to believe that the scorned wizard Susnam Evyndd's personal creatures not only survived the strange kingdom into which you insist they were exiled for all time, but have returned equipped with unsuspected powers." One arm rose to encompass their environs. "I believe that the return of spitefully cheerful color to this conquered country is their doing."

Wide-eyed, Ratha struggled futilely in her bonds. "That's impossible! They were to be banished from the last kingdom of color, but we saw them destroyed before our eyes!"

"You should not have relied on others to do your work

for you." Kobkale picked something small, green, and not entirely deceased from between his front teeth.

"We had no choice!" Ruut objected. "We were compelled to—"

"You were compelled to do what you were told," the Mundurucu interrupted. "Evidently, not adequately."

"It won't happen again," Ratha stuttered.

"It certainly won't." Raising both hands, Kobkale uttered a string of suggestive phrases incomprehensible to prisoners and guards alike. Then, apparently satisfied, he turned and threw himself with ferocious energy into the churning pile of Mundurucu that comprised the Khaxan. Following the arrival of the last of the two-and-twenty, there was a violent implosion that momentarily sucked the startled onlookers forward, a loud *phut* that sounded like a diabolic entity casually breaking wind, whereupon the Mundurucu vanished. Every one of them. Disappeared, down to the last unkempt hair, exfoliating horn, deeply stained fang, and bilious eye.

Uncertain what to do next, the handful of guards eyed one another in confusion. Then Ratha screamed; a ghastly, quavering sound whose timbre trembled at the very edge of human audibility. She was echoed by her mate Ruut, and finally, though he fought frenziedly against it, by the defiant-to-the-last Quoll.

Very little there was capable of horrifying the fighters of the Totumakk Horde, but what unfolded before their eyes on that open platform near the topmost floors of Castle Burgoylod caused even the most hardened among them to recoil in terror.

Writhing and twisting, emaciated black worms began to emerge from the convulsing bodies of the three prisoners. Wracked with pain, they collapsed to the hard stone, every muscle in their bodies twitching and spasming, causing them to jerk and flop about like gaffed fish. Too lost in agony even to scream, they lurched and quivered like that for some time, until finally, mercifully, they lay still. Not black worms but the axons, the actual nerves, had erupted from their bodies. Now these lay in stagnant, lifeless coils about the motionless corpses of three former servants of the Khaxan Mundurucu.

Even in death, the red eyes of a certain maniacal marsupial seemed to burn with hatred for everything living that was not a quoll.

TWENTY-ONE

Cezer and Cocoa were locked deep in conversation. Taj was in the kitchen trying to catalog what edibles remained in the pantry. Samm was busy helping Mamakitty repair a few bare spots on the roof. As for Oskar, he was sitting in his favorite place, dining on bread and a meat roll on the front steps of the house, when an ascending whine pricked his ears. Rising, he cast a puzzled glance in all directions. At the same time he became aware that he was not alone in his perceptions. Similarly intrigued by the peculiar noise, his friends were coming to join him.

The whine ceased with a resounding thump as a tightly packed column of short, stocky, and exceedingly ugly creatures tumbled out of the open sky to land in a clumsy heap in the middle of the lawn. Recovering from their plunge with extraordinary dispatch despite arguing and scrapping among themselves, they gathered together in a milling but disciplined mass that sought a focus for their venomous energy. Multiple eyes shining with malevolence caught sight of the pair of former felines, the giant, and the two figures working on the roof before they came to rest, finally, on the solitary guardian of the front door. Surprised by the abominable apparition, an apprehensive Oskar took an instinctive step backward. His bread roll dangled absurdly from one hand.

A goblinlike figure slightly larger than the rest detached itself from the fractious, squirming mass of its fellows. "So these are the creatures of Evyndd who have been causing us problems. Seeing them makes one marvel at the incompetence of Quoll and the others. Just look at them! You can sense that they don't even know how they did it. They have no lore of their own. Animals! Aided by a simple posthumous transformation spell." His squashed nose twitched. "You can smell their innocence and ignorance. We are dealing with mere afterthoughts here." He grinned most unpleasantly. "Scraps to be swept up and thrown away." When he raised both hands high, so did his one-and-twenty kinfolk. The awful symmetry of the gesture was frightening to behold.

"This won't take long," Kobkale announced confidently. "Give them back their simple animal forms. Then we can be on our way and about the business of reversing this nonsensical, and temporary, flush of loathsome color." He glared contemptuously at the silent house, as if its former occupant could somehow hear the challenge. "The Khaxan Mundurucu do not suffer lightly their hexes to be trifled with."

"Look out!" Oskar yelled as he dove for the wholly inadequate shelter of the modest picket fence that enclosed a struggling flower bed. It was the only cover within reach.

He didn't make it.

It felt as if his insides had suddenly been caught in a wringer, wound and twisted about themselves until they were ready to snap. He tried to gasp, but could no longer feel his mouth. Momentarily suspended in midair, blinded by the flash that had completely enveloped him, every one of his muscles paralyzed, his last thoughts were for Mamakitty and the others. If the Mundurucu were concentrating their malignant energies on him, maybe one or more of his friends would have a chance to escape.

Then he hit the ground.

Panting hard, he discovered that he could roll over. His hands were gone, replaced once more by paws. Fragments of human clothing clung ridiculously to his legs. The Mundurucu had done it, and with seeming ease: he was dog once more.

His fur looked as he remembered it: the same mixture of silver and gray. But something was different. His paws were larger. Much larger, as were the claws that grew from them. He rose on all fours: the ground struck him as being farther away than usual. When he looked back at the rest of himself, he saw a coat that was smoother and less kinked than the one he recalled.

Something roared softly behind him. Turning, he almost jumped out of his skin. An immense lion stood nearby, magnificent in mane and claw, staring back at him in complete bewilderment. Moving up to flank the great cat were a pair of spectacularly muscled female leopards: one with normal leopardish coloration, the other completely black—save for a most peculiar and unlikely white patch on her nose.

"Mamakitty?" He swallowed hard. "Cezer? Cocoa?"

"The Master's enchantment has been expunged," the black leopard replied in the language of humans, "and we have been returned to our previous condition—but with a difference."

"Some difference," growled Cezer. "What's happened to us?"

"We've grown, and not just in size. I suspect it is a consequence of how we grew during our travels, of what we endured, and of what we have learned. All that is reflected in this change. We have—matured." Padding past Oskar, Mamakitty confronted the assembled Mundurucu. They looked uncertain, as if a perfectly familiar, ordinary spell that had worked time and time again had suddenly gone haywire. It was as if a magician who had spent years pulling rabbits out of hats unexpectedly found himself holding a cobra, and was now unsure how to let go of it.

"I don't know how much the rest of me has matured," Cezer rumbled, deep within a throat that could easily have swallowed whole the house cat he had once been, "but my teeth sure have!" Letting loose with a roar that reverberated through the surrounding trees, and before Mamakitty could caution prudence, he leaped straight at the assembled Mundurucu, covering half the distance between them in a single bound.

Uttering a collective shriek, the panicked Mundurucu scattered. The decision on what to do next having been made for them, Mamakitty and Cocoa followed Cezer into the fray, sending squat bodies flying in all directions. Several of the Mundurucu fled for the cover of the nearest trees.

Something shot out of the bushes to hit Krerwhen, who was in the forefront of the flight, with such force that it snapped her spine. Jerking the limp body off the ground, the forty-foot-long reticulated python that was Samm shook the body like a rag-doll even as a massive coil wrapped itself around the deceased's outraged, poisonous sister Kelfeth. Unobserved by the arriving Mundurucu, the snake-man had quietly slipped off the roof and into the woods to get behind them, only to find himself transformed into the king of all serpents.

Stunned by the ferocity of his companions' counterattack, Oskar stood and wondered how he could best assist in the clash. Starting forward at a trot and then breaking into a run, he resolved that if he could only chomp down on a single Mundurucu leg and hold it in place, he would have done his part.

As soon as he decided to move, it seemed as if he was flying across the ground, clearing whole sections of lawn with each stride. It was only as he leaped into the midst of the fracas that he caught the briefest possible glimpse of himself, reflected in the water of the small fishpond that marked the farthest reach of the old homestead's formal landscaping.

Expecting to see the scrungy, scruggy mutt he had once been, he was startled to find himself looking down at the most enormous wolf-dog that ever there was. He was even bigger than the two leopards, and nearly as massive as Cezer himself. If further confirmation of the "growth" he had undergone was needed, it was plain to see in the terrified eyes of the Mundurucu among whom he landed.

It was only when a furious and badly frayed Kobkale managed to gather a dozen of his brethren together to form a desperate goblinish pyramid, with himself at the apex, that the struggle turned in favor of the intruders. Ringing out across the field of battle, the words of the surviving Clan froze the combatants in their tracks. Hexed into submission, Oskar suddenly discovered he could move only his head. His legs would no longer respond to his commands. His tremendously powerful lupine jaws were stained black with Mundurucu blood.

Surveying the lawn and the fringing forest, Kobkale trembled with fury. No less than half a dozen of his kinsfolk lay dead upon the grass, torn to pieces by wolf fang and cat claw or crushed by the coils of an immense snake weighing hundreds of pounds. That now-paralyzed serpent glared at the nominal leader of the Mundurucu out of unblinking eyes, wishing only to be allowed to wrap a single small coil around the squat body. But Samm had been as thoroughly immobilized as his four-legged friends. Frozen by the hastily scribed spell, he lay motionless on the bloodied lawn.

"Pox upon you!" Kobkale screamed, nearly insensible with rage. "Malisons and murder, blood and bone!" From the assembled hands of the inhuman pyramid, stubby fingers thrust forth at the anesthetized animals. "You're going to die, die, die!" Safe now, protected by his riven incantation, Kobkale hopped down from the crest of his willing but none too stable platform. The rest of the surviving Mundurucu followed close behind him.

Approaching the helpless Cezer, who if free to move could have killed the Mundurucu with a single blow of one massive paw, Kobkale stuck his face inches from that of the disabled lion. Yellow cat eyes glared murder back at the Clan leader.

"Do you know what we're going to do, cat? First we're going to cook and eat your gonads. Then your tongue, and then your eyes, and then your insides, one organ at a time. Only then, maybe, will we let you die." Straightening, he swept his short, thick arms in a wide, all-encompassing arc. "Then, just for the pleasure of it, we're going to lay waste every cat and dog in these miserable lands, so that there will be none and nothing left to remind us of the slaughter you have made here among our kinfolk." Stepping back, he turned to face the house of the wizard Susnam Evyndd.

"But first," he fumed softly, "we'll wipe this wretched dwelling and all it contains from the face of the earth, so that it and everything in it that stinks of that beggarly sorcerer are consigned to his soon-to-be-forgotten memory." Raising one hand, he was joined in the gesture by several of his colleagues.

At their chant and urging, a fist-size ball of flame appeared. Drawing back his hand, Kobkale flung his fingers in the direction of the cottage. Obediently, the fire followed the line of his throw, to land on the thatched roof that a human Mamakitty had been so recently engaged in repairing. The dry roofing ignited quickly. Within minutes, much of the cottage was engulfed in roaring flame.

A sudden realization made Oskar struggle harder than ever against his invisible bonds. Taj—Taj was still in the house!

The crackling horror was a delight to the Mundurucu, who clapped their hands and made disgusting comments about the sight as they danced in perverse celebration. Sick at heart, Oskar could only exchange a glance with Mamakitty. In her eyes he saw that she, too, had remembered.

With a splintering roar, the roof caved in, inciting a whoop of satisfaction from the hideous, cackling spectators. Their cries of delight ceased, however, as something was seen to rise from among the ashes. Oskar's lower wolf jaw fell as far as the evil enchantment that held him in place would allow, and even Kobkale was stupefied into silence.

Ascending from the center of the now completely engulfed house was a bird. It was not a canary. Nor was it a hawk, or even an eagle. It had wings of coruscating golden flame burnished with azure and shot through with crimson, a head from which projected long feathers that were tongues of orange incandescence, and eyes that burned with unnatural intelligence and perception. When it fully opened its wings, they overspread the house on either side.

"Firebird!" a terrified Kmotho cried.

His croak of warning was taken up by a dozen other inhuman throats. Unnerved, the Mundurucu looked to Kobkale for leadership. That cunning creature was, however, momentarily paralyzed by the unexpected sight before him. As he strove to consider how best to respond, the firebird that was Taj rose clear of the burning house, swept forward to perch on its still intact forepeak, opened its imposing, effulgent beak, and spat.

To Kobkale's left, the Hairy Kwodd burst into a ball of flame. Shrieking and waving flaming arms, the Mundurucu staggered madly about, finally collapsing onto the picket fence and setting it ablaze. A second Mundurucu was transformed into a flaming torch, and then another, and another. Oskar found that he could move his forelegs and tail. As more and more of the Mundurucu perished, the weaker became the immobilizing hex they had cast.

Retreating to the edge of the forest, Kobkale and his surviving kin gathered themselves for one last stand. But this time, when the most eminent among them raised his arms and began to intone a most horrific rune, even his hideous brethren shrank away from him in horror at the conjuration he was crooning.

Kobkale's desperate chanting had opened the gate into one kingdom of light the travelers had not visited—had not visited because it was as unknown as it was inaccessible, and as feared. No one would go there even if they could. It was a place not of ultimate evil but of ultimate indifference. And its denizens had no love for anything from anywhere else.

From out of the portal to the Kingdom of Black emerged bloated, lumpen shades of unadulterated gloom. They had no faces and, for that matter, no heads. Arms of flaccid blackness dragging the ground, they lurched slowly forward on legs of shadow that reflected neither color nor light.

From his flaming perch, Taj sang at them. Gouts of flame erupted in front of and around each of the figures.

Like the light that fell from the sun, these individually hurled conflagrations were absorbed into the dark corpus of each interloper, sucked right up and away much as a sponge would do with water. For all the damage the exalted flame did to their intended targets, Taj might as well have been spewing birdseed.

With a wrench and a wheeze, Oskar felt himself break free of the last of the thaumaturgic restraints. Nearby, he saw that his friends had been similarly released from the pernicious enchantment. Teeth bared, he started toward the cowering knot of surviving Mundurucu—only to find his path blocked by one of the lumbering black shapes. It manifested no overt threat, carried no weapons, and raised no hands in anger. But the hackles rose on his back, and he halted. To step within the grasp of one of those tenebrous shapes, he sensed, would be to vanish forever from the realm of the living.

A streak of feline duskiness shot past him, heading straight for the nearest intruder from the Kingdom of Black. It was Mamakitty. *"No!"* he snarled at her. Either she didn't hear, or she didn't care. With a single spring, she was on the creature.

And then, just like that, she was gone.

Off to his right, Oskar heard Cocoa wail in dismay. Samm emitted a passionate hiss of despair. But from the congregated Mundurucu, there rose whoops of delight accompanied by a surge of revitalized, depraved laughter.

"Now then," growled a rejuvenated Kobkale, "as soon as this malign firebird has been reduced to a small, burned-out cinder, we will deal with the rest of you as I promised. Boiled cat and fried cat, cat filleted and buttered, cat loin with wolf-dog fritters. That'll be our supper, with strips of sautéed snake for a side dish, and firebird drumsticks for dessert." He started forward, taking care to use the odious dark shapes he had called forth for cover as he advanced.

Something made him pause and glance upward. A look of puzzlement crossed his face. One by one, he was joined by the rest of the Mundurucu. Tilting back his head and shading his eyes, Oskar found himself squinting in the same direction. There came a noise. First a noise, and then the screaming.

The crimson mountain that fell out of the dull gray sky was notable not so much for its size as for its unexpected familiarity. A startled Oskar recognized it immediately: there was no mistaking those enormous vermilion eyes, the supercilious rocky lips. And there, too, wonder of wonders, was Mamakitty, clinging to the edge of the upper lip, one arm wrapped tightly around a projecting spear of stone. With the other hand she was waving wildly at her friends. The warning was unnecessary: they had already begun to scatter.

Caught entirely unawares by the astonishing apparition, the stupefied Mundurucu failed to react fast enough. Plummeting down through the clouds, which tried but failed to get out of its way, the red-tinged mountain landed in their midst with a resounding boom that reminded Taj of a whole storm's worth of thunderbolts all rolled up together and set free at one go. Dust and debris filled the air as a sizable section of forest opposite the charred ruins of Susnam Evyndd's abode was instantly flattened.

Half the surviving Mundurucu died then and there. Shrieking as they scattered in every direction, the others were picked off one by one, sucked down an enormous and inescapable stone gullet. Humping about like a gigantic clod of motile clay, the red-tinged mountain slurped them up with lips of glistening gneiss, like a corpulent anteater making a leisurely meal of its tiny prey. Indiscriminate in its appetite and urged on by Mamakitty, it swallowed the bewildered, stumbling visitants from the Kingdom of Black as enthusiastically and effortlessly as it did the surviving Mundurucu.

"*Yum!* I was right," the Red Dagon rumbled. "Things of other colors *do* taste different than those that are red and orange!" From atop the busy upper lip, the voice of Mamakitty could be clearly heard.

"Like I said, *fssst*—I keep my promises!"

When the last of the Khaxan Mundurucu had been expunged from the earth, pancaked by the hungry Red Dagon or snatched screaming into its inscrutable maw, Mamakitty jumped down from her perch on the upper lip to land on what remained of Susnam Evyndd's badly abused lawn. Naturally, she landed on her feet. As Oskar and the others rushed forward, they could see her lips working as she whispered to the red-eyed, river-drinking mountain that had for all eternity occupied the border between the Kingdom of Red and the Kingdom of Orange. Before they could reach her, there was a mighty whooshing of displaced air and earth. When they opened their eyes again, rubbing dust from them, the Red Dagon was gone. But not the great raven cat who had arrived with it.

Bouncing with delight, Mamakitty's companions surrounded her, rubbing their sides against hers and making contact muzzle to muzzle. A jubilant Samm embraced her lovingly, and had to be reminded to ease off so that she could breathe. Flaming softly so as not to singe his friends, Taj fluttered down on great fiery wings from his perch at the front of the house. The massive supporting timber crashed inward moments later, exhaling a brief, transitory cloud of sparks.

"What happened to you?" Oskar stepped back from his old friend, who was unable to suppress a pantherish grin.

"When you jumped that dark intruder and disappeared into it, I thought we had smelled the last of you for sure!"

Mamakitty's smile widened, showing teeth that were startlingly white in her ebon jaws. "There was no time to think. I remembered something Master Evyndd had once said—that in sorcery and magic, it's a black cat that commands the darkness, and not the other way round. That it is a magic that should be inherent and inherited within me. I had to find out. So I embraced the blackness, and lo, I found it a comfortable enough place—though I wouldn't want to live there." She paused meaningfully. "There was nothing else but to try the thing."

Cezer's huge, heavy paw reached out to ruffle the fur on the back of her head. "We shouldn't be here if you hadn't, Mamakitty."

"What happened to you after you were swallowed up by the blackness?" Cocoa was plainly enthralled by her friend's experience.

The long muscles of Mamakitty's powerful back and shoulders were starting to unkink. "Though I found myself in a land where there was no light at all, I discovered almost immediately that I felt perfectly at home. You see, I had been trying hard to think of who, or what, might help us in our hour of need. I remembered a promise I had made, near the start of our quest to find the white light. A promise is a powerful thing." She eyed each of them in turn.

"Do you remember what the Red Dagon said when I swore that if it let us go free, one way or another, I would bring to its attention something that was not red or orange?"

Cocoa's eyes widened slightly. "It said to call out to it, and whatever kingdom of color we were residing in, it would come."

The black-furred head nodded. "But for it to respond, I had to be standing not in our world but in a kingdom of color. That's why I jumped that visitant from the Kingdom of Black. I didn't know if doing so would take me where I wanted to go. Fortunately, it worked."

Samm hissed in consternation. "If your ploy had failed, you could have been lost to us forever, or killed."

Her response took the form of a resigned shrug. "Better to be trapped in a kingdom where all black cats are ultimately welcome than to die at the hands of vermin like the Mundurucu."

Cocoa frowned. "I see how you were able to bring the Red Dagon to our aid, but how was it able to return to its home?"

Mamakitty turned to her, grateful to be able to talk again cat to cat. "By the same incomprehensible means it used to journey here from the borderland between the kingdoms of Red and Orange. How a mountain can make itself travel through space and time I do not know, any more than I understand how it can drink down the ever-flowing volume of an entire river without becoming saturated. I know only that, having tasted its fill of new colors, the Red Dagon went home." Her expression turned wistful. "I hope it will be happy now, with nothing to quaff again but red river."

"I think it will," Cezer rumbled contentedly. "It will always be able to taste the memory of other colors. Bitter colors, as the Mundurucu must have been, but that shouldn't matter to it. I don't imagine that the palate of a mountain is particularly cultivated."

After a while, fatigue took the place of exultation. Carrying water in their mouths, the animals were able to extinguish the small fires that flaming, fleeing Mundurucu had set around the house. Only one blaze, at the edge of the forest, threatened to get out of hand, and Taj dealt with that by setting an exceedingly precise backfire.

But they could do nothing for the house itself, for the dwelling that had been their home since before any of them could remember. The wooden part of it, together with all it contained, had burned to the ground. As for the portion that remained in the cavern beyond, the heat had reached into every nook and crevice once occupied. Nothing combustible had escaped the conflagration, including the wizard's study, his library, and much else of inestimable value. With its destruction, the memory of Susnam Evyndd would perish forever from the Gowdlands. His accumulated writings and lore, an incalculable wealth of arcane knowledge—all had been lost.

"Well, that's done, then, and nothing for us to do about it." Flopping down heavily onto the burned and bloodied lawn, Cezer stuck out his tongue and began to clean himself.

"Perhaps not quite entirely." Mamakitty was looking at Oskar. "Haven't you begun to wonder about your own recently transformed self, Oskar?"

His response reflected his confusion. "In what respect is the question asked?"

"Look at us." She gestured with a forepaw. "Samm is gifted with greater strength than ever, myself with the ability to dictate to the darkness. Taj has become the mythic firebird, able to command the flames. Cezer has become truly a king of beasts, and Cocoa the master of lean power." Yellow eyes peered searchingly into his own. "What about you, Oskar? What is your gift, beyond the ability to inspire a few trees in a far place? Wherein lies your newly given forte in this world?"

He shrugged diffidently. "I don't know. To be this wolf-creature, I suppose."

"That is a consequence of the magic, not a commanding of it." She continued to stare at him. "In my recalling and my rushing, I remembered something else Master Evyndd once said. Something about dogs, and what they truly mean to the house, and to the home."

Tongue lolling as he panted, he shook his head in bemusement. "I don't follow you, Mamakitty."

"I speak of that which is magically inherent in each of us, thanks to the wondrous ministrations of the Master Evyndd." She stepped to the side. "Go and lie in your favorite place, Oskar."

Wolf brows drew together. "You mean, on the stone stoop by the front door?" When she nodded, he shrugged a second time and loped off to comply. He did not wish to argue with her, and had nothing else to do anyway.

Pacing around an ever-tighter loop, he finally reached that mystic moment known only to settling dogs, whereupon he laid down, head to tail, and with a sigh of contentment closed his eyes. They blinked open not long thereafter, though, as a brightness filled them.

It came from all around him. No, he corrected himself. It came from within. From within *him*. Soft and warm it was, with a fragrance of old fireplaces and hot stoves, of running water splashing in a sink and food baking in an oven, of well-worn furniture and fresh linen. It was the essence not of house but of home—which, as those who are privy to such secrets know, are two entirely different things.

Behind him, within the ardent radiance that emanated from himself, the abode of Susnam Evyndd was restoring itself. Curtains and walls, carpets and floors, windows and collapsed chimneys, all became as they once had been, reborn from the depths of his dog soul and memory. When all was at last once again as it once had been, his jubilant

companions padded and slithered and hopped over to rejoin him.

"I don't understand." Oskar was gazing in astonishment
at the miraculous resurrection he had unaccountably
wrought. "What happened? What did I do?"

"It's an enchantment that resides within your transformed
self," Mamakitty told him. "I thought it might be so. Don't
you understand, Oskar? It's a thing you keep safe within
you at all times. I heard the Master say it often, always
with sincerity and feeling. 'Home is where the dog is,' he
used to say."

"So we have a home again. That's a good thing." Cocoa
gazed in contented astonishment at the reborn dwelling.

"You all do," Taj agreed, "but what about me?"

Mamakitty considered the vigorously radiating firebird,
at once new legend and old friend. "You do present a problem, friend Taj. I don't think your old cage would suit you,
and I don't believe I could sleep comfortably within a house
knowing that you were dozing above me on a wooden and
flammable roof. Surely we can find you a nice, cozy, in-
combustible cave that connects to the main cavern in the
rocks and exits separately to the outside."

The firebird nodded sagely. When it did, flecks of flame
fell like shorn whiskers from the underside of its blazing
beak. "That should do me well enough. Speaking of doing,
what are we to do with ourselves, now that we have carried out the Master's wishes and restored color to the Gowdlands?"

"Time enough to decide such matters." Cezer yawned
enormously, his great leonine jaws gaping wide. "I'm not
concerned with the immediate future, since I intend to spend
it sleeping and eating. And maybe doing other things long
put off." He lifted an eyebrow in Cocoa's direction. For
once, she did not respond with insult or sarcasm. Observ-

ing the eye contact and correctly interpreting its significance, a host of conflicting emotions rushed through Oskar. He fought down the choking sensation in his throat. Magic or no, some things were not destined to be. Love was one intangible even the strongest sorcery could not always put right.

"Odd as it may sound, I think Cezer is correct." Mamakitty inspected the renewed edifice approvingly. "We can't exactly go wandering into the nearest village in these bodies. Perhaps, with time and careful perusal of Master Evyndd's restored store of knowledge, we can learn how to switch more efficiently between our animal natures and our human selves." Tilting back her head, she began to yowl.

It was a striking ballad of joy and triumph that she sang, one famous among cats. Cezer and Cocoa joined in. So did Samm, hissing euphoniously, his metronomically weaving head keeping time to the music. Taj, of course, had no difficulty participating, individual bursts of fire bursting forth from his throat as he warbled sonorously, singing fireworks as well as harmony, a veritable symphony of light and sound unto himself.

It was only when Oskar joined in, throwing back his head and letting out a piercing, crockery-rattling howl, that the others hastily ceased their chanting. The wolf-dog had always been able to carry many things, but a tune was not among them.

In addition to matters of the heart, there are some things even great magic cannot fix.

A thousand years before the events of THE SECRET TEXTS, the Dragons rule an empire that spans oceans and more than 3000 years of history. In this world of wondrous magic, fueled by cruelty and evil, a young man named Wraith, who can neither use nor be used by magic, befriends Solander, the son of one of the most powerful Dragons in the empire, and together they discover the source of the power that feeds their world.

Driven by a thirst for justice, and their vision of a better world and a better way, they attempt to right the wrongs they find. Two young men, a mission of mercy—and the fury of the greatest empire and the mightiest wizards in the world of Matrin arrayed against them.

The conflict that follows will reshape their world forever.

━━━━━━━━

VINCALIS THE AGITATOR
(0-446-67899-6)
by Holly Lisle

FROM WARNER ASPECT

THE VIEW FROM THE MIRROR SERIES
by Ian Irvine

A SHADOW ON THE GLASS (0-446-60984-6)

In ancient times the Way Between the Worlds was shattered, leaving bands of Aachim, Faellem, and Charon trapped with the old humans of Santhenar. Now Llian, a Chronicler of the Great Tales, uncovers a 3,000-year-old secret too deadly to be revealed—while Karan, a young sensitive, is compelled by honor to undertake a perilous mission. Neither can imagine they will soon meet as hunted fugitives, snared in the machinations of immortals, the vengeance of warlords, and the magics of powerful mancers. For the swelling deluge of a millennial war is rising, terrible as a tsunami, ready to cast torrents of sorcery and devastation across the land . . .

THE TOWER ON THE RIFT (0-446-60985-4)

The ancient city of Thurkad has fallen, and all who gathered there for the Great Conclave are scattered. Driven mad, the young sensitive Karan is left for dead. Her lover, Llian the Chronicler, is captured by the renegade Aachim, who plan to use the Twisted Mirror for an act of millennial vengeance. The great mancers, including Magister Mendark, flee, die, or are rendered powerless, and even the conquering sorcerer Yggur is threatened by a growing fear of what is to come. For the path of all heroes and villains will meet in the cursed desert called the Dry Sea. And there, in a lost fortress of power, terrible forbidden magics will merge with desperation and folly—and unleash forces that can shatter the destiny of worlds . . .

and coming in July 2002, DARK IS THE MOON (0-446-60986-2)

AVAIlABLE FROM WARNER ASPECT

VISIT WARNER ASPECT ONLINE!

THE WARNER ASPECT HOMEPAGE
You'll find us at: www.twbookmark.com then by clicking on Science Fiction and Fantasy.

NEW AND UPCOMING TITLES
Each month we feature our new titles and reader favorites.

AUTHOR INFO
Author bios, bibliographies and links to personal websites.

CONTESTS AND OTHER FUN STUFF
Advance galley giveaways, autographed copies, and more.

THE ASPECT BUZZ
What's new, hot and upcoming from Warner Aspect: awards news, bestsellers, movie tie-in information . . .